BLOOD BARGAIN

CAMELLIA CARROLL

Blood Bargain by Camellia Carroll

Published by Camellia Carroll
CAMELLIACARROLL.COM
Copyright © 2024, 2025 Camellia Carroll

THIS IS A WORK OF FICTION. This book is set in an alternate earth. Though names of real,
existing locations or historical figures may be used, the depictions of these places and all characters in
the story are entirely fictionalized. Any similarities to real people are entirely coincidental.

Cover and title illustration by Camellia Carroll
Chapter graphics by Camellia Carroll using Canva assets

ISBN: 978-1-971243-00-9 (print)
ISBN: 978-1-971243-01-6 (ebook)

Printed in USA
Second Edition

Bless Your Heart
Blood Bargain
CAMELLIA CARROLL

ALSO BY CAMELLIA CARROLL

APPALACHIAN MAGIC SERIES

Blood Bargain
Blood Marriage
Blood Memories (Coming Soon)

STANDALONES

Weaver
A Touch of Death
Ambrosia Rising (Coming Soon)

VISIT CAMELLIACARROLL.COM
FOR THE MOST CURRENT LIST OF WORKS

FOR MY APP STATE GANG.

THE MOUNTAINS WERE CALLING, AND WE ANSWERED.

IN WHICH ELLIE CONJURES A DEMON

Ellie carefully drew a sigil in ashes on the bare brick floor of her small home. She followed the swirls and lines from her granny's notes with a steady hand before placing red, black, and white candles in a circle around the sigil. The only light in the room was a small oil lamp on the table, all the curtains closed and the doors bolted. No one would disturb her now.

She looked over the ashes, sigil, and candle placements, making sure everything was exactly as it was supposed to be, and fought not to fidget with her long, silver-white hair tucked back in a thick braid. It had been a habit of hers to play with her hair when she was nervous ever since she was a girl. Tonight, there wasn't time for nerves, though. Tonight was decision time.

The rain pounded outside her window. Not the best night for a conjuring, but certainly a good night for covering her tracks. She wouldn't want the rest of the community figuring out what she was doing.

The wind whipped outside, sending sheets of water smacking against her roof, and Ellie closed her eyes against the wash of memories of another rainy day, two long years ago.

Everyone said witches shouldn't wear white. It was bad luck, apparently. Ellie thought it

was silly, though, and her hair was almost white anyhow. She was certain it couldn't be that much bad luck.

Her granny agreed, slowly fastening the buttons that ran down the back of her simple dress. The storm raged outside, but neither of them minded. The Sader women had always been inclined towards gloomy weather. It made them feel safe, they said, tucked in away from the elements.

Another bolt of lightning flashed, and Ellie shook herself out of the memory.

Even as she looked over the sigil in the light of the oil lamp, Ellie wondered if this was a good idea. A conjuring was a drastic approach, though not as drastic as it might have been forty years ago. Back then, if you wanted a spirit's help, you needed to conjure them.

Technically, Ellie had the option of walking around in a major city till she came across one. Spirits in corporeal form, colloquially called Others, were everywhere these days. However, she decided that trying to call out to someone who had the specific tools to help her might be more beneficial than finding any Other on the street willing to help for a price. There were plenty who would take advantage of people that way, humans and Others alike, and the trip down the mountain was too long to risk. If she didn't find anyone, which was likely, she'd lose time and be right back where she started.

The Others hadn't been on earth that long. At least, not in a physical sense. Sometime in the 1880s, Granny said, spirits had begun to show themselves in physical form. Not just here and there, though. Not just to those who sought them out. No, they showed up *everywhere* and to *everyone*, and they wreaked havoc on the entire system of humanity as it was.

Demons and vampires roamed the streets. The Fae found children in the woods and led them astray or led them home, depending on their mood. Countless spirits in physical form roamed the earth, causing chaos and inserting themselves slowly into human culture. Some, they said, could take physical form even before the Appearances began. Those that were particularly strong, at least, could manifest physically and walk among humans. When they did, their children with humans were

called witches—unpredictable fonts of magical power with varying combinations of human and Other traits.

Most witches came from old bloodlines established far earlier than the Appearances. In those cases, the start of the Appearances coincided with a drastic awakening of powerful magic sleeping dormant in their very blood and bones. Approximately one in four witches were first or second generation, their power coming from one Other parent who Appeared with the rest of them. The general superstition was that the stronger the Other blood, the stronger the witch, but even that rule had its exceptions.

Perhaps it was an antiquated word, but Ellie didn't mind being called a witch most days. She wasn't really sure where the Other ancestry in her blood traced back to, but it was certainly there. It had been there a long, long time, through her daddy to her granny and on back. Granny sometimes said that her magic was as old and reliable as the mountains itself, but Ellie had no way to confirm or deny that.

Most humans didn't like witches, of course. That was more of a historical fact than an observation of society, from burnings, hangings, and exiles around the world on into modern times. However, humans liked witches even *less* after it was clear they were very, very real, or so said Ellie's granny. Humans-only communities popped up here and there, and witch-only communities echoed the sentiment, self-isolating from each other out of fear and prejudice on both sides. Most of the Others floated around somewhere in the middle, in mixed communities or cities known to be friendly to all sorts of beings, though it was possible for an Other to disguise themselves as human in those places if they really wanted to and were careful about concealing their abilities.

Mixed cities were fine. Middle ground. They weren't harmonious havens, but most of them weren't hotspots of violence, either. They still had their quirks, though. Even places like Boone that didn't officially regulate the population had their share of tensions. In 1928, almost fifty years after the Appearances began, tensions still hadn't ceased. In some places, they'd lessened. In other places, entire cities had split themselves into human, Other, and Witch sections in an attempt to make room for an incredible influx of new residents and assuage the fears of fully human residents.

Some people were still nice about it, though. Every now and then you found someone who treated you like a person, regardless of your ancestry.

Ellie cursed under her breath as a set of boxes went tumbling from her arms and onto the sidewalk. There wasn't anything breakable inside, but it would be trouble to get them all back up to her house in the little witch community outside Boone, especially without any transport.

"Need some help?"

He had mousy brown hair that flopped over his eyes and a kind smile, and Ellie jolted in surprise as he started to help pick up the fallen packages from the ground.

"Thank you."

"I'm Ben. I've seen you in town a few times. I remember the hair," he said with a laugh. "It's... nice."

Her cheeks grew warm, and she looked away, eyes glued on the brick sidewalk running down King Street. Most people said her silvery hair was a sign of the devil, or sometimes worse.

"Ellie," she said quietly, extending her gloved hand. "I live up in the ah... commune," she said carefully. His eyebrows raised as he shook her hand, but he didn't shy away.

"Oh, yeah, I hear about that every now and then. Kinda far ways to walk, though."

"No choice," she said with a shrug and a half smile.

"I could give you a ride? If you wanted," Ben suggested. "Just dropped off a load from the farm, so I've got the truck, and I'm headed that way for a while."

"R—really?" Ellie's eyes widened. "You don't have to. I know people are... Well, they're scared."

Ben's expression softened. "I've seen people run away from you when you've never bothered 'em once. You don't seem like a scary ol' crone to me, just somebody trying to get by like the rest of us."

"Thanks," Ellie said softly. "A ride would be nice. I'd like to get back to my granny before dark."

"Her hair the same as yours, then?" Ben asked, his broad smile giving away that he was clearly joking. Ellie couldn't help but laugh along with him.

Biting her lip so hard she tasted iron, Ellie lit the candles one by one as tears unrelated to the pain dripped down her face. She did her best to keep them off of the ashes, drying them with a handkerchief that she placed on the table, away from the candles and sigil.

Gritting her teeth, she picked up the clean herb harvesting knife from beside the box of matches and dragged the blade over the back of her forearm until blood welled up and dripped down. As it dropped into the center of the ash sigil, she muttered her scripted words under her breath.

The incantation was half prayer, half command, part Latin and part English, both beseeching and demanding, but it made one thing very clear: Ellie was willing to bargain, and she sought someone who was prepared to make a deal.

When she finished the incantation, Ellie grabbed the tearstained handkerchief and wiped away the blood from her arm. She also dabbed briefly at her lip where her teeth broke the skin, wiping away the metallic tang before it could dribble down her chin and onto her spellwork. There was no telling what any extra ingredients might do to the magic.

A beat passed in silence and stillness. For a moment, Ellie wondered if there would be any response at all. The only sounds were the thunder outside and the rain against the roof. And, if she concentrated, the slight sizzling of...

Wait.

Ellie jumped as she realized the edge of the handkerchief had caught fire from one of the candle flames, dropping it as a reflex, barely avoiding burning herself. It landed in the center of the sigil made of ashes, right where her blood had dripped, and continued to burn.

"Ellie..."

The voice echoed through the empty sanctuary of a log church. Thunder rumbled in the background, momentarily obscuring the sound of water dripping into a tin bucket in the corner, flowing down from a small leak in the roof.

"Stop telling me he's not coming. He'll be here."

"He can't, Ellie."

She turned around, finally, looking at the preacher as he walked through the door. The man's face was pale and his mouth flapping open and closed as he shook his head.

"I just spoke with the Sheriff. They found a body."

The cotton cloth burned completely to ash, leaving a pile in the middle of the sigil. She fought not to curse, to cry, to knock her ritual tools aside. Another beat passed, and Ellie almost decided it was time to give up hope, rip the faulty conjuring page out of the book, and never look at it again.

Then, suddenly, all nine candles went out at once.

The oil lamp went out, too, leaving Ellie in pitch darkness in the middle of the room. The only faint light came from the dying embers of the handkerchief, glowing every so softly on the brick floor.

"Nine is an interesting number," a masculine voice said.

Ellie had never considered herself to be someone who screamed when danger called. She'd been talking to ghosts since she was four years old. She grew up in the deep woods living with the things that called it home, both dangerous and benign. She'd seen her share of incidents out there, too.

And she *didn't* scream at the sound of that voice, to her credit.

She did, however, instinctively swing out with a left hook that jammed hard into something that felt like... it was *meant* to be flesh. It wasn't, but it was *supposed* to be. It was something else.

Something Other.

"Is that really any way to treat your invited guest?"

The oil lamp flared back to life, and Ellie realized that the person standing beside her had caught her punch, his fist closed over hers in the darkness as he stared down at her, eyebrow quirked.

Ellie was not short, but this man was exceedingly tall. He was well over six feet in height, his coarse, snow white hair pulled back into a high ponytail. His eyes seemed blue at first glance, but they flashed gold when the light from the oil lamp flickered just right. Two short, black horns poked through his hair, just enough to notice, and a curious scar pattern ringed his neck. His ears were slightly pointed, just enough to make you look twice, and his teeth were... sharp.

Very, very sharp.

"Where am I?" he asked, looking around the room as he dropped Ellie's hand. He adjusted his battered black jacket, fiddling in his pockets for something.

"Outside Boone. Out in the woods a good ways."

"Specific," he scoffed.

"Whaddaya want, latitude and longitude?" Ellie snarked back, her Appalachia accent becoming stronger in her annoyance.

"It would help," he deadpanned, looking curiously over at the strings of herbs hanging on the far wall of the kitchen.

"Boone is forty-two degrees and three minutes North, ninety-three degrees and fifty-three minutes south. Average elevation is 3,333 feet above sea level. We're basically Northwest a few miles from there. Figure it out." Ellie crossed her arms over her chest and raised an eyebrow at the man, who turned towards her with a puzzled expression.

"You just... know that?"

"I have a good memory," Ellie grumbled, cheeks reddening. "And I'm Southern, not dumb."

"Well hello, 'Southern, not dumb.'" He extended his hand. Ellie stared for a long moment, and then shook it.

"Mark the demon down for terrible jokes. Got it." She was speaking mostly to herself, but the tall man raised his eyebrows like he was appraising her.

"Want to tell me your name, or do I keep calling you 'Southern?'" He asked in a lazy drawl, leaning back against the kitchen table.

"Ellie," she said, tone clipped.

"That your full name?"

"No." She did not elaborate.

"I'll need your full name if you want to bargain."

"And I'll give it to ya... right after we figure out the terms."

She was not oblivious to the fact that he didn't offer his name, either. Instead, he shrugged noncommittally and crossed his arms over his chest, leaning against the kitchen table where the now extinguished candles still stood.

"Fine. What do you want, then? Sex? Power? A love spell, maybe? People always want to bargain for a love spell. Or they're just lonely and want company... even temporary company." He sounded

completely and utterly disinterested as he rattled off the string of items like it was a rehearsed speech, tapping his foot impatiently.

Ellie blinked, brows furrowing. He was a demon, that much was obvious by the horns. Demons also, just from the records they had, tended to be more willing to make deals with humans or Witches. She was expecting a demon, and that wasn't necessarily a surprise. But... this was odd. This felt a little too *expectant.*

"What kind of demon *are* you, again?" she hazarded, blinking.

He blinked, an almost imperceptible flicker of shock crossing his face before he schooled his expression back into a mask of disinterest.

"You conjured me, and you don't know?"

"I was looking for somebody willing to make a deal. Species seemed like a secondary problem." Ellie shrugged, hands on her hips. It was a true enough statement— as long as whoever responded was willing to solve a murder that the locals had long given up on, she didn't care about their origin.

The man snorted. "I'm an incubus."

Now it was Ellie's turn to hide her shock.

An *incubus?* Ellie had met very, very few full-blooded Others, but incubi were the stuff of Witch legends near and far. Some called on them as a patron for love spells or sex magic, while others claimed to have incubi lovers (though Ellie had never seen any evidence of that at all). Most texts described them as dangerous and depraved servants of evil.

That would, at the very least, explain why he assumed she wanted either power, sex, or a love spell.

"Oh," she said, utterly failing to hide her shock in any way at all.

"You can call me Kaz, if you want."

"Huh." She nodded very, very slowly.

Kaz muttered something under his breath, openly rolling his eyes. "... Unless you were hoping for a Fae to make a deal with? Can't advise it. Tricky little beings."

"No, that's not—" Ellie protested, jolted back to reality.

"Great, then let's cut to the chase so I can get this over with," Kaz said, clapping his hands together. "You called me here for a deal, so tell me what you want, and I'll name a price."

The interruption raised her hackles, but on top of that, he seemed more than happy to simply assume what she wanted from him, and that irked her even more. She didn't know how often he answered conjuring calls from witches or made bargains with people on the street, but she wasn't interested in anyone putting words in her mouth. There was enough of that around here already, as far as Ellie was concerned.

"Listen, lemme just be very clear: I don't need help with any of that stuff. I'm not here for... sex... things," she fumbled, waving her hands awkwardly.

"Mmm. Judgy, but fine."

"Not judgy, just— *dammit*!" Ellie slammed her hand down on the table so hard that the plates shook. "I don't need romance help; I need you to *catch me a murderer*!"

There was a long pause between them while Ellie did her best to maintain composure, breathing hard as wave after wave of rainwater continued to strike the windows. Kaz, for his part, took it in stride. She could tell by the stillness, by the slight widening of his eyes, that something was different now, but he didn't show any obvious signs of shock. Rather than looking disinterested as he had before, he instead seemed... almost intrigued.

Almost.

"Well," Kaz said slowly, tilting his head as a small smile crept across his face, "*Now* I'm listening."

IN WHICH THERE IS A BARGAIN

"Two years ago, a man named Benjamin Mathers was murdered in the woods outside town," Ellie said slowly. She walked towards the kitchen, where she'd preemptively placed a copper kettle on the stove to heat. Steam poured out the spout, and she grabbed it before it could start to whistle, putting it to the side as she grabbed mugs from the shelves.

"You're a witch. Use that Other blood and ask his ghost," Kaz said, rolling his eyes as if that should be obvious. "Don't make me do your dirty work for you."

"First of all, not all witches have the Sight, but thanks for assuming," she grumbled. "Second of all, I *do* have it. I've been talking to ghosts since I learned to talk. You really think I didn't try that right off?"

"And?"

"Killer came from behind, according to the Sheriff. He couldn't have seen," she said softly, eyes suddenly glued on the brick floor. "Besides, he's a little... Ghosts with sudden deaths, they don't... they don't move on easy. Talkin' to 'em about their passin' moments is hard, to say the least." Shaking her head like she could shake off the memories, Ellie grabbed a few herb jars from the shelf on the wall and a little cloth bag, putting pinches of dried plants inside.

"What are you doing?"

"Making tea. I make tea when I'm nervous. You want some?" she asked. When Ellie glanced over, she saw him in a position that looked defensive, like he was ready to bolt at the first sign of any magic. "Trust me, I'm not gonna use magic on a non-consenting, non-hostile subject. I don't care if you're a human or a witch or someone else, that's all the same to me."

Kaz's shoulders relaxed a little at that, but he hesitated, squinting at the little cloth bag in her hand. Ellie just snorted, undoing the drawstring to let him peek inside. He took it from her and peered into it like something might jump out from it and bite him.

"It's chamomile and calendula, with a little valerian to help me sleep. It won't poison you. I can even add some peppermint if ya want a stronger taste."

He sniffed at the bag cautiously before handing it back to her with a nod. "Yes. Tea sounds... nice."

"Have a seat." She gestured to the two empty chairs beside the kitchen table. Kaz slowly perched on the edge of one of the wooden chairs, still obviously tense and suspicious, though Ellie couldn't figure out why. As far as she was concerned, he had the upper hand here, and not by a small margin.

"Can't say anyone's offered me refreshments while hashing out a bargain before," he muttered, watching as Ellie poured water into the mugs, dipping a little cloth bag in each one. "It's more common they try to bind me in a summoning circle until things have been set."

"Well, that seems rude to do to somebody ya want help from," she said firmly. "I refuse to let anyone say I'm a bad host. Even to demons."

She sat one of the two steaming mugs down in front of him, wondering if he'd be suspicious. He did sniff at the brew again, but he seemed perfectly willing to sip on it once it cooled. She hadn't lied— there was nothing dangerous in there, but his paranoia rang alarm bells. Not for herself, of course. She simply wondered what happened in the past to make him so careful.

There would be time to ask that later, though.

"Now, back to business," Ellie said, taking a seat at the table beside Kaz. "I need your help finding a murderer. I'm not equipped to do this all

on my own. It's not a one-woman job no way, no how, but it's especially not a one-woman job for me. There's barely anybody in town who will even talk to me about it."

"Prejudiced against witches?"

"Somewhat, yeah. They like my medicine, though, so I don't think it would be so bad if they didn't think I killed Ben myself."

"Why the hell would anybody think that?" Kaz's brow furrowed and nose scrunched as he frowned.

"Anybody in their right mind *wouldn't*, and besides, the pastor knows exactly where I was all morning long that day," Ellie sighed. "Anyway, that's why I need your help. We'll go into town tomorrow and get started. Any questions?" She stood from the table with her mug in one hand, and Kaz followed suit.

He walked a little closer, looking her up and down in a way that seemed almost suspicious, but he was silent for a long moment until he reached out and grabbed her arm. It was too fast for Ellie to protest, and she found herself just *waiting* as he examined her, wondering what on earth would come out of his mouth next.

"Why did you cut the back of your arm?" he asked, squinting at the thin red line across her skin. "Most people go for the palm, you know."

"That's stupid. Palm cuts are hard to heal and extremely painful, and I'm gonna have to cut it later anyway," Ellie snapped, snatching her hand back. "Blood is blood."

"And you didn't consider that the pain might be part of the sacrifice?"

Shit.

She *should* have known that. There was a way with these things—balance, as in everything. The give and take of the world was an essential part of how magic worked. However, she'd never read anything about *intangible* sacrifices.

"So if the sacrifice wasn't right, why are *you* here?"

"I was curious about whatever stupid human would conjure a demon for a bargain using the potency of their own tears," he said with a shrug. "The blood from your arm was nothing. But those tears and that blood from your mouth... Well, they had bite."

13

Ellie's hand went to her lip, feeling the broken spot where her teeth had drawn blood. She had wiped the tearstained handkerchief across it before it burned... the handkerchief that was never meant to be a part of the ritual in the first place.

"That was a lot of pent-up pain. A lot of pent-up love, too. You were probably bound to snag an incubus dangling *that* out into the ether no matter what you did."

"Any *other* questions?" she asked quietly.

"Why is a witch raised on Christian folk magic desperate enough to try and conjure a demon to bargain with?"

Ellie's nose wrinkled. "How did you know I—"

"Bible on the mantle. Old family Bible, by the look of it," he said, gesturing. "There's a bottle on the shelf with a tag that says 'holy water,' not that I couldn't tell what it was from here. Also, the walking stick by the door has a cross carved into the top."

"Is that gonna be a problem for you?"

"You planning to force me to convert?" He raised an eyebrow, but didn't seem alarmed.

"No." No point in that, as far as Ellie was concerned. Live and let live.

"Then we're fine," Kaz said with a nod. "In truth, I find religious practices fascinating, and I'm a somewhat... unaffiliated demon, if you must know."

"Unaffiliated?"

"Mm. We can talk about it another time. The point is that I want to know why you called a Demon."

"Just from what I've heard, out of any Others, Demons are most likely to strike a bargain with a human or a Witch, from what I heard. I would'a been okay with a Fae, too, if I'm honest. Don't really care about a tricky bargain."

"You probably should. No one makes it out of a careless Fae bargain without consequences."

Ellie swirled the dregs of her tea in her mug, smiling wryly. "I was never planning on making it outta this alive, honey. All I want is justice served. Then..." her shoulders slumped and she sighed. "Well, at least I'll be at peace."

Silence settled in around them like a thick blanket of snow, Ellie's eyes glued on the wood of the kitchen table. It was true, as much as she was... not ashamed, but perhaps loathe to admit it. The grief and the guilt had gnawed at her for so long that it had left a hollow wound somewhere in the middle of her chest, and it wasn't healing. It was only getting bigger with time.

"You... just called me honey."

Ellie blinked furiously. She hadn't even realized it, though it was just like a demon to be more surprised at a southern endearment than an admission that death didn't phase her in the slightest.

"Aw, shit," she hissed. "Sorry, that's a thing I do with everybody, just without thinkin' most of the time. My granny does it, too. I won't if you don't want me to."

"No, it's... fine," he said, a little stiffly.

"So... what do you want outta this?"

Kaz took a deep breath, slumping in the wooden chair. "Honestly, after being stuck in this plane for close to half a century, I'm at the point where I'd almost do it for the entertainment value."

Ellie looked at him carefully over the rim of her mug.

"Almost," he repeated. Ellie nodded, understanding. There was always a price for these things. She expected it by now— it was part of the same balance that she should have considered when making her blood sacrifice in the first place.

"You said you'd name the price. Tell me what it is," she said calmly, trying to remain as detached as possible.

"I'm not feeling generous enough to give you something for free, but... I admit, I'm intrigued. So I think I'll give you a discount," he said with a smirk that showed his sharp teeth.

Ellie braced herself. She wasn't sure what the price would be, but there had to be one. Balance. Give and take. Bargaining with Others wasn't the safest route and they weren't known for their merciful streaks, but after exhausting all other options on her own, this was her best shot at answers. She was prepared to negotiate the price down from anything that involved her soul.

Beyond that... Ellie would pay if it would solve this case, if it would stop the hole in her chest from eating her alive.

"I'm going to need food and lodging while I'm here."

"By food, do you mean..." Ellie trailed off, gesturing awkwardly. She knew enough to know that incubi and succubi didn't exactly subsist off normal bread and cheese, but she couldn't bring herself to ask out loud.

"Sexual energy?" he asked, smirking. "No. My physical form can survive just fine off human food, and though I can absorb sexual energy in lieu of eating, I won't take it without consent."

"That's... okay," Ellie said slowly, nodding. Nice, even. "Is that why you had your, uh... speech when you arrived?"

"That's why I usually jump on bargains when I feel the pull, yes," he said with a shrug. "It's nice to have an energy reserve to pull from if I need it, especially if I'm going to be working magic."

"So... room and board? That's all?"

"No."

"Dammit," she muttered, and Kaz chuckled.

"I need something from you. Something precious, irreplaceable. Something that only you can give me."

"What good would that do you?"

"Mouthy woman, aren't you?" He crossed his arms over his chest, glaring down at her.

"Get used to it," she muttered.

"Treasured items are useful in a myriad of ways. It's always a good idea to have something truly unique on hand for magic, as I'm sure you know. Consider this my lenience on you. A non-specific treasured item and a vacation room for the course of the investigation. Then we're even."

"Deal."

"Good—"

"Just one more condition before we seal it," Ellie said quickly. Kaz sighed, motioning for her to get on with it.

"I need you to swear that you won't purposefully harm me as part of the bargain terms," Ellie said. "I'm not holding double standards— I'll swear the same thing to you, but I want it done."

He seemed to weigh his options for a moment, and then he seemed to scrutinize Ellie for a moment. She didn't blame him. This wasn't her preference, swearing not to harm someone, just in case he

turned out to be a corrupt son of a bitch, but she was fairly sure that the only way she'd be able to get him to agree to it was either agreeing to mutually swear or upping the payment to some extreme that she'd probably regret later.

"I consent to that, if you also swear," he also said. "It seems reasonable considering the amount of time we'll be spending together, and I understand wanting to guarantee your safety with a stranger. I'd like to do the same."

"Done."

Kaz picked up the knife from the table and handed it to her handle-first. She knew well enough what came next. It wasn't something she'd seen often, but occasionally blood bargains took place between witches. She dragged the knife across her palm, wincing as it made a shallow cut.

Ellie watched as he drew one of his sharp fingernails across his palm, silver blood that reflected the light like liquid metal welling up from the cut. Her eyes widened— though she technically knew that Others had different blood colors, it was her first time seeing it in person.

"Kazerin," he said, holding out his bleeding hand.

"Rafayelle," she echoed, grabbing his hand with hers. One of Kaz's snow white eyebrows raised, but he didn't break script.

"I so swear to aid in the investigation of the murder of Bejamin Mathers in exchange for food and lodging during the course of the investigation. On successful completion, I am owed a unique treasured artifact that only Rafayelle can give. Both parties swear not to purposefully harm the other for the duration of this pact."

Ellie turned the wording over in her mind, looking for any tricks or catches or strange turns of phrase. She didn't notice anything the first time or the second time through. The third time through, she still couldn't find anything no matter how carefully she pulled it apart.

"I agree to these terms," Ellie said, giving his hand a slight squeeze. Kaz nodded firmly.

"We have a blood bargain."

IN WHICH KAZ IS SORE

The storm raged through the night, never letting up once.

That was fine with Ellie. She had books and simple food and enough apothecary work to keep her busy, and if she got bored with that, she could always go back to her sewing for a while. She could buy clothes in town, sure, but going to town was a hassle, and when you spent your life in the woods, there was almost always mending to do.

Her new demon... *friend*... sat in the single old armchair by the front window. Ellie didn't have guests often, so she didn't have much need of extra seating. In fact, she didn't have much need of extra anything.

The little two room house was a standard kind of space for Witches living in her small community. Most families expanded on the house when they had children or just moved to a bigger home if it became available, but Ellie had never expected to need more than this.

Well... Only once had she expected to need something more. Those hopes were gone now.

The two rooms in the house were a kitchen space and a space for everything else, plus a bathroom off the back of the house that operated from well water. Though, calling the place two rooms was a bit of a stretch. It was more like two distinctly decorated spaces with an iron stove in the middle dividing them up, but it was really just one large room.

Upon entering, the right half was the kitchen. There was a plain wooden table with two chairs, the basic iron stove for heat, a gas stove and oven combination for cooking, a sink, and counter with storage underneath, and a small cabinet with dishes. The far right wall, however, held shelves absolutely packed with baskets, bottles, bags, and jars of dried herbs. Bundles of drying plants hung from the ceiling rafters, from strings attached to hooks on the wooden walls, even above the doorway... though, Ellie kept those there for a little protective boost.

The left half was... everything else.

The house was designed so one stove could heat the entire space, so the full bed was tucked into the far left corner to save space, a woven rug covering the brick floor near it. A trunk at the foot of the bed held most of Ellie's clothes, a cabinet by the door held her outdoor supplies, and one armchair sat by the window next to a small table. That was the chair that Kaz now occupied, the oil lamp on the table burning bright. Beside the table, an overflowing bookshelf held Ellie's favorite volumes.

"Rafayelle, was it?" Kaz asked softly as he riffled through a book on medicinal herbs. It wasn't the most interesting reading on her shelf, but it was certainly informative and would acquaint him with plants of the area.

"It's Ellie. Unless you want me to go around calling you Kazerin, that is."

"Why the distaste? I would think you'd like being named after a powerful angel."

Ellie just snorted as she pulled extra blankets out of the closet.

"It's a little early for backstories, ain't it?"

"Humor me."

"Okay, short version: my momma was a pastor's daughter from down the mountain."

"And?"

"And that's all you get," Ellie said with a smile. "I told you it was the short version."

If that bothered him, he didn't show it. Everything seemed to roll off his back like the rain rolled off the windowpanes of the house. Kaz stretched his arms dramatically and shrugged off his leather coat, laying it over the back of one of the two kitchen chairs.

Then, without preamble, he crossed the room and flopped his entire body across Ellie's bed.

Feet dangling, Kaz toed off his shoes and let them fall to the floor before he crossed his legs, looking for all the world like he wasn't planning on moving. His eyes closed and he rested his head against one of the pillows

"Uh... that's my bed," Ellie said slowly.

"Well, there's only one and you promised me food and lodging, so I suppose it's *our* bed for the foreseeable future."

Something felt like it cracked open inside Ellie as she processed that statement, like a lightning bolt straight to the skull or a cold chill you couldn't shake.

"Wait— *here*? You're staying here? I thought you meant at a local boarding house or something." She was floundering and she knew it, but she didn't care.

"Do you really want to go through the questions that would cause?" He didn't even glance at her, eyes still closed as he lounged against the pillows.

Ellie opened her mouth, already poised to argue, shoulders tense and finger pointing.

Then she closed it.

She lowered her hand.

She let her shoulders slump.

As much as she was loathe to admit it, he was right. A demon in a witch community was one thing, but a demon staying in town, especially one with visible horns, had the potential to draw too many questions or even cause outright panic among the locals.

For the most part, Others were tolerated in and around Boone. *Accepted* would be an overstatement, but generally the residents left Others well enough alone so long as they didn't cause any trouble. Demons were an exception in many ways. In a town deep in the Bible belt, suspicions and superstitions ran deep. Even Ellie didn't quite trust Kaz, and she was the reason he was here in the first place.

"... No," Ellie grumbled, pursing her lips.

"Good, then that's settled."

"I'm sleeping on the floor," Ellie grumbled.

"Your choice. The bed's big enough for two."

"I know it is." Ellie sighed and started unlacing her boots. "The least you could do is turn around while I change."

Kaz responded by placing a pillow over his face, eyes still closed. "Will this work?"

Ellie bit back a laugh. "That works."

She probably shouldn't find it funny. In fact, she really shouldn't. This was a serious situation, and she'd be in serious shit if anyone found out what she was investigating.

As quickly as possible, Ellie unbuttoned her shirt, slipped on her nightgown, and then wiggled out of her pants while she was still fully covered. She looked over her shoulder at Kaz the whole time, and he didn't even twitch. It was weirdly comforting, in a way, though she was still self-conscious enough to cross her arms over her chest over the thin nightgown as she finally spoke.

"Okay. You're in the clear."

Kaz removed the pillow, opened his eyes, and gasped dramatically. "How scandalous! A calf-length nightgown. How will I survive the shock?" he sighed.

Ellie just rolled her eyes. "I've known you for an hour and you're asking me to get into bed with you. Give me just a little bit of wiggle room here."

"I've known people for less time that asked *me* to get into bed with them," he pointed out, and she had no doubt that was true.

"I'm not those people, but thanks anyways." She wanted there to be a bite to it, but there was none. She just sounded tired, even to herself. The exhaustion was creeping into her bones, and sleep would likely take her soon.

Ellie had no problem with the concept of one-night stands, and that wasn't the issue here. Truly, she didn't even care that he kept implying he expected her to want sex— that seemed like more of a personal thing for him, and she wasn't about to press him on it.

The issue was that the only person she'd ever shared a bed with for any length of time was dead, and she didn't even know who killed him, and she couldn't bring herself to even think about sharing a bed with somebody else that wasn't him. It made her chest tight just to think about it, not to mention that she didn't trust Kaz. They were allies, yes, but also strangers. Sleeping next to a stranger was not something she wanted to do.

"You need sleep. Conjuring is draining."

"I know." The basic principle of conjuring was that, once answered, the spell drew on both parties to guide the conjured spirit to the conjurer. In truth, now that the adrenaline had worn off, she was completely sapped.

That didn't mean she'd sleep in a room with someone she didn't trust, though. Swear or no swear. Ellie was used to keeping her guard up, and a little fatigue was something she could deal with. Even drained and walking on shaking legs, she refused to compromise if she could push through.

Instead of continuing the conversation, she brushed out her hair and re-braided it for bed.

"Why did you call a demon if you don't plan to trust me?" Kaz asked. She turned towards him to find his eyes wide open, staring at her like a puzzle he couldn't solve.

"Does a blood bargain require trust as a spell component?"

"Not strictly, no," Kaz mused, "but you're asking for a prolonged investigation. We're going to be together for a while."

"It's not because you're a demon. Well, not entirely," she said, nose scrunching a little. "I admit I don't know anyone who's had a good experience with a demon, but I know a couple of people who've pissed off some fae and a couple more who claim to have had their own scrapes with angelics. I'm as suspicious of you as I would be of any stranger whose help I needed."

"... Reasonable," he said softly. "Quite reasonable."

"I'm not asking you to trust me, either, for the record." She grabbed a blanket from the trunk at the end of the bed and threw it around her shoulders. "Do people usually trust you?"

"I haven't yet found a middle ground between humans who are overconfident in their ability to control me and humans who are far too trusting for their own good. Though... I do find those areas have quite a bit of overlap. Maybe there isn't a middle ground at all."

"Shit on a stick..." Ellie muttered, taking a deep breath through her nose.

23

Kaz tilted his head slightly, watching her every movement as she took a pillow from the bed and started to calculate the least terrible place to sleep on the brick floor. It was probably on the rug, but she'd risk getting stepped on that way, and it would be warmer next to the stove. She could move the rug, though. That could be an option.

"... Hey," he said softly, just as she was turning all this over in her head.

"Yes?"

"I meant it when I said I'm not going to do anything to you that you don't consent to. We're bound by a blood bargain. Even if I wanted to hurt you, I couldn't until the terms are fulfilled."

That should probably make her feel better, but she wasn't convinced. Just because he couldn't do her purposeful harm didn't mean a damn thing, and she knew enough about wiggle room in wording to know he could probably find ways around it if he really wanted to. She could, too, for that matter. However, there was one phrase in particular that made her pause.

"Even if you wanted to?" She echoed. At the very least, it implied that he wasn't interested in harming her, and wouldn't have been in the first place. That was... Well, not all Others were interested in harming or subjugating humans. That was just prejudice and horror stories and a few real stories that were particularly bad.

She certainly did have someone *interesting* in her home, though, and for the smallest moment, Ellie allowed herself to believe that some form of good luck had finally come back around to her.

"What can I say? It's the most interesting job I've been offered in a long time. I don't plan to let it slip away so easily." He sounded nonchalant, but so had almost everything else he'd said that evening. Just as Ellie thought about questioning it, Kaz groaned, stretched, and stood from the bed, stalking back across the room to the armchair.

"You staying up?" she asked, brow furrowing.

"I was engrossed in that book before you started talking my ear off. Think I'll go back to it."

Kaz plopped down in the chair sideways with his long legs draped over the arm and the lantern at his back, shining light on the worn, yellow pages of *The Flora of Appalachia*.

She wondered for a moment if he was... being nice.

A *nice* demon. That sounded opposite to everything she'd ever heard and read about demons. Yet... here he was, sitting in the armchair by the lamp, book in his lap. As though he felt her staring, he looked up.

"Are you planning to sleep or stare at me all night?"

Without a word, Ellie snuggled down under the comforter, throwing the blanket that had once been around her shoulders on top of the others for a comforting, warm weight. She turned so her back was to him, less as a show of trust and more because she really did not think she could sleep if she was facing someone else.

"Put out the lamps before you sleep, please," she said softly. "Blankets are in the trunk if you get cold."

"Mm."

"... Thanks," Ellie whispered after a long moment.

There was no response, and she wasn't about to say it again.

He hadn't planned to spend the night in the armchair, he really hadn't. Kazerin couldn't remember a single time when someone had actively refused to let him into their bed, especially a human interested in bargaining. That was outside his experience, but he was truly serious about what he told Ellie: he would not do anything without her consent, including sleeping in the bed.

It was stupid of him to answer another bargain, but he was looking for an excuse to get out of town, to find a new life for a while, anything that would distract him. Anything that would break up the monotony. Accepting bargains was almost like a drug addition. It gave him a little distraction for a little while, just long enough to make him feel better before he jolted back to reality.

And then, after a while of sitting in that reality, you came to want the distraction again. It didn't even matter how shitty the recovery period might be.

Bargains were funny things. Conjurings in general were funny things. For a summons, you had to have someone specific in mind, and those usually went to higher-tier demons with more famous histories,

often Abrahamic ones. Summoning would get you exactly *who* you wanted, but there wasn't a guarantee they'd do *what* you wanted.

Conjuring, on the other hand, was like sending out a little lure out into the universe and hoping someone took the bait. It wasn't a guarantee that you'd get any response at all, but it did widen your net drastically, and if you got a bite, there was a better chance it was the bite you needed to get the job done.

On his end of the process, it felt like... a ringing in his ear. A pungent herbal scent that wasn't coming from anywhere around him. A tingle on his skin, a taste on his tongue like blood and grief and salt. The blood was par for the course. Blood sacrifices were standard. The grief was not uncommon, though plenty of people conjured from anger, sorrow, lust, greed, or guilt. Kaz didn't have a preference for emotions most of the time, though with the number of calls he'd answered in the last fifty years, the taste of lust and greed on his tongue made him want to retch. Those were the ones he tasted the most right before answering, the ones that wanted to bargain for power or love, the ones that would pay the highest price for what they wanted.

This one was... different. It was the salt that tipped him off, at first. Iron was one thing, the tang of human blood having its own specific taste, but salt was not normal for a sacrifice. And he only ever tasted the sacrifice— that was the *point* of the taste to a conjuring call, he'd learned over time. Smells were specific to the conjurer, but the taste... why was there *salt*, he'd wondered?

It took him a moment to discern that it was from tears. It took him a moment to discern that there was blood, yes, but the majority of it wasn't potent. It was numb, offered by rote. But the tears... the blood wiped off a self-inflicted wound not made by a knife... Something about that called out in a way that twisted in his chest.

Loss.

It sang a song of loss.

So he reached out with his mind and his magic, pulled on that invisible thread, and tugged as hard as he could.

The next thing he knew, he was standing in a tiny kitchen, staring back at a woman whose grief was plain on her face. That was fine. The grief wasn't new. Dealing in heartbreak was practically a specialty for

incubi, considering they often possessed powers that humans at least assumed would solve their problems. This, though... this was strange.

This was *off*.

She wasn't responding to his flirting and bit back at his jibes, and that was strange. He could tell if someone was playing hard to get or ignoring their own body— he could smell arousal like a perfume on them. This woman genuinely wasn't interested. She was afraid, to an extent, or perhaps it was better to call it distrustful, and that seemed to feed into her biting remarks, but he didn't mind. It was better than simpering for power.

As far as Kaz was aware, he'd been looking over a dry but informative botanical text, turning all of this over in his mind, and then suddenly he was sitting in a chair by a long-extinguished oil lamp, listening to a rooster announce the morning and attempting to move his stiff and sore neck.

It was the smell that really woke him, though. He could hear something sizzling softly, and though it took him a moment to remember where he was, his nose and his stomach seemed to be far ahead of his conscious mind.

Ellie was already awake, dressed in long pants and a simple shirt as she stood in the kitchen. There was a canvas bag on the table with jars and boxes stacked around it, ready for packing, and a few jars of canned goods out with the breakfast materials.

"Why are you up so early?"

"Checking the brews. I've got stuff to take to town when we go today." More glass jars clanked, and then he heard sizzling. "That, and breakfast. We're gonna need a good meal if we're walking to town."

He hadn't taken note of the little stove and oven combination before, but now it was at the forefront of his mind as the smell of frying meat wafted towards his nose. His stomach audibly growled, but Ellie barely seemed to react.

"You want bacon?" she asked, throwing another piece of salted pork into the pan. "I went and checked the hens while you were asleep. We've got bacon, eggs, canned fruit, bread— what'cha want?"

Kaz just opened and closed his mouth like a fish, trying to process both how she could be so chipper so early in the morning and how he'd managed to sleep that deeply in an old armchair in a house he'd never

been in before. Finally, he shook his head like it might clear the morning fog from his brain, stood, and painfully rolled his shoulders.

God, that's a terrible plan, I'm never sleeping there again.

He tried to ignore the subtle cracks and creaks of his bones as he walked towards the kitchen table, continuing to stretch as he went. Ellie, seemingly unperturbed, continued cooking breakfast. She grabbed a jar from one of the shelves seemingly at random. They all looked the same to him, and he thought it might have something to do with the food, but he was wrong.

"Here," Ellie said, plonking a mason jar with a tied-on label down on the table in front of him.

"What's this?" Kaz picked up the jar and squinted at the thick, slightly oily substance inside as he sat in one of the wooden chairs.

"My guess is you've got a crick in your neck from sleeping in that chair. This should help. Put a little on your fingertips and massage it in."

"What's in it?" He opened the lid, popped the seal off, and sniffed at it. The stuff was pungent, but it didn't smell *bad*.

"Nothin' that's gonna poison ya," Ellie said with a snort. "People always think I'm using some kinda black magic because my recipes work so well, but I'm just learning from the folks around us. Usin' things other people wouldn't use."

"Like what?" Almost against his better instinct, he dipped his fingertip into the substance in the jar and began to rub it on the back of his neck. She was right, his muscles were screaming, and he was willing to take a chance on a remedy rather than be in pain all day.

"The Cherokee know a lot more about working with mountain plants than we do, even after my family's been in these woods for generations. You always want to listen to 'em when they pass through. We trade recipes sometimes," she said with a shrug. "There's a few Black families up in Fancy Gap that know African plants real well. They visited here when I was a teenager and I got to know their daughter pretty good. Name's Miriam. We sent letters back and forth for years, and now we send plants back and forth, too. She's got a knack for makin' things grow here that nobody else can, and she's plannin' to pass that on to her kids."

"What about you?" Kaz asked carefully. Bargain or not, he barely knew anything about this woman, and it would be in his best interest to find out anything he could. Just in case.

"What about me what?" Ellie asked around a mouthful of bacon and eggs.

"Kids? Things to pass on?" he asked casually. As he spoke, he noticed a slight warming sensation on the back of his neck, where he'd rubbed Ellie's balm into his skin. Though he was well aware of witch abilities and limitations, he... hadn't truly expected it to work quite so well. There was a pleasant heat to it and the pain slowly faded as he once again rolled his shoulders, and Ellie smirked like she knew exactly what he was thinking.

Blessedly, she didn't comment, though. she just took the jar, put the lid back on, and placed it on the shelf it came from.

"You see any babies running around this house?" She gestured broadly to the open space. "You think I'm hidin' kids in the walls?"

"Could be grown by now," he suggested. He didn't know how old she was and he wasn't about to hazard a guess. Witch aging had gone haywire in unpredictable ways since the Appearances began and their Other blood activated.

"You think I look old enough to have grown kids?" Ellie spluttered.

"Your... hair?" Kaz gestured to her long braid with his free hand. It was completely silver from root to tip, and her hair went easily down to her hips, even braided.

"Oh." Ellie paused, like she'd forgotten her hair color was even odd. "My hair's been growing this color since I was born."

"How long ago was that?" He briefly caught her eye as he put the lid back on the glass jar, looking for any tiny ticks or tells on her face, but he couldn't catch any at all in the dim morning light.

Ellie smirked. "Wouldn't you like to know?"

He let the subject drop, watching as she grabbed a few ingredients from the shelf and mixed them into a bowl. Moving back and forth between taking strips of sizzling bacon out of the pan and mixing something in the bowl, Ellie hummed absently as she worked. It wasn't any specific tune, just humming, and Kaz found it oddly peaceful.

When a loose dough had formed in the bowl, she carefully portioned it out, put a little extra oil in the pan, and began to cook it.

"You want fry bread?"

"Fry... what?"

"Told you we got a lot to learn. It's good, trust me. It's a Native tradition, and I can't make it as nice as they do, but I like it for mornings." The oil in the pan sizzled as she dropped the dough in, and a mouthwatering smell wafted through the air as it cooked. "There's a Seminole version with squash, too. It's a good way to spice up your canned veggies when you're damn sick of whatever you canned by spring."

"Simple living..." Kaz said slowly, not quite conscious he was speaking aloud.

"Again, you got a problem with it?" Ellie asked, obviously bristling. "We're way outside town, and the only way to get to the town with any kind of ease is one train line. It's a new one, too. We do what we can out here. We grow as much food as we're able, installed a water pump and pipe system, and we look after each other."

"I certainly understand the need for self-sufficiency, trust me, but.. . why not make your own town elsewhere, somewhere with better amenities? Or move in with other witches closer to cities?"

Ellie scrunched up her nose. "That's something only a city slicker would ask," she said with a sigh, but there was no malice in her tone. "If we had more people, maybe we could make our own town, but it's not practical right now. And this is home, anyhow. I won't leave the woods and the mountain just to have a little bit of an easier walk to the general store.

"Not wanting to leave your home is something I can certainly understand."

Ellie paused, eyes narrowing slightly as she peered at him, like she might be able to see into his very soul if she stared hard enough.

"Care to elaborate?" she asked carefully.

Kaz just shrugged. "It's a little early for backstories."

IN WHICH KAZ LIES

Ellie re-braided her hair into twin plaits, then pinned them around her head like a crown. There was no point in keeping her hair down at all for a journey to town— up and out of the way was the best way to go. She wore a tank top as an undershirt and an oversized wool sweater, thick corduroy pants, and wool socks under tall, laced up leather boots.

"My guess is you're a light traveler?" Ellie asked, raising an eyebrow as she slipped her arms into her overcoat.

"Good guess," Kaz said. "I don't tend to drag much around with me. I get what I need when I need it, and when I don't need it anymore, I sell it. It's easier that way."

Traveling light certainly was easier in some ways, but Ellie herself couldn't fathom never putting down roots. Her own family ties ran too deep into the mountains.

"Got cash?" Ellie asked, fishing in her trunk for a scarf.

"That won't be a problem. Why?"

"It's March in Boone. Up here, that counts as still winter. We should pick you up some warm clothes while we're in town, and it would be a good idea to grab a few groceries, too. We can store things up here if they're canned or salted, and we got chickens, but best to have a little extra on hand for another mouth." She held out the scarf to him.

"Didn't know I was trouble," Kaz snapped, huffing, but he took the scarf.

She could hear an echo of... *something* in his voice. An echo of give and take, of calculating value. Of figuring out what he could ask for and what he could live on. Though she knew very well that their lives weren't the same, a hint of that pain was familiar. It was the pain of being an outsider, of understanding that you had to fend for yourself first and foremost, and Ellie knew that well.

"You're not trouble," Ellie said gently. "Well, not any more trouble than you're worth. It's just if I don't have anything to feed ya, I *can't* feed ya." Before she thought too hard about it, she reached out and patted his arm.

Kaz looked at her like she was a talking raccoon.

"Come on. I've got a spare hat, too, and you can use it till we get you a good leather one down in town."

"Demons don't exactly run cold," he said skeptically.

"Better safe than sorry," Ellie said with a shrug. "It's a long walk to town, and I don't think those city slicker shoes are gonna be kind to ya in this weather." She glanced briefly down at his basic loafers. The ground would be terrible today, considering the rain last night, but she knew a few paths that were usually less soggy than others.

"That's twice you've called me that."

"What? City slicker?" Ellie raised an eyebrow. "Y'are, ain't ya?"

"It sounds like an insult," he huffed.

"Keep your britches on, it just means we can tell you're from the city and ya don't know how things work around here," she said with a laugh, waving him off.

"It's *not* an insult?"

"Can be, depending. But I could call ya a pretty Georgia peach and it could be an insult depending on how I say it. If I wanted to insult you, trust me when I'd say you'd know," she said with a soft smile. "I'm known for many things. Subtlety is not one of 'em."

Ellie packed her canvas back quickly and thoroughly, writing down notes in a small book as she counted jars and bags. After filling it, she pulled the drawstring tight and hefted it over her shoulder, ready for the long walk to town.

"Okay, ground rules while we're out," she began, adjusting her wide-brimmed leather hat. "Don't tell anyone in town you're a demon. I wouldn't recommend telling any witches you're a full-blooded demon, either, but that's just me. They'll be all over you in two seconds flat, and I'm assuming you're not in the mood to tell your life story."

"Not particularly, no," he said, shaking his head.

"On that note, I'd also recommend you keep that hat on as much as you can. Conceal the horns."

"Noted..." Kaz placed the knit hat on his head, and thankfully it was roomy enough and thick enough that his horns didn't show through. He couldn't say he was particularly fond of the large pom at the top of it, but it would do for now. "What do we tell anyone who asks why I'm suddenly here, though?"

"We'll figure it out on the way to town," Ellie said with a shrug. "It's a long walk."

"You aren't concerned about your neighbors?"

"More that they aren't concerned about me," she grumbled, blowing a stray strand of silver hair out of her eyes. "Let's just say I'm a black sheep to most of the place, 'cept to Granny. And Granny is off on her yearly trip down the mountain, so we're in the clear there."

It was early enough that not too many people were out. Ellie hadn't wasted time this morning, partly because she didn't want to deal with a thousand questions from nosy people seeing her walking around with someone who wasn't Granny. She was almost always alone, and while seeing her with someone else wasn't an immediate red flag, it was unusual enough to see Ellie accompanied by a stranger that it might raise some eyebrows. Most people wouldn't ask, thankfully. They'd just gossip a bit and give her time to come up with an explanation.

"Let's go. We'll get onto the trail and then we'll talk."

Walking stick in hand and shouldering her canvas sack, she locked the door behind them, then moved quickly and quietly towards the iron gate that marked the edge of her yard. The whole world seemed wet and soggy from the storm, but that was alright. There were worse things than a little mud.

As they exited the yard, Ellie made directly for the village entrance, leading Kaz by a few private homes whose windows were still

dark, the community building (a large, open, multipurpose room), and past the chicken coops. As they passed the softly scratching chickens, Ellie caught the briefest sound of humming and flinched.

Someone was awake.

Normally that wouldn't be an issue, but it was the flash of fiery red hair at the edge of the coops that really made Ellie want to move along quickly. There were only a couple of witches with that color hair around here, and she didn't feel like talking to any of them at the moment. Her stomach sank with dread as she glanced to the side, barely catching a silhouette moving from coop to coop.

"Fuck," she hissed, squeezing her eyes shut briefly. If they were quick and lucky, they'd be able to get around talking to anyone and go on their way to town unmolested by any nosy neighbors, but this was possibly the worst person that could be out to see them.

Steps inevitably sloshing in the mud left behind by the rain the night before, they made it approximately twenty feet before a voice called out behind them.

"Mornin', folks!"

Ellie cringed. They were not lucky.

"Dear Lord above, save me from this haint of a woman," she muttered under her breath, moving just a little faster. "Keep walkin'," she hissed to Kaz. He matched pace without question, but it was of little use.

"Hey! Wait a second, Ellie—"

The sound of footsteps coming after them was more than enough to let Ellie know that they probably wouldn't be able to escape questioning. She briefly wished she'd thought this through, but it was rare that anyone would be awake so early, and even rarer they'd comment on what they saw. Really, there was only one person in the village who would even bother.

"Nosy bitch," she muttered under her breath, plastering a false smile on her face that did not reach her eyes as she turned to face the woman chasing them down.

The redheaded witch was a few years younger and a few inches shorter than Ellie, her hair wild and curly around her delicate face, framing genuinely pretty high cheekbones and pouty lips. She had a penchant for wanting to know everyone's business as though it

were *her* business, and absolutely no qualms about nosing into things. Occasionally, she very literally nosed her way into things.

This particular witch had a magically sensitive nose, allowing her to identify the biology of a plant, animal, or person from smell alone, and Ellie had no doubt she could smell the strong Other blood on Kaz. If her own nose couldn't identify something, she could also use her talent for animal speaking to ask whatever squirrels or raccoons in the area for information. It was up in the air if she could identify him as a full blooded demon or not, but she absolutely knew a handsome outsider with strong magic when she smelled one, and Alice could never let something like that just lie in peace.

"Hi, Alice," Ellie said in a clipped tone, the false smile still plastered on.

"Who's this new man you got here? He a... *friend* visiting from town?" Alice asked, batting her eyelashes incredibly indiscreetly at Kaz. She'd barely even given Ellie a second glance, which normally would be fine, but this time she was being used as an intermediary.

"Mm," Ellie said noncommittally, fighting not to roll her eyes. Best not to give any solid responses till she'd worked out the story with Kaz later. "Bye, Alice."

But Alice wasn't having it, trotting along beside them as they quickly walked towards the front gates. She was carrying a basket in her hand, and Ellie could see a few eggs carefully tucked inside.

"Well, you know, I'd be happy to show him around sometime. Save you the trouble of being a guide at all," she said quickly, struggling to keep up with their longer strides.

Ellie snorted. "I'm sure you would. Now, if you excuse us, we're in a hurry."

"Why don't I come along? It'll be like a fun party," Alice said, clapping her hands together. "Just let me put these eggs away—"

"That's kind of you, but Ellie has things under control," Kaz said firmly. Though she appreciated him piping up, Ellie knew that likely wouldn't deter Alice. The redheaded woman just carefully adjusted her basket of eggs and continued to bat her eyelashes.

"It's not a problem. I love meeting new visitors," she called, tossing a lock of bright orange hair over her shoulder as she spoke. "And it's not

like you two are *together*, you know? You're free to explore all you want. Whoever you want..."

The look on her face made it very clear *exactly* what she'd like to see Kaz explore. Thankfully, Ellie could deduce that this kind of thing likely wouldn't work on Kaz as a distraction, and she'd only known the man twelve hours... a good chunk of which she'd been asleep.

He might be an incubus, but she also thought he was a decent man, and... Well, one that didn't seem particularly interested in sex. Odd, based on what she'd heard and read, but she could respect that, and she was sure it probably got annoying being propositioned after a while. In fact, rather than looking intrigued by Alice's clear proposition, he seemed a little put off.

"We are *not*—" Ellie snapped, but not quickly enough.

"Together, yes, we are." Kaz interrupted, grabbing her hand suddenly and intertwining their fingers. "I thought it would be nice to spend some time where Ellie grew up."

Ellie shot him a look that could only be described as pure, unadulterated panic, but Kaz seemed calm as he pulled her a little closer to his side. Her heart hammered in her chest, and not in a pleasant way. It felt more like it wanted to escape her rib cage and head for the hills.

Forcing her expression back to some approximation of neutrality, Ellie risked a glance at Alice. The woman's painted-on smile fell just a little as disappointment clouded her gaze.

"Didn't think you'd ever bring a man home after... you know..." She shifted into a whisper. "... What happened to Ben?"

Blood flashed in Ellie's mind. A mangled body soaked from the rain lay motionless in the dirt, light brown hair stained red, far too red. His chest too still, not a single breath shaking his form.
She'd tried to avoid telling Kaz about the details, even managing to avoid telling him that Ben was her fiancé. Ellie didn't want to relive it, and he didn't need to know the specifics... at least, not right off.

"That's great, Alice, we gotta go—" Ellie tried, pushing down the bile rising in her throat, but Alice wouldn't let up.

"You know, it was just... it was horrible, and... we worry."

There was some hint of genuine concern in her voice, Ellie thought, but she couldn't focus on it, couldn't keep herself grounded.

"Ellie! Ellie, don't touch him, the police are still—"

But she was already there, kneeling beside the body, shaking him as if she might be able to wake him from the most final of all sleeps, white dress turning brown from the mud and red, red, red streaked all over from everywhere she touched him.

A scream ripped from her throat and her vision blurred. She felt hands pulling her back, pulling her away, but she couldn't let them. She couldn't leave him, not like this.

"Ellie," Kaz's voice cut through the fog for a moment, but not long enough.

"What do you mean she's a suspect?" Pastor John asked incredulously. "She physically couldn't have done it. I was with her in the church all morning—"

"We don't know what all her kind can do," the Sheriff insisted quietly, but not so quietly that Ellie couldn't hear. "I'm covering all my bases."

"Her kind? Feel like expanding on that, Sheriff?" John spat, bristling.

The Sheriff opened his mouth to respond, then quickly shut it. It wasn't wise to go up against the local pastor, not in a small town, and everybody knew it. They were at a standstill.

"I don't care what you think of me," Ellie whispered, knuckles white as she clutched the fabric of her ruined dress, still soaked from the storm. "Just... just find the bastard who did this."

"Breathe!" Kaz snapped. He reached up and smacked her lightly on the cheek twice, grabbing her shoulder with his other hand.

Ellie's eyes went wide from the slap as she gasped in shock, gulping in lungfuls of crisp mountain air. It wasn't hard enough to leave a mark or even hurt, just enough to shake her, eyes refocusing on Kaz as she jolted out of the memory.

"Thanks," she panted. "Needed that."

Alice glanced between them as Ellie's vision swam back into place. Her brow furrowed as she stared, but again... Ellie couldn't be sure of her motivations. Alice was under her mother's thumb, and just as likely to act concerned to make herself look attractive as show actual concern.

"Goodbye, Alice," Ellie said softly, all her anger exhausted.

"Oh, dear," Alice began, a flash of something Ellie couldn't identify in her eyes. "Let me get—"

"I've got you. Lean on me," Kaz interrupted, just a little louder than Ellie thought was necessary. He snaked his arm around her waist as though he was supporting her, but it mostly just brought them very close together as they walked.

In a way, that was fine. Ellie was only slightly surprised to find that he was preternaturally warm, not to mention a wonderful shield against the mountain winds. She also did still feel a little wobbly, and she'd take the support while she could get it... Not that she'd ever admit that out loud.

"Where did you go back there?" Kaz whispered as they walked towards the entrance to the village. Ellie's legs seemed to become stronger with every step, the cool morning air grounding her in reality, far away from the nightmares of her past.

"I... somewhere I don't want to be."

"You looked like the soldiers that came back from the war just then." Kaz sighed as he shook his head. "I've seen enough of them to know what trauma looks like."

"I just wasn't expecting... I'm fine," she said, taking a deep breath through her nose.

"Do you panic like that every time someone mentions Ben?"

"No."

"How often?" he pressed.

More often than she would like to admit, so Ellie simply dodged the question.

"Alice is... a special brand of bitch," Ellie whispered distastefully. "Her whole family thought I was squandering my talent by marrying into a fully human bloodline. Her sense of smell is supernatural, too, so I bet she could smell how strong the Other blood is in you from the get-go. Of course it had to be *her* out this early."

"Are there no men in your community?" he asked, brow furrowed. "Is she that desperate for a partner?"

"There's plenty, yeah. Maybe four out of every ten are boys, most from distant enough lines that we don't have to worry about intermarrying too close, or they can submit a letter to the council and look for a match

somewhere else. The dream is to marry a full-blooded Other for a lot of 'em, though, or at least have a baby with one."

"Why not just... let people be happy?"

"That's the money question, ain't it?" she huffed, blowing a stray strand of hair out of her face. "They think that if they marry into a line with strong magic, it'll give them some kind of infinite power or enhance their own power or give them... I don't know, infinitely powerful children whose lives they can control. Some weirdo shit like that." Ellie rolled her eyes, finally standing.

"And you?"

"I think they're a few sandwiches short of a picnic," she grumbled, tapping her forehead meaningfully. "Come on, let's get outta here."

Kaz threw a glance over his shoulder as they reached the gate, and when he looked back towards Ellie, there was a wicked grin on his lips. It was practically possible to hear the wheels turning in his mind, to see the plan forming in his head as they took step after step down the wide dirt path towards town.

"On the upside, I think we've found the perfect cover," he whispered into her ear.

"Besides having quiet conversations because we're standing too damn close, you're gonna have to break down the other benefits for me," she muttered.

"In time," he said, drawing her a little nearer. "Let's put some space between us and this place first."

IN WHICH OUR HEROES WALK TO BOONE

As the dirt road away from the village widened and moved farther into the woods between them and Boone, Kaz shifted from walking with his arm around Ellie's waist and instead moved to hold her hand. She still wasn't entirely happy about that development, but at least she could walk a little more freely now.

"Are we far enough away that you can let go of my hand?" Ellie asked approximately half a mile away from the village.

"I'd say so, at this point. I'm more concerned about your reaction to Ben than my explanation to Alice, though." Kaz dropped his hold with a sigh and Ellie immediately put distance between them.

"So what?"

"Seems like something I need to know if I'm going to help you solve this case," he said, his tone surprisingly gentle. "How did you know him? Be honest."

Ellie went silent. She kept walking down the road, boots squelching in the mud. The early morning bird calls echoed through the woods around them, and the sound of the wind seemed as loud as thunder.

She didn't want to talk about it. She'd talked about it enough that everyone thought she was crazy. Even Granny thought she was a little crazy, somewhere deep down, but... Kaz

was right. If he was going to elp her, he probably did need to know at least the bare bones of the story.

Ellie took a deep breath and steeled herself, rehearsing her words in a way that put them outside herself, outside her body, off into a place where it didn't hurt to say them.

"He was my fiancé," she finally whispered. "He was... so good. So genuinely, truly *good*."

She kept walking mechanically, the words coming from a place that was somehow her and not her all at once, a place just distant enough numb things.

"He always treated me well when we met in town. He never judged anyone based on their ancestry. His whole family runs a farm not too far away, and they're down to earth kinda people. Ben was the best of 'em all, though. He had a big heart."

Keep walking, she thought. *Just keep walking*. Ellie wasn't really sure where she went when she talked about Ben. It wasn't somewhere good, but it wasn't somewhere as bad as it could be, either.

"The morning of our wedding, he never showed up. At first I thought it was a fluke, maybe he just got caught in the rain and the mud and was running late, but then hours went by and the Sheriff found a body in the woods."

"Ellie," Kaz said.

One step after another. She could do this. It wouldn't take long to get through it.

"I guess I just—"

"Ellie, stop."

Kaz put a hand on her shoulder, literally stopping her in her tracks. She turned around to look at him, snapping back into her body from that vague somewhere else that kept the pain out.

"You don't have to relive that experience so I can understand," Kaz said firmly, grasping her hand. "Stay in the here and now. I don't need every detail if it hurts you."

Ellie frowned, narrowing her eyes at him. "Has anyone ever told you that you're kinda weird?"

"Is that... What does that mean?"

"It's a good thing," she mumbled, shaking herself. Ellie took a long, deep breath of cool mountain air before she continued. "Now, want to explain why tellin' people we're 'together' is a good cover and not a red flag to the whole world?"

"Admittedly, I said what I said in the moment because I wanted to explain two people in a house with one bed," Kaz said with a sigh, "but knowing that you live in a community of people who *want* Others in their midst not only legitimizes my presence, it makes them less likely to question me."

"Okay, I follow that," she said, nodding slowly.

"In town, I would think it would be less likely we'd draw attention related to Ben's case if you're clearly involved with someone else."

"Or they'll burn me at the stake," she deadpanned.

"I will not let that happen to you," Kaz snapped, his tone icy. "Not on my watch. I've heard enough about the shit that happened here a couple centuries ago. There's no need to repeat it."

"If you're thinkin' Salem, the one down the mountain ain't that one," Ellie said, smiling despite herself. "That's up in Massachusetts. I feel very supported by the big, strong demon, though, so thanks."

"I... there's another one?" He blinked. Clearly he'd meant "here" as in "this world," not thinking that Ellie knew the exact location.

"Yeah. Moravian town, old place. No public executions, though." She paused. "... 'Least none that I know of."

"Noted," Kaz said, nodding as if he wasn't quite sure how to respond to that.

"You've... seen your share of shit, too, huh?" Ellie said slowly, looking over at him.

"I understand what it means to want to protect your own," he confirmed. "As far as I'm concerned, that includes you for the duration of this bargain."

Yeah, he was a weirdo alright. Ellie cast a sidelong glance at him as they walked, a few strands of his white hair that weren't tucked into the wool hat blowing in the breeze. He didn't push her to talk, and she appreciated that.

"I'm sorry," Ellie murmured.

"Mm?"

"I'm not gonna tell ya I trust you. That's not what I'm saying... but I'm sorry I assumed the worst of you from the start."

Kaz seemed to think on this for a long moment.

"I accept that as a peace offering."

Ellie let out a deep breath that she didn't know she was holding. It was odd to her that she felt so... friendly towards someone she'd expected to hire to help her, but Kaz was... nice. Against her expectations, he was sensitive and a decent person, and he had treated her better in the last twelve hours than most of Boone had treated her in the last year. She thought that deserved some credit.

"Why did you really say yes?" Ellie asked suddenly. "When I called. Why did you say yes?"

"I thought it might make me feel alive again to do something like this."

"Take a bargain? Thought you did that all the time."

"Not like this," he insisted.

"I suppose demons aren't asked to help with cold cases a lot," Ellie said with a shrug.

"It's more likely that we're the ones asked to do the killing," he said, nose wrinkling in distaste. "It's not... pleasant."

"Why do you do it?" Ellie asked, brow furrowed. "If you don't like it, why do you take bargains? The book said you had a choice about responding to me, and you could'a said no when I asked."

"I did have a choice." He sighed, stuffing his hands in the pockets of his worn leather jacket. "I suppose the easy answer is that everyone has to make a living somehow."

"What's the hard answer?"

Silence.

"Okay, okay," Ellie said, holding her hands up in surrender. "I won't push."

"Thanks."

"Wait, stop here," Ellie said suddenly, holding out a hand.

"What's this?" It looked to him like a small clearing on the side of the dirt road, particularly muddy and soggy with rain and rotting leaves. The road curved a little, but otherwise there wasn't much to distinguish this place from any other place they might pass on the way to town.

"This is... this is where he died."

Fuck.

Kaz fought not to curse out loud. No wonder she was feeling shaky— she had to walk past the spot where her fiancé died every time she left her home. There was only one road out, as far as he'd seen, and this was it. Ellie looked off into the distance, squinting into the trees, and then she stepped off the path.

"I need to check something," she mumbled, carefully picking her way through the leaves. A few steps off the road, she turned back to Kaz.

"I couldn't find squat when I checked, but I think the rain had washed away most everything by the time I made it up here. Can you...?" She trailed off, and something about the hopeful tone in her voice made his chest ache.

"My methods are limited. I can't look into the past or read minds, but I can detect leftover energy signatures..." he mumbled, eyes scanning the clearing. He followed in her footsteps, losing track of where she was walking as he closed his eyes, trying to focus on his sixth sense, on the sensation of the energetic imprint of the place.

As he was afraid of, there wasn't much. Outdoors and a long-abandoned crime scene, he wasn't expecting to find any traces, but he did pick up the slightest pinprick.

In the distance, Kaz could feel more than see the softest imprint of leftover *red*. Not blood, no. He wasn't sensitive to blood or biology, but as an incubus he could sense emotional imprints very easily. If it was a two-year-old imprint, it had to be strong to leave even a little trace behind. Very, very strong.

He followed the trail, feeling that pinprick get hotter and louder as he drew closer, until finally he could feel it under his feet, buried in the roots of a large tree.

Careful to disturb the plant as little as possible, Kaz picked his way through the mud and the leaves, fingers gently prizing the roots apart

as he dug out the object calling to him from under the tree. He wasn't sure what he was expecting to find, but when his fingers finally touched something that wasn't dirt or a tree root, he wasn't quite sure what he'd found.

"Odd," he murmured, dragging the small, squashed object up from the roots. After brushing the dirt off, he could tell it was a smashed bundle of thin wire.

"Does that mean anything to you?" he called, holding it up. Ellie scrambled over towards him, plucking the wire from his fingers.

"There's fabric in this..." she muttered, squinting at the wire as she took it from him. "Not a lot, but... looks like burlap, maybe? Hard to tell under the dirt, and it's half decayed from being buried."

"It has... something on it," Kaz said helplessly. "Part of it is the woods. It's been here long enough that a lot of the energy that once was on it has been returned to the earth. There's something that's clinging to it, though."

"Any idea what it could be? Looks like some baling wire to me."

"Rage," Kaz said quietly. "That's all I can get from it, and it's faint, but to cling on after two years..."

"It had to be strong," she said, nodding as she tucked the wire in her pocket. "Thanks. That's more than I was able to dig up out here."

"Still not much..." he muttered, scanning the clearing once more.

That wire was the only energy signature calling out to him in the entire clearing. It was almost unusually clean... but it *had* been two years, and the earth had a way of taking back and cleansing energy all on its own. It was nice, in a way, and it kept the balance. Kept energy moving constantly.

"Was there blood when he died?" Kaz asked.

Ellie paled in a way that almost made him regret asking, but it was one of the few options they had left.

"Yes. A lot," she said, voice shaking slightly.

"In that case, I might have a contact who can help," Kaz said carefully, looking off into the middle distance. "She doesn't often stay in one place for long, but if I can get a hold of her, it might be helpful in more ways than one."

"What do you need to contact her?"

"Some paper, a white candle, a wax seal, and a few basic spell ingredients. Usually, I'd need something that belongs to her, too, but I can work around that."

"You can do it without a tag lock?" Ellie asked, impressed.

"Only if I know the person well. It takes extra energy and there is technically a low chance it won't be delivered correctly, but it's a useful back door to know in a pinch."

"Let me know if you need anything specific from town. We can send the message when we—"

Ellie suddenly went stock still, staring off into the distance. At first, Kaz didn't see anything at all. However, if he squinted, it was possible to make out a figure that seemed to be made of mist.

It was human-shaped, maybe a little under six feet tall if he had to guess, but he couldn't see specifics. It was like staring at a cloud of fog for him, but he imagined that Ellie's Sight showed her every single detail of the spirit in front of them.

"He's here," she whispered, placing a hand on Kaz's arm.

"Is that..." he breathed, eyes widening slightly.

"Hey, Benny," she said softly, walking towards the hazy mist in the vague shape of a man. Kaz didn't know what she was seeing, if it was more detailed than the ghostly whisp he could make out, but she didn't seem afraid of it. "How ya feeling, sweetie?"

"I— I don't know. I can't... it's like I can't think. Why am I out here?"

Hearing a spirit of the dead speak was something Kaz always found a little uncomfortable. It wasn't quite like hearing something in your ears. It felt more like cold fingers caressing your mind every time they spoke, like hearing a voice that wasn't meant to be heard any more.

It didn't seem to bother Ellie, though. Her eyes shone with tears, but she continued to carefully move towards the spirit, putting on an encouraging smile. She was trying to be careful with him. That much was obvious, but Kaz wasn't quite sure *why* she wanted to be careful.

"It's okay, hon. I'm right here, so you know you're fine with me. The woods are my place, remember?" She spoke slowly, carefully, every word carefully calculated.

"Yeah. Yeah, that makes sense." Something about the tone softened, relaxed.

"Why don't you come back to the road with me, huh? You can go back home." Ellie was calm in a way that made it clear she was not calm at all, her tone too even, her voice too soft, her words too practiced.

"I should help with supper. It's gettin' late," he said softly, the hazy mist moving closer.

"Yeah. Come on, I'll get you back on the road, baby," Ellie said softly. She didn't reach out to touch the mist, but she did check to make sure he was following as she walked back towards the main road. The shape followed along slowly. Kaz couldn't see if the spirit took any kind of discernible steps, but it did follow towards the road. It didn't pay any attention to Kaz whatsoever, single-mindedly moving towards Ellie like she was the only thing he could see.

Ellie stepped onto the muddy track, watching as it followed her, but the second that the foggy shadow of Ben's spirit floated over the main road, it vanished.

Ellie's shoulders slumped and she let out a breath, shaking her head. "Let's go," she whispered, beckoning him on.

She started walking without another word, and Kaz had to scramble to catch up. She was moving fast now, and he didn't blame her. That seemed like something anyone would want to run from, and he credited her for holding it together as much as she was.

"He doesn't know he's...?" Kaz asked gently.

"No, he doesn't seem to," Ellie said with a huff, biting her lip.

"Why?" Kaz asked, looking at the space where Ben's spirit had once been.

"People who go suddenly don't always have the most peaceful passing. It does something to their mind, to their memories. Going unprepared like that does something to them. Sticks them... somewhere," she said, shaking her head quickly.

"So you come out here to... soothe him?"

"When I see him pop up, yeah. It's about all I can do for him. I give him some peace when I see him, but I'm not entirely sure what would happen to his mind if he... if he *knows*," she said pointedly. "I don't want to have to exorcise him, and I've seen ghosts turn unpredictable and violent when they're in that state."

"Is there anyone else with the Sight you could ask about this?" Kaz mused, scratching his jaw absently.

"Just Granny," Ellie said sadly, "and hers comes and goes. Some days it's good, others she can't see anything at all."

"How rare is it?"

"Rare," Ellie deadpanned. "Rare enough that I don't know anyone else in the state with the Sight. I'd have to write the Council and ask for records access to locate someone."

"I'm sorry," Kaz said slowly. Ellie just blinked at him owlishly.

"For... what?"

"I imagine it's lonely."

"It... kinda is," she admitted.

"Do you know any psychopomps?" Kaz asked, scratching his jaw. "I wonder if they might be able to help him reach a stable state or guide him where he's meant to go, even if they're stuck on this plane."

Ellie hummed in the back of her throat, tilting her head from one side to the other. "It's not a bad thought. Miriam knows a Dullahan who does rounds up in Virginia and pops by sometimes, but I don't know how well she knows him."

"Psychopomps do seem to keep to themselves," Kaz muttered. "Let me think on it a while, see what I can do."

"Thanks," Ellie said. "I know we have a blood bargain an' all, but I'm... glad I'm not doin' all this alone."

It occurred to him, in that moment, that he wouldn't want her doing this alone. It had been less than a day and he was already attached, it seemed. Ellie was different than the kind of people he was used to, and it caught him off guard.

He knew there were good humans. There were good demons, so the least he could do was give humans some credit and assume not all of them were terrible. He rarely answered calls for good humans, though.

He wasn't used to someone who would think of his comfort enough to give him a pain remedy for his neck. He wasn't used to someone who would ask opinions on groceries or care if he had the right

shoes for the weather. Ellie was a natural nurturer, and he was afraid that he could get used to that a little too quickly.

It made him want to... return the favor. To give back.

It made him want to trust her, even though he knew that was a mistake. Bargains and trust did not mix. Bargains and emotions did not mix, he reminded himself, his fingertips moving to trace the scarring around his neck. He'd already learned that the hard way too many times, and he wasn't about to make the same mistake again.

6. IN WHICH ELLIE VISITS A FRIEND

They finished the walk to town in silence. Surprisingly, Ellie didn't feel pressured to speak, which was new for her. She was accustomed to being around people who felt they had to fill the silence with conversation, that there was no point to being around others without talking. Not Kaz, though. He seemed content to walk together and keep to his own thoughts, which was fine with Ellie. She had things to stew over, too.

Mostly, she stewed over the idea that the Sight was a lonely gift to have. That conversation played in her mind over and over again, each time a little more vivid than the last.

Ellie had never thought of it as lonely, not really. The Sight guaranteed that she, more often than not, always had someone or something around her, so she'd found it almost stifling as a child. It was part of the reason she enjoyed living out in the woods, too. There were spirits out here, yes, but less human ghosts asking for attention or favors or closure. She could only do so much as one person.

Now that he mentioned it, though... Ellie had to admit that there was something to it. There was something to being the only person who could see these things, some kind of pain in understanding that you could see a part of the world that most other people missed.

There weren't many spirits in town like there were in the woods, though. As the dirt road turned to concrete, electrical power lines strung from pole to pole came into view. Sidewalks appeared around the packed dirt and gravel road. The buildings that lined King Street were sturdy and brick, some with large glass storefronts and others with smaller windows. The entirety of the downtown district was no more than one mile on this one street, but it was more than enough for Ellie. She never liked cities. A mile's worth of a shopping district was as much as she wanted.

"Welcome to downtown Boone," Ellie said with a smile. "We've got a few stops to make. Don't mind if people look at ya a little funny. It's probably me."

Hopefully there wouldn't be too many people around today. It was a long walk to town, but they'd left not long after sunrise. Most places would be busier in the afternoon, when their errands should be finished.

"We're heading to the bakery first, then we'll stop by the Sheriff's office and pop into Mast before we head back."

"Mast?" He frowned. "Like a ship?"

"General store," Ellie said, adjusting her bag. "They've got about everything you'd need, plus a few more things. Not the friendliest of the locals, but they're polite enough if you're paying, and there's not many places to pick from to shop."

King Street had almost everything you might need, but Ellie knew well enough not to linger long. Not everyone was friendly to witches, and even those friendly to most witches were not always friendly to *her*. There weren't many people out today, so with luck, she wouldn't have to explain to Kaz why people actively avoided her on the streets. However, it was emotionally exhausting to stay out shopping for too long.

Thus, Ellie marched down the street, almost clear to the opposite end. She went past the post office, past the general store, and entirely ignored the meat market in favor of going directly towards the town bakery. The sign on the large glass window read "Jones Bakery" in a beautiful script, with advertisements for cakes, breads, and more painted underneath.

"Emmaline!" Ellie called, the bell dinging as she pushed open the door to the bakery. "Y'all back there?!"

"Ellie!"

A blur with blonde hair shot out of the bakery's back room, launching at Ellie and almost knocking her over with a bear hug. She was short and just a little plump with round cheeks and a kind smile, and Ellie hugged her back just as tightly. Emmaline Jones was one of the kindest souls in town. She and her husband owned the bakery, and they'd always been good to anyone who walked in their shop.

"Hi, Ellie," a masculine voice called cheerfully before a large man stepped out from the back, his dark blue apron covered in flour. "Good to see you."

"Good to see you, too, Tom," Ellie said with a wide smile.

"Oooooo, did you bring a goodie basket for me?" Emmaline asked, eyeing the canvas bag slung over Ellie's shoulder as she finally released her hold.

"Yeah, I guess, if you count a sack full of medicine as a goodie bag," she said, laughing as she put the bag up on the counter, contents clinking slightly. The rucksack was full of medicines and herbs, freshly brewed, bottled, and bagged.

"You know I do!" she said excitedly, clapping her hands together. Before reaching into the bag, though, she paused and turned to Kaz. "Who's this?"

"He's. Um. He's my..."

"Fiancé," Kaz supplied.

Ellie fought not to glare, but even around Emmaline it was best to keep their cover. She was a trusted friend, but she tended to let things slip out of her mouth when she wasn't thinking, and even a small detail that contradicted their story could be dangerous.

Emmaline raised an eyebrow, turning towards a wincing Ellie with her hands on her hips.

"Are you being blackmailed?"

"No."

"Are you sure?" she asked, eyes narrowing.

"Yeah," Ellie groaned.

"Did Jeannie finally win that ongoing argument?"

"*Definitely* not," she scoffed. "Let's just say Kaz is still... leaning the right human terms for things. Relationships included," she offered. Hopefully that would suffice as a compromise.

"Oh, you're an Other," Emmaline said, nodding as though that was the only explanation she needed.

"Are there many in town?" Kaz asked.

"Like you? A few here and there, yeah. Boone doesn't require papers from anybody who moves in, so as long as nobody's causing trouble, Others go in and out of town as much as they want." She gestured broadly as she spoke, talking as much with her hands as her mouth, blonde curls bobbing as she tilted her head from one side to the other.

"Generally folks don't like it when we ask, so... we don't. I don't blame 'em for being twitchy when humans outnumber Others five to one, and more in areas like this." Tom shrugged. "Sometimes you can tell by the way someone looks."

"Like me," Ellie muttered.

Kaz paused for a moment, giving her a strange look. "And... me," he said slowly, pulling off the knit hat to reveal his short, curved obsidian horns.

"That'd do it, yeah," Emmaline said with a sigh. "Dragon traits aren't too common, though, so don't be surprised if you get some stares. Sorry 'bout that in advance."

"Demon," Kaz supplied, casually slipping his hat back on his head.

"What's that?" Tom asked, moving behind the counter to wrap up a few loaves of bread.

"I'm a demon, not a dragon," he said simply.

Emmaline's eyes went wide.

Ellie glared. "What was rule number *one* of the ground rules?" she asked through gritted teeth.

"I was trying to be supportive!" he said helplessly. "And I couldn't let them think I'm a dragon shifter."

Ellie's expression softened, but only slightly. "I appreciate the support, I do," she said, patting his shoulder. "If I could hide my hair and get around explaining anything at all, though, I would."

"L—listen, she's right," Emmaline said quietly. "Don't go sayin' that in town. I trust Ellie, we both do, so if she says you're safe to be around, that's fine. But you're deep in the Bible belt right now, and folks won't hesitate to judge you as harshly as they can."

"Isn't the whole thing supposed to be forgiveness?" Kaz muttered, brow furrowed. "What have I ever done to them?"

"Keep asking that. It's a damn good question," Ellie scoffed.

As she and Kaz spoke quietly, Emmaline slipped behind the counter, pulled something out from a hidden shelf, and bustled back over to them.

"Here's your cut from the last delivery," Emmaline said, extending a thick envelope towards Ellie. "Tom, honey, you got her bread order?"

The tall man nodded from behind the counter as he held up a large paper bag. Ellie couldn't help but smile a little as she took the envelope from Emmaline, but when she looked inside her eyes went wide.

"Are you sure you're makin' profit off any of these medicines? This seems like way too much..." Ellie said, eyebrow raised as she carefully counted the bills.

"Oh, trust me, we are. You just don't set your prices high enough, so I corrected it for you," she said with an overly innocent smile. "I can't keep your stuff on the shelves. The folks at Mast keep askin' where I get it, but I've kept it quiet like you wanted."

"I'm flattered," she said, shaking her head. "I'm just glad for the extra income. Thank you, really."

"Ellie, you know I'm serious," Emmeline said softly. "This stuff will sell out in a day as soon as word gets out it's in stock. You could make a living doing this, and a good one."

"I'd like to," Ellie said softly. "But you know Jeannie. I need to have Council approval for a business up in our area, and they won't give it to me. Even selling outside the village through you is a bit of a stretch. For now I'm stuck where I am, just helpin' with the gardens and the odd jobs."

"Then move out!" Emmaline huffed, throwing her arms up dramatically.

"And stay where, honey? I love you, but you've got two littles and a husband at home, and you don't need another body in that house."

"We'd make it work," Thomas insisted. "I still say you saved our little girl's life when you treated her flu a few years back. We owe you."

"You don't owe me a damn thing and you know it," Ellie sighed. "There's no way I'd let a little youngin' slip by me who needed help. Y'all were just some of the few who *let* me help ya."

"Still, she made it through. A lot of other folks weren't that lucky. You don't just forget help like that."

"I haven't once felt forgotten around y'all," Ellie said softly. "You're good folks. I'm just glad to have people I trust in town."

"Just... think about it. Please?"

"I'll think about it." She said that every time. And she did think about it, more than she'd like to admit. However, the possibility was so low of it ever happening that she didn't want to entertain it most days. Maybe if things had worked out with Ben. Maybe if she'd been able to really move out and get away, even just a short ways away...

But that was a bygone dream.

Ellie tucked the envelope in an inside pocket in her coat, bid her goodbyes to Emmaline and Thomas, and ushered Kaz out of the bakery. She turned left down the street to head towards the general store and the Sheriff's office with him on her heels, but her mind was somewhere else.

She wasn't entirely sure what made Kaz jump from "together" to fiancé, but maybe it really *was* a cultural difference. Either way, it felt oddly uncomfortable, like a sock that slid down in your boot too far. Not so terrible it's impossible to walk, but a damn annoyance all the same.

Together was one thing. *Engaged* was another, and that would be a separate conversation to have back at the house.

""The Council won't *let* you?"" Kaz repeated. Lost in her thoughts, Ellie almost missed that he spoke at all.

"Huh? Oh," Ellie said, shaking her head as if to clear it. "How much do you know about witch communities and how they're organized?"

"Some," he said, waving his hand vaguely. "I know there's some sense of overall organization for the purposes of protecting registered witches and witch settlements."

"That's the gist, yeah. Each village has a lead witch, and then villages register with the appropriate Council so everyone can kinda... keep track of each other. Keep each other safe. Well... on the good days."

"What happens on bad days?"

"Don't get me wrong, I ain't never seen two witch communities fight. There's too few of us not to at least make an attempt at a united front," she said slowly. "But there's definitely a kind of... internal competition, if you will."

"Wanting to be the biggest and best, I assume. Demon communities aren't terribly far off from that in some circles."

"Sort of. Think about as which ones are more powerful," Ellie explained. "Size helps. Sheer numbers can only get ya so far if you're a community of weak witches, though. That's part of why they don't like me much," she said quietly.

"You... I'm sorry, you successfully conjured a demon and they think you're *weak*?!"

"Keep it down!" Ellie hissed, looking over her shoulder to see if anyone appeared alarmed. Very few people were out on the street, thankfully, and no one was within an earshot, but that could have gone bad very quickly.

"Conjuring takes an immense amount of energy. I know enough to have seen it knock witches unconscious by the time I arrived to answer the call," Kaz scoffed. "Not to mention that the ash blend used is incredibly complex and includes some dangerous components."

"I did fuck up the sacrifice, to be completely fair," she muttered, crossing her arms over her chest.

"Not really," Kaz said, shrugging. "You caught my attention. I think it worked."

A slow flush crept over Ellie's cheeks as he looked down at her, gaze locked on her face. Something about the way the light made his sharp cheekbones stand out, something about the gold flash in his eyes made her stomach twist in a way she hadn't felt in a long time.

And she cleared her throat, and shoved that twisting feeling deep, deep down.

"A— anyway, I'm kinda the family black sheep. I'm good with medicines, but I can't do much in the way of power display."

"You *talk* to *spirits*," Kaz insisted incredulously.

"They want me to be able to conjure fire, control water, make plants spontaneously grow, talk to animals, or anything else flashy that you can think of," she snorted. "Hell, they might even like it if I used the Sight

for seances, but I won't. The dead deserve more respect than being called on for cheap tricks."

"No rabbits out of top hats for you?" He raised an eyebrow.

"I am horrible at slight-of-hand tricks. Real spells are fine, though." She moved the canvas sack to the other shoulder as they walked, boot heels clicking on the brick sidewalks. "Any witch can do spells if they've got the energy reserves, the time, and the patience. That's not too hard."

"Can anyone in your village do the... flashy things?" Kaz fluttered his fingers vaguely.

"Jeannie can, a little. She's good with fire. Her divination is pretty shit, though, and she can't concentrate on writing a spell for more than two minutes at a time." Ellie's nose scrunched as she frowned.

"Tell me what you really think, please!" Kaz laughed, a genuine smile on his face.

"I can't a say a whole lot," Ellie said, smiling despite herself. "She's been a good aunt. Had her share of hard knocks, too, like everybody."

"Even Alice?" He elbowed her in the side gently.

"Oh, somebody's got jokes, I get it," Ellie snorted, rolling her eyes. "Yeah, even Alice, in a way. She has a bunch of siblings and she's used to being... a little overlooked at home, I think. Might be why she tries so hard to draw attention to herself."

"That's awfully generous, considering you called her a special brand of bitch earlier," Kaz said, rolling his eyes. Ellie had to admit that he had a point, but that was just the way things worked out here.

"Just because I don't like her don't mean I can't understand her a little," she said with a shrug. "She ain't exactly a friend, but she's part of the village, and if we don't take care of each other, no one else will. It's complicated."

When you only had each other to depend on, whether you liked someone and whether you trusted them not to fuck you over were different things. Even though some days she didn't *want* to trust Alice, in an emergency, they had each other's backs.

"I get it. I do." Kaz shoved his hands in his jacket pockets as they walked. "I've seen communities of Others do the same thing. They put aside their differences for the sake of survival, though they generally aren't as organized as the witch system."

"Why aren't you living in one of those, then?"

"Let's just say it never felt right."

"Okay," Ellie said, nodding. "I can understand that."

They continued their walk towards the general store in silence, the same comfortable silence as the walk to town. It occurred to Ellie that perhaps it should be an awkward or oppressive silence, but she didn't feel that way at all. She felt welcome to be silent, to understand she wasn't obligated to bare her soul if she didn't want to. It was oddly comforting, and she'd take any comfort she could get right now.

7 IN WHICH OUR HEROES HAVE STEW

"Of *course* the Sheriff is on a damn vacation," Ellie grumbled, unlocking the door to her small house as the sun disappeared behind the mountain. "At least we got you a few winter clothes and a decent hat, though."

"I must admit, I do like this one better than the knit one," Kaz said as he adjusted the wide-brimmed leather hat on his head.

"Looks good on ya," she said with a smile. "I hope they were tellin' the truth when they said they'd get the rest of your stuff up on the delivery truck tomorrow."

Though their trip to the Sheriff's office had been met with more setbacks than progress, Ellie and Kaz had at least managed to place an order at Mast General Store for a few things that Kaz needed. Winter clothes were among the most important, along with a couple of extra blankets and a basic portable camp bed. It wasn't fancy, but it would at least temporarily solve the sleeping quarters issue. Plus, if anyone found bringing in another small bed odd, Ellie could always say she'd bought it to use with her tent on long trips rather than the plain bedroll she was used to. The full load was too cumbersome to walk up the mountain themselves, so they'd arranged for it to be on the weekly delivery truck up to the village.

The bone door hanger jingled as Ellie shut and locked it

behind them, happy to be in the privacy of her own home and to put down her load. The canvas bag wasn't too heavy, but it was a long way to walk carrying it and her shoulders protested the trip.

She tugged off her hat and overcoat to hang on a hook by the door, gesturing for Kaz to do the same, and got to work unloading supplies.

"While we wait for the Sheriff, it might be wise to question some of your witch neighbors," Kaz suggested, hanging his new hat beside Ellie's battered one.

Ellie paused, staring for a moment while her mouth opened and closed. "I'm not sayin' *no*, but I don't really get why a witch would kill Ben."

"I think we should investigate every possibility. Just to be safe." He leaned against the wall, eyebrows raised as if daring her to question him. Ellie raised her hands in surrender, wiggling her fingers just slightly before she went back to dealing with supplies.

"Not sayin' you're wrong, but... Most of 'em see humans as '*beneath them*,'" she said, rolling her eyes. "They don't mind full-blooded humans as long as those humans don't mind them, but it's like they're... flies or something. Not worth botherin' with."

"Noted," Kaz said with a nod, "but I'm still curious if anyone saw something suspicious. The witch community spends more time in the woods than the average Boone resident, correct?"

"Fair point. I guess they could've seen something out on the road that day, but I'd be surprised if someone saw something obviously important and just didn't tell me."

"Why's that?" he raised an eyebrow as Ellie hefted their packages onto the kitchen table.

"We don't look like it, but witches are pretty organized, even out here. We have a formal code for communities under Council protection, and we all know that the most sacred rule is protecting our own." She refilled jars of herbs from paper packets and placed them neatly on the shelves, organizing dry goods and bread as she went. Kaz just watched, sitting down in a wooden chair and tapping his fingers absently on the table as he thought out loud.

"What makes someone one of your own?"

"Blood kin, most easily," Ellie said with a shrug. "Marriage, too. You can formally renounce someone or claim someone under the right circumstances, but it's hardly ever done."

"Did you plan to claim Ben?"

"Already had," Ellie said with a sigh. "I sent papers to the Council ahead of time— dropped 'em off at the post office myself instead of waiting for weekly mail delivery to town. The approval papers didn't arrive until.. . *after*, though."

She shook herself, fighting not to lose her faculties to the current of past memories speeding by. The papers were still in her house, and she knew exactly where. They were in a box with her old engagement ring, with a stack of old letters, with a few precious pictures. She wasn't ready to let go yet, and she wasn't sure she ever would be.

"I'll stoke the fire. You pick what's for supper," Ellie said, already kneeling in front of the woodstove. She'd banked the fire before they left, but it wasn't too hard to open the bank and stoke the smoldering embers to life.

"Anything with vegetables," he said with a shrug.

"Deer stew, then." She hoisted two extra logs into the stove and shut the door. "There. That should warm it up in here pretty quick."

"*Deer* stew?"

"Never had deer?" Ellie raised an eyebrow, but wasn't too shocked. "I know a lot of folks avoid it, but there's a lot of 'em up here and not much room for grazing cows. We eat what we can get. I promise there's veggies, too. We've got beans, carrots, peas, and potatoes to go in it, though we'll be eatin' it tomorrow too, probably. Makes a big batch."

"I didn't think you had a refrigerator. Will it keep?"

"I've got a cellar under the house for cold storage, and there's community cold storage with an icebox. In this weather, there's no need to worry about it, though," she said with a shrug. It would easily be close to or below freezing temperatures the next few nights. "I'll go get the meat from the cellar. You start choppin' potatoes."

"Yes, ma'am," Kaz said, already reaching for the potato sack.

Warm food always hit the spot after a long walk to and from town, and venison stew was no exception. It took a little time to cook, but it was worth it, and the heat from the gas stove and the fire together helped to ward off the chill.

Truthfully, it wasn't as cold outside as it could be, but Ellie had never been a fan of winter. She liked snow, but at this time of year they were out of the season of fluffy white snow drifts and into the season of sad, soggy, freezing rain. There was always the possibility of a late season snow storm, of course, but at this point she was just waiting for the mercy of spring.

"You're a good cook," Kaz said around a mouthful of stew. His spoon clinked against his bowl as he scooped up another bite.

"Thanks. I can make simple stuff, but Granny is teaching me some of the family recipes. Always said I needed to know how to cook for a big family..." Ellie sighed, the same familiar, dull ache in her chest coming back to life.

Kaz silently put a hand on her shoulder, briefly catching her eye with a look that didn't need words. There was nothing Ellie hated more than feeling like she had to explain herself over and over, always justifying her right to live and love how she wanted, always justifying her right to simply exist in a space with people who were different than her. With Kaz... he didn't need that explanation.

Even if he didn't understand, he hadn't pushed her to speak. He hadn't tried to pry open old wounds and peer inside for the sake of his own curiosity. She respected that. It made her feel secure in a way that she hadn't felt in a long time, and she found herself considering the calm warmth that sparked in her chest.

Ellie cleared her throat, trying and failing to push away the red flush to her cheeks. She'd known him all of two days. That shouldn't be enough to unlock anything she'd sealed away inside her.

But... Ben's kindness had broken her open just as quickly.

Briefly squeezing her eyes shut, she pushed away the memories and locked them down tight, along with any strange emotions she might be feeling. Kind people existed in the world. Maybe she'd just forgotten that.

"B— by the way, why on earth did you go spouting that you're my *fiancé* to the town?!" Ellie huffed in exasperation, dropping her spoon into her empty bowl. "I just went with it at the time, but now we gotta figure the rest out!"

"I thought we agreed we were together romantically as cover?" Kaz, to his credit, looked genuinely confused... so much so that Ellie couldn't help but feel a little bad for snapping at him.

"Being together isn't the same as *seriously planning to get married*," she said very slowly, careful to keep her tone even and patient. It might be different for demons. She didn't know.

"Would you prefer I said I was courting you?"

"No—"

"I could call myself a gentleman caller?"

"*Please* do not do that—"

"Boyfriend?"

"That sounds like a teenager."

"Or I could say I'm your long-distance lover," he supplied, gesturing vaguely.

"For the love of mercy, please do not do that," she sighed. "Okay. I get it. I accept fiancé. Just... give me a minute to adjust, and I've gotta figure out a plausible way out of it before you leave."

"Fine. We'll stage a public breakup if we need to," he agreed. "We can do it in town, if you want."

"... Maybe not *that* public," she said with a sigh. "Have you ever been in a place with this few Others around before?"

"I haven't," he said, shaking his head. "The witch population here is exceedingly high, but I'm certainly used to more full-blooded Others in larger cities. It's a little odd, but I'm perfectly capable of fending for myself." Kaz shrugged and pulled at the leather tie keeping his hair in a bun. White hair fell in rumpled waves just past his shoulders, softening the look of his sharp jaw and somehow making his blue-gold eyes look even brighter.

He was beautiful, Ellie thought momentarily, almost like a painting. That wasn't unusual for Others, though. Many of them had gorgeous appearances, especially vampires.

Realizing she was staring, Ellie picked up the dishes from supper and brought them to the sink. The water was ice cold and would take a while to heat, but she could at least rinse them for now before putting the stew leftovers in the cellar for tomorrow.

"Hey..." she said softly.

"Hmm?"

"What if we can't do this?"

"You're choosing now to doubt my abilities and not *before* the bargain?" he asked, but there was a slight lift to the corner of his lip, just a little humor in his tone. It was enough that Ellie's shoulders relaxed, but not enough to ease her mind.

"I'm serious, Kaz. What if we really can't figure out who killed him?" She bit her lip, avoiding his eyes.

"Then I suppose we'll need to start planning a ritual to nullify a blood bargain," he said with a sigh. "It's not *easy*, but it's doable. Or, supposing we don't want to bother with that, we officially agree to close the investigation and leave the unfinished bargain in place."

"Would that balance?"

Balance was the way of the woods, the way of witches. Everything had a give and take. Some people said that all magic had a price, but Ellie didn't think of it that way. All magic was an exchange. If you wanted to get something, you had to give something. It kept the cycle going, kept the world moving, and made sure nothing went so far out of balance that it couldn't be put back into place naturally, if need be.

"It should, in theory. Room and board in return for the investigation. A treasured item for finding the killer. The bargain is set in two parts, and neither of us added anything beyond the typical restrictions of not harming one another." He scratched at his jaw absently as he spoke. Ellie noticed the slightest bit of white stubble on his cheek and wondered briefly if all the hair on his body grew white.

Then she pushed that thought very, very far away.

"That... doesn't sound too bad," she said, clearing her throat.

"It doesn't, no, but it's still technically incomplete. It would require a second bargain to truly close the loop, unfortunately, and it would leave us... There would be a sort of unresolved tether in place between us," he said slowly.

"Never mind, don't like the sound of that," she quickly amended.

"Most people don't, myself included," Kaz admitted. "Blood bargains are favored for their binding potential, especially among powerful parties, but leaving one in place long term can have unknown and unintended side effects. Best to nullify it entirely if it comes to that."

It suddenly dawned on her that he didn't need to give her this information at all. He could very easily have twisted everything he knew to his benefit, but he chose not to.

"You know... y'ain't so bad. For a demon," she said softly.

"Think of it as saving my own skin, if it helps."

"You're thinkin' of me, too, though. I appreciate that," she said with a small smile.

Ellie slowly walked across the room, footsteps padding across the cold brick floors as she walked towards the bed and fished underneath it. There wasn't too much storage space in the house, but it was easy to tuck her camping supplies under the bed, and she really should have thought of the supplies tucked there the night before. Maybe exhaustion had scrambled her thoughts, but for now, at least she knew where the camp bedroll was.

"You take the bed tonight," Ellie said, pulling out the soft, rolled mat. "I can handle the floor with this till the camp bed we ordered comes in."

"It's your bed. You sleep in it," Kaz said, crossing his arms over his chest. He sounded grouchy, but that armchair did not sleep well. Ellie knew that well enough— she'd spent many long nights sitting there, too exhausted to move, too uncomfortable to sleep, and too numb to feel. She wouldn't wish that on anyone.

"Seems only fair we alternate," she said with a shrug, fluffing out the mat and grabbing a pillow from the bed. "I got it last night. 'Sides, can't catch a killer with a crick in your neck. I should'a got the bedroll out last night, but I... well, I forgot." She rubbed the back of her neck sheepishly.

"It's not a problem. I've slept on worse than an old armchair."

"Well, you'll sleep on better tonight," she said with a soft laugh. "Go get some rest. We got work to do."

IN WHICH KAZ TOURS THE VILLAGE

Kaz had to admit, the bed was much more comfortable than the armchair. The camp bed wasn't terrible, either, though he'd been suspicious of the rickety thing at first. It was his turn in the real bed, though, and he was grateful for it... even if he didn't quite understand Ellie's insistence on sleeping separately.

It was just a sleeping space, wasn't it?

It had been a solid two days since their trip to town. Another rainstorm turned the ground to mud pits all around the village and practically washed out the road, making it nearly impossible to get to town and incredibly inconvenient to attempt to question anyone in the village. Since the rain kept people mostly inside, and they were trying very hard not to ring any alarm bells by asking questions, it seemed like a bad idea to go around knocking on doors. It was at least an equally bad idea to stand out in the cold rain and wait for people to pass by, so Ellie and Kaz had found themselves stuck inside with only each other for company.

He might ordinarily consider it a waste of two days, but in this case, he found he didn't mind so much. Kaz didn't consider himself a homebody by any means. He liked wandering and traveling, and he'd absolutely taken an umbrella and gone out to stretch his legs even as the pounding rain passed through,

just to ease the cabin fever. But... Ellie was good company. Being stuck inside with her wasn't as draining or tedious as he was afraid it might be.

Ellie, on the other hand, had plenty to do inside. After coming back from his soggy walk, Kaz found her sorting through dried herbs, boiling down syrups, measuring tea blends, and heating beeswax and oils in the gentle heat in front of the stove for balms. It was impressive how she could keep so many tasks going at once, and he found himself asking about the ingredients and effects of her medicines as she worked with them.

The house still smelled like a strange assortment of pungent herbs, but it wasn't a bad smell. It simply wasn't what he was used to waking up to, but... he liked it. Against his better judgement, he liked it.

The little house was different than the oversized hotel rooms he was used to, though he'd also stayed in his share of shitty, rat-infested apartments. This wasn't either. This was entirely different, somewhere far away from cities. It reminded him of his home in a way that made his chest ache, in a way that he could forget around large crowds and tall buildings. Here, there were lots of opportunities to think about the agrarian community in which he grew up, to think about his shared family home.

There were lots of opportunities to *miss* home here. He thought he would hate it. The first day or two, the ache in his chest had been overwhelming every time he made a comparison to his old life. However... just at this moment, he thought that perhaps it was starting to hurt a little less.

Ellie snored softly from where she slept, curled up on the camp bed near the stove with a blanket thrown haphazardly over her body. Kaz let his gaze linger on the way the morning light caressed her silver hair. She kept it tightly braided or pinned up during the day, but at night it was either loosely tucked back or entirely unbound, falling over her sleeping form like a curtain of starlight.

He hadn't thought of her as pretty when they met, not conventionally. Her skin was covered in freckles and permanently tanned in strange places, presumably from working outside often. She had a little more roundness to her tummy and thighs than most humans liked, but

Kaz liked the clear muscle it showed. She was stronger than she looked, physically and emotionally.

He shouldn't be watching her like this, he thought, but he couldn't tear his eyes away. She was so vulnerable and peaceful like this, even if only temporarily. It was... captivating.

That thought was enough to jolt him back to the present, and he huffed as he threw off the blankets and climbed out of the bed. No point in distractions. Ellie might be beautiful. She might even be kind. That wasn't enough to guarantee anything, though.

He thought other bargain partners were kind, too, and in the end that had almost cost him everything. It wasn't worth the risk.

The magic was almost too strong for him.

He'd underestimated both the magical strength and moral integrity of the witch he made the bargain with, and now it might cost him everything. The witch, a man who once looked on Kaz with smiles and fondness, clamped an iron shackle to his left wrist, forcing Kaz to his knees in the middle of a binding circle drawn in white chalk.

"Why are you doing this?" he choked out, tasting his own blood and the man's greed on his tongue. Both his hands and neck shackled, he had little range of movement, but he could at least shift enough to see the face of the man he once called a friend.

"Power, mostly," he said with a shrug and a cruel smirk. "But also, to show that I can. To show that no one need fear Others when there are witches as strong as me."

Kaz screamed as magic coursed through the shackles, binding magic burning his skin and boiling his blood, lashing out with everything he could against the spell—

Ellie's yawn interrupted his thoughts.

Kaz took a deep breath. Ellie wasn't the same as... *him*. Every time he thought she'd back down or snap back, she proved herself to be softer and kinder and more capable than he thought. Kaz couldn't risk letting his guard down just yet, though. There was too much at stake, he reminded himself, reaching up to touch the scar pattern ringing his neck. If he made a misstep like that again, it could cost him more than he imagined.

It did not help his thought process that she was incredibly endearing when she was sleepy... but that was fine. Kaz knew his own habits well enough. He could handle a temporary infatuation, and it wouldn't be the first one, either. It would fade in a few days, after he knew her a little more and had time to realize that Ellie was inevitably not as unique or pretty or kind as she seemed.

As a distraction, he grabbed the tea kettle and decided to heat up some water. Ellie would probably want her usual morning brew when she woke, and he'd become oddly fond of it, himself.

How... domestic, he thought, and the idea wasn't unpleasant.

"You up already?" Ellie mumbled, rolling over as she pulled the blanket close. The click of the gas stove lighting likely woke her.

"The rain finally stopped. Since the Sheriff is still out of town, we should question the other witches."

"Sounds good to me. I'm not up for another walk to town for a couple of days, what with the road like it is, and there's plenty to do here." Ellie yawned again and stretched, sitting up on the camp bed and rubbing at her eyes.

It was... oddly cute.

"Ah, yes, you have approximately seventy-three potions to bottle," he said with a laugh, mentally smacking himself for staring.

"Hey, I have *eight* to bottle." Ellie said, yawning again. "And they're *medicines*, not potions. No magic in 'em, just good ol' mother earth."

"Well, get up and start bottling. I'll help."

"Really?" Eyebrows raised, Ellie swung her legs off the camp bed and stood, rolling her shoulders.

"The sooner you bottle things, the sooner we can eat," Kaz pointed out. "I'm hungry."

"Golly gee, you poor, starving demon," Ellie deadpanned, rolling her eyes. "It's been a whole twelve hours since you've eaten. Maybe even less."

"I know. I'm wasting away," Kaz said dramatically, putting one hand over his heart. Ellie rolled her eyes.

"Psh. Fine, 'wasting away,' go get some bacon from the cellar while I change clothes."

"Anything for you," Kaz said with a bow and a grin. If he wasn't mistaken, the slightest hint of a flush crept into her cheeks before he turned away.

◆

With breakfast consumed and both of them dressed in warm clothes, Ellie and Kaz made their way outside. It was still a muddy mess, but at least the sun was shining, and it gave him a better chance to get a look at the village.

It was a cozy place, he thought, a cluster of buildings tucked away in the middle of a mountain forest otherwise uninhabited by humans. There was no way to completely flatten the land, but at least the slopes weren't too steep to walk in this area. The layout was a little odd, a combination of working with the landscape and an attempt to create some sort of reasonable community structure. Slopes too steep to walk had been slowly carved down as the trees were cleared away, the timbers used to make the houses. Some buildings extended back into the mountain itself, and Ellie explained that the parts built into hillsides were used for cold storage.

"The main road goes from the gate all the way to where the mountain gets too steep to walk on," she said, gesturing to the wide path made of brick-lined gravel that ran through the middle of the village. Smaller gravel paths clearly meant for foot traffic spider-webbed off the main road, moving towards other houses.

"Where's the property border?" Kaz asked, adjusting his wide brimmed hat.

"Tree line, pretty much. Not sure how much of the land beyond where the trees get thick is owned by the community, but where there's trees, it's the woods. Where there's not, it's the village," she said with a shrug. "There's room to expand if we need to build a new house, but we're not gonna go clearin' trees and disturbin' things where we don't need to."

"How many houses total?" He squinted into the distance, but he couldn't make out all the buildings, nor did he know which ones were inhabited.

"Mmmmm... not sure," she muttered, "I think we've got about a hundred and fifty people livin' here, give or take. That includes families of all sizes, though. Granny has her own house, but we've also got couples with six kids under one roof."

Kaz tried and failed to get a quick estimate on the number of homes. It was difficult to tell when some buildings were for community use and others were private residences, especially since they were all unevenly spaced. Some of the houses had large outdoor spaces while others were practically built on top of one another, and he could even see two barns near the tree line on the west side. Any available land was put to use, it seemed, either as a garden or a grazing space for animals. There wasn't enough farmland to feed the whole village, though, and it seemed inevitable they'd have to supplement their food stores.

Ellie guided him towards the center of the village, or at least something close to the center. It was a gathering area with wooden benches arranged around a large bonfire pit, though the ashes and charred wood left over from the last fire were now soaked from the rain and useless.

"Workshops should be open soon. We can start at the woodshop and say hey to Simon, maybe make our way around to the metalworkers and glassblowers," she said, walking towards a large building that looked a little like a barn. There were no animals around it, though, and the open doors showed a group of men sawing logs and sanding chairs.

"Carpenters?" Kaz asked, peering through the open doors.

"They do a little of everything. Houses, furniture, you name it. Most of the people that come up here from town are comin' to buy pieces from them or the potters. We also got a decent gunsmith up here, but he likes to sleep late sometimes. Might not be in the shop till later."

"The village survives off trades..." he murmured. "Wait. You said they wouldn't let you have an apothecary, though. That makes no sense if the main income is trade shops!"

"Tell me about it," Ellie sighed. "Our working theory is that medicine is too close to sellin' magic for the Council to be comfy with it, but plenty a' plain ol' humans sell medicines with no trouble."

"*Our?*" Kaz asked, eyebrow raised.

"Jeannie. My aunt— also the Lead Witch here. She takes care of sendin' reports to the Council, organizing village income, and generally acts like you might expect a mayor to act. Except, ya know. With magic."

Keeping a brisk pace in the cold air, Ellie led him towards one of the large workshop buildings close to the bonfire area. The door was already open and, like the other building they'd passed, woodworkers were already up and bustling around the place. The smell of sawdust pervaded the air as men and women alike worked with chisels, saws, and measuring tapes. A blazing fire on the far end of the open space provided a little warmth, but it was still quite chilly in the workshop at this hour of the morning.

"Mornin', Ellie!"

A boy with neatly cropped dark hair waved in greeting, flashing a wide smile in their direction. He wore blue jean overalls over a heavy flannel shirt, thick gloves protecting his hands as he worked at a sawbuck to cut a thick branch into pieces. He sounded wide awake and full of energy despite the decently early hour.

"Hey, Simon," Ellie said fondly, walking over the boy on his shoulder. Kaz wasn't sure he was *technically* a boy by human standards, but he wasn't quite fully grown either, maybe nineteen or twenty years old. It was one of the few genuinely friendly welcomes he'd seen so far, though, and that was a comfort.

Simon paused in his work and sat down his saw, giving Ellie a quick hug in greeting before he turned to Kaz, looking him up and down as though calculating if he'd seen him before. Though his hat covered his horns, his white hair was a bit of a standout feature, and after a moment Simon seemed to come to the conclusion that they had not, in fact, met before.

"Who's this? Visitor?" he asked, removing his gloves and tucking them in the front pocket of his overalls.

"Kaz." He tipped his hat.

"I'm Simon. Nice to meet ya," he said, extending a hand.

Kaz hesitantly let his magic stretch out towards the boy as they shook hands, slipping the lock off his sixth sense so he could taste the emotions in the air between them. He didn't like to rely too much on his abilities, but it was undeniable that they would be useful in this scenario, and it was best to monitor everyone they met indiscriminately.

The taste of leafy greens and citrus bloomed on his tongue when he looked at Simon. Admiration, chiefly. There was also a healthy dose of affection, laced with lust. *Pining*, he thought distastefully, and fought not to frown. Ellie patted his shoulder like a younger brother, but he looked at her like she held the moon in place.

"How long ya in town for?" Simon asked.

"A while," Kaz replied, reaching out to grasp Ellie's hand. He twined their cold fingers together, still concentrating on the boy's emotional shift.

Grief. Embarrassment. Shock. The bitter flavor of over-brewed black tea filled his mouth, tinged with the slightest hint of iron, salt, and a healthy dose of peppermint. However, what he did not sense was rage. There wasn't even the slightest little bit of anger, only that sadness... and then... something brought that citrus taste back at the last moment.

Simon's mouth opened and closed twice before any sound finally came out, but when words finally came, he smiled.

"You deserve somebody," he said softly, nodding towards Ellie. The salty taste swelled again for a moment, blending with the citrus.

"You're a sweet boy," Ellie said softly.

"I keep tellin' ya, I'm not a kid," he mumbled, shaking his head as he turned back to the wood he'd been carving.

"I know, but I remember when you were born!" she insisted, shaking her head. "We'll see ya later, Simon. Just wanted to stop in for a minute."

"Y'all have a good day," he said with another wave. As Ellie turned to leave, Kaz noticed that the boy sighed wistfully as he pulled his gloves back on, but he couldn't pick up on any signs of the emotions that were clinging to that bundle of wire and fabric scraps.

When he caught up, Kaz found her staring into the woods, looking with interest at something far past the tree line that marked the end of the village proper. Kaz walked up to stand beside her, but at first he couldn't pick out what she was staring at.

"Hey. Look over there." Ellie said quietly, pointing into the trees.

He followed her gaze to find four deer of varying sizes picking their way slowly through the underbrush. Their brown coloring almost blended into the woods, but after catching a hint of movement, he could see the group. Kaz went quiet and still so as not to startle them.

They were graceful animals, even the smaller ones that looked a bit unaccustomed their long legs. They didn't seem to notice Kaz and Ellie watching, or if they did it didn't bother them, and he thought it odd. Animals often seemed attuned to his presence and automatically wary of him, but perhaps these deer were used to magic and humans both, considering they lived very near the witch village.

"It's been a long time since I've been able to see things like that," he whispered.

There weren't deer in his hometown, of course. There weren't any earthen animals on his entire home plane. Even so, there was plenty of wildlife, and he missed the sense of harmony that came with living very closely in harmony with the animals around them. This was a refreshing sight after decades of witnessing no local wildlife save city pigeons, squirrels, and rats.

"Where were you... before?" Ellie asked carefully.

"Before the bargain?" Kaz asked. "Or before the Appearances?"

"Either," she said with a shrug.

Kaz appreciated that she let him choose. No doubt she was curious about the Appearances. Anyone would be. However, he liked that Ellie didn't press him to share when he wasn't ready. He took a deep breath through his nose, thinking back over the last fifty years. His pattern of travel was tiring, but it had kept him alive and... at least mostly stable.

"Cities, mostly. More people to bargain with, more opportunities to hide. Easy to get in and out without making too much of an impact."

"You like this better or worse than the cities?"

"Most days I think it's both," he said sadly. "But I have to admit that here... It reminds me of home. My home... before."

"It reminds you of... *Hell*?" Ellie's nose wrinkled and eyebrows raised.

"No," he said, laughing. "Just a different plane of existence than this one. I didn't grow up in the Hell you're thinking of."

"But you're a demon."

Kaz just shrugged. He'd heard these same misconceptions before, and they usually sent a prickle of impatience down his spine. With Ellie, though, he didn't mind explaining. Perhaps because she'd proven she would listen to him.

"There are many different kinds of demons from many different worlds. I call myself an incubus because that's the term your world uses for a demonic creature that feeds off sexual energy, but trust me when I say that I don't come from the Christian hell you're used to hearing about. My origin is different."

"What was your world like?"

Kaz opened his mouth to respond, but before he could, the wind picked up. A sudden breeze snatched his hat from his head, sending it spinning off several feet through the air before it crashed to the frosty ground. Luckily, it didn't blow any farther away, and he was able to retrieve it quickly, but his train of thought was long gone.

"Horns?" he heard from behind him as he picked up the hat. "How unusual."

Placing the hat back on his head, Kaz turned to see a tall, willowy woman looking at him curiously. She wore work clothes with a practical, slightly soiled apron and heavy gloves, and her red-brown hair was falling out of its neat bun. A few early silver strands of hair glinted in the morning sun as she tilted her head slightly, hands on her hips in a way that seemed oddly familiar to him. He stood and extended his hand, and the woman shook it without hesitation.

"I don't believe we've met," he said with a polite nod.

"Hi, Aunt Jeannie..." Ellie interjected awkwardly, moving to stand beside him.

"Friend of yours?" Jeannie asked.

"Meet... my fiancé," Ellie said slowly. "This is Kaz."

"Fiancé?" Jeannie's eyes lit up. "Oh, Ellie, that's wonderful! Show me the ring, go on."

"It's... in the mail," Ellie supplied. Kaz barely had time to make a mental note that they should probably acquire some kind of prop ring before Jeannie was six inches from his face, prattling excitedly.

"Full blood?" Jeannie asked, nodding towards Kaz. "Don't see many 'round here."

It dawned on him that the reason Jeannie seemed familiar was because her body posture mirrored Ellie's almost exactly. Even some of their facial features were the same, he could see, though Ellie's features had a roundness and a softness to them that seemed to have worn away with time on Jeannie's face.

"I thought it was considered impolite to ask," he said, genuinely confused as he glanced back and forth between Ellie and her aunt.

"Well, you certainly don't need to disclose anything that makes you uncomfortable, but it's not considered odd to ask in witch communities. After all, we survive based on ancestry," Jeannie said with a shrug. "It's a smart choice to marry into a witch family, if I do say so myself."

"Why would that be?"

"Protection, of course," she said as though it was obvious. "You strengthen our bloodlines, and the witches all look out for one another. Everybody wins."

"Has anyone else in this community married an Other?" Kaz asked, innocently wrapping his arm around Ellie's waist and pulling her towards him. He hoped the motion might mask his question as pure curiosity, and true to his hopes, Jeannie's eyes followed his hand as she answered.

"Mm? Nah, not a full blood one. We have a few witch gentlemen here with strong bloodlines, but no true Others, and that'd be all the more reason we'd *love* to have you stay." She smiled almost too brightly, turning back to Ellie. "Now, how did you two meet?"

"I wrote to the Council a while back," Ellie said smoothly. "Figured it was time, and I'm not gonna find anybody else 'round here."

"Oh, sweetie, I wish you'd told me! We could have celebrated." Jeannie sighed, frowning slightly.

"We're taking it slow," Kaz said, looking down at Ellie with a soft smile. She mirrored him in a way that seemed almost instinctive, leaning her head against his chest. He could sense a bubble of rising emotion just then, but surprisingly, it wasn't from Ellie.

"Well, ain't y'all the cutest," Jeannie sighed, but the sweet tone of her voice did not match the bitter, woody taste in Kaz's mouth. *Jealousy*, he thought. *She's jealous... but why?*

"I would love to meet more of Ellie's family while I'm here," Kaz said, painting a false smile on his face.

"Oh, well, we're all family up in the woods, but if you're lookin' for blood kin, I'm afraid it's just me, my momma, and Ellie." A wash of something else overtook the bitter taste momentarily, something that felt a bit more like salt and ash. *Grief.*

Kaz nodded slowly, unsure of what to say.

"Our family's gonna grow, don't you worry," Ellie said softly, reaching out for Jeannie's hand. The older woman smiled sadly, the salt and ash and woody tastes only growing stronger, but Kaz was distracted by the implication of Ellie's words.

Growing family... children... Children with *him?*

The idea should not have been powerful enough to make his brain momentarily short circuit. Sex was one thing. It was a perfectly natural impulse and he hadn't ever been shy about it, but something about the idea of a child with Ellie's silver hair and eyes that flashed gold in the light made heat rise in ways he wasn't prepared for.

I'm over four centuries of life, there had been many people Kaz found attractive, many objects of lustful flings or even romantic relationships. However, only a handful of them ever made him even want to consider the true long term. It wasn't often he could picture having a family with someone else, and it never seemed to work out in the end when he could.

Ellie, though...

He thought he could get used to the idea of helping her with her medicines, of learning to cook a little more than he could, and he even liked the prospect of having a garden again as he had in his own plane. Not to mention that the thought of her carrying his child was—

"Kaz. Kaz?" A hand waved in front of his face, and the motion was enough to catch his attention.

He blinked, clearing his throat.

"You okay, there?" Ellie asked.

Jeannie had seemingly disappeared, leaving them standing alone near the bonfire circle.

"Where...?" he muttered, gesturing broadly.

"She walked off a full minute ago. You went... somewhere?" Ellie grabbed his hand as he spoke, pulling him off towards an area with more residential buildings. The gravel crunched underfoot as they walked closer to individual homes,

"I'm fine." He adjusted his jacket a little, unzipping it halfway to let the cold air ground him in reality.

"You looked a little..." Ellie's nose wrinkled as she tried to find the right word, gesturing vaguely in midair.

"What?"

"Your eyes turned gold. Looked like you were ready to bite somebody."

"Sorry. I didn't mean to scare you, I was just lost in thought."

"I mean, I didn't think you were planning to bite *me*," she said with a laugh.

Oh, the irony...

Ellie led them down a path that went towards a large garden, or at least what was clearly used as a garden in the summer months. The houses were closer together in this part of the village, so much that they nearly obscured anyone on the path from view. In fact, Kaz heard the voices from around the next corner before he saw the people they belonged to.

"That Sader girl needs to find her place and stick to it," a muffled, ruffled feminine voice snapped from around the corner.

"I agree," came the reply.

The tone annoyed him, but otherwise Kaz considered it a stroke of luck. This might be one of his only chances to get unfiltered opinions out of people in the village, and he wasn't going to waste it.

"Hide," he said quickly, reaching for Ellie's hand. She made a tiny squeak as he pulled her along, but she did follow.

Unfortunately, there weren't many places to hide, and those footsteps were rapidly approaching. The nearest potential cover was an alley between two houses, partially obscured by tall, prickly climbing bushes. It wasn't much, but it would have to do. The alley was the only place he could see that would hide them quickly enough.

Then again, it wasn't an alley, not really. It was more of an awkward space between buildings, too small to hold anything useful but

large enough to warrant cleaning now and then. The gap was perhaps two and a half feet wide, well obscured by the climbing bushes. It would be a squeeze, but it was their only option at the moment.

"That's too small!" she hissed.

"We'll fit, come on—" Kaz cut off quickly as he pulled her into the small space with him.

They slipped between the climbing bushes, the branches snatching at their clothing and skin as they slid by. The pliable plants easily bent back into shape when they passed, concealing their presence from the oncoming group.

"They're around the corner. They wouldn't have seen us if we just stayed put."

"No guarantee they won't walk this way. Best to be cautious."

"You're just trying to feel me up," she grumbled.

"Never," Kaz whispered, drawing an X over his heart with his pointed finger even as he grinned. "Unless you want me to, that is."

"I'm good, thanks," Ellie huffed, but she relaxed a little at his joking, some of the stiffness falling out of her shoulders. "Has anyone ever mentioned that you're *very* warm?"

"Shouldn't you be used to the cold?"

"Used to it ain't the same as likin' it," she murmured, gently leaning her head against his chest. His heart jumped into his throat for a moment as he shifted his grasp from her waist to her hips.

A tiny trickle of red dripped from a scratch on Ellie's forehead. One of the sharper branches must have swiped against her skin as they moved into the small opening, though it didn't seem like she'd noticed yet.

"You're bleeding," he said, wiping the drip away from her skin with one finger. Instinctively, he popped his finger in his mouth and licked the blood away, tasting iron on his tongue and triggering a pleasant kind of emotional head rush he hadn't felt in a long time. Kaz wasn't usually fond of blood, but a taste now and then... that was nice. He hadn't trusted anyone enough to taste blood outside of a bargain call for a long time.

"I'll live," Ellie said quietly, but her eyes were on his mouth. It took far more control than he would ever admit not to draw her in closer,

but this wasn't the time or place, and the fear of breaking her trust loomed over his every action.

They both flinched as a clattering noise came from around the corner, pulling apart as much as the space would allow.

"He's a real cutie, for sure," a feminine voice said, finally clear enough to make out words.

"I think it's good she finally caved and found someone else. She really lost it there for a while."

"Yeah, but why did the Council give *her* a full-blooded Other match?" the first voice whined. "I want one."

The voice was unfamiliar, but the emotional wave coming from the group was enough to make Kaz pause. The taste of cinnamon so strong that it burned his mouth made him suck in a breath,

"You okay?" Ellie whispered. Kaz only nodded.

A third voice came from around the corner, a little deeper than the others, but still feminine. Kaz recognized it as the person who insisted Ellie was out of line in the first place. "Well... Affairs happen. Not too hard to start, either."

Something about that implication raised his hackles.

Kaz didn't necessarily mind being the subject of gossip, especially gossip that wasn't true, but something about the idea of insinuating that it was *normal* and *acceptable* to betray your partner made his blood boil. He gritted his teeth and stayed silent for the moment, though, hoping to catch truly useful information while concealed.

"That's true..." but this time it sounded more hesitant.

"All you need to do is bide your time. Don't you worry. He'll get tired of her."

Though there were enough emotions in the air that it was starting to feel like a thick, indistinguishable wash, Kaz couldn't help but note the overwhelming rage coming from those voices. It was the first hint of it he'd felt in the village today, and that was his only lead so far.

"Do you know who those voices belong to?" he asked softly. He couldn't tell based on his minimal interactions with the residents thus far, but with such a small town, it was likely Ellie might recognize them.

"I'm about to find out," Ellie muttered, eyes narrowed as she pushed away from him and slipped out from their hiding spot. "Stay here."

Kaz very much did not stay put as she marched out towards the voices with long strides, right on her heels and not planning to stop. Something about her commanding tone both annoyed him and made him want to—

He shook himself, swallowed hard, and pushed that thought far away as they rounded the corner, walking towards the voices and no longer trying to hide the sound of their steps crunching on the gravel path.

Three women with curly, fiery red hair stood stock still, two young women and one a little older. Kaz recognized one of the figures as Alice, hair tied in a messy bun and knees of her loose pants already dirty. Her hands were over her mouth in shock or shame or both, and she seemed to instinctively step back as Ellie moved closer. The other young woman clutched the fabric of her long skirt in surprise, mouth hanging open.

The oldest of the four figures wore long skirts and carried a basket, a long braid of red hair hanging over her shoulder. Her expression was stern, but she had the good grace to at least look slightly embarrassed, as confirmed by the same peppermint taste filling his mouth that had come from Simon earlier.

"Good morning to you, too, Mrs. Little," Ellie said with a smile that didn't reach her eyes.

That was when Kaz noticed that the cinnamon taste he'd previously felt coming from the direction of the three women had shifted to Ellie. It wasn't as painful, but it was strong, and he realized that this might be the first time he'd seen Ellie truly angry.

"Good morning, Miss Ellie," the older woman replied. She opened her mouth to continue, but Ellie wasn't having it.

"You do know he's a *person*, right?" She put her hands on her hips, glaring as she tossed her long, silver braid over her shoulder. "He's a whole thinking and feeling being, and you don't need to talk about him like he's not there."

"Ellie..." Alice murmured, brow furrowed and biting her lip. "It's just—"

"It's just *nothing*," she snapped. "I don't give two shits if a person has Other blood or none at all. Kaz treats me well. He's nice, and he's

more considerate than any of y'all by leaps and bounds. Look at'cha, sneaking around in the shadows like rabid raccoons."

"Momma. Let's *go*," Alice whispered, gently tugging on her mother's sleeve like a child, but Mrs. Little roughly elbowed her away.

"No one said a single thing that isn't true," Mrs. Little snapped. Ellie just scoffed.

"Sure. Whatever," she spat. "This mountain is my home, but I just because it's home don't mean I'll sit here like a knot on a log and tolerate your bullshit. You just keep your pie hole shut 'bout things you don't know, y'hear?"

"You two got anything to say for yourselves?" Ellie asked, taking another step forward. Alice squeezed her eyes shut and turned her head away, but the younger woman that Kaz could only assume was her sister met Ellie toe to toe. They were close to the same height, and the fury sparking between the was almost palpable, even without Kaz's incubi senses.

"Don't talk to my momma that way," she growled, stepping in front of the older woman. "You really want to start a fight with us?"

"Liz, just drop it! Let's go home," Alice hissed, reaching out to gently pull at her sister's hand. Liz wasn't having it, either.

Kaz's brow furrowed. It was... odd to see the contrast in place between Alice and her family. Rather than looking like she wanted to fight, Alice looked like she wanted to run. Mrs. Little and her elder daughter stood their ground as Ellie glared, though.

"I don't start fights. I do finish 'em, though, if I need to," Ellie snapped. "You can say whatever the hell you want 'bout me, but you do *not* get to pass judgement on him."

At that moment, Kaz decided it was time to intervene.

He wasn't sure if it was the warm feeling spreading in his chest from Ellie's desire to intervene on his behalf, or some other, instinctual desire to want to protect her, but she he would not let her handle this alone. He reached out for her hand and pulled her towards him in a gentle hug, not even bothering to look at any of the three figures watching.

"That being said," Kaz declared, eyes firmly on Ellie's face. "Affairs *don't* happen, not with me."

He wrapped an arm around her waist, pulling her flush against him as he leaned in close. Ellie's eyes went wide as she automatically looked up at him, her hands moving to his shoulders for balance.

"Forgive me for this," he said under his breath, and he had just enough time to see her give the smallest of nods before he kissed her full on the lips.

It was not the smoothest of kisses. Her lips were chapped and her posture stiff for a bit longer than a real couple might have found natural, but the small noise of surprise she made when his mouth met hers made him want to drink in every little noise she'd ever make like that.

He slipped his tongue into her mouth when she parted her lips for air, barely holding back a throaty moan as he tasted both her body and the sweet flavor of rising arousal on his tongue. Her arms wrapped around his neck and he nearly lifted her off her feet just to get her closer, closer, *closer*.

Something was wrong with him. Something had to be wrong with him for Ellie to have gotten under his skin so quickly. Maybe he was just starved for affection, not used to working with decent people, or maybe it was something else entirely, but this was not what he expected to feel from someone on the other end of a bargain.

The kiss only lasted a few seconds, but when he pulled away, Ellie's lips were parted and her eyes were slightly unfocused, and he didn't dare move his hands from her waist until his breathing slowed.

"Are we clear?" he rasped, throwing a glance at Mrs. Little and her daughters, but he barely saw them. He was more concerned with the fact that Ellie seemed to be letting him hold her. She hadn't pulled away, hadn't shifted, just stood there against him and stared like she couldn't comprehend what had happened.

At some point the sound of crunching gravel signaled that their audience had retreated, but Kaz didn't move. The moment felt delicate, like something would break beyond repair if he approached this the wrong way.

Ellie was the first to move, gently removing her hands from his shoulders and taking a step back. She did not, he noted, run for the hills. She also didn't slap him, and he'd been fully prepared for that outcome as well.

"That was... something," she whispered. "I thought we were planning a public breakup later, not... uh... whatever that was."

"It wasn't planned," he grumbled.

"Uh huh," Ellie squeaked, eyes still wide.

"Are you okay?"

"I... am," she stuttered. "Are *you*?"

"I'll manage," he said softly. "Let's go home."

"H—home," Ellie said slowly. "Right."

9

IN WHICH ALICE CONFESSES

Hours later, he couldn't get the taste of Ellie's lips off his tongue, and it was driving him *insane*.

It was stupid of him to kiss her. *Beyond* stupid, it was dangerous. He was already having a terrible time keeping his emotional impulses in check, and it wouldn't help having the memory of her soft mouth on his every time he looked at her.

He couldn't help but wonder how many other parts of her were just as soft, and how those parts might feel pressed against him. One minute his mind was on a murder investigation, and the next he was thinking how she might feel if he pulled her onto his lap instead of letting her sit in the other hard wooden chair...

Kaz fought not to groan in frustration, running a hand through his loose white hair. He felt like a teenager battling both his urges and incubi magic for the first time.

Lust was easy to brush off. He was used to that. It didn't take much for him to walk away from someone attractive in favor of a less volatile food source. Humans and half humans and even plenty of Others became emotionally entangled in things so easily, and Kaz wasn't looking for energy to feed on that contained even a whiff of emotional involvement. He'd rather settle for subsisting off physical

food and ambient, leftover sexual energy in clubs or bars than worry about someone chasing him down the next day.

This was... harder to ignore, though. Ellie was harder to ignore.

"I wouldn't call that a productive day, but at least we got to talk to a few people," she grumbled as they walked inside, plopping down in the armchair to unlace her boots.

"I would," Kaz countered, running his hand through his hair.

"Eh?" She paused, briefly looking up from her shoes. "You *enjoyed* hearing about marriage politics and furniture making?"

"I have a much better idea of the personalities living around here, and not only that, but how they view you," Kaz said thoughtfully. "Besides, you know I can sense emotions well due to my nature as an incubus. There are some... interesting people living here."

"What did you sense?"

"As far as people we passed? A decent amount of shock and lust for the most part, with some greed sprinkled in there," he said distastefully. "Not that any of those are unusual."

"I'm sorry," Ellie said softly.

Kaz blinked, jolting a little. "For... what?"

"It's just... I know I get frustrated with people who make snap decisions about me before they know me or based on rumors," she said. "Not that I'm not guilty of it, too. I did that to you at first. But..."

"But?"

"I think I'd get real sick of people real, real fast if all they ever wanted to do was use me."

Kaz stepped closer, putting his fingers under her chin so she would look up at him, meeting his eyes. If she'd let him read her emotions, he would gladly take full advantage of the opportunity. After all, it was the easy way out for him. All he needed was a small excuse, something just solid enough to help him lock away these strange surges of. .. *something*... he felt around her.

It was as easy as breathing to undo the lock on his abilities and let his senses flow through Ellie. If he wanted to, Kaz could sense the emotions of anyone within half a mile, but the larger the radius, the harder it became to identify which emotions came from which person. When he focused on someone specific, his senses became sharper.

Clearer. Ellie's heartbeat pulsed loudly in his ears as his senses attuned to hers, and he breathed in slowly, letting his eyes close while he concentrated.

He was... moderately shocked to feel a kind of gentle warmth coming from her. As his hand moved to trace down her arm, trailing along gently until his fingertips found her calloused palms, he expected to feel a swell of arousal or embarrassment. They were there, somewhere, buried underneath stronger waves of feelings. He could taste the familiar flavors on his tongue, but only if he tried very hard to look for them. They weren't primary motivators, but an unconscious body response. The primary emotions crashing over him in waves were something else entirely.

Guilt. Fear. And... something that tasted very much like *affection,* something that tasted like *calm* when she instinctively wrapped her fingers around his hand, settling their palms together. It was almost overwhelming, and he wondered for a moment how she could feel things so intensely and stay as steady, stable, and practical as she usually was.

Shaken, Kaz pulled away and took a step back, eyes snapping open. He typically made it a habit not to rely on his empathetic abilities too much. Even people who held you in fond regard could be dangerous, he'd learned, but Ellie... Something about the openness around her frustrated him to no end. He could have gotten all that information from her face if he wanted to, and that... that was not normal. That was not what he expected. Above all, he hadn't expected the incredible *intensity* of everything she was feeling.

Instead of an excuse to lock down tight, he found the edge of a cliff leading to unknown depths.

"You sure you're okay?" Ellie asked, eyes narrowing slightly.

Kaz opened his mouth. Closed it. Opened it again.

And then he changed the subject.

"Your aunt— Jeannie, was it? She had an interesting combination of emotions when we spoke. Shock, joy, jealously... quite the cocktail," he said suddenly, taking a deep breath as he fought to distract himself from the intoxicating and intriguing blend of emotions still lingering around Ellie.

Normally it would be child's play to turn the sensations off, to ignore them or shut them down, but he wanted to look again. He wanted to make sure that what he sensed was real.

It rattled him to the core.

"Jeannie has had it rough," Ellie explained. "Rumor has it she never showed as much natural talent as my daddy, and now even though he's up and disappeared, she's still gettin' compared to him. She got married when I was little, but she found out she couldn't have kids, and not long after that her husband left her for another witch in a different community."

"Damn..." Kaz huffed, rubbing the back of his neck.

"She's been good to me. Helped Granny raise me some when I was little."

"How did she feel about Ben?"

"Mmm... She warmed up to him," she said with a shrug. "Wasn't crazy about bringing a human into our village at first, since she's the Lead Witch and all, but I didn't back down. It's not against the rules, and she knew it."

"Has she been the Lead Witch long?"

"Mmm... Yeah, about as long as I can remember. She's pretty much the strongest here. 'Cept for Granny, that is."

"The strongest or the flashiest?"

"I think most people say she's both," Ellie said, rolling her eyes. "She's not too bad, though, and I can understand why she wants to hold onto that position."

"Sometimes I think you can understand other people a little too much for own good," he muttered.

"What's *that* supposed to mean?" Ellie snapped, hands on her hips.

"Are you suspicious— legitimately suspicious— of anyone at all? Do you have any ideas about who might have done this?" Kaz asked, gesturing broadly.

Ellie paled.

"... No," she admitted. "That's why I called you."

"You... make me *insane*," he said with a huff, rubbing at his temples. Ellie's cheeks turned red and her shoulders hiked, an argument

obviously already on her tongue, but Kaz just kept talking. "It's a good thing you called for help if you're looking at humanity through rose-colored glasses. You'd wind up getting yourself killed on your own."

"I would *not*!" she cried, mouth hanging open.

"Well, you certainly won't *now*. I'll make damn sure nothing happens to you."

"Th— thanks," Ellie said softly. "That... um, that wasn't in the bargain."

"I know," he breathed. "It wasn't in the bargain that you stick up for me, either."

"That's just what decent people do," she said, waving him off. "It doesn't bother me if it's me, but..."

"It bothers you if it's someone else?" he suggested.

"Yeah. You don't deserve to get caught up deep in the bullshit. You're just visiting." Ellie's gaze dropped to the floor.

He *was* just visiting. It was important to keep that at the front of his thoughts. This was not a permanent arrangement— Ellie needed assistance and he needed a distraction from the drugs and parties and lights in big cities. That was all. That had to be all.

It didn't matter that he'd started to notice a strange tightness in his chest when he looked at Ellie that couldn't solely be attributed to physical attraction.

"I hate to ask, but would it be possible to question Ben's ghost at some point?" Kaz pulled the question from thin air, hoping to change the subject, to brush away the sudden awkwardness. Ellie looked back up at him, blue eyes narrowed.

"He doesn't know anything. You've seen him."

"I know. I just thought... maybe he'd be able to tell us something helpful from when he was alive." Kaz rubbed the back of his neck a little uncomfortably, hoping he hadn't crossed a line.

"I..." Ellie began, cutting off with a sigh. "Listen, his memories are scrambled. I don't want to do anything to cause him more pain."

"My Sight isn't as thorough as yours, but I'd still like to speak to him."

Ellie worried her lower lip with her teeth, thinking for a long moment.

"I'll take you to the gravesite when the road clears up, but if I say the conversation is done, you're done. Got it?"

"Clear," he said with a nod. "Is there... anything I should know about him first?"

She hesitated, just for a moment. It was easy to see that talking about him was painful, but some part of Kaz wondered if she'd ever been *allowed* to talk about him after all was said and done. Did she have anyone to share stories with? Did she have anyone to help her grieve? Would it actually be *good* for her to go through those memories?

"Ben grew up on a farm," Ellie said softly. "He was somebody who always tried to see the best in people. He worked hard, and he was real protective over his younger sisters."

"He liked cats. I'm more of a dog person, and it was a running joke because of the whole... witches and black cats thing," she said with a soft laugh.

"I know I've asked before, but do you know of anyone with a vendetta against him?"

"Not a serious one," she said, shaking her head. "His family wasn't crazy about the idea of us leaving town to find a home somewhere else, but that wasn't the end of the world."

"His own family wouldn't have killed him because they didn't want him to leave," Kaz murmured. "That's a bit counterintuitive."

"No, you're right about that," she sighed, resting her chin on her hands. "We just wanted to poke around a little, do some traveling... Maybe even come back."

Kaz scratched absently at the slight stubble on his jaw. If they'd been planning to come back eventually, that almost negated any motives surrounding their plans to leave town. The more he learned, the more it sounded like very few people had a reason to dislike Ben. He could understand why Ellie had been stuck on this for so long, and in a way he could even understand why the town suspected Ellie. There were too few people with motives to kill him.

A knock at the front door interrupted his thought process. He shot a confused glance towards Ellie, but she only shrugged and peered through the peephole.

"What the...?" she muttered, but she moved to unlock the deadbolt.

The door opened to reveal Alice standing in the cool night air, lantern in hand and looking a little lost. The shadows obscured most of her face, but it was easy enough to identify her.

"Hey," Alice said softly.

"Can I help you?" Ellie's tone was carefully neutral, and Kaz stepped up behind her, muscles tense as he surveyed Alice through the door.

"I'm sorry," she said, fiddling with a stray curl of red hair. "'Bout earlier, I mean."

"Can I help you...?" she asked again, a little more firmly. Kaz noticed that she didn't accept the apology, though she still maintained politeness, and he couldn't blame her for it.

"That's... all I wanted to say," she said softly. "Have a good night."

Alice turned and started to walk away without saying another word, but there was a particular flash of the lantern that seemed to catch Ellie's eyes as she moved. Her brow furrowed as she called out.

"Hey, Alice... come into the light real quick, will ya?" Ellie said hesitantly, beckoning her forward. Alice paused, and for a moment it seemed that she was going to keep walking. However, the young woman turned and slowly picked her way back towards the door until she was standing in the threshold, the light from the lamps inside the house revealing what Ellie had seen the smallest flash of.

A mottled red and purple bruise bloomed on Alice's jaw, unmistakable even as she turned her head to try to hide it. Kaz hadn't noticed it from his perspective, not when she was standing in the shadows, but in the light from inside the house, it was clearly a fresh wound.

"Get inside," Ellie said in a tone that left no room for argument.

Kaz backed up and let Alice in, squinting at the bruise while Ellie shut and bolted the door behind them. Now that he could see it in the light, it wasn't just a bruise. It was also a set of scratches. Not deep, but they certainly didn't look comfortable.

"You want to talk about how you got that?" Ellie's eyes narrowed as she crossed her arms over her chest, leaning against the bolted front door. Alice just shook her head, eyes glued to the ground.

"You want something for the pain?" Ellie tried again.

Alice nodded very slowly. "Please."

"Anything broken?"

"Don't think I'd be talkin' if it was," she mumbled. Kaz thought that was a decently fair assessment, but Ellie looked skeptical.

"Kaz, go grab the coldest thing you can find from the cellar," she said with a sigh. "I'm gonna make tea."

"Can you make something caffeinated?" Kaz asked over his shoulder, already heading for the door. He might need it if this was going to be as long a conversation as he feared it might.

"Not this late at night, and we don't wanna give Alice the jitters." Ellie guided their visitor towards a chair as she spoke, having her sit down before moving over to the shelves of dried herbs, flowers, and leaves. "Chamomile and peppermint. Maybe some lavender... and I'm gonna need the witch hazel."

"Witch hazel... tea?" Alice asked, blinking.

"Witch hazel to clean up your face," she said, nodding towards Alice as she picked jars off the wall. "Don't want that gettin' infected, especially if those scratches are from what I think they are."

Kaz turned towards Ellie questioningly as Alice continued to look down, twiddling her fingers in her lap. Ellie caught his eye and made a shushing motion, but then she flexed her hand at him, wiggling her fingers as she made a swiping motion across her own jaw.

Nails. Ellie thought the scratches were from human nails.

He got to the cellar as quickly as he could, picking out a random canning jar with glass that felt icy to the touch. It looked like either squash or peaches, but he really couldn't tell in the poor lighting.

The kettle was on when he made it back upstairs, and Ellie was sitting across the table from Alice with a strange, carefully neutral look on her face. The kettle wasn't chirping yet, but three empty mugs sat on the table. Alice held one between her hands, perhaps just for something to do with them besides hold them in her lap.

"I hate her," Alice said quietly, gripping the mug so tightly her knuckles were white. "I know you shouldn't hate your own momma, but I hate her."

"Has she hit you before?" Ellie asked, reaching out to take the jar of preserves from Kaz. "Thanks, honey."

"No, this is the first time." Alice sucked in a breath through her nose. "She's... sharp. She's loud. She has high expectations for us. She never..." her hand went to her jaw, fingertips ghosting over the scratches.

"It doesn't get better from there," Kaz said sadly.

"You ready for me to clean it? Might burn," Ellie asked, dipping a clean cloth in a jar. Alice just nodded, turning her head to give better access to her jaw.

"I don't have anywhere else to go," Alice said softly. "If I get married, I could leave, but the Council won't match me with anyone because they favor witches with stronger magic than a sensitive nose and animal speak."

"Is that why she hit you? Because the Council didn't match you?" Kaz asked carefully.

"She said I had to be a weakling if they sent you a match and not me, that God saddled her with a magical cripple," she muttered. "And... she said I betrayed her today when I tried to just leave."

"I'm sorry," Ellie said softly, and Kaz didn't have to be telepathic to know what she was thinking. It was a lie that the Council had matched her to anyone at all, just a story to provide cover for their investigation. As soft hearted as Ellie could be, he worried that she would blame herself for Alice's abusive mother.

"*I'm* sorry," she said, shaking her head. "I've been horrible to you because I was tryin' to survive my momma. I tried not to make it too harsh, but... I was awful, and I know it."

"She *wanted* you to act like that?" Ellie exchanged the cloth for the canning jar, pressing the cold glass against the bruise. Alice winced, but reached up to hold it in place.

"The short version is... yeah, she did. The long version is that it was a combination of that and me being convinced I was somehow better. Then I realized... I won't ever be good enough for her."

"Today?" Kaz asked. "After what you saw?"

"I want what y'all have," Alice said quietly. "I think it's pretty clear that whatever I've been doing isn't the way to get it."

Kaz and Ellie exchanged glances, but he couldn't read the emotion on her face. He didn't dare reach out to sense it, either, almost afraid of what he might find. For now, it was more than enough to know that Alice thought their act was the real thing, and that thought kept circling in his mind long after she'd made her way home for the night.

Alice thought it was real... and he didn't mind.

10   IN WHICH BEN TALKS

It took another two days for the road to dry enough that there wouldn't be trouble traveling into town or down the mountain to the cemetery grounds.

Ellie traced her hand over her lips for the thousandth time in those two days, biting back yet another nauseating wave of guilt and fear and confusion. She hated that kiss. She loved that kiss. It made her feel wanted and special and completely, totally horrible all at once.

Logically, Ellie knew that if she looked at the situation from an outside perspective, if all this had happened to someone else... she'd want them to take another chance on finding love.

However, the guilt gnawed at her mercilessly, and she wasn't sure that letting feelings develop towards someone she had a business relationship with was the best idea. Kaz wasn't planning to stay, and she needed to keep reminding herself of that. It was nice to have company, nice to wake up to conversation in the morning, and nice to know someone else was with her so she wasn't alone at night, but that was all it was.

It didn't matter that over the last couple of days, he'd taken to helping with building fires and drying meat. He even watched Simon skin a rabbit from one of Ellie's traps, and asked if he knew how to preserve the hide.

Simon gave Kaz the skin, in the end, saying to clean it and take it to Abraham in town to learn how to tan it properly. In thanks, Ellie made rabbit stew for all of them that night. The leftovers were in the cellar, and they'd have some after returning from their trip out today.

Ellie took a deep breath of cool air, and tried to clear her head. She'd only known the man a week, and yet it felt so *natural* to see him around her home.

... However, she'd only met Ben a few times before they started seeing each other, too.

She couldn't think about that too hard, though. She couldn't think about Kaz and Ben in the same breath, or she'd start thinking about how Kaz understood her magic, how he knew what it was like to feel almost alone in the world, and how it was refreshing and calming and made her feel things she hadn't felt in two years. She wanted to curl into his arms and sleep there for a long time, the deep sleep of someone who feels protected and secure.

Ellie's boot made an awful squelching noise as she stepped in a mud hole that hadn't quite dried after the rain. At the very least, it gave her an excuse to think about how she'd have to clean her shoes later instead of thinking about Kaz.

"Wouldn't it be more efficient to rent a room in town for a few days than walk all the way there? Especially if we'll be investigating for a while?" he asked from behind her, boot splashing into, no doubt, the same muddy mess she'd just stepped in.

"Probably," Ellie admitted, "but it would also raise a whole lotta eyebrows if it's not clear why I'm in town for a few days. Everybody knows everybody here, and they know I never spend more than a day in town. Besides, the cemetery isn't as far a walk as town is."

The cemetery was really about half the distance to town. They couldn't make much more progress until the Sheriff came back, and they didn't need to run any errands in Boone proper today. It would be better to spend a little longer at the grave and use the extra time at home to prepare a few more things to drop off to Emmaline in a couple of days.

"I don't mind walking," he said with a shrug. "More time for conversation."

Ellie breathed in through her nose and forced her shoulders to relax. Conversation meant getting to know each other, and while part of her was thrilled at the thought, another part was certain that it would emotionally kill her if she got any closer to Kaz and had to let him go when all this wrapped up.

"Fine," she conceded, trying to keep her tone light. "Do you have a job? I mean, besides making bargains."

"Making bargains is enough of a job in itself," he laughed. "It pays well, too."

"Does it?" Ellie raised an eyebrow, turning towards him, but the smile faded from Kaz's face.

"Desperate people always pay well. It doesn't matter what your line of work is."

"How do you pick what to charge?" Ellie asked. "I know that sounds kinda stupid, but is there a standard?"

"Yes, it's one soul per heinous crime," he deadpanned, unable to keep the sharp-toothed grin off his face, but then he grew serious. "No it's... . For the magic, it's more important that there is an exchange at all than the inherent value of items or services. Worth and value are very different concepts."

"Such as...?" She shook her head. The information made sense, in theory, but she'd always thought about magic as requiring a cost equal to what was gained.

"Mothers like to keep baby teeth as they fall out, but when children grow up, do you think those teeth have any value to them?" Kaz offered, eyebrow raised.

"No. They can't do anything with 'em."

"Exactly," he said with a nod. "However, to me, those teeth are an especially potent ingredient in certain spells and curses, far more potent than any adult tooth pulled with pliers. They're lost innocence in a convenient capsule, and rather tricky to obtain."

Ellie squinted at him, frowning. "You... bargain for baby teeth?"

Kaz only shrugged, like it was a question he answered often enough and had no qualms with. "Sometimes. What's more important is the worth that I place on the trade rather than the monetary value or the apparent value to the person offering the item to me. If we both agree that

what we earn from the trade is of equal value, it's enough to satisfy the magic."

"So it's different than doing it alone..." Ellie murmured. That made sense.

If you cast a spell on your own, the only emotion and opinion going into the working was yours. There was no outside perspective to balance. It made perfect sense that adding someone else into the mix changed things, but it was interesting that the items exchanged only needed to have worth to the people asking for them.

"It's very different. And, since the people who make bargains with me are typically people who see what they want as worth an infinite price, I can charge almost anything I want without worry." He paused. "I don't actually take souls, though. That seems rather crude."

Interesting. Ellie bit her lip for a moment, the gears in her mind turning over and over. She supposed that not everyone would really have use for souls— after all, she wouldn't know what to do with one. Maybe demon society wasn't all that different after all, or at least maybe it wasn't where Kaz came from.

"What *do* you take?" she asked hesitantly, unable to cage her curiosity.

"Cold, hard cash is never a bad payment. Sometimes I'll bargain for rare spell ingredients, like the teeth. Once, I even acquired an entire estate that I sold a few years later for a pretty penny, after I got tired of living in the area."

"Holy shit," Ellie said slowly. "You're one of those weirdo rich guys."

Kaz scrunched his nose in distaste and Ellie laughed loudly, the sound echoing through the trees. It was enough to get him to loosen up a little and smile, but he didn't look at her as he spoke.

"I can't deny that I have a... sizeable bank account stashed away," he admitted, "but I'm actually a writer. Or... I was," he said with a sigh. He sounded so despondent that it made her heart ache, and she found herself moving a little closer to him.

"Was?"

"Would you believe I wrote romances a long time ago?" he asked with that sharp smile and a hesitant glance.

"Not a bit." She smiled back.

"You'd lose that bet, then," he said, laughing. "People love a novel with scenes that make their toes curl and their heart rate rise."

"Scandalous," Ellie gasped, dramatically throwing her hand over her forehead.

"You don't seem to be a fan, yourself. I didn't see any on your bookshelf."

"I don't mind 'em." Ellie waved her hand noncommittally. "I like a good love story, and I'm not offended by a steamy scene. Sex is sex. It's human, people do it, and I'm not gonna act like they don't or pretend I'm a precious flower," she said with a snort. "It's just been... hard to read 'em lately."

"Understandable." Kaz nodded, and there was some measure of comfort in knowing that was all the communication they needed about the matter. She didn't have to constantly open old wounds around him. They actually had a chance to *heal*.

"What happened after?" Ellie asked, quickly returning to the previous subject. "After you were a writer, I mean."

"Well, I worked in..." he paused, tilting his head back and forth. "I think the best way to describe it is that I worked with people who were in mental or emotional distress for a long while. Got them back on their feet, that sort of thing."

"Sounds nice," she said, glancing off into the trees. "What happened?"

"Maybe I just took a sudden liking to making bargains with idiotic humans for a living," he bit back, but there was little real malice to it. It was just enough to know she'd hit a nerve.

"Yeowch, kitty has claws," Ellie muttered. "Maybe another time, then." She reached up and patted his shoulder gently, picking up her walking pace just a little.

"... You are, for the record, the least idiotic human I have ever bargained with," he muttered from behind her.

"Considering you've known me all of about a week, I'll take that as a high compliment." Ellie flashed a bright smile over her shoulder, a little surprise to see his mouth drop open for a moment before he composed himself.

"You might be surprised. This is a long trip for a bargain."

"Usually in and out?"

"For the most part. Some take a little more finesse, but most are finished in a day. The longer ones take a week, two at maximum."

"Oh, so I booked you for a big job, huh?" she asked, veering left off the main path and up the hill that led to the cemetery. It wouldn't take them long to get there now.

"In a sense. I have to admit this is one of the... more pleasurable trips I've made." He sounded almost... but no. There was no way Kaz felt *shy* about that, but when she looked back, he wouldn't meet her eyes.

Ellie blinked, brow furrowed. "Are you serious?"

"Why would I lie?"

Ellie did not know that demons could make puppy dog faces, but she certainly would never doubt that fact again.

"It's just... There's no sex and no parties out here, and it seems like everyone has some kinda weird inhuman reaction when they look at ya," she said, nose scrunching as she frowned.

"You don't," he murmured.

As they spoke, they crested the hill. The cemetery was on high ground, just as it needed to be, which was why it was so far away from the town proper. It was a huge swath of land divided into various family plots and church sections, all ringed by a black iron fence with a large gate at the front.

"Yeah, well, I'm the local weirdo," she said with a shrug. "What can ya do?"

Kaz opened his mouth to speak, but as Ellie tugged on the gate to open it, the sound of the rusty hinges screaming in protest drowned out whatever he'd planned to say.

She turned to Kaz, suddenly serious.

"I don't know who's gonna be around today, y'hear? We get in and get out, and don't talk to anyone but Ben," she said, maintaining eye contact. "Clear?"

"Are these spirits dangerous?" His brow furrowed as he glanced between Ellie and the graveyard beyond.

"Mostly, no, but if you agitate 'em, they can be. Any spirit can be dangerous, especially if you clearly have no intention of givin' what they

want. Best not to engage," she said quietly. They were a decent distance from the nearest graves, but as soon as they stepped over the threshold of the iron gate, they would be in spirit territory. Best to keep her voice low... just in case.

Kaz nodded silently, and then he did something she didn't expect. He held out his hand.

Ellie blinked. She poked his palm with her index finger, trying to figure out what he wanted, but Kaz just scoffed.

"Hold my hand, please," he said, rolling his eyes. "You're a formidable force on your own, but any hostile spirits certainly won't bother me."

"Confident," Ellie grumbled, cheeks turning red as she took his hand and walked off at a pace that was probably too fast, practically dragging him along behind her.

Ben's family plot was about halfway back. The plot was almost full, too. Their family had been in these mountains almost as long as Ellie's, and it was actually a little surprising they hadn't met sooner... but they *did* run in different circles.

Ellie could clearly see a few spirits milling about. It was a myth that spirits were more active at night, but it was certainly harder for people without the Sight to see them during the day. For the most part, there weren't many restless souls in the cemetery. She could think of five, maybe seven at most, which truly wasn't bad in a rural town where accidents sometimes happened and not everyone died a peaceful death. Still holding Kaz's hand, she marched deliberately past those half-corporeal forms made of mist and shadow, keeping them in her peripherals but careful never to look directly at any of them. It was not a good idea to let ghosts know you could see them if you were unprepared. Ellie had learned that as a young girl, and she's never forgotten.

A rectangular outline of stones, clearly placed by hand, marked the Mathers family plot. Taking a few steps forward, Ellie guided him towards the nearest marker. The state of the simple stone markers made it clear which one was most recent, even without checking the dates, but Ellie didn't need to look at the stone slab to know what was carved on it.

BENJAMIN MATHERS

1894–1926

THE LORD IS MY SHEPHERD

She almost dropped Kaz's hand, but he must have felt her grip go slack and tightened his hold.

"I've got you," he said softly, nudging her towards the grave.

"The other spirits probably won't bother us now. You can let go," she whispered, but Kaz shook his head.

"That's not why I'm holding on now. Though..." he trailed off, gaze sweeping over the cemetery for a moment. "If my holding your hand is still a deterrent to them, it's an extra benefit."

They stood in front of Ben' tombstone for a moment while Ellie closed her eyes, concentrating on the sound of the wind in the trees and the energetic presence of the other spirits around her. If she wanted to, she could identify where every spirit in the graveyard was with her eyes closed. However, she was looking for only one specific presence.

"You there, Ben?" she whispered, reaching out with that sixth sense she'd always known.

If asked to describe it, Ellie might say she could touch without feeling, see without seeing. It wasn't exactly one sense or another, and yet it was more than her other senses... and less. Trying to describe what it felt like to sense spirits, to sense *magic*, was like trying to describe the color green to a blind man. You could get close. Very, *very* close... but there would never be anything exact enough to describe what it really was.

"I ain't seen you before," a familiar voice said. Ellie whirled towards the sound, relieved to see Ben's semi-transparent silhouette taking shape. He leaned against a nearby tree trunk, looking at them curiously. "You a friend of Ellie's?"

"Yes," Kaz said with a nod. Something about the confidence in his tone made her chest feel warm.

"Hey, Benny. We just dropped by to say hi. How ya feelin' today?" Ellie asked, taking a step closer. She tried to drop Kaz's hand, but he held tight.

"I... don't know," Ben said, brows furrowing. "It's like I'm there and then I'm not. I think I'm okay. But I can't... I can't remember how I got here."

"What's the last thing you remember?" Kaz asked carefully.

"I... saw Ellie in the woods. She told me we'd walk home. Now..." Ben frowned, then winced, pressing his hand to his forehead. "I don't know how I got here from there. When was that?"

"It's okay," Ellie whispered, trying to soothe him. "That was a couple days ago now. Don't try too hard if it won't come to ya." She moved within a few feet, instinctively reaching out... and then dropped her hand suddenly. Ben's eyes followed her hand as it came to rest at her side, a slow understanding dawning in his eyes.

"Ellie..." he said softly, wringing his hands. "Somethin' happened to me, didn't it?"

"Yeah, sweetie. It did," she whispered.

"Do I want to know what it was?"

"I don't know. Do you?" Ellie's tone was even, but she had to fight to keep her voice steady.

"I trust you. Do you think I'm ready to know?"

"I..." Ellie paused, then shook her head sadly. "No. I'm sorry, baby, but I'm scared to put the pieces together in the wrong order. We should focus on other memories first."

Ben nodded slowly, looking resigned as he stared off into the middle space at something she couldn't see. At this point, she was happy to let Kaz take the reins, though. He had questions to ask, and Ellie... Well, she'd already asked about everything she could think of in two years' time.

"Ellie says everybody in Boone likes you," Kaz said carefully, and Ellie was not oblivious to his use of present tense. She'd have to thank him for it later. "Is there anyone at all you have tensions with?"

"Mmm... honestly no," he said, shaking his head helplessly. "It's a small town. Everybody's had a spat here an' there, but nothin' that lasts long."

"No one has problems with you two together? At all?" Kaz blinked, looking back and forth between Ben and Ellie.

"Didn't say that," Ben said with an awkward chuckle. "Ellie can tell ya as well as I can that Jeannie had her feathers ruffled for a while, but she smoothed out the closer to..."

He trailed off, as though trying to remember. A cold spear of panic prickled in Ellie's mind. *The wedding.* She couldn't let him think too hard about it—

"Anyone else?" Kaz prodded.

"If I'm honest, my uncle never liked it, either, but Ma shut him up real good about it one night and he at least wasn't as... Well..."

"Openly prejudiced?" Ellie offered.

"That," Ben agreed, wincing.

"Why haven't we talked to him yet?" Kaz asked, brow furrowed as he briefly turned to her.

"He's on *vacation*," Ellie hissed through gritted teeth.

Kaz opened his mouth for a moment and almost immediately closed it, eyes wide and brow furrowed. "Ah," he grunted, nodding in understanding.

They were going to have to talk about that one on the way home for sure... but she'd hoped that it wouldn't be necessary to hash it out before they actually met the man. It would be bad enough just going in and asking for the files. Having to explain it all somehow made it even worse.

"Hey..." Ben's spirit said, turning towards Kaz. "Can you look after her for a little while for me? I'd do it myself, but I think I'm... stuck here for now."

"Stuck..." Kaz muttered, tilting his head slightly, but before he could dive too deeply, Ellie took a step back and forced a smile.

"I'm okay. Really," she insisted.

Kaz and Ben seemed to share a glance that she couldn't quite interpret. She wasn't sure how strong Kaz's sight was, but some kind of understanding passed between them in that moment.

"I will," Kaz said with a nod.

"Good. If she's happy, it makes it... easier. All of it."

"Seriously?" Ellie asked, eyes narrowing. "Y'all gonna talk like I'm not here?"

"I know ya hate it, just like I know you hate people takin' care of ya," Ben said firmly. "I'm not a skin' permission. I'm askin' you to know when ya need help."

"You know I'm not good at that," she grumbled, eyes dropping to the dead grass and muddy earth in front of her boots.

"Well, then, it's a good thing I asked *him*, ain't it?" Ben smiled in a way that made something deep inside her ache a little, but she thought that perhaps the smile this time was more of a comfort than it was a knife opening old wounds.

Ellie closed her eyes and took a steadying breath. She could do this. It would be okay. They'd figure it out, she would find her closure, and things would go back to normal... Even if she wasn't entirely sure what "normal" meant any more.

"Ben—" Ellie began, but when she opened her eyes again, his spirit was gone.

The place in front of the tree where Ben once stood was empty, only shadows where his spirit had been. She should have been used to it by now, as his spirit often came and went at odd points, but it was always a little jarring every time.

They made their way out of the cemetery in silence, walking pasts the other ghosts as deliberately as they had the first time. The old iron gate squeaked and squealed their exit into the woods beyond the graveyard fence, but there was no one there to hear it. It was eerily quiet out here. Even the animals seemed to be hiding from the soggy weather.

They started up the road a little more slowly than they'd walked before. It was, in part, because they were walking uphill, and that was always a little slower. It was also because Ellie was lost in thought. She shot a glance or two at Kaz and thought he might be, too. If she looked very closely, it might be possible to see little gears in his head turning behind that puzzles expression.

For a few minutes, only the sound of their boots on the road kept them company, but Kaz still did not let go of Ellie's hand.

"About Ben's uncle," Kaz began, taking the turn off the cemetery path to go back to the village.

"His uncle is the Sheriff, yeah," Ellie huffed, adjusting her hat.

"And you didn't think it pertinent to tell me this sooner?"

"I was gonna burn that bridge when we got to it!" she said helplessly.

"*Cross* the bridge, you mean?"

"Nah, I definitely burned it," she muttered, shaking her head. "He uh. He kinda, probably, *definitely* thinks I killed Ben. We haven't really talked since he put me in jail."

"He put you *in jail?*"

"Arrested me soon after they found him, but there wasn't enough evidence to keep me and Pastor John vouched for my alibi. Still took him a damn week to let me out, though, and by then the rain had washed away anything I might have found."

"And we're talking to him... *why?*" Kaz asked, his tone clipped and gruff. It was almost more like a growl than speech.

"He's the only one who can legally let us access the case files," Ellie said, groaning. "That's the shitty part of small town livin', Kaz. Ya got the one guy, and if the one guy hates you..."

"The we access the files *illegally*," Kaz said calmly. Ellie's jaw dropped, but he sounded like it was the simplest thing in the world. "I do think we need to talk to him, though, if only to make sure he isn't the perpetrator."

"Why would he kill his own nephew?" That made very little sense to her. Even though he was an ass, Matthew had always been good to Ben. If he was going to kill anyone, Ellie thought she made more sense as a murder target than Ben.

"Why would he jail someone with a clear and obvious alibi besides to throw suspicion off himself while you were in hysterics?" he countered.

"... Okay, point taken," she said slowly, shoving her hands in her pockets. "We'll question him."

"It makes you feel terrible to suspect people, doesn't it?" Kaz asked, looking over at her curiously.

"... Yeah," Ellie muttered. "It's a small town. Everybody knows everybody, and I don't know if that's good or bad. I want to believe that everybody has some kinda good in them."

"Then you let me deal with the suspects," Kaz said firmly, suddenly moving to wrap his arm around her shoulders as they walked down the road. "

"I need to pull my weight. Can't put the whole investigation on you," she sighed.

It was important to her to participate in this. It was important that she have something to do with it. However, she couldn't deny that Kaz was right in a way. It was weighing her down after only a week. Reliving old memories was bad enough, but the pinching sensation she had started to feel every time she looked at Kaz was just making things worse.

Or... maybe better.

She wasn't quite sure.

"Just... let me take over for a little while. Just a couple of days. Please," Kaz said, gently squeezing her shoulder for a moment as he continued to hold her next to them while they walked.

It was nice being beside him. It wasn't just the warmth, as she'd tried to tell herself. He felt safe and strong and like someone whose word she could trust, and she loved it and hated it and never wanted it to end.

"Yeah," Ellie finally said. "Yeah, okay."

What if it broke her when he left?

IN WHICH HOLY WATER RAINS DOWN

It didn't take too long to make it back to the village, but Ellie felt like the exhaustion seeping deep into her bones and settling there was incredibly disproportionate to the amount of movement they'd done. Usually a walk to Boone left her a little tired, but not entirely beaten. By the time she got back to her door after the walk back up from the cemetery, only half the distance to Boone and back, Ellie was more than ready to sleep for the next year.

Her eyes were half closed and her muscles ached as she turned the key in the lock, Kaz right behind her. That was good, considering he could catch her if she collapsed. Maybe there would be time for a nap later, she thought as she pulled open the door—

Only for a deluge of water to pour out on top of them both.

It rolled off the edges of their hats, mostly, but both Kaz and Ellie's clothes were entirely drenched in moments, the already soggy ground becoming a little more like a small, dirty lake in front of the house. Ellie stood with her mouth open, jaw slack from sheer shock as she looked from her soaked clothes to Kaz and back again. A flash in her peripheral vision barely alerted her in time to dodge the bucket that fell from under the

eaves on her roof overhang, and it smacked to the ground with a harmless splash.

"What... What the living *shit* was that?" She spoke through gritted teeth, struggling to at least keep her volume down even if her tone was not at all even.

"Prank, most likely," Kaz said, removing his hat as he squinted up towards the roof, already scouting for the source of the water.

"Who dumps water on someone in this weather?!" Ellie screeched as a gust of cold wind kicked up, tearing right through her soaked clothes and down to her skin. It wasn't cold enough for a freeze, but it certainly was not warm, especially with raging mountain winds kicking up every thirty seconds.

Kaz didn't seem to mind the wind, though. Instead he looked at his dripping sleeve, moving his arm back and forth as if seeing it from a different angle might reveal new information about the water.

And then he licked his sleeve.

Ellie blinked, eye twitching slightly. She was an herbalist and not a stranger to licking objects to identify them, but this was *water*. Even with his demonic abilities, she wasn't really sure what extra information he planned to glean from tasting his own clothing.

"Mm. Holy water," he said softly, smacking his lips. "Too much salt, though."

Holy water?! Ellie went cold with dread for a brief moment before she realized that Kaz looked completely fine. He was wet, sure, but he didn't seem any more affected by the water than she was. On the upside, it made much more sense why he'd thought to lick his sleeve.

Holy water involved exorcised water and blessed salt, so normal water *would* taste different than holy water. It also, thankfully, helped the shelf life. Curious, Ellie brought the back of her hand to her mouth, licking it hesitantly. It was, indeed, salty.

That wasn't enough for Ellie to confirm it was holy water by itself, but Kaz certainly would have been able to. Ellie looked him over, but besides appearing wet and reasonably annoyed, he seemed fine. That was. .. odd.

"It... it doesn't *bother* you?" she asked slowly. Based on everything else she'd heard, most demons found it unpleasant at minimum and toxic at worst, but Kaz actually *rolled his eyes*.

"Why would it bother me? Besides drenching my clothes in cold weather, that is," he scoffed. "I've already told you that I'm not from the Hell you're thinking of. I have no quarrels with your God, so why would Their blessing bother me?"

Okay, that made sense. Ellie nodded slowly, still jumping through mental hoops to make this logic work as Kaz continued to look for the mechanism that triggered the deluge.

"Then how do you know it's holy water?" Ellie asked, eyebrow raised and hands folded across her chest.

"They boiled the hell out of it," Kaz said very seriously.

Ellie blinked.

A tiny laugh bubbled up from her chest. Then another. Then suddenly she was doubled over laughing, shaking her head as she smiled. It might have been the sheer ridiculousness of his answer, the surprise of the water, or the emotional stress of their visit to the cemetery finally cracking her open, but she couldn't stop laughing.

"That's not funny!" she protested, still giggling, now wiping away a few tears as she righted herself.

"Clearly it is!" Kaz also laughed, a wide smile on his face that showed his pointed teeth. "In all seriousness, you know I can sense emotion left behind on objects. That extends to blessings, to a degree."

That... actually made sense.

"Come on. Let's get inside, it's cold," Ellie said, wrapping her arms around herself. As she opened the door, a feminine shriek cut her off.

She turned to see a familiar face scrambling towards them, basket in hand and loose red curls bouncing in the wind. Alice's eyes were wide and she had her skirts hiked up to her knees to move faster, picking her way around the worst of the puddles and mud holes as she came closer.

"Oh, good lord! What happened?" Alice scurried up to the wet mess in front of the door, looking back and forth between Ellie and Kaz. To ger credit, she seemed genuinely concerned.

"Prank, I think," Ellie said with a shrug. "Annoying, but harmless. We're okay."

"And salty," Kaz added, holding up his drenched sleeve.

"Who the hell keeps *this much* holy water just out and about?" Ellie muttered, squeezing some of it out of her braid. Even she and Granny only ever kept a couple of cups at a time around for light cleaning. "Guess my yard is nice and blessed now, at least..."

"Holy water?" Alice gasped, eyes wide as she looked from the puddles to Kaz. "You could have been hurt!"

"A bucket falling on our head is hardly an issue," Ellie scoffed. "I've had worse. Thanks for checking on us, though, hon."

She patted Alice's shoulder with a small smile, which the younger woman hesitantly returned.

"No, I—" Alice cut off, biting her lip. "I meant Kaz. I thought... with the holy water..."

"I'm fine, I assure you," he said firmly.

"That's good," she said with a sigh. "They say enough holy water can outright kill a demon, and I don't want Ellie to go through the worst again."

Kaz grew very, very still for a moment, eyes going wide. He shook his head, pursed his lips, and started to pace back and forth through the muddy mess at the front of the house, disregarding the fact that he splashed dirty water everywhere in the process.

"Kaz? You alright?"

"It's not about him," he said suddenly, an almost manic tinge to his voice as he turned to Ellie. "It's not about him at all. It's about *you*."

"Me?" Ellie squeaked. Kaz grabbed her hand, pulling her back inside the house. She barely managed to say goodbye to Alice before the door shut behind them.

"We have to look at our suspects again from a whole new angle," he muttered, hanging his hat on the hook. "We've been looking at this like someone had something against Ben, but we need to be looking at who had something against *you*."

Kaz pulled a legal pad from the shelf and began scribbling, mumbling to himself as he wrote.

"Just— gimmie a minute," Ellie said, walking to the tiny bathroom to strip off her wet clothes. They stuck unpleasantly to her skin, but it was warmer getting out of them. However, she was so concerned about getting

the soaked clothes off that she hadn't pulled anything from her trunk to put on, so instead she slipped into a bath robe and tied it securely around her waist.

After she hung her soaked clothes over the side of the bath to drip dry, Ellie emerged from the room and found a blanket to wrap around her body over the robe.

"Are you not cold?" she asked, plopping down in the kitchen chair beside where he was still writing, making notes and crossing out things at the speed of light.

"Not enough that it's dangerous. My body temperature runs high," he mumbled.

She would have protested, but he seemed incredibly absorbed in what he was doing. Pencil in hand, he scribbled and crossed out a series of notes on the legal pad, dripping holy water all over her brick floor as he wrote. At least the floor was nice and cleansed now, she supposed.

... Did it count if the holy water dripped on it from the body of a demon, though?

Maybe not.

"The way I see it, here's our short list," he finally said, passing her a list of names. "It could be someone else, but these are the people that are most likely out of who we've talked about so far."

Well, it certainly was a *short* list. There were only four names circled, though the names of everyone Kaz had met so far were scattered around the page, plus a few people he hadn't met. Some were crossed out. Most notably, "Granny" had a significant scribble through it. "Simon" was not crossed out entirely, but there were question marks nearby.

The four names at the top read: ALICE. MRS. LITTLE. JEANNIE. SHERIFF.

"Alice? And Jeannie, too? *Seriously?*" Ellie raised an eyebrow.

"She's already admitted to acting on her mother's orders. We can't rule her out entirely," Kaz said, hands on his hips. "As far as Jeannie, it's the same. We know she was, at one point, opposed to the marriage."

"Okay... Well, the Sheriff I think is at least reasonable, probably, if you're going by who doesn't like me and had a connection to Ben. Mrs. Little might be a stretch."

"Mrs. Little is the only person I've come across so far with the type of rage residue we found on that wire bundle," Kaz said pointedly. "It could be from someone else, but it's too significant to rule out. Besides, they wouldn't be a very good murderer if they were too obvious. Everyone on this list has just enough to keep them out of suspicion if you don't look too closely."

Ellie sighed, biting her lip as she stared at the list of names. "Lemme think a minute. You should change clothes."

She heard, but barely registered the sound of Kaz's footsteps as he walked towards his trunk, now placed next to hers near the bed. The creak of the hinges and thunk of the lid closing washed over her somewhere on the edges of her thoughts, but with every moment Ellie grew more distant from reality. The list of names turned over and over in her mind, growing bigger and louder with every second until only one thought looped over and over.

It's all my fault.

It's my fault my fault it's my fault this is my fault.

The thought surged and swelled and crested in her mind until it crashed over her in a wave she couldn't run from. Her hands shook and her eyes burned. Hot tears sprang to her eyes and ran down her cheeks. It felt like the room was spinning, like she could see everything and nothing at all.

It's my fault.

The dull thump of footsteps in the background and a warm pressure on her shoulder made Ellie realize that her eyes were squeezed close, that her teeth were gritted, and that her palms were clenched so tightly that her nails had left little half-moon marks on her palms.

Kaz knelt in front of her, gently prying her hands open as his fingers traced those same marks. They weren't bleeding, but if she'd kept pressing down much longer, they could have been. Her eyes locked on his as she breathed slowly, trying to focus on catching that flash of gold among the blue. It was enough to bring her back to reality, but not to stop the tears blurring her vision.

"It's because of me," Ellie whispered. "If someone did this to get to me, to punish *me*, then... If I'd left him alone and never gotten close to him, would he still be alive?"

Ellie clenched her teeth so tightly that her jaw hurt. Her thoughts were foggy and spiraling, wandering down a long, dark path that she'd tried to keep herself away from for two long years. It hurt to even think about. She squeezed her eyes shut and more tears streamed down her cheeks, threatening to wash her away in the process.

"*No*," Kaz snapped, loudly enough that Ellie flinched. "No, it is not your fault. It's the fault of whoever decided to kill him. You didn't do that."

The hand on hers squeezed gently, his thumb stroking the back of her palm, but that only coaxed out another wave of tears. Kaz reached out with his free hand and put his fingers under her chin, scrubbing away a few stray tears with his thumb.

"Look at me," he insisted, forcing her to raise her head. "This is not your fault."

Ellie tried to speak, but it came out as a broken, gasping sob.

"Does it... ever... ever stop hurting?" she whispered, voice shaking.

"I don't know," Kaz said, running his hand through her hair. "I think it gets a little easier over time. Maybe it doesn't go away, but we grow around it and learn to carry it. We find new meaning."

"I can't keep breaking down if we're going to solve this," she said, voice finally steadying a little.

"You're reliving significant trauma that you never completely healed from. I told you that I used to help get people back on their feet. I can handle a little crying." He patted her shoulder gently, flashing a small smile. Ellie gave a watery laugh, wiping her nose with the sleeve of her robe and clutching the blanket more tightly around her body.

Kaz made her feel warm and safe. She felt herself cracking open for him like a flower turning towards the sun right before it blooms. He was... something else. Disarming in a way she hadn't expected. Before the conjuring, Ellie expected a business partner, not someone who would dry her tears and treat her like a friend and... kiss her like something other than a friend.

"Hey, Kaz?" she whispered, voice a little raw from crying.

"Mm?" He hadn't moved from his spot kneeling on the floor, one hand still holding hers.

"Can you... maybe not kiss me any more?" she asked softly. "I know we have to keep up the bit, but I don't think I can take it when it doesn't mean anything."

Kaz paused, taking a deep breath. He moved his other hand to hold her free one, but he dropped his gaze.

"What if it did mean something?"

Ellie didn't know if it was confusion from crying, from panic, or from something else entirely, but her heart felt like it couldn't take the range of emotions fighting for dominance in her chest. "Does it?"

Kaz looked up, hesitantly meeting her eyes. He didn't seem inclined to pull away, but there was some kind of tension between them. She wasn't sure what to do with it, though, until Kaz finally decided to speak.

"It... could. Maybe. If you wanted it to, that is."

"I've barely known you a week," she whispered, but it was a futile protest.

"Oh, it's been at least a week and a half," he said with a smile that showed his sharp teeth, and she had to fight not to smile back. "How long do you want to know me?"

"L— longer than that," she mumbled.

"So you want me to stay," Kaz said with a slow smile.

Ellie's mouth dropped open. She was half mesmerized by that smile and half terrified at the implication.

"I won't force it on you. I promise," he said softly. Finally, he let go of her hands and shifted to stand, but something in her mind seemed to click into place in that moment, and Ellie thought that if she didn't take advantage of it right now, it might slip away forever.

"Wait."

He immediately froze in place, blue eyes locked on hers. Ellie reached out slowly to touch his cheek, letting her fingers trail across his temple and over his horns. He leaned into the touch, eyes fluttering closed for a moment.

It felt like her heart was going to burst. Things were too hot and too cold, moving too slowly and too fast.

"I'm scared."

"That's okay." He reached out to carefully take her hand, twining their fingers together. "I'm not going to run because you're scared."

"Am I betraying Ben?" she whispered, squeezing her eyes shut.

"You knew him better than anyone. What would he say?"

"He... he always said he wanted me to be happy," she choked out, sniffling. "He even said we could leave and find somewhere else to go if it would make things easier, but I didn't wanna pull him away from his family."

Kaz just nodded, pressing his forehead against hers.

"So many times we almost left... So many times. Maybe he'd still be here if we had."

"You can't think like that, rosebud. You can't turn back the clock, and you're only torturing herself by acting like you can," he murmured, rubbing gentle circles on her back.

"What do I do now?" she asked helplessly, leaning her head against his shoulder.

"I can't make that decision for you. I promise you that we'll figure out who did this to him, though."

"I know we made a bargain—"

"No," he said suddenly, pulling away to look in her eyes. "I am not saying this because of our bargain. This is me, Kazerin, promising you that I will do this for you because I... care about you."

As Ellie reached out to hug him, burying her face against the soft fabric of his flannel shirt, she thought that might have been the most beautiful and terrifying thing he could ever say to her.

12

IN WHICH THE SHERIFF RETURNS

If Kaz could have held Ellie all night after seeing her cry like that, he would have. She insisted she was fine, though, and he didn't want to push her.

In the two days since then, she'd been eerily quiet. Instead of laughing loudly, sometimes at his terrible jokes, she'd been tapping her fingers on the table and scratching down notes with a pencil. He'd tried to ask if she was alright, but there was a delicate kind of tension between them that seemed like it might snap at any moment.

More than anything, Kaz wanted her to open up to him. He'd been so afraid that she'd pull away after his admission that he... cared more than might be appropriate for a bargain. She hadn't, but she wasn't moving closer, either.

He also felt stuck, to be fair to her. It wasn't entirely Ellie's fault that they were emotionally hanging in midair. It took two.

Yes, he'd voiced that it was possible for this to be... *more*. He could even admit that he wanted it. However, he could also see that pushing any more might be a terrible decision. They were balancing on the edge of something, and neither of them were ready to jump. It was endearing, frustrating, and devastating all at once to know that they were both, in their own ways, afraid to move forward at this point.

Yes, he wanted to hold her all night, but Kaz still couldn't bring himself to hold her *hand* without an excuse. There was some sort of order to things, and it couldn't jump too far too soon. He needed that logic. It kept him sane. His practical mind was all he had some days, his calculations his only company. If he couldn't logic his way out of this situation, then... then... Well, Kaz wasn't sure. He did think that it might be futile to apply logic to the living tornado that was Ellie, though.

She was wild, soft, and beautiful, and he had absolutely no desire to tame her. In fact, it would make Kaz very happy to see her embrace herself a little more, but as they walked down King Street towards the Sheriff's office, it was easy to see why her natural light was a little dimmer than it might be.

This time, more Boone residents were up and moving around King Street than the first time they'd gone to town. People actually crossed the street to avoid passing her on the sidewalk, and they didn't even try to hide it. Their movement patterns were more obvious due to sheer numbers. Most of the residents gave Ellie a wide berth, and those that acknowledged her presence did so at a distance.

"Emmaline, Thomas, and Abraham are about the only ones who get too close to me," Ellie said with a sad smile. "We gotta go see Abraham on our way outta town, too. He can take care of that rabbit skin for ya."

"How can this not bother you?" Kaz shook his head. More people crossed to the other side of the streets, nervously looking over their shoulders or keeping their heads down entirely.

"They all think I went crazy when Ben died," she said softly. "I can't blame 'em, either. I lost it for a week or two."

Ellie, for her part, looked accustomed to it. It wasn't that it didn't bother her, he realized, but she had experienced this for long enough that it rolled off her. The harm was already done, and she'd developed a thick skin because of it. Anger flared to life deep in the pit of his stomach, a raging fire that wouldn't die down. She didn't deserve this.

"They can't allow you a week or two after *your fiancé was killed*?" Kaz asked incredulously.

"I know it sounds harsh, and... it is," Ellie said slowly, "but when you're like me and you're flagged as different, it's easy for little things to spiral into bigger things. And I'm not gonna say it's fair or right, but..." she

trailed off, heaving a sigh. "It's just that I'm tired a' fighting. That's all. Sometimes it's easier to just let it roll off your back and do what ya can than push against it."

Kaz could understand that, but some part of him ached for her. She'd been reduced to just wandering through life. He'd seen glimpses of a beautiful, passionate fire inside her, and he wanted nothing more than for Ellie to embrace it. She was incredible. Every day made him want to stay a little longer, to learn a little more about her.

He was afraid, yes, but... Maybe there was a chance.

The entry bell hanging on the doorknob of the Sheriff's office clanged loudly as Ellie pushed open the front door to the small building. It was small and brick on the outside with whitewashed concrete walls on the inside. The reception area included two rickety chairs and one large desk, behind which sat a disinterested deputy who barely looked up from his magazine to see that someone had walked inside.

"Can I help you?"

"We're here to talk to Sheriff Mathers," Ellie said, crossing her arms over her chest.

"What if he don't wanna talk to you?" the deputy drawled, looking up briefly to glance back and forth between Ellie and Kaz. His faded name badge read "GRANT" in white paint.

"Then I think he'd better come out here and tell me that himself," she snapped, glaring.

"I think that's a perfectly reasonable request, don't you?" Kaz asked, reaching up to remove his hat and hold it against his chest. The gesture itself was peaceful, almost pleading, but that was not the point of removing the hat.

The deputy's eyes went wide as his gaze landed on Kaz's short, black horns. The hat covered them perfectly, which was why he typically kept it on everywhere except in the comfort of Ellie's home. Right now, though, it made his point perfectly clear: If the deputy didn't abide that reasonable request, he might be forced to take an *unreasonable* action.

"He's in the back," Grant grumbled, gesturing to the far door. "Knock first."

The deputy went back to his magazine, resting his feet on top of the desk as he did so. Fighting the urge to roll his eyes, Kaz walked to the

far door and rapped on the wood several times. He had little doubt that whoever was inside could hear everything happening in the front office, but he might as well knock for show.

"Come in," a gruff voice called from inside.

The Sheriff sat in his desk chair with a cup of coffee in one hand, but he stood when he got a good look at Ellie's face. His gray mustache was perfectly waxed and curled, a sharp contrast to his thinning and greasy gray hair. The Sheriff's tan, button-down uniform shirt stretched taut over his bulging belly, tucked securely into matching pants hitched up by an overworked leather belt. His already beady brown eyes narrowed even further as he frowned, looking back and forth between them. Even though he was Ben's uncle, Kaz was doubtful there was any resemblance between them.

"Can I help you, Miss Sader?" he asked with a sigh as he sat down the coffee cup with a clunk.

"We need to see Ben's case files. Please," she said firmly. It was impressive how she could keep her expression so calm and distant when she had enough preparation. That was something Kaz had slowly learned— Ellie didn't do well with surprises. Too much at once could crack her, but if she knew even a little of what she was walking into, he was convinced she could handle anything at all with a straight face.

"Who's he?" Sheriff Mathers gestured to Kaz.

"Do you need to know that to grant access to the files?" Ellie raised an eyebrow, hands on her hips. She was ready for a fight if need be.

"Maybe," he said, mustache twitching.

"Kazerin," he said, extending a hand. Sheriff Mathers looked at his hand suspiciously, but did not shake it.

"Kaz'rin who?" he sniffed, glancing between Kaz's face and his hand.

"Just Kazerin," He smiled in a way that made his pointed teeth visible. Just to make the moment even more uncomfortable, he continued to hold out his hand until the Sheriff finally reached for it. He had the grip of a wet noodle and an expression like the action was akin to reaching into garbage, but the Sheriff *did* shake his hand.

Kaz adjusted his jacket, determined not to show a single sign that he'd been annoyed at all, especially not after the way that deputy talked to

126

Ellie. Composure gave you the upper hand. It was a lesson that he'd learned many times, and it did make more sense why Ellie had wanted assistance now. It wasn't just about the outside perspective. It was about power.

And, luckily for Ellie, she had a demon on her side.

"The files, if you please," Kaz said with a nod.

The Sheriff made a noncommittal grumbling noise somewhere between a groan and a snarl. He didn't move to retrieve any documents. he only stared back and forth between Ellie and Kaz, like he was waiting to see who would crack under pressure first.

"It's a cold case, and they aren't sealed. You don't have any legal right to keep them from us," Ellie said in that same careful, even tone. "And, if you remember, I was already legally designated next of kin before Ben passed."

The Sheriff outright glared at that, his frown deepening as he huffed. He mumbled something under his breath that Kaz couldn't make out, and then reached for a large ring of keys on his belt, fishing through them until he came to a small silver one.

"I'll let you see the files, but you're gonna look at 'em here, in my office, *where I can see ya*," he snapped. "We clear?"

"Fine." There was a slight tick in Ellie's jaw as she spoke, but otherwise she did not show her annoyance. It was clear that the Sheriff thought they'd try to tamper with evidence or destroy the records— after all, Ellie already mentioned that Mathers thought she was the killer, or at the least was prepared to implicate her. Though Kaz didn't like the idea of looking over evidence in the presence of a suspect, they didn't have much choice.

Sheriff Mathers opened one of the drawers of the file cabinet behind his desk with the small key, riffling through it until he pulled out a thick manila folder. There were pieces of oddly-sized papers stuck out the sides, a couple of smaller folders obviously tucked in the larger one, and Kaz could see that the label read "Mathers, Ben [CLOSED, COLD]."

The Sheriff turned back towards them, but he didn't offer the folder to them. Instead he looked at Ellie for a long moment, like he was trying to see through some kind of façade that didn't exist.

"It's been two years. Why now?" Mathers asked, eyes narrowing.

"It's been two *weeks* since your office declared it a cold case, and then you left on vacation," Ellie said pointedly, extending her hand for the files. "Forgive me if I thought I'd pick up where you left off. Besides, you know I've looked at the files before."

Mathers snorted derisively, but he put the thick folder in her hand.

"I've seen most of these already," she said to Kaz, placing the folder down on the Sheriff's desk so she could thumb through the files. "It never hurts to look again, though, just in case. It's good to have a fresh set of eyes, too. Maybe you'll catch somethin' I missed."

"What's most important?" Kaz asked, looking over her shoulder as she sorted the documents into two piles. One contained records of suspects, police investigations, and anything else that was a bit more distant from the grisly details. She sorted the photos of the crime scene, the coroner's report, and eyewitness accounts of the investigation from the day of the murder into a separate pile.

Ellie handed him the second stack.

"There's one part in particular I'd like you to look at. I hate to ask, but... I never had the guts to read it," she admitted as she handed him the papers. She took a slow, controlled breath, and Kaz heard her voice shake for the first time that day as she spoke. "It's the coroner's report."

He nodded, mentally steeling himself. It was obvious why she wouldn't want to look at any of these, especially since she'd seen the body herself. Everything in this pile of papers outlined the crime scene in ways that would be painful to relive, but they were important details for him to know. Ellie didn't need the trauma of that day heaped on her over and over again, so he was glad to be able to do this for her if it would help the investigation.

The black and white photos didn't show as much detail as he would have liked from the crime scene, but it had been raining, overcast, and foggy that day. There wasn't much that the cameras could capture clearly simply due to poor lighting and the deluge of water everywhere. The most the pictures showed were body placements and the distance from the main road.

Police reports and accounts from the day of the murder were little help. Someone on a delivery from Mast found the body on the way back

by coincidence. The driver stopped to relieve himself on the side of the road, and was met with a bloody surprise instead. It was even difficult to narrow down the time of the murder, considering that the rain and mud affected the state of the body. They knew for sure that Ellie left that morning at 8:00AM. Ben's body was discovered at 2:00PM. Beyond that, it was difficult to narrow anything down.

As far as the manner of death...

"*Fuck*," Kaz hissed as he finally made it to the coroner's report, eyes going wide.

Ben hadn't just been killed. He'd been utterly *mangled*, stabbed to death in a manner more consistent with a hate crime or a psychotic serial killer than a small-town grudge. There were *eighteen* stab wounds on various parts of his body, and worst of all, the coroner was convinced that the most lethal ones were the last strikes. There were notes about blood flow and blood loss and the state of the surrounding tissues, but even if Kaz didn't understand all the technical jargon, he understood the end result. Someone wanted Ben not just to die, but to *suffer* before he went.

That was unfortunately inconsistent with his previous best theory. There was no point in killing Ben slowly if the point was only to make *Ellie* suffer, so there must have been more to the motive than he realized. Too many theories swirled around in his head as he looked over the notes, until finally he noticed a note at the end of the coroner's report.

"No signs of struggle reported at the scene?" Kaz murmured, squinting. "Really?"

"And?" Mathers asked, sipping his coffee.

Brushing a lock of white hair out of his face, Kaz opened his mouth to respond... and quickly closed it. If Ellie hadn't been able to bring herself to read the coroner's report, it was because she knew how brutal the murder was. She'd seen the body. She didn't want details. He wasn't about to take that choice away from her.

"Are you sure you want to hear this?" he asked Ellie.

She bit her lip and clenched her fists, but she nodded. "I do."

"The report says that the most lethal wounds, the ones that targeted vital organs that would have made him collapse or pass out from blood loss, were very likely the last ones the killer made," Kaz said slowly.

"I don't think it's very likely that someone would sit there and let themselves be actively stabbed, do you?"

Ellie clapped her hands over her mouth, hanging her head for a moment. Her throat tensed and she made a strangled noise as she gagged, but she ultimately managed to hold her stomach.

"That... is a more reasonable sentence than I expected from you," Sheriff Mathers said slowly.

Kaz elected to ignore that statement for the sake of his own sanity. That, and he was far more concerned about Ellie's reaction.

"Breathe. Slow," Kaz said softly, placing a hand on her back before he turned back to the Sheriff. "Ellie said it was storming that day. Is it possible that the rain washed away any signs of a struggle before the body was found?"

The Sheriff stroked his mustache, tilting his head back and forth as if considering.

"It's possible, but the coroner didn't find any signs of it, either," he finally said. "Besides the stab wounds, there was no bruising or scuffs or anything that looked like he tried to run."

Why would a man stand there and let someone stab him repeatedly until death? Kaz's brow furrowed and he shook his head. There was a missing chunk of the puzzle that no one had found yet. It might be time to call in help once they made it back to the village. He had a few contacts that would likely jump at the chance to catch a murderer.

"Thank you for your time," he said to the Sheriff, tipping his hat. "We'll be on our way."

He needed to review the case with Ellie again. In private.

Kaz packed the files neatly back into the folder, turning the details over and over in his mind. The stab wounds on the shoulders had been first, then the legs. The killer avoided major arteries and vital spots while making certain that Ben would still bleed. Had the blood loss killed him, then, or one of the later wounds to his neck or stomach? Was it even possible to tell?

As they walked out of the back office, the door clicking shut behind them, Kaz politely waved to the deputy at the desk. He was still absorbed in whatever magazine he had in his hands, and for a moment it

wasn't clear that Grant even registered the visitors leaving. Just before they reached the front door, though, he finally spoke.

"Ben's case, huh?" Grant asked lazily, not even bothering to look up at them. "Prob'ly killed him yourself, if the rumors are true. Shouldn't have let ya out of the clink that day."

Ellie stiffened slightly, just a little flinch, but she kept walking as though she hadn't heard him. It was more than enough just to see that tiny flinch, though. This day was hard enough for her. This *entire investigation* was hard enough for her. She didn't deserve false accusations on top of that.

"What did you say to her?" Kaz growled, and he could feel that his eyes flashed from blue to gold as he whirled towards the deputy.

"Kaz—" Ellie began, but she wasn't quick enough.

"Feel like repeating that?" Kaz asked, smacking his palms down on the desk hard enough that the deputy's coffee cup shook.

"I said *she did it,* just nobody knows how 'cause she's a damn witch!" Grant snapped, voice echoing off the cinderblock walls of the small room.

Before he had time to consciously think about it, Kaz surged forward, picking the lanky deputy up by his shirt collar and pushing him against the concrete wall. The man yelped as the chair he'd been sitting in clattered to the floor. His back smacked against the painted stone wall with Kaz holding him up by the collar with one hand and pinning his shoulder back with the other.

"What in blue blazes—" the Sheriff grumbled, opening his office door. Kaz didn't bother to look towards him.

"Sh— Sheriff—" the deputy began, stuttering and eyes wide as he looked past Kaz. Grant's free arm flailed for a moment, and then Kaz heard a click. A round shape just the right size to be the barrel of a pistol nudged against his torso, barely wedged between him and the man against the wall.

There was a feminine gasp from behind him, followed by the cold press of metal against his stomach, but Kaz didn't even flinch. There were some mortal weapons powerful enough to kill him, but the little pea shooter the deputy possessed wasn't enough to even come close. It might hurt like hell, but he'd survive.

"Don't look at him. Look at *me*," Kaz said slowly, letting the gold color flash in his eyes. Grant's gaze slowly moved back to him, and all the color slowly drained from his face. "Good. Now, how effective do you think a little bullet like that would be on me?"

"Enough to make it worth the risk," Grant said through gritted teeth, pushing the barrel of the gun a little harder into Kaz's stomach.

"You really want to find out?" he asked calmly, eyebrow raised. There was a flash of fear and indecision in Grant's eyes, his lips twitching in a frown or a sneer or some other unreadable expression.

"Kaz," Ellie insisted, placing her hands gently on his shoulders. He relaxed a little at her touch, but he didn't let the deputy move, still firmly pinning him to the wall. "Let him go. He's a smartass, but he's harmless."

"It's not harmless to accuse someone of murder," he said through gritted teeth, gaze never moving away from his target.

"You know the truth," she said firmly. "*You* know. And wherever he is, Ben knows. That's enough right now."

"Grant," the Sheriff snapped. "Drop your weapon."

"But—" Grant stuttered.

"*Drop it.* You shoot him, and we got a whole case on our hands. *Put your goddamn weapon down!*"

It was possible that the building next door could have heard Sheriff Mathers bellowing out orders. Grant obeyed, either from shock or fear, and the gun clattered to the floor. Kaz bared his teeth in a snarl just to watch him flinch, and Grant yelped again, kicking out with his legs. The kicks hit his shin, but Kaz's skin was stronger than any human flesh. He barely felt it.

"Put him down, honey," Ellie said softly, giving his shoulders a gentle squeeze. It felt like the anger drained out of him at the sound of her voice. He didn't *want* to let the man go, but... Well, Grant looked scared enough.

"You are lucky that she is more patient than I am," Kaz growled, but he loosened his hold and backed away, brushing his hands together as though rubbing off dirt from touching the deputy.

"Y— you just assaulted an officer—" Grant stuttered, knees shaking as he knelt to pick up the pistol. He didn't get a chance to reach it before Kaz kicked it out of the way, sharp teeth bared and muscles tense.

"After *you* accused someone of murder with no evidence?" Ellie stepped in front of Kaz before the situation could escalate again, putting her arm out to stop him surging forward. "I think we'd best call it even. Don't you agree, Sheriff?"

Sheriff Mathers bit his lip, looking back and forth between them for a long moment. Kaz was not oblivious to the fact that he was weighing his options. Small town politics weren't like city laws, and if there was too much trouble, an outsider might be called in by the state to take his place.

"You're barely bruised, Grant. Get up," he finally said, sighing as he stroked his mustache. "You two see what you need to see?"

Kaz and Ellie exchanged a glance, then nodded.

"Good. Have a nice day." The Sheriff walked to the door and held it open, the entry bell swinging wildly as he did. That was enough of a cue that this conversation was finished.

Ellie didn't hesitate to grab his hand and start out the door, clearly ready to leave this office and the town of Boone behind for the day. It was very possible that she'd be furious with him later, and he couldn't say he'd even blame her for it. Though it was possible his actions crossed a line, he wasn't about to let her be verbally beaten and battered without fighting back. It wasn't in his nature, and he thought it wasn't in hers, either. She just wasn't used to fighting for herself any more, so Kaz would simply have to do it for her until she remembered how.

"I think it would be wise if you didn't spread unsubstantiated rumors in the future, don't you?" Kaz threw over his shoulder as he adjusted his hat, managing to cast one last glance at the terrified Grant before the door closed behind them.

13

IN WHICH WILD TURKEYS FLY

Ellie was far too lost in her thoughts to speak much on the way back to the village. Her emotions felt all over the place, anger and gratitude and shock all mingling in a horrible storm that left her reeling. However, more than anything, Ellie realized that she felt... protected.

Kaz had been rash. However, she wasn't used to someone defending her. Ellie typically preferred to fight her own battles, but she'd been far too tired for that ever since Ben passed. It was nice, in a strange way, to have someone who would take up for her as surely as she wanted to defend him if he needed it.

"Are you... angry with me?" Kaz asked softly.

"What?" Ellie turned, giving a surprised squeak as she almost tripped over a rut in the road.

"You haven't said a word since we left town. I thought I might have crossed the line," he said sheepishly, tucking his hands into his jacket pockets.

"You... sorta did," Ellie admitted. "I didn't mind, though. It's been a long time since anyone's done somethin' like that for me."

"I'm happy to do it, as long as it doesn't bother you," Kaz said with a small smile. "It just... it made me..."

"Snap? I get it," Ellie sighed. "Emmaline takes up for me in her own way, too. She's a real firecracker, but thankfully Tom usually calms her down."

They took the last fork in the path up to the village, veering left and up. The gates were only about a half mile away, but the last leg of the path was steep. It was on high ground, which was good for rain, but both sides sloped sharply off the road, surrounded by dense mountain forest. Every now and then, a few bushes sprang up and provided a place for small animals to hide, but their roots also helped keep the road from washing away too quickly.

A shifting sound in the trees made Ellie stop cold on the path, throwing her arm out in front of Kaz to stop him moving forward.

Seconds later, an enormous wild turkey flew out of the underbrush and across the road. Kaz's eyes went wide, but it wasn't an unusual sight for Ellie. She was more concerned about why the turkey might be motivated to expend energy on flying.

"Weird..." Ellie mumbled, following the turkey with her eyes. Wild turkeys were a common sight in the mountains, but they didn't usually take off flying unless they were seriously startled. Something must have spooked it.

Just as she was considering if there was something else among the trees that they should be wary of, maybe a bear or a bobcat, the sound of a gunshot rang out through the woods.

Ellie wasn't shy around guns, having grown up learning to hunt and trap game. She knew what a rifle sounded like. Normally, that wouldn't have bothered her. People had to hunt to survive around here.

However, she also knew that shot was damn closer than it should have been.

"The hell—" she hissed, peering into the trees to try to see who was out there, but another shot almost immediately rang out.

Kaz cried out in pain, dropping to one knee.

"Fuck!" he cursed, pressing a hand to his shoulder. When he lifted his palm, it came away bloody.

"Shit, shit, *shit*—" Ellie's eyes were wide, words spilling unconsciously out of her mouth at the sight of Kaz's sticky, silver blood. It looked like liquid mercury staining his clothes and skin, and it sent cold chills down her spine, shock halting all thought.

"Run," Kaz hissed. "*NOW!*"

Kaz grabbed her hand and yanked her along the road, moving as fast as he could. Ellie was at a full sprint trying to keep up with his long legs. Another shot echoed through the woods, but it missed. The shooter must have been far enough away that their aim was off. Ellie could take a wild guess that there were too many trees in the way, and the shooter probably didn't have a scope to help with the distance.

"There's no cover if we stay on the road!" Ellie panted, hunched over and trying to move as quickly as possible.

"No other choice. We need to get back to the village, and *fast*." Kaz grunted, clutching his shoulder with one hand and pushing her ahead with the other.

It wasn't exactly easy to run uphill, and especially not when they were trying to seek cover where they could, but they managed to avoid another shot from the woods.

"I see them!" Kaz huffed. "They're getting closer—"

Ellie briefly turned to look as she scrambled up the dirt road, but all she could see were trees. Kaz might have been able to use his empathic abilities to locate the shooter more easily, but she couldn't make out even the barest notion of a silhouette, especially while trying to flee.

"Down!" Kaz cried, pushing Ellie to the side as a second shot rang out.

She yelped as she crashed to the ground, safe but stumbling. Knees stinging and palms burning, Ellie struggled to her feet as another shot sounded. Behind her, Kaz cried out and stumbled, and she whirled towards him. However, as she turned, her foot caught a muddy patch off the side of the road, sending her careening off the clear path and into the woods, down the side of a steep slope.

Ellie screamed as she rolled uncontrollably down the mountainside, unable to stop herself from flying downward through the trees. Roots and branches grabbed at her hair and clothes, scratching her skin and slowing her descent as she slid through dirt and mud and debris. It was only a few seconds of disoriented tumbling, but it felt like an eternity before she hit the bottom of the hill.

The bottom was much, much worse.

Ellie barely had a chance to register what was happening, the world still spinning around her, before a sheer cold shock stole the breath

from her lungs and the movement from her muscles. A scream ripped from her throat, but it was muffled by water.

She landed in a half-frozen stream, crashing through the paper-thin layer of ice and into the dark, frigid water below. At first, the cold water shocked her so much that she couldn't move, head spinning from the downhill slide, eyes and nose burning as she struggled to identify up from down.

It was deep for a mountain stream. This part of the water was over her head, forcing Ellie to fight her sodden clothes and swim for the surface. The cold was so sudden and strong that it was painful, like knives everywhere on her skin as she fought to reach air.

Flailing and kicking, Ellie managed to get her head above water long enough to take a deep breath, but something hard rammed her in the back of the head almost immediately. She swallowed a mouthful of icy water and was knocked back under, dazed and disoriented from the head wound.

"Ellie!"

She could hear Kaz calling to her from somewhere, but she couldn't tell where he was. Gasping for air, Ellie fought her way to the surface and tried to swim for the side of the creek. The water was still deep and the bank was too steep to climb, but at least she wouldn't be flowing freely downstream.

With stiff and frozen fingers, she reached out for a thick tree root hanging over the bank, barely managing to grab on as she gulped in lungfuls of air, lungs burning and heart pounding. She scrabbled for a foothold on the bank, but the muddy ground slipped and caved away under the toes of her soaked boots.

"*Kaz!*" she screamed, gasping for air. Her legs were starting to go numb from the water, and every muscle in her body screamed for mercy. She couldn't pull herself up. She didn't have the strength, and every second she lost a little of her grip on the root.

Tears sprang to her eyes when she saw a familiar silhouette appear over the bank. He slid to lay on his stomach, reaching down for her with his uninjured arm.

"Come on, I've got you!" Kaz cried. "Hang on for me!"

"You can't pull me out like that, just go get help—"

"I damn well can, just *hold on!*" he insisted, yelling over the sound of the water.

It was all Ellie could do to reach for his hand and force her frozen fingers to grip tight. Kaz moved slowly, but he never once let up, dragging her out of the water and up the steep, muddy bank until she could clamber up the rest of the way, both of them panting and groaning from exertion and the cold. In the process of pulling her out, Kaz wound up half-soaked himself from the frigid water sloughing off Ellie.

"You... really strong..." she mumbled, falling to her knees in the dead leaves and dirt.

"Come on, there's no time," Kaz insisted, pulling her to her feet. Her frozen limbs screamed in protest, but she knew he was right. The shots had stopped, but there was still someone out there who had *very clearly tried to kill them.*

As Ellie turned towards him to ask where he wanted to go, she noticed a metallic silver blood stain spreading across Kaz's white shirt. It was a second wound, this one to his stomach, and on a human it would be lethal.

"Oh, god," Ellie gasped. "You're gonna be fine, we just— we have to stop the bleeding."

"I know *I'll* be fine," Kaz said quickly, brushing her off as though a bullet to the stomach was a papercut. "This is nothing. You, we need to get inside."

Leaning on each other, they picked their way up the steep hill and back to the road as quickly as possible. It wasn't far from the village, but they were both exhausted and moving slowly. Every single sound had Ellie on edge until they reached the gates to the village.

When they finally reached the entrance without hearing another shot, Ellie swung the massive gate closed behind them and leaned against the old wooden boards, breathing hard and head still spinning. She couldn't fully feel her body yet, but what she could feel *hurt.*

That was about when she noticed that there was a small crowd of people who had stopped cold from their daily tasks to stare at them. Most of them weren't moving, but two figures in particular rushed towards them.

"What the living hell happened to you?!" Simon cried, sprinting towards them as soon as he got a good look at their bloodied, muddied appearance. He caught Kaz under the arm to support him before he collapsed.

"Oh, my god, *Ellie*?!" Jeannie shouted, right on Simon's heels. "We were just about to go check out the shots—"

"Someone... woods..." Ellie began, her body starting to shake with cold or shock or both.

"Stay put. I'll get blankets and bandages," Jeannie said, eyeing the bloody spots on Kaz and Ellie's clothes.

"No time," Kaz said through gritted teeth. "Come on, Ellie's soaked and we have to move."

"Agreed," Simon said with a nod, helping Kaz straighten up a little. "Let's get y'all inside. Can you walk?"

"Yeah, let's go," Ellie stuttered, nodding.

They shuffled to her front door as quickly as they could, Simon supporting Kaz while he put pressure on his stomach wound and Jeannie helping Ellie balance on frozen, soggy feet. Fingers shaking, she managed to unlock the door and let it swing open, stumbling inside.

"Let me help—" Jeannie began, but Kaz brushed her off, shaking his head as he straightened.

"We'll be fine. We can take care of it," he said firmly. "Thank you for your help."

"Are you sure?" Simon asked. "Y'all look... rough."

"Let us take care of it. If it makes you feel better, come back and check in later," Kaz said through gritted teeth, still keeping pressure on the wound.

He closed the door behind them and locked it without another word.

"Clothes off," he said urgently. "I'm sorry, there's no time for modesty, and I didn't think you'd want them watching."

Ellie nodded, stripping out of her sodden sweater, shirt, and undershirt as Kaz worked her boot laces loose. The curtains were closed and the lighting was dim, but it all still felt incredibly exposed. She wrapped her arms around her bare chest for just a little coverage, but he

kept his eyes firmly on the floor as he pulled off her shoes and tossed them to the side.

As Kaz dealt with her shoes, Ellie inspected herself for injuries. Now that she could feel a little besides the numbing cold of the water, she could tell that most of her body was scratched and bruised, and there was a bloody gash in her side where some debris or other caught her as she slid downhill.

She winced slightly, gently prodding at the still bleeding wound to see if anything was clearly stuck inside. It didn't feel like there were any splinters and it probably wasn't deep, but she balled up her wet shirt and used it to apply pressure anyways.

"Socks off," Kaz commanded, tossing her boots to the side. "I'll get the fire going."

"You need to sit the hell down," Ellie snapped. "You've been shot, probably with a hunting rifle, too."

"I'm aware," he grumbled. "I'll make it."

Muttering under her breath, Ellie stood and stiffly walked to the bed to grab a dry blanket, wrapping it around her shoulders. Under the blanket, she finished stripping off her wet garments and let them fall to the floor with a sodden *smack*. She dropped the shirt with them, assuming she could deal with the gash later.

Blanket trailing a little as she walked, Ellie took a metal cookie tin, towels, and a few jars from the kitchen shelf, arranging them on the wooden table. The sizzle of a match flaring to life let her know that the fire had been started, and perhaps now he would listen to her.

"Shirt off," she said, glaring as she mimicked his previous words.

Kaz huffed, looking her up and down for a moment, but after glancing back at the fire once more, he began unbuttoning his shirt.

"This is nothing to worry about," he protested, but the wounds appeared to be bleeding.

"Can't be comfy," she countered, reaching for the box of matches to light the oil lamp on the table. "We need to stop the bleeding. Bullet still in ya?"

"Went right through." Kaz shook his head and Ellie sighed in relief, standing to peer around to his back. Sure enough, there was an exit wound for both the stomach wound and the shoulder wound, though she

wasn't sure if that was better or worse. More blood loss, yes, but at least it was a clean pass, so there was no bullet to remove.

"Definitely a hunting rifle," she mumbled, using one of the towels to apply pressure to the wound. "Here, you put pressure on the other one."

Some small, manic part of her wondered how to get silver blood out of cloth, but the small part of her rational mind that was still conscious pushed it away.

"Have you treated a gunshot wound before?" Kaz asked, eyebrows raised.

"A few times, yeah," she said, nodding, but her eyes never left the wound. "Sometimes hunters are idiots while they're out, and people get hurt. This is the first time I've ever seen anyone huntin' *people*, though."

The good news was that the wound to his stomach wasn't as serious or as centered as she thought it was at first. It was more to the side, less lethal, and not bleeding nearly as badly as she'd feared. However, it was still possible the bullet had struck a kidney or a lung or some other vital organ...

"Don't look at me like I'm about to die, please," Kaz said with a small smile. "I'll make it."

Ellie took a deep breath, nodded, and held her hands in front of the iron stove for a moment, trying to urge some warmth back into her fingers. For now, all she could do was believe him. He wasn't delirious from the pain or losing enough blood that he'd passed out, so those were both good signs.

"Look. It's stopped bleeding already," Kaz said softly, wiping away excess blood with the towel. It left behind a strange, metallic shimmer across his skin, but that was all. No more blood seemed to be welling up from the wounds.

"How is... how is that possible?" Ellie murmured, brow furrowed as she leaned in. It really *had* stopped bleeding, and the shoulder wound had as well.

"Demon," he said with a shrug. "A little food and I'll be good as new soon."

"Let me clean it first, and then we'll see about food," Ellie said with a little half smile, reaching for the jar of witch hazel.

"That is not what I meant—" Kaz said with a sigh.

He scooped Ellie up in his arms and brought her over to the armchair, seating himself first and then settling Ellie on his lap, ignoring her squeaks of protest. Her head rested against Kaz's bare chest, legs tucked up on his lap as he cradled her close. His skin was warm against her cheek, and she didn't quite understand *how on earth* he could still be this warm when he'd gotten wet, too.

"I know it's not the most comfortable, but my body runs warmer than yours," he said quietly.

"You're *hurt*, you idiot," she protested, trying to wiggle out of his grasp, but it was useless. She was weak and his grip was like a vice.

"And you patched me up beautifully. My constitution is stronger than yours."

"But—"

"Let me do this," he said softly. "I'm not bleeding, and I can clean the wounds soon, but if we don't warm you up, you're in danger of hypothermia."

"... Okay," Ellie finally conceded, relaxing against him. She kept one eye on his shoulder wound, checking for any signs that it was getting worse, but his breathing was steady and the wound appeared to be... attempting to close?

Other biology was *amazing*. Ellie was a quick healer, herself, but nothing on this scale. As she was enjoying the warmth and wondering if Kaz would mind a few questions about his healing speed, his grip tightened a little on her and he took a shuddering breath, hanging his head.

"I'm so sorry," Kaz whispered. "I know that doesn't cut it, but I am so... truly sorry."

"For saving my life?" she asked, eyes blinking open.

"It's my fault you fell."

The grief in his voice broke her heart. Ellie worked her arm out of the blanket cocoon to reach for his hand, thumb stroking gently over the back of his palm.

"... Because you saved me from getting' *shot*? I'll take the water, thanks," she mumbled, settling back against him. "You didn't do this. The person out *shootin' at us* did this."

Kaz let out an uneven breath. His mouth opened and closed for a moment as he stared off into the middle distance, twining his fingers together with hers.

"I don't know what I'd do if something happened to you," he admitted, voice so soft she almost couldn't make it out. "I don't know... what you did to me, but..."

Ellie did not know what to make of that.

She felt the same way. If there was such a thing as fate, she was glad it led her to Kaz. He'd dug up old wounds and helped her heal all in one, and while the healing wasn't finished, she'd realized she was stronger than she knew. She realized that she'd healed more than she knew in the last two years, was ready for more than she knew.

And... he was *good*. He was genuinely protective and funny and an empathetic person, more than plenty of the humans she'd met. If it was another time, if she wasn't utterly terrified to lose someone else, maybe it would be possible for... more.

"Do you... really want me to go?" Kaz asked, as though her silence made him nervous. "If you do, I will when the time comes, no questions asked. If you don't want me to leave, though, I... I don't have to."

Maybe she could let herself dream of having more, just for a little bit. Maybe she could be honest with herself and honest with him.

"I hate being alone," she admitted, eyes fluttering closed once more, "and I like being with you."

"Can I stay a while, then?" Kaz leaned his forehead against hers, their breaths intertwining for a moment.

"I'll let ya," Ellie mumbled, nodding. "Y'ain't so bad. We could always set'cha up a house here somewhere. Or maybe down in Boone, if you can hide those horns."

"You think so?"

"Why not? Teacher's college is taking off, too. You might be able to get a job there teachin' writing."

"That's... not a bad idea," he said, nodding slowly.

"I know mountain folk ain't the most personable or cultured sometimes, but we look out for each other up here. You stick here long enough, you're family. Blood or no blood."

Or chosen blood, she thought. Kaz saved her life today. He didn't have to do that, it wasn't in the bargain, and he'd showed genuine care and concern for her wellbeing on top of that. As far as she was concerned, he was her chosen blood. Her heart was cracking open more and more every second he stayed, and she minded it less every day.

"Like the baker?" Kaz gently rubbed circles on her back over the blanket, soothing her stiff muscles.

"Emmaline? Yeah, I reckon she's family by now," Ellie said with a sleepy smile. "Her husband's good folk, too."

"I'm not sure how I feel about the rest of the people in this... place..." Kaz said distastefully, a pinched frown on his face.

Ellie couldn't help but laugh. "Yeah, they ain't the best, but they ain't the worst. At least I know I'm not gonna starve. If I run out of firewood, there's more in the community stock. If I need medicine, I have the supplies to make it. And when I get old, I'll... ah..." Ellie paused, stiffening.

"What?"

"Nothing," she said, shaking her head and casting a glance up at him. "We take care of our elders here, s'all."

"So if I tell you I'm four hundred and seventy-two, am I an elder you need to care for?" Kaz asked, flashing his sharp teeth in a wicked grin.

"Unfortunately, you gotta hit the half millennium first," Ellie deadpanned. "We witches are long-lived suckers."

"I... truly cannot tell if you're serious," Kaz admitted, laughing softly. The sound reverberated pleasantly in his chest as Ellie leaned against him, and she thought she wouldn't mind hearing it more.

"I'm not," she admitted, smiling. "Not entirely, anyways. Granny's old, older than a normal human should be. She said she stopped aging when the Appearances started. Got stronger, felt better."

"Stopped... aging," Kaz said slowly, "Like some Others."

"I don't know if it's all of us. I don't even know if it was just a side effect of everything going to hell in a handbasket. Fifty years is a while, but it isn't... we don't know enough."

Kaz looked at her very, very carefully for a long moment.

"How old are you?" he asked.

"Thirty-two."

A pause. Kaz frowned slightly, almost like he knew exactly what she was implying.

"How long are you going to be thirty-two?"

"I don't know," she admitted. "People tend to stop aging somewhere between twenty-five and thirty-five, but it's hard to notice. There aren't symptoms or anything. It's just that, we think... right when you reach your peak, right when you would normally stop growing and start growing old, you just don't. You just stop."

"Have you reached yours?"

"I did last year," she sighed. "No more changin' for Ellie."

Kaz shifted her weight in his lap so he could put his arms fully around her waist, her back to his chest and his chin on her shoulder. It was like he could tell she felt conflicted, like he knew she wondered what the world would be like when everything stood still for her.

After all, he'd experienced it himself, hadn't he? Four hundred years of it.

"That's good," he murmured, his voice sending shivers down her spine that had nothing to do with the cold. "I like you just the way you are."

Four hundred years...

Logically, she heard him say his age. Practically, it took a moment to sink in. Her life span was bound to be long, *unknowingly* long. She'd been so set on the fact that if she ever married someone, it was likely they'd die of old age long before her. Not Kaz, though. He would likely live as long as she would.

It suddenly occurred to Ellie that perhaps, if this worked out, they would not have to lose each other after all.

14 IN WHICH ELLIE STITCHES

Ellie didn't realize she'd fallen asleep until she woke up tucked securely into bed. The house was toasty warm, and the blankets were heavy on top of her slightly flushed body. She stretched groggily and started to push the blankets off, but she quickly realized that the blanket closest to her body was all she was wearing. It was still wrapped around her from when she'd...

... When she'd been sitting on Kaz's lap, she realized. If her cheeks hadn't already been red from the heat, they certainly were now.

A clanking sound from the kitchen caught her attention, and she looked over to see Kaz fiddling with a cast iron skillet near the gas stove. He'd pulled his white hair back with a leather tie, and he seemed intensely focused on whatever was in the pan. While Ellie slept, he'd clearly taken the time to change clothes, now wearing loose linen pants and a nightshirt.

"Kaz?" she called.

"Ah, she's awake," he replied cheerfully, glancing over with a small half-smile. "How are you feeling?"

"Like a horse trampled me on the way down the mountain," she sighed, rolling her shoulders, but kept the blanket tucked securely next to her body. "Grab me a nightgown when you get a sec, will ya?"

"It's on the side table," Kaz said, turning back to his cooking. "Come get food. I won't look."

Ellie glanced over to find that a bundle of white fabric was, indeed, on the side table, along with her faded red robe. Checking to make sure that Kaz was still focused on the pan, Ellie grabbed the gown and slipped it over her head while still under the blankets, wiggling the fabric around her body till she felt covered. She grabbed the robe next, pulling it partway around her shoulders when she suddenly paused, realizing what Kaz just said.

"You *cooked?*" she asked, bare feet silent on the brick floor as she padded towards him to peek in the pan.

"Badly, I think, but yes," Kaz said. "It's never been a special skill of mine, but I can manage."

Two plates sat on the table, both loaded down with toast and some slightly overdone sausages. In the pan, he carefully flipped two portions of fried eggs. The smell made Ellie's mouth water, and though she wasn't sure if the hunger gnawing at her belly was from sheer exhaustion or the smell of his cooking, she was happy he'd taken the time to make something.

"Not bad," Ellie said, smiling brightly. "How's the shoulder? And the side?" She reached out to pull aside the neckline of the nightshirt and check his stitches, but Kaz smacked her hand away, shaking his head.

"I'm not bleeding through my shirt, so you can wait until after we eat for that."

"... Fine," she conceded, eyes narrowed. "I'm puttin' the kettle on, though. We'll need hot water."

The food that Kaz cooked was actually *good.* She had to hand it to him— it wasn't just the fact that they were tired and hungry and in need of a good meal. He'd made the eggs fluffy, and she didn't mind a little char on her sausages. He'd even managed to find a jar of marmalade in the cellar, and Ellie decided they deserved it as a treat after the day they'd had. Survival did funny things to your head, she thought.

After they'd eaten, she rinsed the plates and took care of the crumbs, putting the dishes in a pile to clean in the morning. As long as there wasn't food on them, they could wait a few more hours. Ellie took a knee and fished under the sink for a moment, pushing aside the blue

checked curtain that hid her storage to reach for a jar she kept far, far in the back.

"What's that?" Kaz peered around her as she pulled out a large mason jar. There was a slightly foggy liquid inside, and she couldn't deny it looked a little suspicious, but it was perfectly safe. In fact, they were probably going to need it for stitches.

"Emergency moonshine," she said. "Want some?"

"I thought that was illegal in this country," Kaz said, squinting at the mason jar.

"It is." Ellie shrugged. "Mountain people make do. Now, drink up. I can do a little for the pain with what I have on the shelves, but not as much as this will, and you're gonna need stitches."

"I'll be healed by morning," he scoffed.

"You're telling me stitches wouldn't help *at all*?" she pressed, quirking an eyebrow.

Kaz pursed his lips, silent.

"That's what I thought. Shirt off," she scoffed, making a shooing motion with her hand. While Kaz pulled off the nightshirt, leaving it in a rumpled heap on the table, Ellie poured two mugs of moonshine for them, dropping a few herbs and orange peels in the mugs with the alcohol.

"Are those for pain, too?" he asked, looking at the concoctions warily.

"Nah, that's for taste," she said with a smile, turning to examine his wounds.

He'd done a decent job of bandaging himself, though it was clearly a temporary solution. The bandages were only slightly bloody when she gently removed them to check the wounds, and the bullet entry and exit sites looked appropriately dry. The blood was clotting as it should be without excess liquid oozing from the wound, which was a good sign. However... it did look a little strange to see metallic blood clotting. The color of the surrounding skin was different, as well as the shade of the bruising around the injury, which made sense. It also made her nervous, though.

"Yeah, we're stitchin' that," she said with a sigh. "Just to be safe."

Kaz grumbled something unintelligible, wincing as Ellie peeled the bandage off his side. She found the second gunshot wound in much the same state as the first, also in need of sutures. The cookie tin was still on the table where she'd left it, and she cracked it open to find a needle and thick, waxed thread.

"I promise I'll be as quick as I can, but I don't want that thing bustin' open in the middle of the night. I'm assuming demons can jostle their wounds just as much as humans can." Ellie took a quick sip from her mug to test the taste, scrunched her nose, and added another piece of dried orange peel to both cups.

"I don't think it's advisable to sew a wound closed while inebriated."

"Good thing I'm holdin' off on the rest till after you're stitched, then," she said with a soft laugh, retrieving the heavy needle from the box. "You really think I can't hold one sip 'a liquor?"

She placed the needle in a clean mug, poured boiling water from the kettle over it, and put both the mason jar of moonshine and the second mug with flavoring beside Kaz.

"We'll start with the shoulder. Then I'll need to sit on the floor to get at your side," she said, using tweezers to fish the needle out of the hot water. He grimaced, but he gritted his teeth and nodded.

Ellie did not enjoy sewing sutures. She never had. However, she assumed Kaz liked getting the sutures even less, so she decided it was best to bite her tongue against the strange sensation of pushing a wickedly curved needle through flesh and focus on completing the task as efficiently as possible.

"Drink the moonshine," she said as she worked, gaze never leaving the shoulder wound. "It'll help."

Kaz just grunted, but his slight shift signaled he'd picked up his mug.

He was practically made of muscle, and that was not what Ellie expected. She knew from the first night he arrived that his flesh felt a little strange, like something that was trying to be human, but just could not quite make it there. It felt that way sewing sutures, too. The needle protested every time she pressed it against his skin, like it simply didn't

want to puncture him, like it thought better of the plan and had decided not to do the job.

Kaz's skin was incredibly warm, enough that if he was human, Ellie would be seriously concerned that he had a fever that could kill him. The needle grew hotter and hotter as she worked, too, enough that she had to sterilize a small pair of pliers to help her pull it through because it was simply too hot to touch. By the time she finished the front and back of his shoulder wound, Ellie had to wave the needle in the air to get it to cool.

"How ya doin' over there?" she asked softly.

"I'll survive," Kaz said, taking another sip of moonshine. "This... isn't bad, by the way."

"It gets less bad the more you drink, I promise," Ellie assured him. "Lemme clean the shoulder, then we'll get your side stitched."

Using some of the warm water from the kettle and a clean cloth, she wiped clean the little silver blood that had leaked while she was stitching and sanitized it with witch hazel. In the morning, she could make a poultice if he needed it, but Ellie wasn't entirely sure how demon bodies worked or which remedies they might respond to, so she thought it best to keep things simple for now.

"Moonshine helping?" she muttered. Kaz's eyes were half closed when she looked up, and his mug was empty, so she assumed it was.

She thought about continuing on without warning him, but the poor man looked half asleep, so she thought it best to tap his uninjured shoulder gently before she started stabbing him with a white-hot needle again.

"One more," she said softly.

She knelt on the floor beside his chair to stitch his stomach wound, putting her roughly eye level with the injury so that she wouldn't have to constantly bend over. Partway through stitching the entry wound, she looked up to find Kaz's blue-gold eyes wide and trained directly on her. His lips were slightly parted, either from the pain or the alcohol or both, and he looked a little woozy, but she couldn't help but think he looked like a painting in that moment. He looked like a statue that should be staring down at her from a museum, not a person gazing at her in awe.

It was then that the expanse of skin on display really and truly hit her, and Ellie's cheeks flushed. Normally, she could remain detached during medical work without issues. She had a habit of hyper focusing on the injured area and somehow managing to ignore the rest of the patient's body. Not this time, though. This was different.

Taking a steadying breath, she went in with the needle once more.

"Is it difficult?" Kaz asked.

"Wha...?" Ellie blinked rapidly, glancing up at him for a moment as she carefully pulled the thread through. His eyes were still on her face, though, not her hands.

"To sew the wound," he clarified.

"It doesn't... feel like sewing a human," she said carefully. "The needle gets hot fast, and your skin is... different. The feel and the color, both."

"I imagine it is," he murmured. "People say it feels like something unnatural. It's too firm for human skin, harder to break, more like stone."

The irony that Ellie had just compared him to a statue in her mind was not lost on her.

"I don't know 'bout *unnatural*," Ellie muttered, nose scrunching. "Just different."

She finished the stitches without incident, leaving the too-hot needle and supplies on the table. They could clean up in the morning. After the day they'd both had, they deserved sleep. Using another clean cloth and more warm water from the kettle, she gently dabbed the side wound clean of silver blood and patted it dry.

As she cleaned, she finally sipped her own mug of moonshine. Ellie could hold her alcohol fairly well, but there was enough in that mug that it would make her ever so slightly tipsy. She would probably need that liquid courage, too. Neither one of them needed to sleep on the camp bed tonight, not with bruises and slashes and gunshot wounds like this.

Not when there was a real bed that could hold two.

"There. All clean," she said softly, bringing the cloth away from the wound. When she looked up, Kaz's face was only inches away from hers, and there was a look in his eyes that she wasn't sure how to take.

Very slowly, he leaned forward until his lips touched her skin, placing a soft kiss on her brow.

"Thank you," he murmured. Ellie wasn't really sure if that was the alcohol or not, but his touch was gentle and his words were kind, so she wasn't sure she cared.

"I... think you should probably sleep in the bed tonight," Ellie said, trying to smile, but it didn't quite reach her eyes.

"When it's not even my turn? Is someone having pity after stabbing me with a needle, hmm?" Kaz slurred, taking another sip of the moonshine right from the jar.

"If I can trust you to save my life, I think I can share a bed with ya," Ellie said as she tied off the stitches. Then she snatched the mason jar from Kaz's hand and put the lid on tight.

"Hey!"

"Hey, nothin'. You've had more'n enough of that. It's stronger than ya think it is."

"I'mma demon, it'll go *riiiight* through me," Kaz insisted, even as his eyes closed and his head tilted to the side.

"You're a demon who needs a damn drink of water," she muttered, filling a cup from the sink. "Here. Down the hatch."

"Don't want that, I'm fine," he muttered, standing on wobbly legs. Ellie pushed him back down into the chair, pressing the cup against his lips.

"Drink it, or I'll kick you out of the bed while you're sleeping."

Instead of waiting for him to drink, she took the oil lamp from the kitchen table and moved it to the nightstand, busying herself by putting out the rest of the lights, hanging her robe on a hook on the wall, and adjusting the blankets on the bed more than necessary. It felt like there was extra nervous energy in her bones, like some of the leftover adrenaline from the day had decided to make itself known just at this moment, but she pushed that aside.

It was just a bed. It was just a space. She could sleep on the same soft space as someone else.

One side of the bed was against the wall of the house to help conserve space, so Ellie slid across the mattress closer to the wall. Kaz didn't have the mobility that she did due to his injuries, and she wouldn't have him tearing his stitches after all that, so she made the executive decision to take the far side of the bed.

Kaz didn't slide under the blankets right away, though. He stood by the mattress, just staring for a long moment.

"Are you really sure?" Kaz mumbled, voice a little less slurred as he carefully chose his words. "Thought you didn't want to share the bed."

"It's... complicated. I'll tell ya in the morning," she sighed. "But yeah, I'm sure. We both should sleep somewhere comfy after today."

Ellie turned over so that she faced the wall. It would be easier this way, she thought. Behind her, Kaz put out the oil lamp, sending the room into complete darkness, and the mattress shifted with his weight. Her shoulders went tense as he adjusted the blankets over them, as she grew used to the feeling of a slight dip in the mattress beside her that hadn't been there in two years' time.

"You're shivering."

"It's okay, I'll warm up." She didn't have the heart to tell him that only part of the shaking was from the cold. Her heart rate was higher than it should have been, and Ellie took slow breaths to try to calm it, wondering if she really should have had that moonshine at all.

The mattress shifted behind her and there was a slight shuffling of blankets before she felt a warm, warm arm settle on her waist, a solid heat at her back. She was so shocked at the sudden heat that she didn't even bother to fight the hold, just relaxed and snuggled into... into...

She couldn't think too hard about it.

"You're like a human heater—"

"A demon heater, you mean."

"Mm. That, too," Ellie murmured, shifting her hips to settle into his embrace. Her head was just a teensy bit fuzzy, just enough to tell her she might regret this in the morning, but she was tired of waking up cold and alone, her whole body hurt from today's misadventure, and she desperately wanted this comfort.

"Ellie?"

"Hm?"

"Push me away if... if you don't like this."

Kaz adjusted behind her as her eyes fluttered closed, wrapping his arm fully around her with his hand splayed over her soft stomach, gently

settling one of his legs between hers so they were flush together, intertwined like branches or vines. She felt like she shouldn't like it, but oh lord, it was blissfully warm tucked in close to him, and his hold was so gentle, and she felt so... safe. Her muscles seemed to relax of their own accord, and rather than pushing him away, she found herself wanting to snuggle even closer, if that was possible.

Ellie had just enough time to realize she could feel the slow rise and fall of his chest as he breathed before she slipped into sleep.

✦

Ellie slept like the dead for several hours, locked in Kaz's warm embrace and so tired that she didn't even dream. When she woke, it was still dark. There was still a warm arm over her waist, and there was still gently breathing coming from behind her. It wasn't clear how long she'd slept, but her head wasn't as foggy as it had been before. Her heart rate wasn't as high, either, though she attributed that to finally managing to sleep.

Moonlight streamed through a small crack between the curtains, and Ellie held up her arm to check her injuries. She'd been bruised and scratched after her fall down the mountain, but now her arm looked entirely healed. If she checked the slash on her stomach, Ellie would be willing to bet it had closed already, too.

"What *are* you?" Kaz asked, softly. Ellie jumped, gasping softly. She hadn't even realized he was awake. His voice was a little rough from sleep, just like the mornings she'd woken him from the camp bed, but it was somehow different hearing it right beside her, tucked in under the same blankets.

"I don't know," she said, pulling her arm back under the covers. "I heal pretty quick, but I don't know what else I can do. Even Granny isn't totally sure what kind of Other blood we have mixed in with ours. We just know it's... old," she said carefully.

She curled up in a little ball without thinking about it, tucking her knees to her chest as she sighed, examining her newly healed skin. Kaz shifted on the mattress behind her, pulling the covers over them a little more.

"Are you grumpy about sharing the bed now?" he asked, gently poking her shoulder.

"What? No," Ellie scoffed, but she didn't turn over.

"You said you'd tell me in the morning. It's morning."

"It's barely morning," she protested, rolling over to face him. "Ain't *really* mornin' till the birds start singing."

"Morning on a technicality is still morning," Kaz said, smiling softly. "Besides, I can tell you're stewing over something. You're tense."

She hated that he was right. All the tension from the night before had creeped back into her muscles in a matter of moments. Ellie didn't really want to talk about it... but she knew that she *needed* to talk about it. Even to him. *Especially* to him.

"I've only ever shared a bed with one person. I... It's not that I think you're going to do anything horrible to me in my sleep. Well, not anymore at least," she said with a small smile, clearly trying to lighten the mood. "It's just that... I feel like I'm betraying him by sharing a bed with anyone else."

Tears started to fall before she could stop them. She did her best to keep her breathing steady, to use the early morning darkness to hide how emotionally shaken she felt, but it didn't work. Kaz just hugged her close, tucking her against his chest, legs tangling together as he stroked her hair.

"I feel like a blubbering baby," she choked out, scrubbing tears from her face with her sleeve.

"You're grieving. You're allowed to grieve."

"Two years should be enough, shouldn't it?" Her voice shook more than she wanted, but she couldn't stop it.

"You told me your mother died, too. Did two years fix that?"

"... No," she whispered. "No, it still hurts. It's... dull now. It doesn't feel as sharp or raw as losing Ben, but it hurts."

"I know I haven't known you long, but you're trying to find Ben justice even after he's gone. That takes strength." He absently stroked her hair as he spoke, and the motion was almost enough to stop her shudders. "I don't think anyone would ever ask you to give up Ben's place in your heart."

Ellie cried harder, a new fit of sobs shaking her from head to toe. "I don't want him to go," she sniffed. "I don't wanna lose him again."

"You won't. You have those memories, and they won't leave you... And I won't ever force anything on you. I mean it."

"I know." And she did. The longer she was around Kaz, the more she felt she could trust him.

"Good."

Ellie took a shuddering breath and rolled over so her back was to him. She needed to talk. They both needed this, and she knew it, but Ellie didn't think she could say what she needed to say while looking him in the eye. Just for this moment, she wanted the mercy of closing her eyes and looking away.

"I like you," she whispered, "but it hurts."

"Does it hurt like a knife wound or hurt like antiseptic?" he asked.

Ellie's eyes fluttered open in confusion. She'd never thought about it like that before, but it made sense. The sharp sting of something bleeding and not yet healed versus the slow burn that came after, but with the knowledge that the wound was closing.

"Maybe both, a little. Maybe like takin' out the knife," she whispered. "I know that... I know for someone else, I'd want them to find someone. I would. Like Jeannie— I'd be happy to see her happy. I... I don't think I can lose another person, though. I think it would really end me this time."

"Good thing I've got a damn long life span, then, isn't it?"

"Long enough to let me try to go back to sleep?" she teased, though her voice was still a little watery.

"I think that can be arranged," he said, laughing softly. "Do you want me in the bed or out of it?"

Ellie paused, biting her lip.

"... You can stay."

IN WHICH GRANNY RETURNS

"You are hopeless with an axe, ya know that?" Ellie drawled, shaking her head. "Here, gimmie that. I'll do the splittin', and you chuck the logs in a pile."

"I am perfectly strong enough to split wood," Kaz grumbled.

"Moot point if ya can't aim right." Ellie laughed loudly and took the axe, going back to splitting logs with a vengeance.

The radio broadcast informed them that a late winter storm was headed their way, and now Ellie and all her neighbors were prepping for snow. The town residents were likely doing their own prep in Boone proper, but there wasn't time to make any kind of journey down there on foot today. There was plenty of work to be done in preparation to hunker down inside for a couple of days after the storm swept through.

Ellie and Kaz were splitting logs in her yard, restocking the firewood they'd need for the next several days.

"Hey, Ellie!" Simon called as he walked by the yard. "Looks like Granny made it back just in time."

Ellie went absolutely stiff. She paused with the axe in midair, raised over her shoulder for a strike, and turned to Simon, eyes wide.

"Granny's back *early*?"

She never came back early from her yearly trip down the mountain. *Never.* She said her old bones couldn't take the mountain cold, but Ellie thought she just liked spending time with her old witch friends down in the piedmont.

"Yep. Tyler's off unloading her things from the pickup. Just in time, too! Wouldn't want her gettin' caught in the snow on the way here."

"Yeah, definitely," Ellie said with a shaky smile.

She went back to chopping wood, but the next two pieces were terrible splits. Her aim was almost as bad as Kaz's was, now that her mind wasn't on chopping wood at all.

"Fuck," Ellie hissed as soon Simon was out of an earshot.

"What's wrong?"

"I was hoping to get this... *business*... all tidied up before Granny got back from her trip, but I guess she came back early 'cause the storm's on the way," she muttered.

"And risk getting caught in it on the way up the mountain?" Kaz's eyes narrowed, and Ellie couldn't blame him for being suspicious.

"She's got a ride," Ellie said with a shrug. "She's good with the weather, too. Never was my strength, but you can plant your garden according to Granny and make out just fine every time. She probably knew when she needed to leave."

"If there's a storm coming, couldn't we just... avoid seeing her? If you're that concerned," Kaz suggested, leaning against the fence around Ellie's yard.

"It's either we go to Granny, or Granny comes to us, and if we go to Granny, at least we have the power to walk off and leave if we need to," she said with a sigh, rubbing her temples with both hands. "She raised me, and I love her dearly, but when she wants to talk to ya, you ain't gettin' out of it."

"It can't be *that* bad. She's just an old woman— *hey*!" He cut off as Ellie picked up the besom she kept outside for her yard and smacked his rear with the softer end.

"Don't you talk 'bout Granny like that," she snapped, though there was no real malice in it. "She'll have your hide if she hears you call her old. And while you're stacking wood, fill that wheelbarrow up, too. I'll cut extra and we'll drop some off at her place."

"Bossy mood today, I see."

"Oh, you like having something to do," she said, flashing him a brief smile before going back to cutting wood.

"I do," he admitted. "What can I say? Makes me feel useful."

"See? Even big scary demons want to feel like they're contributing," Ellie said with a grunt as she brought down the axe once more.

"Couple of things you need to know," Ellie said as they walked towards Granny's house on the far side of the village. She pushed a wheelbarrow laden down with wood while Kaz walked beside her. He'd offered to push, but Ellie seemed calmer when she had something to do. "Granny raised me. After my momma passed, she came and got me from our little town, brought me back here, and started trainin' me as a witch."

"And why are we going to see her if you're this stressed about it?"

"Because she's gonna find out you're here one way or another, and when she does, she's gonna be madder'n a hornet that I did a conjuring," Ellie muttered. "It'll be worse because you're a demon, too. No offense." She winced slightly at this, but Kaz didn't mind.

"None taken." He simply shrugged, gaze moving between Ellie's face and her death grip on the wheelbarrow handles.

"I was *hoping* to be all tidied up by the time she got back, but clearly that ain't happening. Might as well bite the bullet, I guess," she muttered.

They stopped outside a small, neatly kept house. It looked about the size of Ellie's, perhaps a little bigger, but the wooden boards that lined the outside were painted a bright, cheery lilac color instead of the faded yellow of Ellie's home. The shutters were dark blue, and there was a wooden cross hanging on the outside of the front door.

Ellie walked past the main door and around the back, stopping in front of a small, nearly empty shed that was obviously used to house firewood. One by one, she loaded log after log into the structure. Kaz helped where he could, but it almost seemed better to let Ellie get out her

excess energy. There was, unfortunately, no way to unload the wood very quietly, and eventually their thumping alerted someone inside the house.

"Ellie, baby? That you out there?" a voice called from inside, slightly muffled through the door.

Ellie swore a blue streak under her breath, or it sounded like she did from the tone. He couldn't make out any of the exact words.

"Dropping off some firewood for ya, Granny!" she called.

"Come on inside the house, darlin'. Lemme look at'cha."

The back door swung open, and a squat woman poked her head out to wave at them, smiling in a way that didn't reach her eyes when her gaze landed on Kaz. Something about it made him suspicious, but he couldn't say why.

"Aw, you've gotta introduce me to your friend, too. We haven't met yet, and I hear y'all are well on your way to... A *special connection*, if you will." She kept that smile plastered on her face, never faltering once.

Ellie looked like she wanted to curse again, but she smiled, a mirror to the older woman's expression, and nodded at her grandmother. "Okay, Granny, be right in."

The back door closed, and Ellie shot him a look like she'd rather be digging up graves than unloading the wood from that wheelbarrow. It didn't take long to finish the task, though, and she seemed to steel herself, take a deep breath, and open the back door.

"Hey, Granny," she called hesitantly.

"Come on in, baby, you're lettin' in the cold," the short woman called.

Kaz scuttled inside after Ellie, shutting the door behind him. Granny ushered them into her kitchen. A steamer trunk and a large carpetbag sat in the middle of the living area, yet to be unpacked, though it looked like there was a fire in the iron stove and the house was toasty warm. Granny seemed to be bustling around doing... something... but Kaz couldn't quite figure out what. There were a number of odd ingredients scattered around the table, many of which he didn't recognize at all, and frankly, he was afraid to ask.

"Now, first give Granny some sugar," the little woman said, opening her arms. Ellie bent slightly to give her a tight hug and a kiss on the cheek, and in that moment Kaz could see the resemblance between

the two of them. They had the same noses, the same blue-green eyes, and something made him think they probably had the same stubborn streak, too.

"Second, what in *blue blazes* are you doin' walking around in plain daylight with a *demon*?!" Granny yelled in a voice almost too big for her small body. Ellie visibly flinched. Even Kaz jumped, a little shocked at how quickly the woman's temperament could swing from one extreme to another.

In the two weeks he'd been here, he hadn't seen Ellie cower often. It was hard to make her cower, he'd learned, and even if she was scared, she wasn't going to show it. With Granny... something was different. Ellie looked like a child caught with her hand in the cookie jar.

"Girl, you got one foot in the grave and the other one on a banana peel, bringing him here!" she continued, pulling a dishtowel off a hook and using it to swat at her granddaughter. Ellie managed to avoid the towel, but only barely.

"You, uh... *heard*?" she asked, cringing.

"I heard the whole damn town talkin', if that's what'cha mean! Said you'd been walking around with a strange man with white hair, and then I get back here, and Jeannie says 'oh, ain't it great, Ellie's brought us a demon, maybe he'll marry in.'"

"I know it's not great, but I had to tell 'em something—"

"So you told 'em you got *engaged*?!"

He tilted his head as he watched them. Truth be told, the longer he looked, the more he could tell Ellie wasn't cowering. She wasn't scared, not truly. She was... something else. The hairs at the nape of his neck prickled, muscles tensed and ready just in case he needed to fight, but... no. Even he could see that Granny wasn't actually going to hurt Ellie.

"I know good and well y'ain't engaged to nobody, nohow! Only Jeannie would be stupid enough to believe that!" Swat. "If you're out there conjuring demons like a dumbass, the least you can do is tell the truth about it!" Another swat.

"Ow!" Ellie jumped away from the second swat with the dish towel as it smacked her shoulder.

"That is the least you deserve!" Granny cried, swatting at her again.

"Hey, hey now— wait a minute—" Ellie protested, trying and failing to dodge the smacks from her Granny. They didn't seem particularly painful, but it was enough to make a point.

"I don't care how old y'are, I should be pickin' a switch and takin' ya out back for a lickin' for this," Granny grumbled, shaking her head as she smacked Ellie's shoulder with the towel one last time, but it seemed a little halfhearted. "Now, make us all some of that tea you're so good at brewing, and tell me why on *God's green earth* you brought a demon to my house."

Ellie jumped to it without questioning, picking up the kettle from beside the sink. There wasn't an iron or gas stove here like at her home, just a fireplace, but she put the kettle on the crane and settled it over the flames as though she'd done it a hundred times before. She probably had, Kaz thought. Granny raised her, so this was probably home for a long time.

"And you," Granny said, making Kaz jump to attention. Something about that woman told him that she was certainly someone he didn't want to cross. "Bolt the door behind you, and sit down at the table. Can you make wards?"

"Yes, ma'am," Kaz said, surprised at himself. Granny was just the kind of person you called ma'am, though. She nodded, expression softening slightly.

"Good boy. You put one around the house so nobody can listen in on us." She paused, squinting at him for a long moment. "I'm watching you. You step one toe outta line, I'll spray ya in holy water just like I'm training a stray hellcat."

"Chamomile?" Ellie asked, as if all of these were perfectly normal phrases.

"Anything that'll knit my poor nerves back into place," Granny said with a sigh, sinking into a chair on the opposite side of the table. "I didn't get'cha too hard with the cloth, did I?"

"Nah," she said, shrugging it off. "Didn't feel it much, honestly."

Kaz closed his eyes as they chattered softly, mouthing the words to his basic warding spell. It only took a moment to set up. Privacy wards could be tricky, but he put them up often. It was a familiar dance to weave the wards in place around the home, especially ones that wouldn't need to last days at a time. An hour would likely be more than enough, and that was hardly trouble for him. When he finished, Kaz caught Granny's eye and nodded. No one should be able to hear them from outside by physical or magical means.

"Thank you," Granny said, putting a little liquid from a bottle on a cleaning cloth to wipe down her window ledges. Kaz squinted, realizing that she was cleaning and warding her home with holy water.

"Do all witches in this village keep holy water sitting around?" Kaz asked, thinking of the deluge that assaulted him via bucket that day. Granny was using a small bottle, no bigger than a quart, but a few gallons had poured out from the bucket and onto Ellie's yard.

"Not all. Mostly me an' my girl here. It's good for cleaning and... emergencies," Granny said in a tone that made it very, very clear to Kaz that *he* was the emergency.

Ellie plonked three mugs full of steaming tea down on the table. She took one for herself, but didn't drink, holding the cup between her hands like a lifeline.

"He listens better'n you," Granny said with a chuckle, turning to Ellie. "Sit, child."

Ellie sat, but did not speak. For some reason, Kaz assumed that Granny would make it known when they were supposed to say something.

"I would say I don't know where to start, but I think we've already covered that one," Granny said after a sip of tea just long enough to make Kaz want to squirm. "Did you bargain?"

"Yes," Ellie said, eyes firmly on her mug. She managed to let go of it for a moment, tucking her hands in her lap instead, but she was clearly tense.

"I hope whatever you're gettin' is worth it," Granny scoffed.

"We're solving Ben's murder," she said quietly. Kaz noticed that her hands were in fists, knuckles white as they rested on the table. Though Ellie didn't look up, Granny stopped with her mug halfway to her lips as though frozen in time.

"That..." the old woman said, shaking her head as she sat the mug down without drinking. "That is about the only explanation you could have given that I understand."

Ellie looked up, her eyes filled with tears and cheeks blotchy. "Really?"

"Don't get me wrong. I don't *like* it," she clarified. "But I do understand it."

Ellie swallowed hard before she spoke, and to her credit, her voice barely shook. "I gotta know, Granny. I can't... It hurts not knowing."

"You think it's gonna hurt less after you solve it? He's still gonna be gone, baby girl," Granny said with a sigh, placing her hand over her granddaughter's.

"I don't know," Ellie said. "I have to try, though."

At that moment, Granny turned to Kaz, eyes narrowed. "What are you charging her?"

"Room and board for the duration of the investigation, plus one treasured item upon solving the case," he said smoothly.

Granny's nose wrinkled as she blinked furiously.

"I know I really shouldn't be telling you that you're undercharging, but... This is a case most demons would want a soul for. Or at least a murder committed as a price for solving one."

"I'm not interested in a blood bath," he huffed.

"And you're not making her sleep with you?"

"Granny—"

One look silenced Ellie.

"I'm not interested in forcing anyone to take me to bed, either," Kaz snorted. "Incubus I may be, but I can find a willing partner without issue if the need arises."

"What *are* you interested in, then?" Granny asked, keen eyes searching his expression. "No one makes a bargain without something in it for them."

"You... have no idea how incredibly boring it is being stuck here for fifty years, do you?" Kaz sighed, rubbing at his temples. "I am so tired of people only ever wanting to make a bargain so I'll sleep with them. I'm sick of love spells and lust spells and power spells, I'm sick of all the awful shit that everyone wants to do to other people just to increase their own power. I thought that it would be nice to do something that doesn't hurt anyone for a change, and Ellie..."

He paused, sighing. What could he even say about Ellie?

"She's restoring what little faith in other people I had left," he finally said.

Granny raised an eyebrow. Her eyes widened very, very subtly as she looked between Kaz and her granddaughter. Ellie, for her part, kept her eyes very, very carefully glued on the floor, hands in her coat pockets and posture ramrod straight.

A shame. He'd have loved to see her blushing at him. Instead the tips of her ears turned slightly red as she looked down, but Kaz doubted that Granny's sharp eyes missed that detail. Instead of waiting for either of them to respond, he kept talking, hoping to disperse some of the nearly unbearable tension building in the room.

"I never got the chance to explain fully to your granddaughter, but I am unaffiliated with any higher power. I come from a hellscape that mostly exists on its own terms, a different plane that still has demonic beings. It's rural village life, for the most part. We're... farmers and teachers. Sexual energy is... yes, it's a part of our existence, but it's a food source. It would be like me only ever calling you to talk about your potatoes."

Granny looked at him for a long, long time. Long enough that it made Kaz highly uncomfortable, long enough that he found himself drinking from his mug of tea to avoid squirming in his chair. When she finally did speak, she let out a large breath and rolled her shoulders, and what came out of her mouth was not at all what Kaz expected to hear.

"You got damn lucky, girl," she huffed.

Kaz breathed a sigh of relief. He hadn't trusted that she wouldn't attempt to exorcise him or something else equally bad. After all, this was a woman who cleaned her kitchen with holy water. He thought it best to expect the worst and hope for the best rather than letting his guard down.

Ellie visibly relaxed as she looked up at her grandmother. The old woman reached over and grabbed her by the ear, shaking gently enough that it wouldn't hurt but hard enough to make her point. "You ever, *ever* go conjuring and bargaining with a damn demon again, I'll douse you in holy water and leave you outside the night of the first frost."

"So... I can conjure a Fae, right?" she asked, a Cheshire Cat smile spreading across her face.

Granny just glared. "You wanna push me, youngin'?"

"No, ma'am," Ellie said quickly, grin immediately dropping.

"Good." The old woman released her granddaughter's ear and hugged her instead. "I was so worried about you, baby."

"I'm sorry to make you worry," Ellie said, voice muffled against Granny's shoulder. "I'm not sorry I called for help finding who killed Ben, though."

Granny pulled away and looked at her for a long moment.

"I know the state ain't gonna do a thing if you write to 'em about this, and the town... is the town. They need some adjustin' sometimes," she said distastefully. "It was a stupid plan, but I understand why you did it."

"So... you're not mad?" Ellie squeaked.

"Oh, I'm pissed as hell, but Ben was a good boy, and I liked him," Granny said firmly, hands on Ellie's shoulders. "I'll help ya if I can."

"Another set of eyes and ears would be useful," Kaz said. "I can blend into shadows and investigate in ways I won't be seen, but I'm only one person, and your village... doesn't exactly trust me."

"Mmm. Other or not, you're still an outsider. As desperate as the witches in this village are to have a full-blooded Other in their bloodline, they won't tell ya to leave, but they damn well only want you to see the sunny side of things."

"Doesn't help that they all hate me," Ellie muttered.

"Oh, they can hush up about that. We all know why they're petty."

Kaz's brow furrowed as he looked back and forth between the women. Ellie seemed to shrink in her chair, shoulders slumping as she sighed and avoided his eyes.

"She didn't tell you, did she?" Granny said with a smile. "Our bloodline might not be the purest or the most full of Other blood, but it's one of the oldest in these parts."

"Ellie said they... found her comparatively weak?" He remembered that conversation very clearly.

Granny snorted. "Child. Stop telling your man lies."

"He's not my—"

"He is for the duration of this bargain, and you best tell him the truth," she said, shaking her head. "Ellie isn't weak. They all torment her because they know she's the strongest witch on this mountain."

"I'm not. You are," Ellie protested. "Then Jeannie right after you."

"Baby, you have so much more locked inside of you than I ever have, you just need to let it be free. On top of that, you know good and well that Jeannie never put in the work to develop her gifts the way she should have." The older woman shook her head and ran a hand through her gray hair.

"Whatever you say, Granny," Ellie said softly, but it was easy enough to tell they'd had that conversation many, many times before. She downed the rest of her tea and put her mug down on the table with a clunk, but no sooner had she done that than Granny made a shooing motion towards her.

"Now that you're warmed up, lemme talk to the boy. Shoo," she said, gently swatting Ellie's shoulder.

"Granny, you know we're not *actually* engaged, right?" She rolled her eyes, but stood from her chair all the same.

"I'm aware," she said firmly. "Lemme talk to the boy. Out. Scoot."

Ellie walked a short distance towards the back door, and then looked over her shoulder, like she was wondering if that was far enough.

"*All the way out,*" Granny said. "Go take your wheelbarrow home and come back."

Ellie grumbled under her breath, but she put her hat on her head and walked out the door, leaving Kaz alone with her grandmother.

"You like her," Granny said, eyeing him pointedly. It wasn't a question.

"She's different."

"I imagine she is compared to the people who usually call Others for bargains," Granny said, finally putting the dish towel back in its place on a hook. "Let me be clear: You hurt her, and I will make you *wish* for Hell."

"I have no intentions to hurt her."

"That's what worries me," Granny muttered. "You break her heart— on purpose or not— and you can forget wishing for Hell. I'll make Hell seem like a spa day."

"I..." Kaz paused, throat suddenly closing. "I want to help her grieve. Anything else is secondary."

"Listen son, I'm old, not blind, and I'm certainly not stupid," Granny said, rolling her eyes.

"I'm older than you are," Kaz said pointedly.

"Does this really seem like the time to be pointin' that out? You want me to tell my granddaughter you're a cradle robbing demon, too?" She shook a wooden spoon at him as she spoke in a way that seemed somehow more threatening than a real weapon.

"N— no, ma'am," Kaz stuttered.

"That's better." Granny smiled brightly, and this time it did reach her eyes.

"I... want her safe," he sighed. "I want her happy."

"What about when it's done? You goin' your own way again?"

"I... like it here," he said slowly. "It hasn't been long, but it reminds me of my home, in a way."

Granny paused, like she was trying to read his intentions in the same way he could read other people's emotions. Hell, she might have been able to read everything going through his mind. Kaz wasn't sure what the upper limits of witch powers could be, and he wasn't particularly interested in finding out by pissing one off. However, it seemed as though they had, for the moment, survived Granny's interrogation. He wasn't sure they gained her approval, but she was willing to help with the case, and that was a start.

"You better take good care of my baby girl, or I'm coming after you myself, y'hear?" she finally said. "Oh, and give her this. I picked up the mail on the way here."

She reached into her pocket and smacked a battered-looking letter down on the table in front of him. It was clearly addressed to Ellie, and though he didn't understand how Granny had managed to get her hands on it, the envelope was still sealed, and Kaz didn't mind being a delivery boy.

"Nice to meet you, Granny Sader," he said with a tip of his hat. Granny smiled broadly at him as he stood from his chair and walked towards the back door.

"Don't be a stranger, boy."

16

IN WHICH SNOW FALLS

Kaz walked slowly back towards Ellie's house, fully expecting to cross paths with her on the way. He had a feeling she was used to things like this with her grandmother, but it was amusing to him as an outsider.

As predicted, he found her rushing back down the path, muttering under her breath with an enraged look on her face. Kaz couldn't help but smile— it was endearing seeing her angry, and he liked the way the sunshine caught her silver hair.

She practically skidded to a stop in front of him, one hand on his shoulder and panting from running.

"Dammit," Ellie sighed between breaths. "I miss all the good stuff. What did she say?"

"She's smart, I'll give her that. Good intuition," he said, adjusting his hat.

"Kaz," Ellie said, eyes narrowing. "What did she say?"

"Oh, this and that. Nothing bad." Kaz shrugged and shoved his hands into his jacket pockets while they walked back towards Ellie's house. He took her hand almost reflexively, pleased when she didn't pull away.

"Granny took me in when my momma passed," Ellie said slowly. "I was real young. Never met my daddy, but Granny said my blood called out to

her just like his did, kin to kin. She tracked me down when momma died and brought me back here."

"I like her," Kaz said as soon as the door to Ellie's house closed behind them. "I can see where you get your attitude from."

"How dare you suggest I am *anything* but a sweet Georgia peach," Ellie said in mock indignation, batting her eyelashes innocently.

"You're a wild mountain rose is what you are," Kaz said with a snort. "Prickly when you want to be, but you can grow and thrive and climb wherever you want."

Ellie stared.

"What?"

"It's just... That was... Sweet."

There was a strange little confused frown on her lips, and the thought crossed his mind that he wanted to kiss it away. That would hardly be practical, though, and instead he shrugged off his jacket to avoid thinking any more about Ellie's mouth, hanging the coat on a hook by the door. As he turned, he noticed the corner of an envelope peeking out of one of the jacket's inside pockets.

"Oh," Kaz said suddenly, glad of the distraction. "This is for you. Granny said she picked it up on her way home." He fished the slightly crumpled letter out of his jacket pocket and handed it to Ellie. She tore the envelope open and plopped down on one of the kitchen chairs to read, elbows resting on the table and an adorable crease of concentration between her brows.

"It's from Miriam," Ellie said softly, eyes scanning over the page. "Should'a guessed. Was due for a letter from her."

"I remember you mentioned her once," Kaz said, taking a seat beside her.

"Mm. She's my pen pal up in Virginia. She's a real sweetie," she said absently, eyes still locked on Miriam's writing. After a long moment of scanning over text, Ellie put the letter down, worrying her lower lip with her teeth as she sighed.

"Bad news?" Kaz raised an eyebrow.

"Her kids are growin' up fine, but there's been a lot of violence towards the Black residents up there. She don't feel safe, and I can't say I blame her." Ellie sighed, folding up the letter. "Don't wanna leave the mountain, though, and I can't say I blame her for that, either. It's home."

"So she's... stuck?"

Ellie sighed, shaking her head. "It's hard to find anyone that will sell land to a witch, a woman, or anyone with darker skin, much less someone who's all three at once. I offered for her to move in here, but she's against Council-ordained witch communities, and even if she wasn't... There's a good chance they'd find a reason to deny her application for residency just because of her skin," Ellie spat. "If I had the option, I'd find a place for us all up here, but... I honestly can't afford land right now, even if anybody *would* sell."

"What about moving North?"

"It's still segregated up there, too. May not be as overt as Jim Crow laws down here, but at least on the mountain she's got a patch of land and some distance between her family and anyone who dares try an' bother 'em." She gazed off into the middle space, staring at nothing in particular. "In a big city, she'd be crowded in with a thousand other folks, ten times as dirty and still not safe."

"Is there... anything I can do to help?" Kaz asked hesitantly. He wasn't sure what they needed, but money was hardly a problem for him.

"I'll talk to Granny about it," she said, folding the letter and tucking it back into the envelope. "I have a little saved up, and I think Miri does, too. If we put our heads together, maybe we can find some land out on the mountain somewhere."

"You said they won't sell to a woman or a witch..." Kaz said slowly. "What about an Other who can pass as a white human man? I have the money."

He would gladly go and purchase the land for them if it would make life easier. Kaz wasn't exactly known for his charity towards humans or witches or... anyone, really. However, it had been a long time since someone had gotten close enough to him to make him feel like acting charitable. Ellie was a good soul who deserved to get out of this community without being driven off the mountain. He imagined that, as well as Ellie spoke of her, Miriam was the same.

It enraged him that someone could be driven out of their home just because of their skin color, just because of their biology. It sounded far too familiar to the humans-only cities that forcibly removed or killed Other residents to establish their own little sanctuaries. Even worse, Miriam and her family were as human as the rest of the earth's natural residents. They belonged here. If Kaz could aid in making the place safer for even one person... Well, he thought that was progress.

Odd, how his heart had softened more and more the longer he was around Ellie. It had been frozen in his chest a long time, hidden behind steel walls and layers of ice, but she hadn't wasted any time in melting all that away with her care and warmth.

"No," Ellie said firmly, shaking her head. "They might sell to ya, but I don't want you to do that for me."

"I'm not really doing anything with the money, to be perfectly honest," he said with a shrug.

"You're living off it."

"I have more than I'd ever need to live off. It's a common payment system for bargains, but I don't gain much from it."

"You're sweet," Ellie said with a little half smile. "I can't accept that, though. It's too much. It would feel like a debt I can't repay, and... Honestly, I don't think rich people get how important stuff like that is to people like us mountain folk."

"I was afraid you'd say that," he sighed.

Ellie frowned.

"I come from an agricultural town, remember? And I live off bargaining. I may not be familiar with human money, but one thing I do understand is debts and payments," he explained.

She visibly relaxed at that, slumping back in her chair like she'd been prepping for a fight that was now over before it began. He could guess this wasn't the first time she'd refused financial assistance. In a way, Kaz couldn't blame her. This was an area where people learned to manage on their own, manage with the help of the town, or generally barter with what they had and get by. Pride was important to Ellie, to the whole community, and he knew it was best to respect that.

"Thank you," she said sincerely, placing her hand on his shoulder reassuringly. "We'll figure it out."

Ellie drummed her fingers on the table impatiently, eyes fixed on a random spot on the wall as she stewed over the letter.

Kaz, on the other hand, felt the spark of an idea forming. Though he knew it might be a long shot, with a little help, he thought he could manage it. If money was the main issue, he could solve that, but he needed to do it in a way that Ellie wouldn't feel belittled by accepting... It might take a while to work out the details, but he thought it should be possible.

A knock on Ellie's door came before he had the chance to finalize his thoughts, but that was just fine. He'd have time to straighten everything out later.

Ellie tucked the letter into a basket of what appeared to be old mail— postcards, pictures, opened letters, etc— on her countertop before she went to open the door. Considering that the number of people who could possibly be coming to speak to Ellie was very small and that his friend from out of town wouldn't be here until after the incoming snowstorm passed, Kaz was only slightly surprised to see Alice on the other side of the threshold.

"Hey," Alice said with an awkward wave.

"Come on in, Alice. You're in time for supper if you want."

"N— no," she stuttered, shaking her head furiously. "I just needed to stop by real quick. Don't want anybody knowin' I came here, and the storm's gonna blow through any minute. It's cold 'nuff out there to freeze the tit off a frog."

"Cold enough to... *what*?" Kaz blinked, suddenly mildly horrified for any frogs in the area.

"City slicker?" Alice asked, turning to Ellie.

"Yeah. He'll get used to it," she said with a shrug. "What's happening, Alice?"

"It's just... I heard my momma talkin' to Ida May. She's the oldest sister," she said, turning to Kaz as she explained. "She sounded... mad. Real mad."

"Seems like she's always all tore up about somethin' or other," Ellie muttered.

"Yeah, that ain't far off," Alice admitted. "This time was different, though."

"How so?" Kaz's brow furrowed as he leaned against the wall, fighting not to tap his foot impatiently on the brick floor.

"Momma always compared me to everyone. To you, too. It's... not an excuse," she said awkwardly. "It's just that I didn't think anythin' of it at first, y'know? But then I noticed she's *real* unhappy with you lately. And Kaz, too. Started sayin' that if Jeannie completes that ritual she's wantin' to do, we'll be on the map and princess Ellie won't be the only special one."

"What the hell ritual was she goin' on about?" Ellie muttered.

"I don't know more'n the man in the moon," Alice said helplessly, throwing her arms up. "Was hopin' you might."

"I got nothin'... but Granny might," she said, drumming her fingers on the table once more. "My guess is Jeannie would want help for anything complicated. She's not patient enough for a lotta calculations. Granny's the best there is for those."

"We can check on that tomorrow," Kaz said. "

"Hey... thanks, Alice. Really," Ellie said.

"I... I'm not gonna lie to ya, I want outta here. Bad," Alice said, taking a deep breath. "I don't think it matters what I do. I can't be good enough for Momma. So... I'd rather be good enough for me."

"I think that's a good plan," Ellie said with a smile.

Meanwhile, the gears in Kaz's mind continued to turn. He wondered just how many decent people there were around here that wanted out of this village besides Ellie. Granny and Alice made two, and then Miriam and her family, if he could swipe the address off the back of one of Ellie's old envelopes and get a letter to her...

This might come together more easily than he thought.

"I... think I'd like to be a veterinarian," Alice continued softly. "Maybe. I like animals. They're nice, and they can tell me what's wrong with 'em. I like farm work, too, though. Anythin' outside."

"Have you thought about the teacher's college? Could take some biology classes, maybe," Ellie suggested. "It would be a start towards workin' with animals, and it'd get ya out of the house."

"D— do I have to cut any of 'em open?" Alice squeaked, looking a little green.

"Well, if you've gotta cut a lil critter open to save his life one day, you wanna know how to do it, right?"

Alice gulped. "Y— yeah."

"Best get used to a little blood in service of a greater good, then."

The sound of the wind howling outside, gusts strong enough to rattle the windowpanes, made them all wince.

"I better get on home," Alice said.

"Be careful. Please." Ellie's voice held genuine concern. It was amazing to him how fluid she was, how she could let herself change opinions on people and work with new information, how much she wanted to see the best in everyone. He wanted to protect that side of her with all he had.

"Hey... I can see you're happier, Ellie," Alice said softly. "I'm glad. I'm guessin' y'all are sticking around for a while, so... Welcome home, Kaz. Officially."

"Thanks," he said softly, but his chest ached as he spoke.

He wanted to give Ellie time, but the uncertainty gnawed at him at night. More and more often he felt like he was standing at the edge of something big, something important, but he didn't want to jump before she was ready.

However, at this rate... neither of them would ever jump at all. Someone had to make a move to break the tension between them, and it seemed like Ellie would let her guilt and grief and confusion hold her back forever if he didn't. If she wasn't ready, that was fine. He could understand. Kaz wouldn't just give up and sit there waiting, though.

As Ellie closed and locked the door behind Alice, he wondered how to broach the subject, but in the end, he simply said the one thing running through his mind over and over, the thing that had been on repeat in the back of his head for days.

"Am I? Sticking around, that is," Kaz asked, moving a little closer to Ellie.

"I was thinkin' about that," she said softly. "And I just... I think if we're gonna do this, if we're gonna... *try*... Then it can't be halfway."

Kaz waited patiently while she clenched and unclenched her fists, struggling for words.

"I'm still afraid that if I let you in, I'm gonna lose Ben," she admitted. "It's not fair to you to keep wafflin' though, and I... I can't... I don't want to lose you, too."

"Are you sure you're ready?"

"No. I mean, yeah, but... I want to try. You make me want to try again. I'm just scared."

"And that's okay with you?" Kaz asked gently, reaching out to run his fingers through her hair. "I'll gladly have you even if you're scared, but I don't want you to regret this."

His voice was calm, but his heart was beating out of his chest. It felt like he could hear very little besides the rush of blood in his own veins, feel very little besides Ellie and the vague impression of the ground beneath his feet.

She was so, so strong. Bold and brilliant and hard-headed and absolutely beautiful, Ellie had tangled herself in his heart in a way that few people had ever managed to do before. He wondered for a moment if this was what people meant when they referenced fate, destiny, or true love...

And then he realized he didn't care. This was his life. It was a choice for the two of them to make together, a choice to compromise and grow together, a choice to make this work. Fate and destiny be damned. He wouldn't leave Ellie behind, not as long as she wanted him in her life. She was already far too important to him.

"Yeah," she whispered, nodding. "You make me feel *less* scared."

Kaz breathed a deep sigh of relief, leaning in close to rest his forehead against hers.

"Please, *please* tell me this means I can kiss you now," he murmured.

"The devilish part of me wants to tell you no," Ellie admitted as a wide, wicked grin crossed her face. "I'm not quite that cruel, though."

"Mm. Generous of you," Kaz said with a laugh, pulling her towards him till they were pressed flush together. "Benevolent, even."

"Well, you know me—" Ellie began, but Kaz couldn't take the waiting any longer, and she cut off with a slight squeak as he claimed her mouth in a searing kiss.

It felt like he'd waited too long for this, like her touch was the only genuine comfort he'd been blessed with since he'd gotten stuck on this godforsaken plane. A kind of dreamy lightheadedness overtook him as he focused on the feel of her soft lips on his, and for a moment he couldn't tell if it was lack of air or sheer emotion making him dizzy.

Maybe it was both.

<hr>

Ellie tried and failed to stop thinking about that kiss the rest of the day. She tried and failed to stop thinking that she admitted she really cared for Kaz. She tried and failed to stop herself from acknowledging that they were a good pair, that they made an excellent team, and that she could see them in the future with... a real life. A real life past the investigation.

Even considering the possibility was terrifying to her. Ellie wasn't good at taking things one step at a time— she needed to know how everything would proceed so that she wouldn't get hurt. The problem was, in this case... she could see a feasible future where things proceeded *well.*

Dressed in a soft nightgown, she pulled back the blankets for bed and tried to ignore her pounding heart, but it was futile. She wanted Kaz to hold her again. That was the best sleep she'd had in months, tucked safely in beside him, and Ellie couldn't help but crave more.

... He was across the room, though, awkwardly loitering next to the bookshelf.

"You stayin' up?" Ellie asked, glancing over her shoulder at him as she slipped under the covers.

"You... still want me in the bed?" The look on his face was oddly close to a wounded puppy, enough that she wanted to laugh and hug him at the same time.

"You got me spoiled now," she said with a shy smile. "I need my heater."

Already dressed in pajamas, Kaz didn't hesitate snuff out the lights and clamber into bed beside Ellie, a toothy grin on his face. She was still getting use to those sharp teeth, but it was endearing when he smiled wide enough to show them. It either meant he had a mischievous plan up his

sleeve or he was feeling genuinely happy, both of which made his eyes shine in a way Ellie adored.

"A Christian witch and a demon sharing a bed," Kaz murmured, settling in beside her. "Who would have thought?"

He had a point, unfortunately, and it wasn't one she'd forgotten. Ellie tucked the covers under her chin as though she could use the blankets as armor, fighting not to curl into a little ball as she spoke into the dark room.

"Does it bother you?" Ellie asked, a little self-conscious. "My religion."

"Not particularly, no," Kaz said as he adjusted the blankets. "I admit that I find it a little ironic considering how many people have immediately assumed that I'm irredeemably evil. It doesn't bother me, though. I told you that I have no quarrels with your God, and I meant it, and I haven't seen you trying to step on anyone else's religion. I think we're in the clear."

"Good," Ellie sighed. "I just... I just wanted to check. I mean, I can see spirits and there are Others out there now, and I think there are a lot more things out there than we'll ever know... but I've picked who I want to align with. And I'd like my... um... what do I call you?" she squeaked, suddenly feeling even more nervous.

"Well, I suppose a fiancé isn't technically accurate," Kaz conceded. "We'll have to think of something, though, because you already nixed 'lover' a long while back."

Ellie just snorted. "I think I would explode from embarrassment if you called me that in public. Or I called *you* that in public." She paused with a slight sigh. "Anyway. You don't have to have the same loyalties I do, but I at least don't want any major conflicts, ya know?"

"Reasonable, I think," Kaz said.

His hand found hers under the blankets, fingertips tracing over her skin until he finally ran his fingers over the wound from their bargain. In the time since their bargain, he'd been with Ellie almost every second of the day. Kaz had seen that scar slowly form, seen every moment of the healing process. It had scabbed over by now and faded to raised scar tissue, but it was still there. She imagined the wound on his palm had nearly healed by now, too.

"Ellie," he said slowly, threading their fingers together. "You asked me once why I took bargains if I don't like doing it."

"I remember." She gave his hand a little squeeze.

"It's... easier this way," he said slowly. "It's easier to pretend this is temporary. If I go from place to place, I never put down roots. I can pretend my roots are at home, that I can go back at any time, that I'm just on an extended vacation. I can pretend I'm not... stranded."

It made her heart ache to think of it, but it made sense. Homesickness was never something Ellie could handle well. It was part of why she didn't want to leave the mountain. She couldn't imagine being trapped far away from everything she'd ever known and having to start over.

"Where all have you been on vacation, then?" she asked gently, pleased to hear Kaz laugh softly in response.

"I've mostly been drifting. A few years here, a few there. Some Others have a permanent home place, but most of them are twitchy around demons. I've seen the world, on the upside," he sighed. "On the downside, I'm pretty tired of it all."

"I can understand that..." she said slowly.

If it wasn't for Granny taking her in as a child, she probably would have been the same way. When Ellie's mother passed away, no one in the town had been willing to take her in. Instead, she was stuck at the local orphanage, and would have remained there if Granny hadn't come calling. Truth be told, even if Granny hadn't shown proof of their kinship, the ladies there would have let anyone take Ellie. They thought she was a curse on the town as long as she stayed.

"Story for a story," Ellie said. "You wanted to know why my momma named me Rafayelle."

"You don't have to tell me," Kaz said, shaking his head.

"S'okay." She shrugged and snuggled a little deeper under the covers, sliding in close to him.

"My momma thought I was gonna be a boy. She was sure of it," Ellie said softly into the darkness. "She just changed the spelling of the name she picked on the fly when I popped out instead. That's why I'm named like I am."

"It's a nice name. At least, I think it is," Kaz murmured, absently playing with a lock of her long hair.

"Just... imagine for a a second," Ellie said with a sigh. "Imagine you're a little girl with a boy's name. Imagine your hair grows silver from the day you were born—"

"Don't have to imagine that one," he muttered.

Ellie elbowed him in the side, unable to stop her slight laugh, but she sobered quickly.

"Now... imagine your daddy's long gone and your momma doesn't talk about him. Imagine everyone tells you that you're devil spawn. Imagine they chase you home with sticks from school till you just start staying home all day long."

She tried not to lose herself in the swarm of memories, but it was difficult. In the end, Ellie's mother had been her teacher for her early years. Granny sent her to school later on, but by that time she was behind the other children her age and it had been difficult to catch up.

"Imagine your momma was a pastor's daughter who had you all on her own. No marriage, or not one recognized by any humans. Imagine it's some kinda sick irony or apology that got you named like that in the first place," she said even more quietly. "Do you like it now?"

"I do," he said firmly.

Ellie blinked, and he must have felt her tense, because Kaz pressed a soft kiss to her forehead before he spoke again.

"It's *your* name. I like *you*," he explained.

The tips of Ellie's ears burned in the darkness.

"I'm nothin' special, but thanks," she muttered, turning onto her side to face away from him.

Kaz sighed, and the mattress shifted just a little behind her until she felt the warm press of his body against hers. He hugged Ellie close from behind in a way that made her relax into him, that made her want to melt into him and never pull away again.

"You are extraordinary," he whispered, his breath against her ear sending shivers down her spine.

She wanted to cry and scream and rail against the feeling of her heart slowly softening towards him. It hurt, it hurt, it *hurt*, like she couldn't stand to lose him. It hurt like she wanted to jump off a cliff.

It hurt like she wanted him to catch her.

God help her, she wanted him to catch her more than anything in the world.

His kiss from mere hours ago replayed in her mind on a loop, and she wanted more and wanted to run all at once. Ellie knew, logically, that it was okay for her to be a little afraid of this. Running for the hills and far away from a relationship wouldn't get her anywhere, and she... she liked him. She liked him so much that it felt dangerous.

It couldn't have been more than a few seconds, but it felt like an eternity before she let go of his hand and turned over to face him.

"Kaz?"

"Mm?"

"I think it hurts like antiseptic," she said slowly. "I think it hurts because it's tryin' to heal."

Ellie inched forward in the darkness, fingertips threading through Kaz's white hair, her thumb gently stroking his cheek. Slowly and carefully, she leaned forward in the darkness and placed a soft kiss on his lips.

Kaz's response was immediate. He shifted his hold to pull her closer, a soft moan sneaking past his lips as he kissed her back. She wanted to lose herself in the feeling of that gentle heat, her fingers tangling in his hair and breath coming in soft sighs. He shifted his hold to kiss her jaw, gentle touches trailing down her neck and arms over her nightgown. Ellie's fingers found the hem of his shirt, her thumb stroking the soft skin underneath more from instinct than conscious thought. When Kaz's hand moved across her torso, the edge of his fingertips barely brushing the side of her breast—

Ellie flinched.

Kaz stopped immediately, resting his forehead against hers instead. A wash of guilt and shame settled deep in her chest, and she couldn't seem to brush it away. It was just... she wasn't ready. She couldn't do this yet. Not this *fast*.

She needed to get used to the idea of letting herself really love someone new before pushing herself— or him— towards anything else.

"That's far enough for now, then," Kaz murmured, kissing her cheek gently.

"Sorry," Ellie whispered, brushing a stray lock of hair out of her face.

"You have nothing to apologize for," he insisted. "Besides, it's... probably best for us both to take our time. Though, if it's alright, I'd be more comfortable without..." he trailed off, picking at the fabric of his loose linen shirt.

"Overheating?" Ellie murmured. "I'm sorry I didn't notice before."

"A little, yes. That and... I feel more comfortable in less clothing. I've gotten used to it, but human clothing conventions are still a little odd to me," he admitted. "You cover yourselves entirely even when you don't need to for protection."

Her throat felt a little dry at the thought, but... Thinking back, she'd been around him shirtless before. It shouldn't be that much of an issue.

"... Be comfy," Ellie finally said.

It only took a moment for him to strip off his shirt and toss it to the floor, and though Ellie couldn't see much in the shadows, she felt the shuffling when he settled back in under the covers. However, she wasn't expecting him to decide they needed to be even closer now that there was even slightly less chance for him to overheat.

Reaching out to grasp her arm, Kaz pulled Ellie half on top of him in a way that was far warmer and much more comfortable than it should have been, her head tucked just under his jaw and one leg slung across his hips. He was still wearing his pants, but it felt like every contour of her body pressed against him. She wasn't shy, necessarily. But it was... it almost felt like a wave of guilt washed over her for feeling this comfortable.

And then a wave of peace as she let out a breath.

"You said 'be comfy.' You're comfy," Kaz murmured.

"Flirt," she huffed, but she settled against him and wrapped her arm around his waist, fingertips trailing across the bare skin of his abdomen. Even though his body still felt a little *off* from true human flesh, his skin was softer than she expected.

"You like it." The smile on his lips was practically audible.

"I tolerate it," Ellie said, yawning. "I do like you, though. Bad jokes and terrible flirting included."

"I'll consider myself lucky, then. Sleep well, rosebud."

As snow began to fall outside, coating the mountains in frozen white flakes, Kaz's comforting presence lulled her into a deep, deep slumber.

IN WHICH A VISITOR CALLS

The morning light came far too soon for her liking, peeking through the closed curtains and lighting the room just enough to see. Ellie closed her eyes against the sunshine, though, knowing that it was well below freezing temperatures outside, the snow was likely still falling, and... Well, if pressed, she could admit she simply didn't want to get up yet.

"Hey." Kaz's rough voice came from beside her.

"Hnnn," Ellie groaned.

"Does that mean you're awake?"

"Mmm." It was a noncommittal sound at best. Awake? Technically. Did she want to be? No.

"Feel like getting up? Or did the moonshine after dinner do you in?"

"I barely had any, ya ol' coot," she grumbled, tucking the blankets up under her chin. "It's just too damn cold."

"You should be used to it. Didn't you grow up here?" Kaz asked, but he shifted closer to her. It was like sleeping next to a heater, and she didn't fight when he wrapped his arms around her to share his warmth.

"Just because I know how to dress for it doesn't mean I like it bein' five below zero when I wake up."

Kaz chuckled, and Ellie felt the reverberations more than she heard them.

"What do you plan on doing today?" he asked.

"No clue. Nobody'll be out on a day like today, not unless they have to. Not much point in workin' on the case."

"We could stay inside?" Kaz suggested.

"I... Mm," Ellie trailed off, shuffling slightly. "Nah. Gotta get up."

She was dead tired, but there were always things to do. That was just how life worked.

However, as soon as she tried to sit up, Kaz tightened his arms around her in a hold that was somehow both gentle and viselike all at once. He hauled her back towards him, cocooning her in his warmth in a way that left little room for argument, mostly because he was too strong to fight.

"What are you doing?" she asked, but she let him pull her back.

"You're burnt out. Take a day. Go back to sleep," he protested, and somehow she felt more than saw that his eyes were still closed.

"Got... shit to do..." Ellie said between yawns.

"You said it yourself— it's unlikely we'll find anyone to talk to today, and we've got supplies to last a week. If you don't stop soon, you're going to get sick."

"I'm not that frail."

"I would never accuse you of being frail," Kaz said, snuggling in close as he wrapped his arms around her, keeping her under the blankets. "On the contrary, it would be a favor if you let me get a little extra sleep, too."

"You can sleep on your own..." she mumbled, but her eyes were already closing again.

"It's much more comfortable this way, though," he protested, but when Ellie grumbled under her breath and tried to get up again, Kaz changed tactics.

"How about a bargain, then? Let me sleep, and I've got something for us to do later," he proposed.

"... You and your bargains," Ellie sighed. "I'm listenin', though." It couldn't hurt to hear him out... especially if it meant staying under the warm blankets a little longer.

"If you want something to do inside today, I... had a thought. Earlier," he said softly.

"Yeah?" She was skeptical, but she'd hear him out. Ellie rolled over to face him, watching his eyes flutter open in the dim light peeking through the curtains.

"If you're worried about losing Ben... Why don't we write your story? Together," Kaz suggested. "I told you I'm a writer."

Whatever she expected him to say, that was *not* it. Ellie was, for the moment, wide awake. It was like a jolt of adrenaline to her system, though Kaz seemed perfectly calm about it.

"You..." Ellie blinked, brow furrowing. "You want to write it? Like... in a *book*?"

"Or a short story. Or a poem. Whatever you think is best. It's been a long time since I've had something to write that felt like it had any depth to it. It would be my honor," he said gently. "If you want, we can even give it a better ending."

It was only a moment before she felt the tears prickling at the corners of her eyes, and she wasn't able to stop them falling onto the pillow. And then she wasn't able to stop them at all, letting a cascade of emotions run down her face— good and bad together, pain and joy, grief... but also an opportunity to move forward.

"Yeah," she said, sniffling. "Yes. Please."

"I've got you," Kaz said softly, hugging her close.

"How do you know how to do this?" Ellie asked, voice muffled against his chest.

"Do... what?"

"Comfort people."

"I told you that I'm stuck here already. The first few years were... bad. They were very, very bad," he said slowly, his hand rubbing circles across Ellie's back. "I did things I'm not proud of. I was a person I don't want to be again. I tried to use sex and money and drugs to fill the void, but nothing worked. It just numbed the pain for a while."

"You're not like that now, though."

"I'm not," he conceded. "And I wasn't like that before, either. I was... grieving. Grieving the loss of my home, like so many of us were."

"What changed?"

"I started to write again," Kaz said softly. "No one would publish it, but I didn't even care. I just... I had to get it out. I had to take it out of my

chest and put it somewhere that I could examine it a hundred different ways, look at it as a journey from the outside instead of from someone caught in the middle of it. It... helped. Made me see what I was missing, got me back on my feet."

"Could you read it to me one day?"

"I can't guarantee it's any good. It's not even finished, if I'm honest."

"That's okay," Ellie said. "Maybe I can help you finish it."

"I would like that." A yawn escaped her lips before she could stop it, and Ellie finally conceded that he had a point about a rest day. "Maybe.. . Maybe after we get some more sleep."

⸺ ◆ ⸺

The late season storm brought two feet of wet snow with it that solidified into a rock-hard layer of slick ice over a few inches of packed powder. Most of the village, Ellie and Kaz included, chose to hibernate inside for a few days, but by the time the third day arrived, Ellie had a severe case of cabin fever.

That morning, she pulled on her boots, bundled up like a human marshmallow, and rammed the front door open. It took a minute to dig her way out enough to get to the real snow shovel, but as soon as she could, Ellie was knee deep in cold, slushy snow drifts and shoveling a path away from her door.

"What poor perversion of snow is this?" Kaz frowned as he finally made his way out the door, looking at the piles of muddy, gritty, slushy ice with disdain.

"Normal," Ellie grunted, sticking the shovel into another pile of slush. "If a big snow blows through here, it's nice for about 24 hours if you're lucky, 'specially this time of year. It's been just warm enough to melt it during the day and then freeze it solid at night, so ya end up with *this shit*," she said, smacking the nearest block of ice with her shovel for emphasis. The metal end of the shovel clanged in protest, but it got the point across.

"Snow is *not* supposed to be like this," he muttered, but he picked up a second shovel and started to help break up the ice.

"You're used to New England snow, I guess? Stays cold up there for way longer. Snow don't stay soft 'less the temps stay below freezing *constantly*. Too much variation down here. It'll be five below this mornin' and nearly forty degrees at noon." Ellie just shrugged. She'd heard people describe the differences when they passed through from the northern or western states, but this was all she knew.

"That is... moderately terrifying," he said slowly, giving up on the shovel entirely as he simply kicked his way through a layer of ice with sheer blunt force.

Ellie let out a breath that fogged in the frigid air, putting her shovel to the side for a moment. There was almost a decent path leading away from her front door, but then they'd all have to work together to clean off the main road that ran through the village. Her cheeks were already red from exertion as she squinted towards the village gates, the bright sunshine reflecting off icy banks in blinding glares.

"Who in their right mind is out hikin' up the mountain in this kinda weather?" Ellie huffed, trying to make out the shape in the distance.

Sure enough, there was a shadowy figure tromping through the snow just outside the village gates. He carried a large bag as he steadily worked his way towards the main entrance, leaving a trail of crunching footprints. It would have been an imposing, almost ominous sight...

If he hadn't slipped on a particularly slick patch of ice and fallen flat on his back almost as soon as he was inside the gates, of course.

Ellie winced on his behalf. That wasn't a fun fall— she'd taken it many times. She didn't recognize the man, though, even as he struggled to his feet and brushed snow and ice off his clothes as best he could.

"Excuse me!" the man called, waving to Ellie as he struggled towards them.

It was early enough that Kaz and Ellie were the only two outside, mostly due to Ellie's aforementioned raging cabin fever. Shoveling snow had burned away some of the restlessness, but she'd felt ready to snap something in half when she woke up that morning, or maybe crawl out of her own skin just to stop the crushing feeling of being stuck indoors.

"Can I help ya, there?" Ellie called.

"Pardon the intrusion," the man said, panting for air. "My name is Hartley Allade, I'm a professor at—" he paused for breath, but there was apparently no need for him to explain any further.

"Hart?" Kaz gasped, dropping his shovel to run over to the man. What?

Ellie sighed and followed along much more slowly, using her shovel like a walking stick to help her balance in the snow.

"Kaz?" the visitor took one more hesitant step towards them, but Kaz was faster.

"What the hell are you doing here?" Kaz asked, shaking his head even as he reached out to hug their visitor.

"Tracking ley lines. Sort of." The man, Hart, waved his hand vaguely as he spoke, and frowned. "It's difficult to explain. What about you? You're usually one for cities— what on earth are you doing out here? And in this weather?"

"Well, if that ain't the pot callin' the kettle black," Ellie grumbled, boots crunching on the icy snow as she walked up to the newcomer.

Now that she was closer, she could make out his face a little more. He wasn't quite as tall as Kaz, but still easily over six feet, body frame almost completely disguised by layers and layers of clothing. Fogging half-moon glasses partly hid bright green eyes, and his pale skin was flushed from the cold and the walk up the mountain. Dark brown, almost black hair hung over his shoulder in a long braid, a bronze-blonde streak peeking through amidst the dark strands.

"This is Ellie," Kaz said as she approached. "She's my..."

He trailed off, and at that moment Ellie also realized that they'd never actually settled on any kind of terms. They both floundered for a long moment before Ellie finally wrapped her arm around Kaz and sighed.

"We're tellin' people he's my fiancé to make it simple," she whispered, shrugging. "Prob'ly better if we talk about that inside, though. You look plum soaked through."

And he was. His boots looked barely used and his clothes weren't appropriate for the weather. He was dressed like someone who had never really spent extended time in show before, but assumed what he would need to wear to prepare... wrongly.

"I... would appreciate a moment inside, yes," Hartley said slowly, letting out a breath.

Ellie wasted no time in leading them back to her front door, mostly assuming they were following her from the crunching sounds of feet breaking through thin ice coming from behind. She rested the shovel against the outside of the house and opened her door to a warm blast of air, ushering them inside quickly.

On days like these, she was thankful for her brick floor. It was hard on the feet, but she also didn't have to worry about the water and slush sloughing off their boots and coats as much as she might with a wood floor.

"Shoes off, hang your coat, have a seat," she said curtly, automatically moving to put the kettle on as soon as she'd removed her boots.

"Hope you like tea," Kaz said with a laugh.

"Oh, I love tea, thank you," Hartley said, and she could hear the scrape of one of the kitchen chairs across the kitchen floor as he pulled it out to sit down.

"How do you two know each other, now?" she asked over her shoulder as she picked herbs out of jars. Today felt like a day for strong black tea, maybe with some cinnamon. Something to warm them up, especially the poor man who looked like he'd barely seen snow before.

"Kaz and I met early in the course of this mess. We were both... having a hard time with the reality of it," Hartley said carefully.

"What he means is that we were kicked out of the same bar and he let my sorry ass sleep off a hangover on his sofa." Kaz, as ever, did not mince words when it came to things like this. He didn't mind telling the blunt truth about himself to someone he trusted, Ellie realized, and she liked that about him.

"The start of a beautiful friendship," Hartley said, shrugging helplessly. "Though I certainly didn't expect to see you here, of all places."

"Long story short, I'm helping investigate a cold case. Murder," he said bluntly. "Actually, since you're here, we could use a little help."

"I'll gladly assist if I can, but I have to admit that my strengths are in healing magic. I don't know if I'd be any help as a detective."

"You're... a witch?" Ellie asked, eyebrow raised. "Nice to meet one from outta town."

"Not a witch, no," Hartley said. "I'm... an Other."

"Don't bother asking what kind of Other. He likes to keep it to himself," Kaz said with a shrug. "All I know is that he's an old, old man with a very pretty face."

"Thank you, I *am* pretty," Hartley said with a soft smile, adjusting his glasses.

"*You're* an old man," Ellie mumbled, elbowing Kaz gently before she went to pour three mugs of hot tea for them.

"Compared to him, I'm probably something like a toddler," he said, but quickly changed the subject as Ellie distributed the mugs. "Are you still on your science experiments?"

"I'm still investigating the source of all our troubles, yes," Hartley sighed, leaning on the table. "The ley line energies seem to lead to somewhere in this area, but it's taken me years to get this close, and I can't narrow it much farther, so it's up to searching on foot."

"Translation?" Ellie asked, eyebrow raised.

"He's looking into the reason for the Appearances in the first place. Hartley's a... little obsessed," Kaz explained.

"Inquisitive," Hart countered, eyes narrowing.

"Fixated." Kaz took a sip from his mug of tea.

"Curious."

"Okay, *children*," Ellie said, rolling her eyes. "Anyways, you in town for a while?"

"I am, yes. The Appalachian Teacher's College was looking for professors, so I took a job there, and the college is planning on expanding. They're building an extended campus for Other studies outside of town, so they recruited me for the program. Luckily, my magic speaks for itself, and they don't mind that I'm not keen to disclose my personal history."

As he spoke, Hartley absently fiddled with a circular pendant on a long chain around his neck. At first, Ellie thought it was a pocket watch. It opened and closed like one, certainly, and Hart wasn't even looking at it as he traced his fingers over the object. However, when he finally moved to open the clasp, she could see it was actually a compass.

The needle moved oddly, centering on a seemingly random direction and holding firm when Hartley looked down at it momentarily. He sighed, closed the compass, and let the pendant rest against his chest.

"You keep a compass around your neck?" Ellie asked, only mildly surprised. She supposed it would be useful, especially for someone doing an extensive amount of foot travel and map making.

"Yes, but... It isn't for navigation, not really," Hart said softly. "It doesn't even point North. I have a different one for that."

"Heirloom?" That would certainly make sense. It wouldn't matter if a purely sentimental object pointed north or not.

"Something like that," he said carefully, taking a deep breath. "It belonged to someone very important to me."

An empathetic ping resonated through Ellie's chest. It wasn't hard to recognize that tone, not after she'd heard it in her own voice so many times.

"I lost somebody, too. I... I get it," Ellie said quietly.

"I... I was hoping I might have a chance..." he trailed off, shaking his head and abruptly changing the subject, looking up at Ellie from over the rim of his mug. "Since I'm here... Are you any good with divination?" Hartley asked hesitantly.

"Kinda depends on what you're lookin' for," Ellie said, shrugging. "I'm good with cards and casting, sometimes books. Never did take to scrying, though."

"Cards will do," he said, nodding. "Would you be willing to look into a matter for me? I... would like to confirm something, and I'll gladly pay you for your time."

"Is it a court case, a date of death, or tryin' to see if somebody loves you back?" she asked with a sigh, leaning her head on her hand.

"N— *no*?!" Hartley blinked, taken aback. "Do you get those requests often?"

"I get more requests for medicine than card readings, but I just wanted to check," she said with a shrug. It was against her personal code of ethics to read for dates of death or to try to reveal someone else's feelings. It seemed like prying without permission.

However, if it wasn't any of those things, and if Hartley was willing to pay, that could be a mutually beneficial arrangement. She wasn't opposed to that.

"... There's somethin' else I could use more than money for payment, though," she said slowly.

"I'm listening." He took a long sip from his mug, humming pleasantly at the taste.

"There's somebody I know who would really benefit from a few science classes at the college," Ellie said. "Think you could maybe look into that for me?"

"Done," Hartley said with a nod. "And... While we're at it, if you all keep any maps of the area around, I'd love to see them. I'm not certain what I'm looking for, but I can't afford to stop searching yet."

"I think we've got a few in the library building. It's a *small* library, but there should be somethin' in there about mapping out the land, building houses..." she trailed off helplessly.

"Is it open?"

"Usually, if the creek don't rise," Ellie said with a shrug. "Jeannie's usually a stickler about unlocking it in the mornings. Kinda toss up in this weather, though."

"If the..." Hartley squinted, looked briefly at Kaz, and then looked back at Ellie.

"Don't think about it too hard," Kaz said with a sigh. "You'll be branded a city slicker."

"Ah... Alright, then," Hart said slowly, rising from his chair. "Well, thank you for the help and for the tea. I suppose I should be on my way if I'm going to continue searching today."

"You're sure that's the best idea?" Kaz asked.

Ellie was inclined to agree with him. If Hartley was dead set on searching, that was one thing, but he didn't seem like he knew mountain weather or mountain slang or mountain... anything. He might unwittingly put himself in danger. Others were strong, but even they could end up in trouble sometimes.

"I... don't know anymore," Hart admitted. "It's the only thing that keeps me sane now, though. We all have our vices. Besides, I haven't been in the area long, so I might as well look around."

"That explains it," Ellie said without thinking. Hartley just blinked at her owlishly. "Your clothes. You didn't pick the best ones for a trip this far out, and your boots look like new. Better be careful with those or you'll rub sores on your feet."

"I see... thank you," Hartley said with a nod. "Perhaps I'll stick to the library today, then. Is there anywhere here I could stay the night, or should I stick to the plan of going back to town before dark?"

Kaz and Ellie exchanged glances.

"You mind sleepin' on a camp bed by the stove?" she asked.

"Anywhere warm is fine with me." City slicker he might be, but at least he seemed easygoing. Not picky, either, which was good this far out.

"The village doesn't get visitors often, so we don't have an inn or anything, but you can stay here for the night if you need to," Ellie said. "Kaz vouched for ya, so it's okay with me."

"I appreciate that very much," Hartley said with a smile. "I wasn't expecting to find friends here." He reached for his boots and started to put them back on, tying the damp laces tightly. A puddle had formed where the slush melted off their clothes, but it was warm enough inside that they were mostly dry.

"Want me to pull cards for you before you leave or...?" Ellie asked, slightly confused.

"I'll come back with the registration papers for your friend. You can do it then," Hart said with a smile as he pulled on his coat. "That way you know I'm as good as my word."

"Good to see you, Hart," Kaz said, holding out his hand.

"You as well. I'm glad to see you're happy," Hart said, looking back and forth between Kaz and Ellie. It wasn't until after the door shut that Ellie realized neither of them ever moved to explain that Kaz was not her fiancé, not really, and it wasn't several hours later that Ellie realized she didn't so much mind not correcting him.

18

IN WHICH THERE ARE PUPPIES

Hartley wound up staying the night after all, though he came in quite late from looking at maps of the area and almost immediately dropped off to sleep. In fact, he probably would have immediately dropped off to sleep if Ellie hadn't tapped into her Southern need to feed guests and insisted he have a little supper before he slept. It was good to see him again for a while, too. All in all, Hartley was a good sort of person. Quirky, but nice.

Apparently the rest of the village thought so, too, as Kaz heard his name once or twice amidst the other residents out doing their morning chores even two days after he'd left. According to Ellie, the village didn't get visitors often, and he imagined someone who asked as many questions as Hartley had made a big impression... especially considering he was a full-blooded Other of some kind or another. That seemed to be a novelty of some sort in this place, though he wasn't sure if that was good or bad.

"You know, for somebody travelin' all by your lonesome, it seems like you've got a few friends in high places," Ellie said as they walked. "Hartley made quite an entrance."

"He does that," Kaz snorted. "Friends in *low* places is more accurate, though. I've had more blackmail victims and bargain partners in high places than friends."

"What about—" but Ellie cut off suddenly as they neared Granny's house, suddenly turning to look in the direction of familiar voices.

It was cold outside, so the windows and doors were closed, but even so he could hear muffled shouting inside the house. Ellie pressed a finger to her lips in warning, catching his eye briefly before she worked her way around to the back of the house. Carefully avoiding errant puddles of mud and slush and muddy slush, she picked her way to the back door and slowly turned the knob. Standing just out of sight, Ellie eased the door open a hair, enough for them to hear what was happening inside a little more clearly.

"—will give us power beyond *belief*. You have to understand what this'll do for us, momma! It'll change lives!"

"Jeannie?" Ellie mouthed, brow furrowed as she leaned in a little closer to listen. Considering there was no other person in town who might call Granny their mother, Kaz could only assume she was right.

"Yes, and for the worse!" That was Granny's voice, and she did not sound happy.

"For the *better*!" Jeannie countered, her voice twice as loud as she.. . Well, it sounded like she slammed her hand on a table.

"Fletcher was *insane*, and you know it," Granny snapped. "He was out of his mind from blood magic and ten million other things when he wrote that godforsaken ritual, and then he *died* trying to complete it, along with four other witches."

"Sounds to me like he was just ahead of his time," Jeannie said cooly. "Otherwise, why would Elias have bothered to transcribe it?"

Elias? Kaz caught Ellie's eye, confused. That was a name he hadn't heard before.

"My dad," she whispered.

"Elias wanted to unravel the construction to figure out why Fletcher died, *not* to repeat it."

"I'm using his notes, don't worry. I won't be dying in the attempt, and neither will anyone else," Jeannie insisted. "But don't think your refusal to participate will stop us."

"Then *I* will," Granny practically growled.

"*I* am the lead witch here, not you, 'member? You turned down the job to focus on raising your granddaughter," she spat. "This is *my* decision."

"This is a mistake, that's what it is. You'll live to regret it."

"I'll live to prove you wrong," Jeannie said firmly.

And at that moment, both Kaz and Ellie jumped back from the door at the sound of footsteps coming towards them. Just before the sound reached the door, Ellie opened it, jumping back with wide eyes as she came face to face with Jeannie. It was a decent impression of being startled, Kaz had to admit.

"Whew, you scared me," Ellie said with a slight laugh. "Hey, Jeannie."

"Hey, honey. Good to see you," her aunt said with a smile, patting Ellie's shoulder as she slipped out the door. "I see the rest of the village hasn't scared off your fiancé?"

"I'll be here for the foreseeable future," Kaz said, letting his smile show his wickedly pointed teeth. He tried and failed to keep his tone from sounding threatening, but after what they'd just heard, he wasn't sure that was entirely possible.

"Y'all stop lettin' in the cold!" Granny cried from inside, thankfully releasing them from their conversation. Ellie ushered him inside, quickly shutting and bolting the door behind them. Granny was in the kitchen—Kaz found her stirring something in a large pot over the fireplace. It smelled like stew, but he couldn't tell what kind.

"Okay, 'fess up. How much of that were you listenin' to through the door?" Granny asked, not even looking up from stirring.

"How the—" Kaz began, but Granny just glanced over her shoulder at him pointedly.

"I know a draft when I feel one, son. Don't matter if it's a crack in the door or a hole in the wall," she said. "Ellie, go get the grimoire. You know where it is, and it's easier for you to look at the bullshit Jeannie wants to try to kill herself with than for me to explain it."

Ellie stood from the table with a nod, shuffling off towards a closet at the side of the house. Only a short moment later, she came back with a massive book in her hands. It was old, sporting yellowed pages and

a worn leather cover, the spine obviously patched and repaired many times over, and it had to be at least two or three inches thick.

"Here," Ellie said, plopping the book on the table.

"Page thirty-two. It's the one with all the papers in it." Granny gestured absently with the spoon as she spoke, a little broth sloshing onto the countertop.

It was accurate to say "*all* the papers." Kaz couldn't even see the writing on the book's pages for the piled of notes squashed in between the fold at that place. The writing was in an elegant, spindly hand, interspersed with questions, crossed out lines, and random extra notes on scrap paper haphazardly clipped to bigger pages.

For his part, Kaz couldn't make heads or tails of the writing. Even at places where he could make out the scribbles, he wasn't sure what they were referencing. He could see words like "catalyst," "sacrifice," and "energetic affinity," but magic had never been something quite so calculated for him. Even on the few occasions he performed spells, Kaz was an intuitive caster. He'd never seen a spell or ritual dissected so *thoroughly*.

"I've seen this..." Ellie murmured. "It's in my copy, too, but dad's notes are all in the pages after, and there's a big ol' warning at the top of the page."

"Then you're lucky you got the organized version," Granny scoffed. "These are the notes he left me the last time I saw him, and I can't make any sense of it. The one in my book is the original version that my brother, Fletcher, wrote... Before he lost his damn mind, and his life, too, that is."

"Fuck..." Ellie muttered. "I glanced at it before, but I didn't know how..."

"Gruesomely twisted it was?" Granny offered from where she sprinkled herbs into her stewpot.

"That. Yeah," Ellie said slowly, eyes wide as she glanced over the ritual.

Kaz shuffled his chair closer to Ellie so he could look at the book pages, putting the notes to the side for the moment. Sure enough, the script on these pages was different than the notes, in a blockier hand that somehow grew bigger, bolder, and spikier as the spell's instructions

progressed. The first page had a title in bold script, a list of ingredients, and a detailed depiction of a magic circle with markers at five points.

"*Ritual of Returning*," Kaz mumbled, squinting at the title. "Returning *what*?"

"Fletcher was... obsessive about magic," Granny said with a sigh. "He didn't have much power in him, but he was convinced that all the power that came from generations before had to have gone somewhere. He thought it built with each generation."

"That doesn't sound like a terribly off-base theory, based on what I've heard from Hartley and seen here..." Kaz murmured.

It was only a loose theory. Fifty years was enough time to test some things about witches and Others and magic, but not many. Substantial information would take generations. Granny didn't contradict him, though.

"You're right. And he was right, too, in a way. The older your bloodline, the stronger your magic," she said, moving to look at the book with them. "But some folks always take to it better than others. Or maybe it's the other way around and magic takes to some folks better. Maybe it *knows* when there's trouble brewing."

"Like Fletcher?" Kaz offered.

"And Jeannie, too," Ellie muttered, fiddling impatiently with her long braid. "Why the hell would she ever attempt *anything* like this?"

"She wants power, same as Fletcher did," Granny said sadly, and then turned to Kaz. "The Ritual of Returning is supposed to return the powers of generations long past to the casters. It draws on ancestral magic from deep, dark places to pull up power and flood it through your veins."

"And it... took his life?"

"Dead as a doornail, and he deserved it too, as sick as the requirements are," Granny said bluntly, not a trace of remorse in her voice. "His mind was long gone by the time he attempted it. I couldn't see anything left of the brother I knew."

Ellie stood and wrapped her arms around her grandmother, drawing her close in a gentle hug.

"It's okay, baby," Granny whispered, but she didn't pull away. "I had my time to grieve, just like we all do. I just can't let the same thing happen to Jeannie."

"So we stop her," Ellie said simply.

"We do."

Kaz raised his hand like a child in school. "How would you suggest we do that?"

Granny rolled her eyes, but he could see she held back a laugh, and counted that as a victory.

"It's definitely not somethin' they can be subtle about doing," Granny admitted. "I don't know when they're plannin' it for, but if we start thinkin' about how to throw a wrench in it now, we can be ready when the time comes."

Kaz opened his mouth to speak, but before he could, an envelope appeared in the air in front of him with an audible pop, hovering for a moment before it flopped down to the table in front of him. Ellie and her grandmother stared as he opened it, finding a brief message in familiar handwriting.

I'll be on the 3PM train. Pick me up. Bringing the hounds.

"How does that even *find* you?" Granny asked.

"Think of it like a magic telegram." Kaz shrugged. It was decently common for quick messaging, though as Ellie pointed out before, most people needed a tag lock to make it work. Hair or nail clippings were best, but most Others knew various work-arounds to the rule.

"Convenient," Ellie conceded. "Weird, but convenient."

"Kids these days," the shorter woman muttered.

"I'll be back by dark," Kaz said, tucking the letter in his pocket. "I need to pick up Harper at the station. She's the vampire I sent a message to about investigating the crime scene for us."

"I can go with you—" Ellie started, but Kaz just shook his head.

"Stay here and read up on that ritual. Figure out whatever we need to do to stop it from happening— I'll be back soon," he said softly, leaning in to kiss her cheek.

Granny raised an eyebrow and Ellie blushed.

"I think I'll just... um... lemme go check my copy. Might be somethin' useful in the notes," Ellie said quickly, standing from the table as

she flipped the book cover closed. She kissed Granny goodbye on the crown of her head and scooted out the door as quickly as she could.

"You ain't gettin' outta this talk, youngin'!" the older woman called.

"Have a good day, Granny!" Ellie said cheerfully, as though she hadn't even heard. Now it made a little more sense where she'd learned the basics of acting.

"Psh, at least ya know she trusts you to leave ya here," Granny said with a chuckle. "Prob'ly thinks I tore you a new one last time, and there's not much else to say between us."

"Is there more to say?" Kaz asked, almost nervous.

"I'm an old woman. There's always more to say," Granny said bluntly. "I'm not gonna detain ya if you've got things to do, though."

"To be honest," Kaz said slowly, "before I go, I had an idea to run by you."

"Oh?" She didn't look up from the soup.

"Ellie had mentioned it's difficult for a witch to buy land," he said carefully, "and that Miriam needs to move. She said she wanted to get a place for all of you set up in the mountains. I'd like to help with that, if I can."

"Help how, exactly?" Granny's eyebrow raised, but the fact that she didn't immediately write off the idea was enough encouragement.

"Trust me when I say that money is hardly an issue for me," Kaz said. "I've been drifting for fifty years and I've stockpiled large sums from bargaining fees—"

"We don't want your blood money, boy," Granny said with a huff. "An' Ellie's too proud to take it, especially when y'ain't even married yet."

"That's why—" Kaz stopped suddenly, the full extent of Granny's words hitting him. "*Yet?*"

"I ain't so old I can't tell which way the wind blows. I know when somebody's attached. Don't matter if it's been three weeks or three years," she said with a shrug. "Now, what did ya have in mind?"

"Can you get me Miriam's address?"

"I can. Why do you need it?" she asked, stirring the soup slowly.

"I have a plan that I think will get around Ellie accepting anything she feels like charity, but should also be able to get her out of the village."

"Okay," Granny said, turning around and placing the spoon on a dish by the stove. Pulling out a kitchen chair to plop down next to him, she adjusted her glasses a little. "I'm listening."

The Ritual of Returning was one of the sickest things Ellie had ever read.

Granny raised her as a witch, yes, but a witch with a strict code of ethics. Meddling in other people's lives without their consent was absolutely prohibited. Love spells were beyond taboo. Don't do rituals that seem too good to be true. Turning lead into gold might be possible if you tried hard enough, but it would also fuck up the local economy and probably the rest of your life with it. Magic was an aid, not a solution.

And, on top of all that, there were prayers before mealtimes, prayers before bed, and prayers in the morning. She had Bible lessons along with her witch lessons, and all of that had only impressed an additional layer of a very, very strict moral code upon Ellie. She learned how to walk the fine, fine line her ancestors walked before her at a very early age.

Fletcher... Clearly never learned anything about lines.

Even if it hadn't involved multiple ingredients harvested from living sacrifices, Ellie could have clocked the red flags in the process from a mile away. The ritual called for five casters, but the language in the Latin incantation only grammatically referred to one practitioner. Her father's notes mentioned this in detail, and his theory was that Fletcher's awful grammar caused the power from the other four casters to flow into his body. The state of his corpse afterward suggested something of a magical allergic reaction, like the power summoned from those ancestral witches simply wasn't compatible with Fletcher on an innate level.

Specifics were important in magic, right down to the word choices. It was a large reason that Granny was quite firm that Latin should never be a primary language choice for spellwork unless you were very, very familiar with it.

Ellie was not. She wrote her spells in English like a normal mountain-dweller.

Outside, the sun was setting. It was about time she started cooking her supper, even if it was something simple. Kaz could fend for himself if he wasn't back soon, she thought, though as soon as she stood from her chair to get started, her front door swung open and a familiar demon swept into the room, a bright smile on his face.

"Where you been, stranger?" Ellie asked wearily as she closed the book. There was little point in looking at those awful pages any longer, and seeing Kaz was like a balm to her frayed nerves.

"Like I told you, I picked up Harper at the station. She needs a little extra escort effort because of her sun sensitivity, so it took some extra time," he explained. "I do have another surprise for you, though."

"A surprise...?" Ellie raised her eyebrows, uncertain if she should be nervous or not. She wasn't typically fond of surprises. They usually brought too many bad things with them.

"Remember how I said I thought it would be helpful if you had a friend with the Sight?"

"... Yes," she said carefully.

"You're in luck." Kaz smiled in a way that showed his sharp teeth and opened the front door wider.

Ellie wasn't quite sure what she was expecting, but it certainly wasn't two utterly enormous dogs followed by five small balls of fur. They trotted into her house and sniffed the air, as if looking for something.

"Smells good," a feminine voice said.

Except... it wasn't a voice. It wasn't a voice in the sense that she heard it in her ears. Instead, she heard it in her *mind*.

"Did you... did you just talk?" Ellie asked carefully, looking back and forth between the two dogs.

"We're perfectly capable of communicating, yes," a masculine voice said as the largest of the dogs turned towards her. *"Hold out your hand."*

Shocked into obedience, Ellie held out her right hand. The dog sniffed it, nudged her with his nose, and then went back to sniffing around the house.

"This is Charlie and Luna, and of course, their new pups. I sent them a message about a week ago," Kaz explained. "I knew they were arriving today, so I went to town to meet the train. They're old friends."

"Y'all just came here all on your own?" Ellie asked, dropping to her knees to talk to them at eye level. "You must be tired."

"Our person is in town. She'll be up once the sun sets," Charlie said, the masculine voice rumbling through Ellie's mind.

"No need to worry, though. We travel often, and the pups are full of energy," Luna said as she nuzzled her mate.

One of the tiny balls of fluff that Ellie now recognized as a puppy tripped its way up to her where she knelt on the floor, sniffing carefully for a moment before putting a paw on her lap. The little brown and black puff of fur seemed to be more curious than their siblings, ready to sniff at Ellie specifically rather than investigating the room with the other pups.

"Hey, sweet pea," Ellie murmured, holding a hand out for the little one to sniff. The puppy nosed at her fingertips for a moment before it slipped under her hand and climbed into her lap. Ellie's heart practically melted into a puddle as the puppy curled up on her thighs, batting at her long braid.

"Play nice," Charlie said sternly. The little one barely flinched.

"Are y'all planning to stay in town?" Ellie's eyes were still on the baby.

"Depends," Luna's voice echoed in her mind. *"It isn't easy for animal spirits to be independent in this world, so we choose homes together with a human-shape for safety."*

"Human... shape?" Ellie repeated slowly.

"Harper. She's an Other with a human form, so... technically, she's not human," Kaz said with a shrug. "She won't be here till after sunset to help with the investigation, but I wanted to bring her canine friends by to meet you."

Ellie's attention went back to the puppy in her lap, who was happily snuggled up and snoring.

"Does this little bean have a name?" she asked.

"We've been tossing some around, but our kind don't often have names in humanoid tongues," Charlie said.

"Your... kind?" she asked hesitantly, finally looking away from the puppy and back to the much larger parents. They just looked like... *dogs,* albeit very large ones.

"They're hellhounds," Kaz said like he was saying the sky was blue.

Ellie's brain seemed to short circuit for a moment as she processed the massive size of the animals, the puppy in her lap, and the telepathic communication. It made sense, it did, but hellhounds were *rare* to come by. She'd never seen one before in her life, and she wasn't expecting... well...

"I... um, I thought hellhounds were... not this cute, honestly. Or nice," she mumbled, words spilling out before she could process them. However, she did have the good grace to blush when she realized what she'd said. "Sorry 'bout that."

Luna chuckled. *"We'll take that as a compliment. Hellhounds can manifest in many sizes and shapes. We like these best."*

"So you can... I'm sorry, I'm still not connecting this with Spirit Sight." She shook her head helplessly, looking to Kaz for assistance, but he just smiled.

"It's our job to escort souls to the afterlife," Charlie explained. *"We make sure to take them where they need to go. If they're lost, we can guide them there, both good places and bad."*

"You see 'em, too," she said softly, processing.

"Kaz says you're trying to help someone stuck in the middle." Luna plopped down on the ground beside Ellie as she spoke, nosing at the little pup in her lap. The baby gently nipped back at her mother, but stayed on Ellie's lap.

"I am," she said softly. "He's... someone I love very much. I want him at peace."

And for the first time, saying she loved Ben in the present tense while knowing she was on her way to developing those same feelings for Kaz didn't feel like a knife in her chest.

"Why don't you let us help you?" Charlie suggested.

"You... don't know me. I'd appreciate it if you can settle him, but I don't expect you to."

"We consider it something of a sacred calling, as far as we're concerned," Luna explained. *"It is our duty to help those who are lost or wandering. I'm sure you understand."*

"... Yeah," Ellie said slowly. "Yeah, that makes sense." She carefully petted the puppy in her lap, pleased when the little fluffball rolled over for belly rubs. The other pups continued to explore the room, sniffing and nosing at objects, and a couple of them came up to sniff Ellie as well or to sit for a quick scratch behind the ears, but none of the others clambered onto her lap.

"When Harper gets here, we can check out the scene together," Kaz suggested. "Ben's spirit may or may not appear, correct?"

"Yeah, it's never a guarantee," Ellie admitted.

"We have time," Charlie said with a canine huff, and Ellie thought that might be the equivalent of a shrug. *"Harper likes to stay places for a long time, and we stay with her."*

"I'm sorry if it's rude to ask, but is it just you two who... talk? Not the babies?" Ellie asked, raising an eyebrow as she glanced at the litter of pups clambering around the room. Though their mental communication wasn't quite rhe same as talking, she wasn't sure there was another good way to describe it.

"Not rude. Our pups aren't old enough to communicate in human languages yet," Luna said, nudging the sleepy little dog in Ellie's lap with her nose. *"She likes you, though."*

"She's a cutie," Ellie said, smiling brightly.

"Our kind sometimes bond with human-shapes," Charlie said, tilting his head to look towards them from his position near the warm stove. "We shall see if there is time, but this bodes well."

The puppy yipped something in a language that Luna apparently understood.

"We'll be here a little while, and you can see her tomorrow, too," Luna said. *"If that's alright with you?"*

"Of course," Ellie said, nodding. From the side of the room, Kaz absolutely beamed as he watched her interact with the pup, and she wondered if this was what he'd hoped for all along.

IN WHICH A VAMPIRE ARRIVES

"Are you sure she's gonna be here?" Ellie asked, checking her watch.

"She said nine 'o' clock sharp, so she'll be here... Well, she'll be here by nine-fifteen," Kaz said with a chuckle.

They stood just off the main road that ran between the witch village and Boone, near the murder scene. Charlie and Luna followed along with their pups, wrangling the little ones into an oddly orderly form that looked a bit more like ducks than dogs as they sat patiently near their parents. The little ones stayed warm by their mother, who didn't seem to be affected by the cold at all, but Ellie and Kaz's breaths came out in foggy clouds of steam as they waited.

It was two minutes past nine, and Ellie was already twitchy. According to Kaz, Harper wanted to meet them down on the trail to avoid explaining her presence in the witch village. Ellie agreed that it was a good idea to keep newcomers out of the village as much as possible, if for no other reason than to avoid suspicion, but there was no sign of her yet. It was almost pitch black outside, but they'd opted not to bring a lantern in hopes that it would draw less attention. That was fine for the hounds and Kaz, but Ellie was a little nervous not being able to see very far in front of her.

The same little pup who seemed to cling to Ellie inside nudged at her foot, and Ellie knelt down to pet her, noticing she was shivering just a little in the cold night air.

"Can I pick her up?" Ellie asked, looking between Charlie and Luna.

"Go ahead," Charlie said.

"Hey, honey," she murmured, gently scooping up the puppy. She yipped happily as Ellie slightly unzipped her jacket, tucking her inside the left side and against her chest, just over her heart. The little ball of fluff calmed almost immediately, front paws and head resting on her shoulder, and little damp nose touching Ellie's neck.

"Warmer in there, huh?" she asked softly, cradling the pup like a newborn.

"She'll fall asleep on you like that, and you'll never get rid of her," Luna said softly, giving a whuff that sounded a little like a laugh.

Ellie thought she'd be just fine with that outcome, but a puppy was certainly a big commitment. It's what kept her from getting a pet in the first place, despite feeling the cold of crippling loneliness sink deep into her bones after losing Ben. She'd take the time with the little one while she had it, though.

"Ah, there's our assistance," Kaz said suddenly, gazing off into the night past the point where Ellie could see. "Right on time, five minutes late. As usual."

"Now, you know well an' good that is *no* way to talk to a lady, Uncle Kaz," came a voice from the darkness. As she drew closer, Ellie could finally make out the shape of who was talking.

She was just as tall as Ellie, but lean and muscular where Ellie was softer and curvy. Golden blonde hair hung in loose, gentle curls around her shoulders, a sharp contrast to her entirely black lace dress and the black parasol in her hand. She looked like she'd dressed for a party more than a hike, even down to cute, black kitten heels peeking out below her tea-length dress.

"Took you long enough, Harper," Kaz said with a snort, but he stretched out an arm and gave her a quick hug, regardless.

Though the cold air made Ellie shiver and hold the pup in her arms a little closer, Harper seemed entirely unaffected. She wasn't even

wearing a thick coat, opting for a lightweight peacoat instead. Her skin had an eerie not-flush to it, looking human and not human all at once, and her irises were as red as her deep burgundy lipstick.

When she smiled, she showed pointed fangs where human canines would be.

"You must be Ellie," she said happily. "I've heard a lot about you."

"Nice to meet ya. Georgia?" Ellie asked as they shook hands, referring to her accent.

"Lilburn," Harper said, grinning. "Born and raised. My momma was pregnant when the Appearances started, so they settled in the first place they found."

"I knew her parents from... before," Kaz explained with a shrug. "We got stuck together. I go back to check on them now and then."

Ah, that would explain "*Uncle*" Kaz, then.

Harper knelt to say hello to Charlie and Luna, taking a moment to pet the pups (minus the one soundly asleep in Ellie's jacket) before she turned back to the woods, squinting into the darkness between the trees.

"This is the place, then?" Harper asked, and both Kaz and Ellie nodded. "Lemme give a listen."

Ellie looked at Kaz strangely, but she only shrugged and motioned for her to wait a moment. Harper, on the other hand, closed her eyes for a long moment and cocked her head to one side. She seemed to be concentrating intensely, but Ellie couldn't tell *on what*.

"I don't know about this one," Harper muttered, nose wrinkling as she looked over the area. "I owe ya for sure, but two years is a long time, and who knows how much animal blood has overlaid it since then."

"Can you see in the dark like Kaz?" Ellie asked. She couldn't see for shit out in the dense, foggy woods. If she wasn't careful, she'd run smack into a tree and end up with a bloody nose.

"Certainly can," Harper said, smiling in a way that flashed her fangs. "Wouldn't be genetically fair to expect me to avoid all sunlight if I couldn't, I don't think."

"Harper is a unique vampire," Kaz explained quietly. "Most Others have a semi-standard subset of abilities, but with vampires, it's a like a random lottery. From what she tells me, Harper hit the jackpot. Night vision is the tip of the iceberg."

"To be fair, I got the worst of the sun sensitivity to balance it," she said despondently. "I pretty much have a permanent parasol attached to my arm."

"Not like you need it now," Kaz muttered.

"Is it bothering you?" Harper asked, twirling the umbrella handle as she batted her lashes at him.

"N— no...?" he said slowly.

"Then hush up, I got work to do," Harper said with a bright smile. She tapped him on the nose gently and Kaz grumbled, rolling his eyes. Ellie bit back a laugh, making a mental note to try that later.

Parasol in hand and dark skirts swishing, Harper sauntered off into the woods. She seemed to float more than the walked, like it was impossible for her to trip even among tangled roots and underbrush. As she stepped farther and father from the path, she tilted her head this way and that, listening for something Ellie couldn't hear.

"I hear it... There's a lot out here, but it's mostly animals," she murmured, twirling her parasol as she spoke. "But there's one..."

Harper closed her eyes, turning in a circle where she stood like a compass needle trying to find North. She took one step forward, then two. More turning in circles. Finally, perhaps ten feet away from the spot where Ellie and Kaz stood with the hounds, she stopped.

Eyes still closed, she bent to the leaf-covered forest floor and worked her hand under the first layer of debris, pushing past twigs and stones, carefully digging her hand into the soft ground, until she suddenly stopped.

"Here."

Cradling the pup close, Ellie took a few steps out into the woods towards Harper, looking through the shadows to see what she was holding. If it was buried in the ground, it was a small miracle she found it amongst the underbrush, leaves, and general debris in the area.

Maybe it was a coin? Maybe a lost possession from Ben's body? Ellie tried to think if there was anything noticeable missing, but there was no evidence he'd been robbed at all. Maybe it was a pin or a button from the killer, or a—

"Holy shit," Ellie muttered, looking at the long, thin, and wickedly pointed bullet between Harper's fingers.

"We got lucky," Harper said, brushing the dirt off the object as she examined it. "Normally the trail goes cold after the blood is washed away, but I think it reacted with the bullet and preserved the bloodsong. Bonded with the metal or some such. It's not unheard of for weapons."

"Is this... I mean, you're sure this is his?" Ellie asked carefully.

"To tell ya the truth, I can't be absolutely sure without the body," she admitted. "I *can* tell you that's not animal blood, though. This bullet went through a human body."

"If you went to the grave, could you tell me for sure?"

She paused, pursing her lips, blonde hair swishing as she tilted her head in thought. "Maybe. Some bodies sing more than others after death, and the burying makes it muffled, but it's worth a shot."

Kaz picked his way through the trees and plucked the bullet from Harper's hand, turning it over and over in his fingers. "Ellie... Does this look like the kind of bullet that a hunting rifle would use?" he asked pointedly.

Ellie pursed her lips. "Yeah, it's about the right size for one. I know where you're going with this, though, and I'm not sure it'll help," she sighed, petting the sleeping pup behind the ears.

"Why?"

"Most people own some kinda huntin' rifle around here. Those that don't can borrow one, easy. It won't be that easy to track down where this came from, or who was shootin' at us in the woods that day."

"Dammit..." Kaz sighed. "Can we match bullets?"

"Did you *find* any other bullets?" Ellie raised an eyebrow.

"We could look."

"Decent idea, but seems like a futile effort," she sighed. "It would be hard to figure out exactly where shots went. Ya know, considering we were pretty preoccupied with *not gettin' shot* at the time. Or *gettin' shot*, in your case." She shuddered at that, frowning. The sight of the bloodstain on Kaz's shirt still haunted her.

"I could probably locate them," Harper said thoughtfully. "If everyone has a firearm around here, though, it wouldn't stop the same person from shooting two different guns to throw us off. It might be better to chase the symbol on the bullet."

Ellie blinked.

"The *what* now?" She asked, bending close to the bullet in Kaz's hand.

"She can't see in the dark like we can," Kaz reminded his vampire friend.

"Right, right," Harper sighed. "Sorry. You'll have to take a look at it in the light, but there's somethin' carved into the end of it."

Kaz placed the bullet in Ellie's palm, and she ran her fingers over the flat end of the bullet. Sure enough, she could feel the indention of a crude carving in the metal, but there was no way she could see it till they were back at the house and in decent lighting.

"Let us know if you need anything else," Harper said. "Or if you change your mind and wanna go bullet scouting. We'll be in town for a little while. The cool weather suits me," she said with a peaceful smile.

"Thanks for your help with this. It means more than you know," she said sincerely, looking back and forth between Charlie, Luna, and Harper.

"Happy to help," Harper said. "The hounds prob'ly told you I like to travel, and Kaz is an old friend. Family, basically. The way he talked about you sounded like he was head over heels, and I wanted to see it in person. Gives me blackmail material," she said with a wink.

"Oh, I *like* you." Ellie gave her a Cheshire Cat smile, laughing.

"I did *not* sound—"

"Don't you even deny it, you grumpy ol' demon," Harper said, wagging her index finger at him. "It's *cute*. You can be a demon and be cute."

"I am over four hundred years old," he said through gritted teeth. "I am not *cute*. I am deadly and imposing."

"I think you're cute," Ellie said, nudging him gently. Kaz's mouth opened and closed like a fish for a moment, sending Harper into a fit of giggles.

"I'm afraid I'll be... *limited* on my movements during the day," she said once she stopped laughing. "Charlie and Luna know they're free to come and go as they will, though, so you might see 'em around a little."

"Our runt has gotten attached to Miss Ellie, it seems, so yes. I think they'll see us often," Luna said. Ellie just smiled down at her.

"I'll be happy to see y'all whenever you want to stop by."

"We'll see y'all soon, then," Harper said, smiling.

Early the next morning, Kaz and Ellie knocked on Granny's front door.

When she was able to see it in the light, it was clear that the bullet *did* have a symbol carved into the end, but it wasn't one Ellie had ever seen before. Still, it was something to look into, and she wanted Granny to know that they'd found another piece of evidence... however small it might be, literally or figuratively.

"We got news," Ellie said softly. "Kaz?"

"On it," he said firmly. Within moments, Ellie could feel his warding magic take over to shield the building. It was a necessary precaution considering the sensitive material they were about to discuss.

"Well, don't keep me waitin' over here!" Granny insisted, eyebrows raised.

Fishing in her pocket for a moment, Ellie's fingers finally landed on cool metal. She put the rifle cartridge on the wooden table with a soft clunk, letting out a breath she didn't know she was holding.

"We found this," she said, trying and failing to keep her voice from shaking a little.

"A bullet?" Granny slipped her glasses on and peered down at it through the thick lenses, holding it between her thumb and index finger.

"Can confirm it went through a human at some point. Working on confirming if it..." Ellie trailed off, unable to finish her sentence. Granny just nodded.

"Do you recognize the symbol on the base?" Kaz asked.

Granny turned the bullet over to check the flat base, squinting at it. "My eyes are better than they were before the Appearances, but I can't say I know it. I can see it's silver capped. I'd say it's a witch hunter bullet, but..."

"But?" Ellie prodded.

"Why would a witch hunter put a sigil on the back of their bullet?" Granny murmured, running her finger across the small, carved design. "Why use witch magic on witches?"

"You're sure it's a sigil?" Kaz asked.

"I know a sigil when I see one," Granny said firmly. "Even a tiny one."

"Witch hunters ain't exactly known for being the most straightforward," Ellie mused, tossing her long braid over her shoulder. "They hate magic, but some of 'em use magic to catch magic, weird as it sounds."

"And yet no witches are dead," Granny said slowly.

"If it's a sigil, what does it mean?" Kaz asked. "It has to have some kind of function, right?"

Ellie and Granny exchanged glances in a way that made him sorry he'd asked.

"It's possible to figure it out. That's the good news," Granny said with a sigh. "Any witch worth their salt writes down a sigil once it's been used, even if it's just stuck in a book and never used again. You don't want to leave your work lying around all untied and unidentified like that."

"I'm almost afraid to ask what the bad news is..." Kaz said, grimacing.

"Ain't worth a hill of beans havin' the sigil 'less you know either the witch who made it or the method they used to make it," Ellie groaned, resting her head in her hands. "Think of it like a padlock with four digits, and we have zero for clues. We'd have better luck huntin' down the grimoire at this point than trying random combinations."

"Four digits would be easier," Granny snorted.

"Thank you for that uplifting reminder, Granny," Ellie muttered without looking up, voice muffled.

She felt utterly defeated. She didn't want to believe it was a witch who killed Ben, much less someone in their village, but the signs were starting to point that way. Their only real evidence was a sigil, the police records, and a scrap of fabric and wire—

Wait.

"That wire," Ellie said suddenly, sitting bolt upright. "Kaz, that wire you found. Was it buried?"

"It's been two years, of course it was buried," he said, as though it should be obvious.

"No, I mean... I'm not askin' if it was covered with dirt, I'm askin' if it was intentionally pushed into the ground."

Kaz pursed his lips, nodding slowly. "Probably. I had to push apart tree roots to get to it."

"Fuck. I'm an idiot. *Fuck*," Ellie hissed, squeezing her eyes shut for a moment before she turned to Granny. "Wire and burlap scraps buried in tree roots."

There was a slight pause while Granny's eyes widened, but to her credit, it only took a few seconds for that implication to process.

"A poppet?" Granny asked, brow furrowed. "You think you found a *poppet*?"

"It was fallin' apart when Kaz dug it up. There's no way to trace what plants were inside it or what could'a been the tag lock, or even if it was a doll at all, but... why else would wire and fabric end up at the base of a tree?"

"Wire and fabric that held on to a lot of rage," Kaz said slowly.

"Is there any reason that land would be used for workings besides Ben's death?" Granny asked carefully.

"No," Ellie said, shaking her head. "It's a random patch of woods."

"I didn't see any other evidence of magic, and Harper didn't scent any other human blood there," Kaz confirmed.

"Then I think we better find out who's responsible for that sigil," Granny said firmly, but then she sighed. "That's gonna be like lookin' for a needle in a haystack, though, even if we narrow to only this village."

"There has got to be a way to trace that," Kaz grumbled, running a hand through his hair.

Ellie just shook her head. "Not really. Sigils leave evidence because you gotta write 'em down to make 'em work, but they don't leave a lot of ties to the witch who made it."

"I have the family book here, but I've never seen one like that," Granny said, pulling a thick, battered volume off the shelf. "You're welcome to double check, but it's likely something designed for this in particular. Makes it harder to trace in case... Well, in case somebody tries to do exactly what we're doin'."

Kaz flipped through the book, scanning page after page, but Ellie was fairly certain it was a useless pursuit.

"I hate to break it to ya, but no witch is going to show any random person their grimoire without a whole lotta questions at minimum. We'll be settin' off alarm bells from here to Tennessee," she said, crossing her arms over her chest as she tapped her foot absently.

"So we don't tell them," Kaz said simply, shrugging like it should be obvious.

Ellie and Granny exchanged glances.

It... was a fair point, she had to admit. She wasn't incredibly comfortable with the idea of breaking and entering, but they wouldn't be stealing anything, and this was information they needed if they were going to solve the case. At this point there were too many loose ends. Even if the answer was that the sigil wasn't from anyone in their village, it would still be a step forward in the investigation.

"Okay... I'm not good at sneaking around, though," Ellie said, shaking her head. "And it's too cold for anyone to be out at night much."

"The spring bonfire's in a few days," Granny said. "Whole village'll be three sheets to the wind and the weather'll warm up, too, if we're lucky. It's a good time to poke around where you can."

"You think Harper would be willing to help?" Ellie asked, turning to Kaz. "It's a lotta houses to search, and I have a feelin' somebody is gonna notice if I just up and disappear for too long."

"I'll ask," Kaz said with a nod. "It seems like the best shot we have to find a solid answer, though."

"I agree," Granny said. "They'll notice if I'm missin' from the bonfire, too, even stone cold drunk, but I'll try to help with keepin' everybody distracted while y'all look around."

"Okay," Ellie said, nodding. "Seems like the best we've got for now."

20 IN WHICH KAZ AND HARPER SNOOP

The morning of the bonfire celebration, Ellie's stomach was in knots. It felt like half the town was already awake at dawn to start cleaning the bonfire area and set up for the celebration, and to Ellie, that just meant they were one step closer to solving Ben's case.

The weather was warmer than it had been, the snowstorm from last week gone like the final LF frigid gasp of winter's dying breath before the arrival of spring. It wasn't warm enough to go out without extra layers, but it was consistently above freezing temperatures, and Ellie was grateful for that. It was one less thing for her to worry about.

"I'm nervous as a long-tailed cat in a room full of rockin' chairs," she muttered, voice low enough that only Kaz could hear.

"Calm down," he whispered back, gently moving his arm around her shoulders.

"Right. Tellin' somebody to calm down has always helped with that," Ellie snorted.

"If you're annoyed, at least you're not nervous," Kaz said with a grin, bending to kiss her forehead.

"Mmm. Sure," Ellie sighed. "Maybe I'll walk down to where Harper's stayin' and see the puppies. I need a distraction."

"I could distract you, I'm sure," Kaz crooned, pressing close as his hand moved from her shoulder to her waist.

"You ruined that chance by *just now* attempting to annoy me as a distraction," Ellie muttered, but her cheeks flushed all the same and she didn't pull away from him.

Kaz sighed dramatically. "Well, in that case, I think you have another option for a distraction. He just walked through the gate."

Hartley, dressed in a light coat for the warmer weather, steadily moved up the path and through the gates, making a beeline for Kaz and Ellie as soon as he spotted them. He had a dark blue scarf around his neck and a messenger bag slung across his chest, which he flipped open and began to dig around in as he came closer.

"I didn't know if your friend would want to register for classes at the main college or in the program for Others starting soon, so I brought papers for both," he said, fishing in his messenger bag.

"Thank you," Ellie said, smiling as she took the papers. "We'll probably pass her today, but if not I'll drop 'em off later."

"Seems like everyone is out today," Hartley said, glancing around at the crowds of people splitting wood, toting food back and forth, and otherwise setting up for the celebration that night.

"Spring bonfire," Ellie explained. "There's gonna be a big crowd here tonight. And moonshine, if you're a party person."

Hartley scrunched up his nose. "I... can't say that I am."

"Homebody," Kaz sighed, but he was smiling.

"Roisterer," Hart shot back, calm as a cucumber.

Kaz just rolled his eyes and ran a hand through his white hair. "Between Ellie's southern-isms and your grandpa vocabulary, I'm never going to know what anyone is saying about me, am I?"

"S'okay," Ellie said, standing on tiptoe to kiss him on the cheek. "We love you anyway."

Hartley sighed. "Leave me out of this one, please," he said with a chuckle.

"Do you, now?" Kaz teased, pulling her in close with one arm and tipping her chin up with his free hand.

Ellie blushed, eyes wide as she realized what she'd said.

"Maybe we should go do that reading," she mumbled, taking Kaz by the hand and hauling him back toward her house. She could hear him laughing behind her as he beckoned Hartley along after them, and thus she promptly chose to ignore it.

The village was small, but they drew plenty of stares walking about towards Ellie's home. A newcomer was unusual, and the same one twice in a matter of a week even more so. Hartley took it in stride, though, waving hello to anyone who even looked at him a little oddly. He was much more gracious than Ellie would have thought to be among the stares, and she admired that. She usually just keep her head down and keep walking, going about her business as peacefully as possible.

Once they were tucked safely inside the house with the door closed, Ellie pulled a box of well-loved cards from her bookshelf, along with a two neatly folded cloths. She gestured for Hartley to take a seat at the kitchen table and pulled the chair around to the other side to sit across from him, gently pulling the cards from their box.

"Okay. What am I readin' on?" she asked, gently running her fingers over the deck. It felt like an old friend to her at this point, and the familiar feeling of the worn surface of the cards under her hands brought comfort and clarity.

"I just... I need to know if someone is alive," he said softly, leaning forward slightly with his elbows on the table.

"You got somethin' I can use as a tag lock?" Ellie asked.

Hartley nodded as he removed the pendant from around his neck, placing the compass in Ellie's hand. "Will this work?"

Ellie closed her eyes and tried to focus on the energy left in the object. Tag locks were tricky. If they were too old or another person besides the original owner had them for too long, the energy could rub off, die out, or just plain be overwritten with time. This compass, though...

"Yes," she said with a quick nod. "This is good."

It was impossible to tell exactly how old the compass was, but the energy signature coming from it was strong. Almost... fresh? From the signal alone, she would guess that whoever this was attuned to was alive, but it was always best to be sure.

Ellie laid a clean cloth out on the table and placed the watch on it, then laid out a second cloth big enough to work with her cards on. They

always shuffled better on cloth, she thought, and she liked to keep them clean.

As she shuffled, she did her best to clear her mind of everything except her question. She needed to know if the person whose energy was on that compass was alive. It wasn't Hart's energy— Ellie knew that for a fact. It was... similar, but different. Close, but very far away.

After dealing the cards, Ellie flipped them over in a line of three. Death. Ace of Swords. The Lovers.

"Alive, yeah," Ellie said, nodding. "I can tell you that much."

"I'm sorry, isn't that card *Death?*" asked Kaz.

"Not literal death, dingbat. Don't scare the man like that!" Ellie said, swatting his arm gently as she chuckled. "It's one of my favorite cards. It means cycles, rebirth. I might be a little concerned if it wasn't upright, but it still doesn't mean *death* death."

"It fits," Hartley rasped, eyes wide and breath shallow. "What are the others?"

"The Lovers," Ellie said, pointing, "and the Ace of Swords."

"The Lovers..." he murmured.

"It can be about love and balanced matches between people, platonic or romantic, but it can also be about choices. It's encouraging you to make the choices that are in your best interest, and tellin' you to be *careful* with your choices. Could be a delicate situation moving forward, but it has good odds to work out for ya."

The front door opened without a knock as Ellie spoke, and besides Kaz, there was only one other person who would enter her home like that.

"Hi, Granny," Ellie and Kaz said in unison, neither looking up from the cards.

"Well, ain't this a merry welcome," she said with a chuckle, walking inside like it was her own house. "Did you put on tea or should I?"

"You can if you want. I haven't put on any yet," Ellie said, gathering up her cards. The shuffling sound drew her grandmother's attention, and she looked over at the spread on the table with wide eyes, toddling over to peek at the spread herself.

"You're *reading?*" Granny asked. "He must'a done somethin' *good* for ya."

"You don't do this often?" Hart asked, eyebrow raised.

"I ain't seen her pick up a card deck for a living person in... years," Granny said, shaking her head. "She'll read for spirits, but not humans."

"Got tired of answerin' the same damn questions," Ellie muttered. "At least spirits have original ones."

"Then thank you sincerely for picking them up for me," Hartley said, inclining his head in a way that seemed almost like a renaissance-style bow.

The more Ellie interacted with him, the more she could understand why Kaz jokingly referred to him as a grandpa. Though he dressed in modern clothes and didn't speak in a particularly antiquated way, there was something about his mannerisms that felt just a little out of time, something about his speech patterns that was just a little too formal.

"You want me to try scrying for her?" Granny asked slowly, eyebrows raised.

"Seriously?" Ellie asked, taken aback, then turn to Hartley. "Don't turn this down. She don't offer to do this much, and I'm shit at scrying."

"How...?" Hartley began, trailing off helplessly, but Ellie knew what he was asking: *How did you know I'm looking for a "she?"*

"Call it a gut feeling," Granny said with a small smile. "I can read the energy on that compass from here. It's *strong.* "

"I'm afraid I didn't bring anything to pay you with—" Hartley said slowly, but Granny waved him off.

"Consider it a favor," she said simply. "I'm curious, so you'll owe me one in the future."

Rather than reply, Hartley looked to Kaz. He seemed tense, sitting ramrod straight in his chair with his eyes narrowed, like he was looking for the answer to a trick or a trap.

"I'd trust her not to abuse it," Kaz said with a slight shrug. "I know we've seen our fair share of bullshit, but I'll vouch for her."

"Flattery will get you everywhere," Granny said pleasantly, gently swatting at Kaz's arm.

"When did you start likin' Kaz?" Ellie said with a laugh.

"'Bout the time you started lookin' less like a ghost," she countered, patting Kaz's arm gently. "Now, let Granny read."

Granny didn't read with cards. She could, but Ellie had never known her to pick up cards when she could work with a scrying source instead. It only took a moment togather supplies— a bottle of ink, a bowl of water, and a fallen twig.

Taking a slow, centering breath, Granny held the twig between her hands and closed her eyes, muttering to herself for a long moment. It could have been a chant or an incantation, but Ellie knew it was a prayer. Once she opened her eyes again, she dropped a tiny bit of the oily, black ink into the bowl and began to stir with the twig. She made seven slow circles clockwise, starting small and becoming bigger until the twig touched the edge of the bowl on the last circle.

Then she stopped, gazing down at the bowl as the ink swirled in strange shapes.

"She's..." Granny said softly. Hartley's breath caught. "Long hair. Short stature. Accompanied by a dog, looks like."

"Is she... safe?" he asked.

"Yes," Granny said without hesitation. "For now."

"Where is she?" His knuckles went white as he clenched his fists, leaning forward slightly in his chair. Granny took a deep breath, eyes still closed, head tilting like she was looking around at something behind her eyes.

"Doesn't matter. You should stay where you are," Granny said, eyes snapping open. "She'll come to you."

"I..." Hartley trailed off, swallowing hard. "Are you certain?"

"It's hard to see the surroundings too clearly when you scry— everything gets a little murky outside the subject— but it felt like looking at a one star in a dark night sky. The only Other in a whole swath of humans. My guess is that it would be bad for both of you to go lookin' right now." Granny settled back in her chair, hands folded neatly on her lap.

"I see," he whispered. "Thank you. I appreciate your time and the honesty."

"Polite boy," Granny said approvingly. "I like this one, he can come back."

"I'm honored," Hartley said with a slight chuckle.

"You seem like a nice boy," Granny sighed, patting his arm. "You should really know that this is bigger than you. I wish it wasn't, if it's what I'm thinkin' it is, but it's bigger than you think. You two got a lot more to do than you know."

"How do ya know all that from scrying?" Ellie asked, nose scrunching.

"I've been gettin' weird pictures for a while. This one matched some of the others I've been seein', and not in a small way." She turned to Hart. "She got wings?"

Hartley paled as he nodded slowly.

"Yeah, those have been showin' up for me here and there," Granny muttered. "We might not know the whole of it for a while yet, but you stay in touch, y'hear?"

"Of course." Hartley sighed, rising from the chair. "I'm glad to know she's safe."

He picked up the compass from the table and slipped it back around his neck, gaze lingering on the slightly wavering needle for a long moment. He held it like a treasure, like it was the most precious object in the world, and Ellie's heart ached for him as she wondered exactly who he'd lost...

... and where she was now.

"We'll walk you to the gates," Ellie said, patting his shoulder gently. "Should help keep people from askin' too many questions about why you're all the way up here."

The group left Ellie's house together, Granny included, and slowly wound their way through the chaos of festival preparation towards the gates. None of them spoke. The moment felt delicate and Hartley seemed... somewhere else. He hadn't let go of the compass once, glancing down at the needle now and then as if to make sure it was still there.

As expected, they did pass Alice on the way out. Luckily, Ellie had the presence of mind to grab the school papers before they left, and she very promptly and pleasantly shoved them in front of Alice without preamble. She skidded to a stop with a squeak, glancing down at the sheaf of papers.

"What... are these?" Alice asked, taking them gently from Ellie so she could scan over the text.

"Registration papers for the college. Thought you could take some science courses if you wanted," Ellie said with a smile.

"H— how did you get these?" Alice gasped, green eyes wide.

"Help from a friend," Kaz said with a shrug, one hand on Hart's shoulder.

"This is Hartley," Ellie said. "He's a professor down at the college, and I asked him to grab some registration forms for ya. You should look into those science classes." She passed Alice the set of papers, but Alice wasn't looking at her at all.

"H— *hi*," Alice said, eyes wide and cheeks flushed. "Good to meet ya."

Good lord, Ellie thought, but managed not to roll her eyes. Hartley, for his part, seemed distant, detached, and a little bit dazed from Granny's advice, though he managed a polite handshake and a half smile.

"I'd best be on my way," Hartley said with a polite nod. "I hope you all have a lovely celebration tonight."

"You could stay for it?" Alice squeaked, cheeks positively flaming red.

"Thank you, but I have prior plans," he said, keeping his tone even and pleasant, though Ellie suspected his prior plans involved a large cup of tea and a book rather than other people.

"We'll see ya later!" Ellie said with a smile and a wave. "Safe travels."

As Hartley waved goodbye and walked towards the gates, leading back towards town and the college, Alice kept staring after him. She looked almost starstruck, different than she had when she tried to overtly flirt with Kaz.

"I know I ain't *your* granny," the old woman said, gently patting Alice's shoulder, "but that's one you should let go."

Alice's brow furrowed as she looked over at Granny, who only shrugged.

"Just trust me on this one. Old ladies know things."

"You ain't old yet," Alice said with a giggle. "Kickin' like a spring chicken."

Granny gave a loud laugh in response, looping her arm through the younger girl's as Kaz and Ellie watched Hartley slowly make his way out of the village, compass clutched tightly in his hand.

<hr>

Kaz crept around the back of the gray house belonging to the Littles, dark jacket zipped and hat covering his white hair as he worked his way through the shadows. Harper followed behind, lock picks in hand.

"I know Ellie said we probably wouldn't need the picks, but if somebody's hidin' something, best to be safe," she whispered.

In the village center, a large bonfire raged. Though the air was a little chilly, there was enough dancing and moonshine to keep the witches warm as they celebrated the oncoming spring. The sounds of shouting, talking, and merry making filtered through the night air, along with the faint strains of music. Night fell hours ago, but no one was asleep yet.

Ellie and her grandmother were at the celebration, generally trying to stay sober and keep an eye on anyone who might catch Kaz and Harper searching around the village. Rather than splitting up, they'd opted to check one house at a time and work as a team. That way, if either of them found something, they'd know to stop searching.

They'd already searched two houses on the outskirts, but neither of them yielded anything fruitful. Kaz expected as much, though. He wanted to test their snooping in places that would provide a little more cover, and they still managed to find and riffle through the family grimoires for those houses. Nothing even resembling the symbol on the end of the bullet showed up in either book, but the night was young. In the best case, they'd be able to check all the houses, but that depended on how quickly they could find the grimoires.

Before checking anywhere else, though, he wanted to check the Littles' home, as well as snoop around Jeannie's house. Both Mrs. Little and Jeannie were at the top of their suspect list, and he didn't want to risk missing the opportunity to investigate them while they were distracted. It was lucky neither he nor Harper needed light to see details in the dark. They could sneak around much more easily since there wasn't a need for a lantern.

"Hmm. Unlocked," Kaz muttered as the doorknob turned without trouble. The hinges creaked softly as he carefully opened the back door and peered inside.

One of the larger homes in the village, the Little residence housed all women. Mrs. Little and the younger four of her six daughters all resided in one building. In the darkness, Kaz could see a familiar iron stove, a basic kitchen, and a living area. The shadow of a set of stairs off to his left led to the second floor, presumably where the bedrooms were.

"Living area first," he whispered.

"You check that. I'll look in the closets and the kitchen," Harper said.

Ellie warned them that any smart witch family would keep their grimoire either hidden, disguised, or both. However... the hiding places in the first two homes they'd searched hadn't exactly been excellent. One was on a kitchen shelf among the cookbooks, easily identifiable by the gold symbols on the spine. The other was simply laying out. Open. On the bedside table.

Kaz was embarrassed for whoever lived in that one.

"So... Ellie's real pretty," Harper said with a wicked grin, searching through kitchen cabinets. "Better be careful, I might try and steal her."

Kaz just glared, not quite seeing the situation in the same humorous light as she did.

"More searching, less talking," he grumbled as he stared at the living area bookshelf.

"You won't let me have any fun," Harper sighed. "I think she's good for you, though. You seem less... sad. Less jaded."

"I do not seem sad and jaded," he scoffed.

"I mean, not any more y'don't. And it's been what? Almost a month? Imagine being with her for a year. Or more."

Kaz froze in place.

Could he imagine staying with Ellie for that long?

He wondered what it would be like to simply... not leave. Take up residence here. After all, he'd told her he planned to stay, but something about Harper's phrasing struck a chord with him.

Years with Ellie. *Years.* Besides his blood relations, it had been a very long time since he spent years with anyone. Romantic relationships in

the past had been relatively quick, with a few serious ones here and there. Romantic relationships on this plane were... either purely sexual or nonexistent. Ellie was an anomaly— a beautiful, sassy one that made him feel more alive than he had for a long time, but an anomaly, nonetheless. It unnerved him a little that his life had changed so quickly, that his perspective had changed so quickly... but he supposed that was just the way Ellie was. She was someone who couldn't help but shake things up a little, he supposed.

"Found it," Harper whispered triumphantly, interrupting his thoughts. "I'll give it to 'em, it's creative to put a book in a fake book box. Thought it was a weird decoration at first."

Kaz watched as she flipped through the book, surprised when a few loose pages fell to the ground. They seemed to be tucked in between random spells, inserted wherever they would fit, but he was most shocked that he'd seen the diagrams on these pages before.

"That's not the sigil," Harper said, peering over his shoulder.

"No... but it is a page of notes on the same ritual Ellie was investigating," he murmured. "I wonder if Mrs. Little is slated to be one of the casters."

Ellie said the spell called for a primary caster plus four others... all of whom had died in the only known casting attempt. Mrs. Little was power-hungry, according to Alice. He wasn't surprised she would be willing to take the risk.

"Isn't that... bad? Like, for momma Little?" Harper blinked owlishly down at the page.

"Yes, most definitely," Kaz said absently. He tucked the pages back into the book and continued looking for anything that even vaguely resembled the sigil from the bullet.

Something in his gut told him that this would be a very long night.

✦

The bonfire celebration had been going for hours.

Ellie was cold, annoyed, sick of all the loud shouting, and most annoyingly... she missed Kaz. She wanted to curl into his warmth and hide away, not sit out here among the ashes and chaos of the celebration.

And the alcohol.

So, so much alcohol.

She didn't mind alcohol, but the level of inebriation among the general crowd was a bit high for her personal comfort. Ellie preferred to stay sober at celebrations like this, so it certainly wasn't suspicious for her to take a warm cup of perfectly non-alcoholic cider and sit by the fire on a large log.

"Hi Jeannie," Ellie sighed, holding her cup of cider close.

"You feelin' okay, punkin'?" Jeannie asked, wrapping her arm around Ellie's shoulder. Judging by the smell wafting from her mug, she'd chosen to indulge in some of the warmed homemade wine that one of the residents brought to share.

"Yeah. Just thinkin' about a lot, I guess," she sighed. "I get in my head on nights like this."

"Mmm, you should be draggin' your man back to bed, not thinking," Jeannie said, rolling her eyes.

Ellie barked out a laugh. "Maybe slow down on that one," she said, nudging her aunt.

"I wouldn't if I were you," Jeannie huffed as she gazed into the blazing bonfire. "Ya never know which way the wind is gonna blow..."

"Jeannie..." Ellie said slowly, leaning her head on her aunt's shoulder. "Have you thought about... maybe dating again? Looking for someone?"

"No point," Jeannie said with a huff. "Council won't match me since I can't have kids."

"Doesn't have to be a Council match. You could maybe find someone in town?" she suggested gently, but Jeannie looked nothing short of repulsed.

"A human?" she scoffed. "Nah. No sooner I start to love him, he'll be dead and I'm still stuck here."

The grief Jeannie felt was palpable. It was understandable that she didn't want to be alone. In fact, Ellie understood the ache of loneliness on a level she wished that she didn't. Jeannie's divorce had taken a toll, changed her, and taking on the role of leading the village had emphasized that change even more. Ellie opened her mouth to respond, but she felt a nudge against her foot.

Looking down, she saw a little ball of brown and black fluff gazing up at her with sweet puppy eyes, tail wagging.

"Well, hey, sweet pea!" Ellie smiled as she bent down to pet the little hound, noticing a scrap of folded, crumpled paper in her mouth. She reached out to the pup and the dog practically leapt into her arms, snuggling against Ellie's chest like she was always meant to be there.

It wasn't too surprising. Charlie and Luna were around with their pups, helping to monitor the celebration as subtly as possible. However, Ellie hadn't seen them most of the evening. This little one must have slipped away, and she knew exactly which pup this was.

"Looks like you got a friend," Jeannie said with a laugh. "Lemme go grab another log for the fire. Looks like it needs one— I'll be right back."

Ellie waved to her aunt as she gently scratched behind the puppy's ears, cradling her gently.

"What'cha got there, hmm?" Ellie murmured, carefully tugging the paper out of the little one's mouth. It was a little damp from puppy drool and evening dew, and part of the page was charred away, but as Ellie unfolded the paper, her eyes went wide.

It was a rough sketch of the same sigil they'd found on the back of the bullet.

Before anyone could question her, Ellie rolled her eyes and shoved the paper in her pocket, faking a little laugh in case anyone had seen. Ellie's heart pounded in her chest as she fought to keep her expression calm.

"Silly goose, picking' up trash," she said, loud enough for anyone nearby to hear. "Gotta keep you outta trouble, huh? Let's get you home before you nose up anything else."

Petting the pup's ears gently, Ellie held her against her chest and made her way back to her small house on shaking legs. She didn't dare let that piece of paper out of her sight for a moment, not till they could check it thoroughly with Harper and Kaz present, but taking the pup back to her house to rest was a good excuse to go ahead and examine it.

Then, as they neared the edge of the crowd, Ellie whispered to the little pup.

"You did so good, little baby. So, *so* good."

IN WHICH NO ONE SLEEPS

In the wee hours of the morning, sometime between 3 and 4AM, Kaz and Harper met Ellie and the hounds in her home. They kept the curtains drawn and the lights low, just enough that Ellie could see, but not so much that it would draw attention.

"Where did you find this, little one?" Ellie asked softly as she spread the page out on the table. The pup yipped in response as Ellie gently scratched behind her fluffy ears.

"She says took it out of the tinder at the start of the bonfire," Luna translated.

"Incredible," Kaz said with a grin. "It looks like it's been torn out of a book. Someone wanted to dispose of evidence... which means someone is onto us."

"Agreed," Harper sighed.

"What?" Ellie blinked owlishly at them from her spot sitting at the kitchen table.

"It's been two years. Why try to burn it *now*?" Harper muttered. "If it was part of a book, they obviously weren't plannin' to tear it out before."

"They *know*. They know we're onto something." Kaz said with a nod, scratching at the faint stubble on his jaw.

"Better figure it out quick, then," Ellie said absently, standing up. Her chair screeched as it scraped across the wooden floor, tottering

slightly as she sighed, moved away from the table, and began to pace in small circles around her house.

"Did you figure out what it does?" Harper asked as she tossed her hair over her shoulder.

"The notes say it's a stillness spell," Ellie muttered, "I don't know what you'd want to shoot someone to freeze 'em in place for, though."

She supposed that anyone hit with a bullet would probably run, as evidenced by her own personal experience. However, wasn't the goal to aim for the kill shot? Why bother with all that stabbing and shooting if the goal was to end his life anyways?

"Recognize the handwriting?" Kaz asked, but Ellie just shook her head, long braid swinging back and forth.

"Not sure. I've seen... probably everyone's handwriting who lives here, but not enough to pinpoint it. We'd need a writing sample to be sure."

Kaz tapped his foot impatiently. His eyes were fixed on a blank spot on the wall, brow furrowed, arms crossed over his chest.

"What all can you do with a poppet?" he asked.

"A lot, honestly, but it's mostly meant for influencing people," Ellie mumbled as she turned around and began to pace the other direction.

"Could it influence someone to walk off the main path for no good reason?"

"That... Wouldn't be too hard, actually," Ellie said slowly. "I don't know one witch who'd fall for it, but we all know what a poppet spell s'posed to feel like."

"Ben wouldn't have?" Kaz pressed, but Ellie was sure.

"No. No way."

Harper hummed softly, tapping her long nails against the table as she thought. The faint clicking sound was the only noise in the room for a moment as they all processed the details, and Harper was the one to finally break the silence.

"So the killer somehow got their hands on a tag lock for the poppet, lured him off the path, and shot him through with a stillness sigil to hold him... while..." Harper's nose scrunched and she frowned, looking like she was trying very hard not to gag and failing miserably. "No wonder the blood was strong."

Dear God.

A wave of cold dread slowly slithered down Ellie's spine, resting deep in the pit of her stomach. This confirmed it. It was not only a witch who killed him, but a witch that lived in this very village.

A witch she likely knew.

A witch she had looked in the face for two years and not suspected.

"I am so stupid," Ellie said softly, resting her head in her hands. Tears pricked at the corners of her eyes, and she found she couldn't hold them back. She'd cried more in the last three weeks than the last two years, and at this point she wasn't sure if that was good or bad or somewhere in between.

"You did the best you possibly could have." Kaz perched on the bed beside her, wrapping his arm around her shoulders.

"I should have known it was a witch. I should have suspected," she stuttered, trying to keep her voice quiet between hiccupping sobs.

"Come here." Kaz wrapped her up in a soft hug, rocking her gently as she cried. Ellie found herself clutching onto him like a lifeline, face buried in the fabric of his shirt as she tried to muffle herself. "I've got you."

"It's just... I grew up here. I thought I knew these people. Some of 'em I don't like, but not liking someone isn't the same as... as..."

Murder. Not liking someone wasn't the same as being willing to kill them for it.

She couldn't bring herself to say it.

Rubbing salty tears away from her face, Ellie felt something tugging on her sock. It was the little pup, barking at her from the floor and running in a slightly distressed circle around her feet. Ellie dropped to her knees and scooped up the baby hound, who didn't seem to mind in the slightest. In fact, she seemed to like being held.

The little one snuggled against Ellie, licking at the tear trails left on her skin and whimpering softly.

"She's trying to comfort you. She likes you," Luna said softly. "And she picked her human name, as well."

"Oh?" Ellie looked back and forth between the parent hounds, waiting on an answer. She was still sniffling a little, but more than happy for the subject change. Her emotions could only handle so much at once.

"*She said she wants to be called Rosemary,*" said Charlie.

"I like that. Hi, Rosemary," Ellie murmured. The pup yipped at her, licking her cheek.

"*If it's alright, she'd like to stay here until tomorrow. She's worried,*" Luna sad, nudging her pup with her nose.

Ellie looked at Kaz, but he only shrugged, flashing her a toothy smile.

"It's your house."

She turned back to Luna, already feeling a little lighter. "I'd like that, then."

<hr>

Harper left the village under the cover of darkness, taking the hounds and their pups with her— except for Rosemary, of course, who slept peacefully beside Ellie and Kaz in the bed that night, snuggled up and snoring slightly.

They didn't sleep much. Ellie was anxious, and every sound seemed to wake her. Even tucked in close to Kaz, she couldn't relax, and her shuffling roused him every time. He didn't complain once, to his credit, but Rosemary was the only one who slept well.

When the sun rose, Ellie slid from the bed and made tea, taking a seat at the table with a notebook and pencil. It was time to go over the facts again. Surely they had enough to draw some kind of conclusion. *Surely.* If they didn't, she worried it might drive her out of her mind at this point.

"Let's look through what we know so far," Kaz suggested, hunting for a loaf of bread and some hard cheese around the kitchen. "We'll compare notes."

"We know... Well, we know about as damn much as at the start," Ellie grumbled, sipping her tea.

"Not true. You've simply been inundated with the details for so long that it doesn't seem like much anymore." He sat down in the second

chair and Rosemary hopped into his lap, unscrupulously trying to steal a bite of cheese. Kaz pinched off a bit for her and chuckled as she licked it from his hands, and the sight soothed Ellie's nerves.

"We know... the records at the Sheriff's office say he died from a multitude of stab wounds, but Harper found a bullet with human blood on it in the woods," she sighed. "We have the sigil from the bullet on a random, half-burned page..."

She trailed off as she smoothed the crumpled paper out one more time, reading over the wording for the stillness spell. It was nothing particularly unusual. It froze your target in one place, rendering them incapable of conscious movement. The shape of the loops and swirls of the letters scratched at something in the back of her mind, though.

She was *sure* she'd seen it before. All she needed to know was *where*.

"Wait," Ellie said suddenly.

She pulled her grimoire off the shelf, flipping to the very first pages as she placed the torn paper from the bonfire beside it.

"I thought that sigil wasn't in your grimoire." Kaz came closer to peer over her shoulder as she flipped pages.

"It isn't. I'm not looking for the sigil," she mumbled. "This is a collection of old pages from my witch family members. Some of 'em were from my dad's old grimoire and got bound into this one. Others Granny wrote for me. Others—"

Ellie paused, picking up the piece of paper and holding it next to a page in her book. It was a simple spell, just detailing how to conjure a ball of light in a lantern if there were no matches to light it, but as she held the sigil page side by side, it was clear to see that the handwriting matched.

"Authored by Jeannie Sader," she murmured, pointing to the signature at the bottom of the page in the book.

"Jeannie's sigil," Kaz whispered. "*She* made it."

"She tried to *burn* it," Ellie rasped. "Jeannie's primary magic skill is fire. *She* lit the bonfire last night, Kaz!" They were lucky that Rosemary managed to pull the paper out of the pile of tinder before the fire started. Otherwise, their evidence would literally have gone up in flames.

"Does Jeannie have a hunting rifle?" Kaz asked urgently.

"Yeah, she does. Knows how to make a basic poppet, too," Ellie choked out, her voice becoming very, very quiet as she flipped forward in the book.

Turning the pages slowly and carefully, the book her only anchor in a spinning room, Ellie finally found what she was looking for. It was Fletcher's ritual page, but this time she wasn't looking for her father's notes. She needed to see the main list of components, right at the start of the spell.

Ah.

There it was, written clearly in black ink.

"Blood of a tortured sacrifice," she muttered, pointing at the list. "It's designated as *human blood*."

Animal blood was listed as a plausible substitute in both her father's notes and the notes on Fletcher's original spell, but Fletcher emphasized the potency of human blood over animal blood. Each caster needed their own blood supply, and it wouldn't be hard to get animal blood without raising suspicion. There was enough game around here to spare and many places to dispose of it, but...

It would explain why Ben had been stabbed so many times.

It would explain the bullet with the sigil holding him in place, so someone could hold a jar and catch his blood in a bottle.

"I'm gonna—" Ellie began, but cut off as she clapped a hand over her mouth and ran to the small bathroom, emptying her stomach into the toilet.

When her stomach was empty, she kept dry heaving, gagging until there was nothing left to give. Ellie spat one more time, wiped her mouth with a tissue, and flushed the mess. Then she tottered back into the main room, still in a daze, and took a seat on the floor in front of the bed. She leaned her back against the footboard for support, grateful when Rosemary climbed into her lap and Kaz took a seat beside her.

They sat in silence for a long moment, Ellie quietly petting Rosemary and Kaz just sitting, breathing slowly, his eyes closed.

"You think we got the right one?" Kaz asked.

"She never liked Ben," Ellie whispered. "Never. I thought she was comin' around there at the end, but knowing this... It makes too much sense."

"I'm sorry," Kaz rasped. "I know that's a nearly useless thing to say right now, but I'm sorry."

"I don't... If she tried to kill you... Why did she do it?" Ellie stuttered. "Why? What was so horrible that she—" she cut off with a choked off sob, but it felt like she was out of tears to cry. Instead, she leaned her head on Kaz's shoulder and reached for his hand, just needing to know he was there to ground her in some way while part of her world crumbled.

"What do you want to do?" he murmured, his breath tickling her scalp.

Excellent question.

She didn't know exactly how to approach someone and accuse them— no, *tell* them they were a murderer. It would take time and planning, though they didn't have too much time. If Jeannie had any idea they were investigating, then she might have recognized that piece of paper in Rosemary's mouth last night. She couldn't ignore that possibility. Considering that, they'd need to act soon.

But...

"I need to talk to Ben," she said softly. "Before... before we do anything else. I have to. I need to make sure he's at peace, and... and maybe see what he even wants me to do." He was the only person she felt had any say over how to deal with this information, over what to do with Jeannie. He *deserved* a say in this.

"Okay," Kaz said, though his fists were clenched by his side. "It's your closure. We'll do this your way."

"Call Harper at the inn. Tell her Charlie and Luna need to meet us at the cemetery."

IN WHICH ELLIE SAYS GOODBYE

Rosemary walked beside Kaz and Ellie as they picked their way down the mountain, moving slowly towards the cemetery that was Ben's final resting place.

Rather than going to inform Granny of their conclusions before leaving the village, Ellie insisted on going straight to the cemetery. Kaz seemed confused about that decision, but Ellie couldn't bring herself to look Granny in the eye at the moment. That was something they'd need to deal with later. Right now, she wanted to know what *Ben* wanted. It felt right to tell him first, in a way.

Charlie and Luna were already at the gates by the time they arrived. Either four legs were much faster than two, or Ellie was simply moving very, very slowly. The world still felt like it was spinning around her, like she couldn't quite believe anything she saw. Maybe it would settle eventually. Maybe it never would.

Ellie was almost surprised to see Ben's spirit already wandering when they entered the graveyard. It was almost like he was waiting, like he knew they'd be coming to contact him soon. Despite having no witch blood in his veins whatsoever, Ben always had an uncanny intuition like that in life, and Ellie wouldn't be surprised if he kept it in the afterlife.

He stood by his tombstone, looking a little lost and a little uncomfortable, but he smiled

when he saw her and waved hello. She waved back, forcing herself to smile at him.

"Hey, Ellie belle," he said, shoving his hands in his pockets, but then he frowned as she came closer. "You... don't look so good, hon."

"I... have somethin' I really need to tell you," she said quietly. "And I don't know how you're gonna take it."

"O...kay?" Ben, to his credit, didn't seem even the slightest bit nervous.

She couldn't being herself to meet his eyes for a long moment. Ben waited patiently for her to pull herself together, to swallow the lump rising in her throat and calm her wildly beating heart. When she finally looked up, his kind eyes almost broke her down again.

"Ben, baby... you're... you've passed on," she said gently, tears pricking at the corners of her eyes.

"I know," he admitted.

"I..." Ellie said slowly. "Why are you still here, then? You've been confused about where you are and what's goin' on every time I saw you."

"I've known for a while. I knew last time ya saw me, if I'm honest. Just wasn't ready to admit it yet," he said, taking a seat on the ground and patting the spot beside him. Ellie sat cross legged next to his ghost, the same way she would have when he was alive. "Wanted to look out for ya a little longer. I remembered a lil' more every time we talked, but I wasn't ready to leave yet."

"You can rest. You don't have to stay for me," Ellie choked out. "You deserve your peace."

"So do you."

She didn't know how, but even as a ghost, Ben's gaze seemed to go right through all her defenses and see deep into the parts of her heart that she didn't want anyone to touch.

"She took you too soon," she whispered, fighting to keep her voice from breaking. "It's not fair."

Ben's eyes visibly widened.

"S—*she*? Do you know who did it?" he asked, taking a deep breath through his nose.

"Yeah. We think so." Ellie paused, took a slow breath, and nodded. "We *know* so."

"Good," Ben said, nodding firmly, but there was a long pause before he spoke again. Ellie fought not to squirm in place in front of him as he scratched at the back of his neck, adjusted the collar of his shirt that was somehow always off center, and scuffed at the cemetery ground with his incorporeal boot. For what seemed like an eternity, he wouldn't meet her eyes.

And then he looked up, a new kind of steely resolve in the set of his jaw and the straightening of his spine.

"Don't tell me who it was," he finally said. "I don't wanna know, an' I think it's better that way. But... I think *you* need to know. I think you need the closure."

He was right.

Something inside Ellie sighed with relief at that. Ben had always been soft and kind, and she was glad to see that death hadn't twisted that into something unrecognizable. He was still the same old Ben on some level, and she could rest easy knowing that.

But he also knew that Ellie wanted that closure— not just wanted, but needed it desperately. She'd craved it ever since the day her white dress was forever stained with his blood. However... she needed to do it in a way that they both could agree on. She wanted to do this for her *and* for Ben.

But...

"I don't think... I don't have the heart to kill 'em for killin' you," Ellie said quietly. "I know the witch laws say an eye for an eye... but I *can't*."

"Good. That means you're still just as soft as ya were before. You're not *you* if ya ain't soft," he said with a smile.

"... Are you gonna be mad if I still wanna kick some ass, though?" she mumbled, wincing.

To her surprise, Ben's spirit let out a rollicking laugh. "Go get 'em with my blessing," he said approvingly. "I trust you to know what's enough for justice. Just don't lose that soft side. It makes you more human than most people, even most humans."

Ellie nodded, a small smile creeping across her face. Ben understood how badly she wanted to go too far sometimes. She knew that

he understood the magnitude of her grief and the subsequent recklessness of her actions. Having his blessing to do something, though, to get revenge or justice or just a little closure in even a small way... that was important.

"Can you do something for me, sweetie?" Ben asked.

"Anything." For him, she would do anything at all without a single second of hesitation.

"I need you to keep living," he said softly, a little half smile crossing his face. "The world doesn't stop turning because I'm not in it, and I know you're gonna be there a long time. You got too much life in ya to stop now."

"That's..." Ellie said softly, swallowing hard.

That's not fair, she wanted to say. *That's not right*, she wanted to say.

Ben was not the first ghost to say something similar, though. Life is for the living, they said over and over. Someone said. Maybe someone who'd never spoken to a ghost, but they were technically right all the same. Wherever Ben had gone, it was to a place she couldn't reach him now. He had his own peace to find and his own dreams to chase on the other side, in another plane, in another life, maybe.

Whatever it was, she just hoped it was beautiful for him.

"You take care of her," Ben said to Kaz, tipping his spectral hat. "She's got a hard head and a soft heart. Needs somebody."

"I'll do what she'll let me," Kaz said, returning the nod. "And... Well, I might do a few things she doesn't want me to do, too. For her own good."

Ellie scoffed and rolled her eyes.

"That's my Ellie belle," Ben said, chuckling. "I always worried what was gonna happen to ya once I was gone. Didn't expect to leave quite this quick, but that's okay. I know you'll make it. And... I'm glad you've got somebody."

"I'm sorry," Ellie rasped, determined to get it out. "I'm sorry you're dead 'cause of me."

Ben looked taken aback, jaw dropping open.

No, not just taken aback, he looked.... Moderately horrified, shaking his head fervently.

"You didn't kill me," Ben said, setting his shoulders in a way that, in life, indicated that he really meant business.

"But if it wasn't for meetin' me—"

"If it wasn't for you, I'd have lost out on a lotta things," Ben said gently. "I'm glad. I don't regret it. And you didn't cut me down yourself, so I deem this not your fault. Ever. Y'hear me?" Ben's eyes narrowed as he examined her closely, in all her guilt and shame, in all her love and grief.

She nodded slowly, biting her lip, unable to put into words how grateful she was for him, for everything, for just the chance to meet him. That was alright, though. Sometimes things like that didn't need to be said. Sometimes... you could say them with other words instead.

"Are you ready to go?" Luna asked, looking between Ben and Ellie.

Ellie took a slow breath, fighting back the lump in her throat. This was good. This was good for Ben.

"Go...?" Ben trailed off, blinking at Luna.

"Somewhere better, I think. Let's get you settled, shall we?" Luna flicked her tail, and it looked as though a streak of light cut through the air, expanding into... a door?

It wasn't clear what was on the other side of the door. It was at once too bright and too shadowy, too foggy and too reflective to see, but that was for the better. Wherever Ben was going, humans weren't supposed to go. Not yet. Not till they were finished on this plane. Ellie might have Spirit Sight, but even she was aware that some places are just for the dead.

"I'll walk with you," Luna said as she sidled up to Ben's spirit. A high-pitched whine came from Rosemary, and she jogged over to stand beside her mother. Luna just nodded at her as Rosemary's tail wagged. *"We will, that is. We'll make sure you don't get lost."*

"I love you," Ellie said. "I'm glad I met you."

"I love you, too," Ben echoed, blowing a kiss towards her. "You'll never lose me, not really."

She couldn't bring herself to watch as they disappeared through that door. It didn't fade once Ben's spirit and the hounds stepped through, but remained for one minute longer. Then two. Then three.

Ellie wasn't sure how time passed on the other side of that door. It seemed like an eternity that she waited there, hands clenched into fists and just staring at the strange light. Finally, though, Luna and Rosemary appeared in a flash of light from the other side.

The door closed behind them.

Ellie looked at Luna for a long moment. "Is... is he...?"

"At rest," Luna confirmed.

A sense of relief like she'd never known washed through Ellie. Her mother had her baptized as a baby, and she couldn't remember the moment at all, but she wondered for a brief second if this was what it was supposed to feel like. It was like a weight lifted off her very soul, leaving her entirely unshackled, too free to laugh or speak or do anything but breathe. Breathe, and allow herself to collapse onto her knees by Ben's tombstone.

For the first time in two years, some of the guilt truly eased away, and Ellie had hope it might not return. If it did, perhaps it would be a little less.

As she sat on the bare dirt and simply tried to breathe, Ellie felt something wiggle under her palm.

Odd. She didn't think she'd put her hand over a mouse or a bug... and she found neither of those things. Instead, growing under her palm, there was a green sprout of a plant with leaves and thorns.

And it was growing *fast*.

In a matter of seconds, Ellie watched the plant grow from a tiny sprout to full size, three feet tall and coughing. Other sprouts echoed its growth, springing to life around Ben's tombstone. The vines gently cradled the headstone without covering it, even showing pods and buds that opened into out-of-season blooms. Deep magenta mountain roses, native to North Carolina, unfurled in a beautiful tribute around Ben's grave.

"Is that... Where is that coming from?" Ellie asked, taking a step away from the tombstone. Where her feet once were, more plants sprung up, more deep magenta roses bloomed.

"You can't tell?" Charlie asked, padding closer. *"It's from you."*

She blinked at the roses, wondering if they were real. This was the kind of thing Granny talked about, the kind of magic that Granny said their family had. It was innate and in tune with the land, it came from the

mountain and her emotions, and it worked with the life and death cycle of all things.

It was also a kind of magic that she had never, not once, been successful with before. Now she had, apparently, managed to perform it entirely unconsciously.

"This is new," Ellie murmured, reaching out to touch one of the roses. As though it was sentient, it bent its stem towards her hand, petals brushing across her fingertips. "I... didn't think I *could* do anything like this."

"Have you ever felt like this before?" Charlie asked as he walked over to her.

"N— no..." she stammered, feeling more tears prick at her eyes.

It was like a dam had broken inside her, like all the things she'd been trying to hold back feeling for the last thirty years were all coming out at once. It was grief for her mother and grief for Ben, anger for herself, fear and hope and love. Everything felt like it could settle now because she knew that Ben was at peace, even things from parts of her life long before she met him. She felt like, for the first time in a long time, she could take a step forward without the chains of her past dragging along behind her.

Ellie breathed deeply, wondering if this was how it felt to have a weight off your chrest.

"What do you want to do now?" Kaz asked, grabbing her hand.

"If we're taking her down, I'm taking her down in a way she will never, ever recover from. Not in this lifetime," Ellie said through gritted teeth, scrubbing away tears from her face with one hand.

"I'm with you. Let me know what you need," he said softly, giving her hand a squeeze that Ellie returned.

"Us too." Luna said. Rosemary yipped.

"We'll have to wait until exactly the right time to do this," Ellie said softly, rubbing a hand across her face. "If we fuck it up, we don't get a second chance."

"Let's head back, then," Charlie said, already turning to walk out of the cemetery. *"We can figure things out from your home."*

Harper and Ellie sat on a soft blanket under the stars. Ellie wore her coat, but the chill didn't seem to bother the blonde vampire at all as they both gazed up at the constellations.

Ellie had set up on an overlook well outside the village, just to keep out of sight of any prying eyes. Though Harper was technically there to meet Charlie and Luna, she insisted it was important to have some "girl time" on their own. Rosemary was, of course, allowed to join at the pup's own insistence, and the little dog snoozed between them as they chatted quietly.

Their group spent the afternoon planning, writing letters, contacting folks. She still hadn't had the heart to tell Granny, still hadn't figured out how to say it. They did have a little time, though. There was another week before the full moon, and thus another week before Jeannie was set to complete her ritual. They just needed to lay low until then.

"How do you feel?" Harper asked.

"Shitty," she whispered. "I don't think I'm gonna fully process this for a long time."

"You get that letter sent off to the Council?" Harper's eyes were fixed on the stars.

"Yeah. Hopefully word'll get back soon," Ellie said. "Stopped by the Sheriff's office in town, too, but we can't do too much without the Council. She's protected as a lead witch. They'd spring her from any jail run by a human in a heartbeat."

"It's gonna work," Harper whispered. "It will. It's a good plan."

"I don't know what I'm gonna do after this," Ellie sighed. "It feels like... I don't know. It's like I've been stuck under a snow bank this whole time, and now I can breathe and feel and *think* again. I... think it's thanks to Kaz that I can feel anything much at all."

Even if a lot of what she was feeling hurt. And it did hurt. It hurt like a punch in the gut that never got better, like a knife in her chest that no one removed, but the hurt was slowly turning into anger and grief, and she was grateful for that instead of the numbness. The numbness was worse.

"I... I know it's easy to numb out," Harper said softly. "I get it. I'm not much older than you, maybe a decade or two, but we've all seen our share of the same shit."

"I don't like feeling too much," Ellie whispered. "It's scary."

"Yeah, it is," she sighed through her fangs. "But if getting in touch with your emotions brought out your magic— if your *closure* brought it out, don't ya think it's worth it?"

"I think so, yeah."

A gentle breeze whistled through the trees as they spoke. Beside them, a leaf landed on Rosemary's nose. The tickling sensation made her sneeze herself awake, the leaf flying off into the breeze.

"You ready for bed, Rosemary?" Ellie asked as Rosemary yawned.

"She's real attached, huh?" Harper said, laughing.

"*I'm* attached." Ellie smiled and let Rosemary jump onto her lap. "Don't know what I'm gonna do when y'all leave town."

Harper paused, pursing her lips, suddenly very fascinated with the blanket they were sitting on. "... About that," she said softly.

"What? You leavin' tomorrow or something?" Ellie asked, taken aback.

Harper's eyes went wide as she shook her head. "No! No, no— it's just. Well, Kaz can tell ya later. We're workin' out details. Might be here for a good long while, though."

Ellie thought she might enjoy that.

23

IN WHICH ROSES GROW

Kaz walked up the mountain trail towards Ellie's house as quickly as he thought he could get away with. He didn't want to raise any alarms, but he also needed to get back as quickly as possible. Not only did he have an important letter to deliver, but he felt like he would burst from the news he'd gotten from a realtor in Boone.

He entered without knocking and kicked off his boots, not noticing for a moment that he'd left the door open behind him in his haste to get inside.

Ellie, for her part, was nervously playing with her vines. It was a habit she'd picked up very, very quickly, and Kaz was honestly surprised that the entire house wasn't covered in out-of-season greenery, both outside and in. While she'd been waiting on word from the Council, Ellie had put everything she had into working on her magic. Any spare moment was practice, both growing things and returning them to the earth. Working with the natural cycle of things, she called it. She said that's what it felt like.

Kaz thought the expression fit her, especially considering how her Spirit Sight had taken off since she finally reached even a little closure over Ben's death. She could see and hear more clearly than ever, and not just human ghosts. Animals, plants, and spirits of the land

appeared to her in flashes, and Kaz suspected that ability would only grow stronger.

He wondered if the years of teasing and isolation had really been the thing suppressing her magic, and maybe now that she had people encouraging and accepting her, it was able to break free. Or maybe he just hoped he had something to do with it because he loved her.

He did.

He loved her very, very dearly.

But she could wait a little longer to hear that, for now.

The hinges creaked as Kaz closed the door behind him, reaching into his pocket to wave a letter in the air.

"Look what I've got!"

Ellie looked up and gasped at the sight. "Holy shit, you're *just* in time."

"Could they have cut it any closer?" he asked, rolling his eyes as he handed her the letter. "That godforsaken ritual is *tonight*. You *told them* to rush."

"Now you see why Miriam hates the Council," Ellie snorted as she tore the letter open.

She scanned through the text as quickly as possible while Kaz waited with bated breath. After what seemed like hours, but was likely only a few seconds, Ellie finally looked up at him.

"This is just what we needed," she said with a slow smile.

Unable to help himself, Kaz picked her up around the waist and spun her around. The joy radiating off her was tangible and beautiful and delicious, and he would never tire of feeling that mix of calm and happiness and love from her. Ellie laughed as he finally set her down, tucking the letter back in its envelope and putting it safely to the side... for now.

"Before we start thinking about tonight, I need to talk to you about something," Kaz said seriously, taking her hands in his.

"You're... not proposing, are you?" she asked, brow furrowed.

"Give me at least another year for that," Kaz said with a snort, but Ellie's shoulders visibly relaxed.

He was glad to see her loosen up over the last few days. She'd always had a strong personality, but now she felt relaxed as well. For the

most part, at least. They still had work to do, loose ends to tie up, but seeing her working her new magic and slowly finding herself again was worth more than he could describe.

"You said before that it would be difficult to find anyone who would sell land to a woman or a witch," he said slowly. "What if I told you I had land?"

"... What are you saying?" Ellie asked slowly, eyes narrowing. "I told you already- I don't want your money. It's too much."

"I'm not offering you money. I'm offering to sell you land," he said with a crooked smile. "Forty acres, if you want that much."

Ellie's mouth dropped open.

"That's... incredible," she whispered. "But I told you, I can't bring myself to leave the mountain."

"That's the best part: you won't have to." The smile on his face only grew wider as he spoke.

Her mouth dropped open. For a moment, she stood stock still and gaping like a fish, processing his words. "How the hell did you get *mountain land*?"

"I pulled some strings," he said with a shrug. "According to Hartley, it's over that direction..." he said vaguely, pointing off at a peak in the distance.

It was some kind of handle, Granny had told him. Or... something like a handle.

Or maybe a peak?

"*Howard's Knob*?" Ellie gasped. "You bought forty acres on *Howard's Knob*?"

"... Is that good? Granny said it was good," he said a little helplessly.

"That's more than good, Kaz. That land is *beautiful*!" She shook her head and laughed, like she just couldn't help it. "There's no way I could have afforded a quarter of that on my own. What on earth are you plannin' to sell it for?"

"I know someone that wants some land," he said with a shrug. "I'll set a price at some point."

"We'll negotiate. You're not sellin' yourself short," Ellie grumbled, pursing her lips together.

"You won't be paying interest. I won't budge on that."

Ellie tilted her head back and forth for a moment, seeming to weigh her options. "Okay, that much I agree to. We're not done talking, though."

"I would never assume," Kaz said, smiling.

❖

It was time.

There was a small wagon packed outside Ellie's house. They didn't need much, mostly the two clothes trunks packed to the brim with anything they could shove inside and a couple sacks tied on top with food and dishware. Ellie and Kaz were both dressed for traveling.

Granny stood with them on the fringes of the crowd gathered to watch the Ritual of Returning, looking rather somber. She took the news as well as it could be taken, and she hadn't doubted Ellie for a moment. For that, Ellie would forever be grateful, but it still felt like a betrayal to take Granny's daughter away from her.

"Granny," Ellie said softly. "I'm sorry."

"Don't be sorry," the old woman said. "You didn't make her decisions for her. You didn't force a single thing on her. She brought this on herself."

"I wish..." she said softly, helplessly, but Granny just nodded.

"I do, too. She sealed her a fate a long time ago when she couldn't get over how jealous she was of your daddy, though." Granny sighed, clasping her hands together. "I wish I could'a gotten through to her before she married that man..."

"You did everything you could," she murmured, reaching out to hug her grandmother. "I love you so much."

"I love you, too, baby," Granny said, kissing Ellie's cheek. "Now go get 'em."

Ellie took a deep breath as she gazed towards the gathering crowd.

It was now or never.

She carefully wove her way through the group on onlookers gathered for the Ritual of Returning, working her way to a place where she could see the entire setup. Jeannie stood at the top of a five-pointed star in the center of a massive casting circle drawn on the ground with the ends of burnt oak branches. A black-robed witch stood at each of the four other star points. Each of them had a basket at their side, presumably filled with tools and ingredients for the ritual.

Bile rose in Ellie's stomach as Jeannie stepped forward to address the gathered crowd. She forced it back down, concentrating on the feeling of the earth's energy around her, of the plants and roots under her feet, of the cycle of nature at work.

It *wanted* to bloom for her, she'd learned. Her heartbeat and the heartbeat of the wild green plant life around her wanted to intertwine to make something beautiful. She just had to give it a little direction.

"Tonight we complete the Ritual of Returning!" Jeannie proudly declared. "Step into the circle with me, friends, and claim-"

"You're not steppin' nowhere," Ellie called out from the crowd.

Green, thorny vines grew from the ground around Jeannie's feet where she stood outside of the casting area, some wrapping their way around her feet and legs while others whipped out to secure her wrists and hold her arms in place.

Wild mountain roses.

They weren't wrapped tightly enough to do any real harm... so long as Jeannie didn't try to move. Ellie stepped forward and walked across the casting circle, purposefully mussing the carefully drawn lines as she went by dragging her feet across the chalk. A wave of whispers and murmurs went through the crowd as she walked, and two of the four other ritual casters moved forward to stop her.

They didn't make it two steps before Ellie flicked her hand and wrapped vines around them, too.

"Anyone else?" she asked, looking around. No one moved.

"Ellie? What are you doing? We *need* this-" Jeannie tried, but it was no use at this point.

"I believe one of those ingredients rightfully belongs to me," she said coldly as she approached.

Ellie bent down to the basket, plucking out a large glass bottle of dark, congealed blood, ignoring the other bits, bobs, and herbs in the basket. She forced herself to breathe slowly, evenly, as she got to her feet to look Jeannie in the eye.

"This is a bottle of Ben Mathers' blood, isn't it?" she asked loudly, holding up the glass for the whole circle to see.

Jeannie was silent, but Ellie could see the color begin to drain from her aunt's face, could see the change in her posture as she started to try to squeeze her way out of the vines.

"I wouldn't struggle if I were you. If you don't want a whole mess of thorns stuck in ya, at least," Ellie snapped. "Now, if you don't wanna tell me the truth, I've got a friend over here that can tell me exactly who this blood belongs- *belonged*- to. It's just gonna get worse the more you make me wait, though."

Jeannie didn't seem particularly inclined to respond to that, but Mrs. Little, still wrapped in her own set of thorny rose vines, tried to protest.

"This is *ridiculous*, Ellie-" Mrs. Little grunted, pulling at the plants.

"I ain't talking to you. Hush up," she snapped, tightening the vines ever so slightly. Mrs. Little cut off with a gasp as Ellie turned back to her aunt. "You needed the blood for the ritual, and you never liked Ben. He was a convenient target, and the only time you were able to catch him alone was the morning of our wedding."

"You have no proof," Jeannie hissed. "The Council will have your hide for this."

"Oh, I *do* have proof," she said. "I have a sigil page in your hand and a bullet singing Ben's bloodsong with that same sigil on it. I have the fact that you own a hunting rifle *and* managed to get to me and Kaz that day in the woods almost a little too quickly. And, I bet if I really wanted to, I could match the decayed fabric scraps from that poppet to a piece in *your* house."

Jeannie was silent, but her eyes blazed as she glared. Murmurs went through the crowd, and it seemed as though the whole village collectively took a step or two back from them.

"You know what I really don't get?" Ellie practically snarled. "You were so determined to leave me alive. Even when you shot at me and Kaz from the woods, you stopped as soon as I got in a pinch."

"You're still my niece," she said through gritted teeth. "I didn't want you dead."

"Oh, but you were fine killing the person I loved? Mm, great judgement there," Ellie snarked, very aware that she held the cards in this situation. It was difficult to control her anger, to control the desire to yell and scream and rip Jeannie to shreds in every way possible, but she knew she had to. She had to stay calm if she wanted to keep the upper hand. "You know else what I found out? You were also fine with makin' sure I could never get a start for my own business. You *never* sent my apothecary papers to the council for approval. I checked. They'd never heard of it. You wanted me dependent on this village- dependent on *you*."

"I wasn't gonna let some *human* fuck up the last chance our line has for a better future!" Jeannie shrieked, pulling against the thorns. The plant seemed to tighten around her almost of its own volition, and streaks of red blood ran where thorns pierced her pale skin. "You're the only one who can pass on our magic— make it *stronger*. I'm not lettin' it die that easy."

"So why shoot at Kaz?" Ellie asked, eyes narrowing. "He's not human."

"Because you couldn't let Ben go," she spat. "You couldn't just *let it fucking go* and live your perfect life! You had to poke your nose into the past instead of burying it, and he was encouraging you. You have *everything*, Ellie! You have everything in the world and you couldn't let one stupid, useless human boy just *die*-"

Ellie took the remaining two steps towards Jeannie and slapped her aunt across the cheek with a resounding *crack*. She thought she heard a gasp in the background, but she didn't care.

It wasn't about their line, not really. It was about power. It was about jealousy. Jeannie didn't inherit the magic that Ellie and her father did, not to the same degree. She couldn't have children, either, and thus couldn't pass on even the smallest bit of power that she did have, and her husband left her because of it. Though it might have started as rage against

Ellie for marrying a human, exactly as she claimed, her motivations had clearly warped and twisted beyond that.

"I don't know what the hell made you think I have some kind of perfect life, but I've got good news for ya: You'll never be a part of it again. I'm leaving," she said with a quiet fury that rang through the cool spring night. "I'm leaving, and you better be thankful I'm leaving you with your life."

"The Old Ways say-"

"The *Old Ways* say you owe me a blood debt for taking one of mine from me," Ellie spat. She reached forward and took Jeannie's chin in her hand, forcing eye contact, squeezing just a little tighter than necessary. "I'm well within my rights to collect on it now. What'cha think, Jeannie? A life for a life sound good? An eye for an eye? That follow your Old Ways well enough?"

The woman paled, eyes wide. "You wouldn't."

"Oh, I don't think you have *any* idea what I'm capable of right in this moment," Ellie said softly. "You're right about one thing, though: the dead don't suffer. And you *will* get your due for this."

And then she stepped back, taking a deep, slow breath. She wanted to fight and scream and let every bit of her anger and grief loose at Jeannie, but that wouldn't do any good. She needed to be calm right now. She needed to show that she had the upper hand.

Oh, and Ellie *certainly* had the upper hand.

"I don't need to follow the Old Ways for you to get what's comin' to ya," she said, loud enough that the surrounding crowd could hear. "I sent a letter to the North American Witches' Council a week ago. You violated our code by taking one of mine from me- one of *ours*, one I claimed as my kin and yours through me. I have the paperwork to prove it, too. Good thing I mailed it myself instead of handin' it over to you."

"The Council will side with me. I was well within my rights to preserve the lineage of our community," Jeannie said confidently, her posture straightening a little

"Funny you should say that," Ellie said slowly, fishing in her pocket, "because they sided with me."

She unfolded the letter that Kaz brought her that morning, waving it in front of the village.

"As of receiving this letter, so- mm, maybe 10AM Monday? You've been stripped of your position as lead witch and this community has been put on formal suspension until a new lead is elected. Council members should be on their way here as we speak to evaluate the situation."

A murmur went through the crowd, louder than before.

"Actually, they offered *me* your job, but I turned 'em down. I ain't staying here, no siree."

"So you're turning me over to the Council for punishment?"

"Nah. Not yet, anyways," Ellie said, and then turned to face the village gates. "Ya get all that, Sheriff?" she called, her voice echoing through the trees.

Sheriff Mathers stepped out from his hiding place just outside the gates, two deputies following quickly behind him.

"Loud and clear, Miss Ellie," he said, tipping his hat.

Jeannie tried again to move, but she failed miserably, screaming as the thorns bit deeper into her limbs and kept her in place. Only once the deputies had her by each arm did Ellie release the plants so that she could move, and she didn't make it half a step before Sheriff Mathers cuffed her.

The entire crowd was dead silent. They didn't know what to do or where to move, or if they should move at all. Ellie was fine with that. She suspected that, somewhere along the way, at least one or two others had been involved in Jeannie's rotten plans.

She hoped anyone who helped happened to be very literally shitting their pants at the moment.

"If you *ever* come knocking on my door- no, if you ever set foot in my neck of the woods, if you ever come looking for me or mine ever again, I will collect what I'm owed. Are we clear?" Ellie asked, eyes narrowed.

"I *am* one of yours-"

"You are NOT one of mine and ya never have been, ya goddamn devil woman!" Ellie took a long, slow breath, let go of Jeannie's jaw, a took

a step back. "As of today, I renounce you. I sever all ties, blood or otherwise. You are a stranger to me."

"You can't *do* this to me-" Jeannie cried, struggling against the cuffs and the deputies, but it was futile.

"I'm not leaving you alive because I'm feeling merciful, Jeannie," Ellie said slowly. "I'm leaving you alive because I don't deserve to carry the weight of your death on my conscience. I'm leaving you alive because you owe me. Anyone who had a hand in this *owes me*. And just in case anybody thinks I might be sweet and merciful, make no mistake: You will never be off the hook until the day you die."

Slowly, very slowly, the residents backed away from Ellie. She finally released her thorny grip on the two casters who tried to interfere, and they both scrambled away. Rather than chase after any of them, though, Ellie just stood where she was.

Her legs shook against her will, and if Kaz hadn't walked up and wrapped his arm around her for support, she thought she would have collapsed on the spot. She felt sick and exhausted and cold, so cold, and leaned into Kaz like he was her lifeline.

Well, he *was* her lifeline. She wouldn't have been able to pull herself out of this without him.

They stood quietly for a long moment, watching the villagers retreat into their homes as Granny and Alice worked double-time with straw brooms to sweep away the casting circle. Simon gathered up the baskets of ingredients and separated them out, preparing to scatter, burn, or otherwise get rid of them.

It was only then that Ellie realized she still had the bottle of blood in her hand. She didn't drop it, though. She wanted to return it to where it belonged.

The Sheriff walked over as the crowd thinned, a somber expression on his face.

"You did good, girl," he said softly, placing a hand on her shoulder for a long moment. "I'm as glad to know who killed him as anybody."

"If you're grateful, get your deputies to stop flapping their jaws about me in town," Ellie said. "I'd like to be able to walk down King Street in peace from now on."

"You brought in my nephew's killer. Least I can do is clear your name." He paused for a moment, frowning. "And... I'm sorry. I'm sorry I thought you killed him."

"Apology accepted," Ellie said, sighing. "It's gonna take time to mend bridges. I hope you know that. This is a big step, though."

"I understand," he said slowly. "If I can ask... where ya goin' after all this?"

"Not sure yet. Can't stay here, though," she snorted. "We'll be gone before sunrise."

"You could always come to the farm," Mathers said, and Ellie genuinely smiled at the offer. The Mathers farm was a long ways out of town, though, and it was already crowded with a whole herd of kids.

"I really appreciate that," she said. "I think we'll find somewhere, though."

"Y'all be safe, then. And stay in touch," he said, patting her shoulder awkwardly before he turned to where the deputies were struggling to force Jeannie into the back of a car.

It didn't feel real, in a way. Kaz's arm around her was the only thing that anchored her to her place, and she couldn't decipher what the mix of grief and adrenaline in her veins meant to her. What was she supposed to do now?

Where did she go now that she knew the truth?

"You don't have to stay, you know," she said softly, looking up at Kaz. "I... I *want* you to, but you don't have to."

Kaz pulled her in close and kissed her, and for once, she didn't care who was watching. Ellie let herself lean into him and wrapped her arms around his neck for balance, a wash of gratitude and sadness and relief rushing over her.

"Does that count as an answer?" he asked, pulling away ever so slightly.

"I just wanted to check!" she squeaked, eyes wide and cheeks flushed.

"I made my decision a while ago. Don't worry," he said, keeping his arms around her.

"What about the bargain?" Ellie asked. "You said if we didn't finish it, there would be something left unresolved that would... connect us."

"Would you be opposed to simply leaving that in place?" Kaz rested his forehead against hers as he spoke. "I don't think it would hurt to have that as a connection point, though I'd argue you've already given me something precious, so I think the conditions are satisfied."

Ellie blinked at him. "Excuse me?"

"I've got *you*. Best bargain I've ever made, if you ask me," he said with a toothy smile.

24 IN WHICH OUR HEROES WALK TO HOWARD'S KNOB

"We got her, Benny. We got her real good."

Ben's spirit no longer resided at his grave, but Ellie wanted to go there anyways. The roses she'd unintentionally grown around his tombstone were still blooming and thriving, looking oddly fresh and lush compared to the rest of the cemetery.

It was important to her that they stop here on the way out of the village. She buried the glass bottle of his blood behind the headstone, or rather... she gave the bottle to the roses, and they sunk it deep underground with their roots, keeping it safely buried with the rest of his body.

She blew a kiss towards the tombstone as she got to her feet and slowly walked out of the cemetery. Though her grieving process was not over, though it might not ever be over, she hoped this would be the last time for a while that she felt compelled to spend time at his grave.

After all, Ben wanted her to *live*.

"Where to now?" Kaz asked as she came closer, reaching out for her hand. He had insisted on being the one to pull the small wagon with their trunks, arguing that it wasn't very heavy and they were heading downhill anyways. Ellie planned to annoy him about it later.

"We could look for a room in town... Or, I mean, we have a

tent and a camp bed. We could go on up to Howard's Knob and camp for a while," she said with a shrug.

"It's a good thing I have a better solution, then, isn't it?" came a voice from behind them. Ellie didn't even have to turn around to know who it was, but she did anyways.

"Granny?" Ellie asked, taken aback. Kaz, on the other hand, just smiled.

"Oh, you didn't think your ol' Granny would let you leave me behind, did you? I just needed time to pack!" she said with a chuckle. "And you should thank your demon for helpin' me with that, too."

"I didn't want you to have to move out into the Boonies when you're safe here!" Ellie said, laughing incredulously.

"Look around! We're already in the Boonies." The older woman gestured vaguely to... everywhere. Trees. Woods. More trees. More woods.

Ellie and Kaz exchanged glances.

"A... Fair. Yeah, fair point," she admitted. "But—"

"WAIT FOR US!"

A shriek of laughter cut through the cool mountain air, and Ellie turned to see two faces she wouldn't have expected.

Alice came tearing down the hill faster than a jackrabbit. Ellie would have said she was toting a wagon, but it looked more like the wagon was toting her. There were three trunks piled on top of one another, along with various sacks and bits and bobs that jingled as it rolled down the bumpy dirt road. Behind her, Simon struggled to keep up, moving at breakneck pace down the hill.

"We're comin' too!" he shouted, waving his arms wildly.

"What the living—" Ellie said, cutting off with loud laughter.

"Granny said y'all were leaving, and y'ain't leavin' without us!" Alice said, holding onto her straw hat so it wouldn't blow off her head as she ran towards them.

"We figured... we..." Simon said between pants, finally catching up. "Figured we... could help out."

"You're okay with this?" she asked Kaz.

He nodded. "I may have had a hand in it."

"Well... come on if you're coming!" she said with a smile. "It's a long walk to where we're going."

———— ✦ ————

It took the rest of the day to trek to Howard's Knob, and by the time they made it there, Ellie did not think she would be up for pitching a tent, making a fire, and generally doing anything besides falling into a deep sleep.

However, as they made their way over the last part of the hill, she noticed a shadow on the horizon. A very large, very *house-shaped* shadow.

"What in blue blazes—" she muttered, squinting into the late afternoon sun.

"Did you really think I'd let him move you up here in a tent?" Granny scoffed. "Gimmie a lil' more credit than that."

A house.

A real house.

... And it was *huge*.

As they approached, she could see it more clearly. Two floors, probably a basement underneath for cold storage if the builder had any good sense, though... the thing *was* shaped a little strangely.

It was a sturdy structure made of logs and brick and whatever else the builder could get their hands on. The roof was clay tiled, the windows different sizes in different shades of colored glass, as though someone had picked them up from a scrap pile and made something new from them. It was absolutely, incredibly, wonderfully *beautiful*.

"Called in a favor," Kaz said, smirking.

"It's... perfect," Ellie whispered.

"There's three bedrooms, an attic, and a cellar, and we can always build more space if we need it." Granny paused. "... I want the attic for my room, though. Old woman's rights and all that."

"Granny, I've never had this much space in my life, and you know it!" Ellie said, laughing. "What am I even gonna *do* with all this?"

"You'll run your apothecary, just like you wanted to do out of the village," Granny said firmly.

"And you?" Kaz asked.

"I'll be over here making sure she doesn't call any more demons into the house. One is enough for a lifetime," Granny joked. "Nah, I'll take care of the gardening and the house, don't you worry. And I can teach ya how to trap and skin game in the winter."

"Can you teach him how to swing an axe first?" Ellie asked.

"Hey! I'm improving," he protested.

"Before y'all get too into bickerin' and flirtin' over there, this s also yours," Granny said, handing Ellie a thick envelope with an official seal and a ribbon.

"What..." she blinked, slowly opening the seal to peek inside.

"It's the deed to the property. You've got all forty acres," Granny said with a smile. "Now, it ain't all flat, of course, but it's enough land for hunting and trapping. Maybe even makin' your own little village if you want."

"Kaz," Ellie said in a warning tone. "I told you I was payin' for it."

"Well. You can pay me later, then," he said, waving her off. "I won't tell you not to because I know it's important to you, but I think room and board for me for the foreseeable future should put a good dent in the price, anyways."

"*Kaz*," she huffed.

"My foreseeable future is a very *long* one, to be fair," he said innocently. Ellie rolled her eyes, though... she was glad his foreseeable future was very long. Hers was, too.

"I... I like this plan," she said softly, a slow smile creeping across her face.. "No Council, though. Keep those power-hungry city rats offa my mountain."

"About that," Kaz said slowly. Ellie raised an indignant eyebrow.

"Don't tell me you registered with the Council. *Please.*"

"I certainly did not," he said, frowning, but he cheered up quickly. "However, if you're up for housing a city slicker professor, I've got someone interested in residency. A vampire, too, but she speaks southern. Oh, and somebody wrote back from Virginia. She wants to move here with her family."

"I think I can handle those *specific* folks," Ellie rasped, biting back tears.

"Just us and some friends. You know, a few good people." Kaz smiled, swinging their joined hands as their little group started off down the road.

"We'll make out just fine," Ellie said as she gave his hand a squeeze. "I've got a good feelin' about it."

EPILOGUE

After Jeannie's arrest and subsequent departure, it was only a matter of weeks before the little witch village outside Boone began to crumble. The Council refused to approve a new lead witch, instead settling on shutting the place down entirely. The residents were relocated to other places, as near or far away as they wanted. Some of them couldn't imagine leaving the mountains, of course, but rumors eventually went around that a few of them had truly taken the opportunity for a new start at the coast.

It took Ellie and her group of family and friends a good year to entirely furnish the new house.
That was fine. There wasn't much they all needed, though there was quite a lot of sleeping on camp beds and hay mattresses in those first few months while Simon and Kaz worked to get real beds constructed for those that needed them. They could transport some things from the old witch village, slowly, especially things abandoned by the previous residents, but even that took time and effort.

It felt appropriate to let the place rest, for the most part, though Ellie was not above suggesting disassembling old village houses so they could use the timbers for new ones. After all, the wood wasn't doing anyone any good sitting there rotting away, and it would be faster than cutting a slew of new trees. They

weren't out to create a new version of the old village, but something about repurposing the old pieces to make something better felt right.

Alice, Granny, and Ellie spent their first months on Howard's Knob establishing a working garden with planned seasonal crop rotation. They also set up a complex ward system in layers around the property. They weren't about to let their new home go unprotected, spiritually or physically.

Hartley took several months to move out to Howard's Knob with the rest of them, as did Harper. That was fine, though. Construction was slow, and Ellie was well aware that the first winter would be a test of endurance for them all. They made it through, though. Kaz learned to hunt and trap from Granny during the colder months, and Alice learned how to can vegetables and preserve meat. Their little community pulled together as best they could.

When it was clear that spring was on the way, Ellie sent a letter to Miriam and arranged for construction to begin on a new house. Simon led the project, establishing himself as a skilled architect as well as a cabinet-maker. He also led the construction project for Hartley's new home, which went up shortly after the house for Miriam and her family was completed.

Ellie, for her part, was happier than she'd been in a long time. Sharing a home with her family in a place that made her feel like she was at home did wonders for her mental health, her energy, and her magical abilities. She was more than happy to keep learning and growing with her family.

Kaz seemed to like it here, too. He loosened up over time, seemed less gloomy, and even managed to finish writing and subsequently publish two books. Almost exactly a year after moving to Howard's Knob, he walked in with a package from town and proudly handed it to Ellie.

"It's here," he said with a smile. "You've read it, of course, but this is the official copy."

Ellie slowly unwrapped the brown paper to reveal a hardcover book. It wasn't too long, but they'd worked on it together, and it was precious to her. It felt... almost strange to have the copy in her hands, to know where the story came from, and to know that the ending was much, much better than what actually happened.

This was her closure in the form of a book, her life for Ben and her love for Kaz all in one. She would absolutely treasure it, she thought, running her hands over the cloth cover.

"Mountain Magic," she read, "by Kazerin Sader."

"I still don't know why you didn't want your name on it," he muttered.

"Well, it kinda is!" Ellie laughed. "My last name, anyways. I guess demons don't have those?"

"I never really needed one before!" Kaz protested, gesturing helplessly.

"So you stole mine?" Ellie teased, standing on tiptoe to kiss him.

"I'd steal it for more than a pen name if you'd let me," Kaz murmured, pulling her in for a hug.

She wasn't sure how to respond to that. Kaz was wonderful. He was so, so dear to her, and she'd gladly have him with her for the rest of her life, but it was difficult to tell when he was teasing and when he was serious sometimes, especially about these kinds of things.

"Hey," Kaz said suddenly, pulling away to take her hands in his.

"Mmm?" Ellie raised an eyebrow as she threaded their fingers together, gently rubbing her thumbs over the backs of his palms.

"I love you," he said firmly, expression turning serious. "I'm not asking you to return that yet, but I need you to know that I'm here. I'm in this for the long haul."

"I love you, too," Ellie said, letting go of his hands only to hug him tightly, resting her head on his chest to listen to his heart beating as she spoke. "And I need *you* to know that there's always a place in my heart for you."

"Does this mean I should start planning the proposal now, or...?" Kaz raised an eyebrow, smiling mischievously.

"Pfft, right, I get it. He's got jokes," Ellie said, rolling her eyes as she took a step back.

Kaz didn't respond, still smiling as he shoved his hands into his pockets and shrugged.

"Kaz?" Ellie blinked at him, watching as he turned towards the door of the room and began to walk away, still smiling, still absolutely silent.

"*Kaz!*"

ACKNOWLEDGEMENTS

Getting this book to its current state has been a journey and a half.

I'd been writing things on my own for years-- original fiction, fanfiction, plays, poems, you name it-- and had never taken the leap to publish anything online. Finally, in 2024, I decided it was time to just take a chance and publish the new project I'd started a few months back about a witch and a demon solving a murder in Boone, NC, where I went to undergrad. Ellie was originally a character in an Old Gods of Appalachia TTRPG campaign in which we never really got to deal with her grief over Ben's death or truly processing having his ghost around, so I decided I wanted to create a whole new world for her so she could solve his murder.

It blew up. I wasn't viral, I wasn't internet famous, but between the first chapter post in March 2024 and December of that year, I'd won the Wattys, won the Ambys, and garnered about 59k reads on the project, which was so much bigger than I ever thought it would be. It really gave me the confidence I needed to move forward with publishing this series, and though I did think about going for a traditional publishing route or looking into a paid online gig, I started to realize that I had the skills to do this myself. I needed someone to copy edit, but I could do my own cover design, internal illustrations, formatting, and set up my own website and online presence. It's a LOT. Indie publishing is not for the faint of heart, and kudos to anyone out there who has gotten all this done, if you have three sales or three thousand.

I wrote Blood Bargain while I was working on my dissertation, and the contrast between the two documents was just what I needed. I like research, but after year of documenting every single assertation you make down to the tiniest sentence, reading every book you can get your hands on, fighting imposter syndrome, fighting university processing so they'll let you put appropriately formatted sheet music in your document, and trying to explain to everyone who asks why a 200 page academic document with intensive citations and several rounds of required committee critique isn't done yet... I was stressed. Badly.

The burnout might not have been as bad as it was, but it came on the heels of a deep depressive slump that lasted almost two years, starting from when I lost all hearing in my left ear in 2022, spanning through my maternal grandmother's passing only a few months later, and creeping into 2023, when I moved 700 miles back home as a 28 -year-old to finish my dissertation and spent months applying to jobs only to be told that I was overqualified for anything that might help financially and underqualified for any teaching jobs until my dissertation was finished.

This book saved me.

I wrote 80,000+ words in two months, which is about the fastest I've ever written a novel. The positive online response and progress that was significantly faster and more visible than progress on my dissertation made me feel like I was actually doing something right. Seeing it come together was a lifeline, and writing about Ellie's grieving process helped me process a lot of my own emotions that I just hadn't taken time to sift through in the chaos. This story needed to come out, and I think getting it on paper saved me in so many ways that I haven't even discovered yet.

And now for the thanks.

Thanks to my family members for not acting like I was crazy for wanting to write books in my spare time. Thanks especially to my mom for always reading my stuff and being an amazing cheerleader, even while I'm still in the writing stages, and for letting me ramble to her about plots. Thanks to dad for being quietly supportive and for all the silly jokes about my typing sounding like a machine gun. Thanks to my grandparents for being patient and loving even when they weren't quite sure what all I was writing about. Love you lots of bunches.

Thanks to my best friend, Hailey, for helping bounce ideas around and listening to me say "oh, I could write a novel about that..." approximately every three seconds on some days. You're very patient with me, even when I hyperfocus so hard that I sit on a different plane of existence for a little bit, and I love you.

Thanks to Ben Meeks. You may not remember me, if you ever read this, but I signed up for your author mentor sessions at DragonCon. I was thinking about trying to submit to agents and genuinely afraid for the process. I remember saying "Yeah, I can do my own cover design, I've done my own internal formatting, I'm not super worried about the editing. .." and he said "So... If you can do all that, why are you submitting for traditional publishing?" And he was right.

And finally, thanks to you. Thank you for reading this book, for coming on this journey, and showing your support. Thank you for reading this work on Wattpad, for telling me this was a project that made you feel something. Thank you for having this book on your shelf and in your hands and on your digital readers, and thank you for giving me the chance to share a story that is very, very close to my heart.

As I type, I am working on the third book of the Appalachian Magic Series. Keep an eye out for future volumes!

CONNECT WITH ME AT
CAMELLIACARROLL.COM